Bird
of
Passage

Catherine Czerkawska

Published by Dyrock Publishing
Copyright © 2020 Catherine Czerkawska

ISBN: 978-0-9557364-1-4

'I was three-quarters of the way through this book ... before it dawned on me that it was *Wuthering Heights* in modern dress. I was tipped off by a couple of sly and amusing references to twigs tapping on windows and ghosts, and by the hero disappearing for twenty years and then returning a rich man. It's not a re-telling, though – it's a re-imagining. A dialogue with the older book, if you like. It asks, would the same story, the same deathless love, be possible in the modern age, and if so, how? ... I was convinced, moved and impressed by *Bird of Passage*. It says that, yes, undying love for another, unrelenting absorption in another, is possible in these days of computers and motorbikes. But, although it's possible, you may not want to pay the price.

Whether you love *Wuthering Heights* or not, if you enjoy an involving, beautifully written book, you'll enjoy *Bird of Passage*.'
– *Susan Price, Awfully Big Reviews*

'There are no pat answers in this story and no neatly contrived solutions. Endings are jagged, situations remain unresolved. Yet at the end of the book there is a feeling of satisfaction that things did work out as they should – at least to some extent. I think that makes the story and its characters all the more realistic and credible. It's hard to pigeonhole this book to a specific genre. It's a love story, yet sometimes defies the label. It's contemporary, yet dwells quite a bit in the past. As to its audience – I think this would appeal to readers who don't need to be led by the hand and who enjoy challenging relationships. Wholeheartedly recommended.'
– *Gilly Fraser, the Indie eBook Review*

'It's not just a cracking read, it's a genuinely powerful one, and once you stumble over the great love story at its centre you won't be able to put this book down. There's real pain here and many different kinds of healing, few of them nice. A story that like *Wuthering Heights* has as many harsh and knotted bits as deliciously sweet ones, you will be taken to a different world by it, but one as real as your own.'
– *Dr David Manderson*

Also by Catherine Czerkawska

— **FICTION** —

The Curiosity Cabinet

The Jewel

The Physic Garden

The Posy Ring

Ice Dancing

A Quiet Afternoon in the Museum of Torture

Rewilding

The Amber Heart

— **NON-FICTION** —

The Way It Was

For Jean: Poems, Songs and Letters by Robert Burns
for his wife Jean Armour.

A Proper Person to be Detained

— **PLAYS** —

Wormwood

The Price of a Fish Supper

Quartz

Burns on the Solway

The Secret Commonwealth

Prologue

THE LAST TIME India saw Finn O'Malley, he frightened her so much that she knew there was nothing to be done except let him be. She was playing at a festival of Celtic music in Oban and she had made the long trip to the island on impulse. It was a cold February day with a stiff breeze blowing in from the west, and the crossing was choppy. She felt sick on the ferry, so she stopped at the village shop to buy some biscuits and a bottle of dry ginger ale (her mother's cure) to settle her stomach, and the elderly woman who worked there recognised her. She had known India's mother when she was a girl and Finn for as long as he had been coming to the island. She had sold sweets to India and Flora when they were children and now she seemed delighted to see India, although slightly overwhelmed by her growing celebrity.

'I miss your mother,' she confided. 'I miss seeing her cheerful face around the village.'

'I miss her too. We all do.'

'It was good to see her and ...'

The woman hesitated, uncomfortably aware that what she was about to say might sound tactless.

'Her and Finn.' India finished the sentence for her. She was long past pussyfooting around the idea of her mother and Finn.

'But it was disturbing as well, you know,' the woman continued, confidingly. 'It was so ...' she paused again, searching for the right word. 'So exclusive. As if they had no time for anyone else in the whole world. Only each other. Him especially, I think. Poor Finn! But then he had no-one else. You would see them walking down the road to the village together, and he would be looking down at her as though he could never have enough of the sight of her.'

She halted, embarrassed by her own eloquence. India wanted her to go on talking, needing to know. But she already did know. There was nothing this woman with her pink cheeks and salt-and-pepper hair could tell her that she had not already imagined for herself, sometimes obsessively and sometimes with simple curiosity.

'And what brings you back to the island, my dear?'

'I was in Oban. I thought I might go up to Dunshee.'

The woman frowned. 'But surely ... he's still up there. Not that we see much of him in the village. God knows what he eats. He drinks plenty though.'

'I know. But I thought I should go and see him.'

'Oh my dear. I don't think he'll welcome you.'

'All the same, I have to go.'

India got back into her car and ploughed on. Max from the band, big, cheerful Max, who was half in love with her, had offered to go with her. She had turned him down, wanting to make the journey alone, but now she began to wish that she had let him come. It would have been nice to have a friend beside her.

On the way to Dunshee she made a detour to the cemetery. There was a single tap with a plastic milk bottle hanging from it. She turned it on, her fingers clumsy with the cold, and stood at arm's length to fill the bottle. The water always came out of the tap sideways and if you weren't careful it would drench you. Nobody ever fixed it. She had bought a bunch of filling station flowers on the way through Oban that morning, but when she got to the grave she saw that somebody had left a posy of evergreens beneath the headstone: holly, ivy and a few larch cones loosely twined together. The vase was a dented metal container inside a square granite casing with R.I.P. in black letters. She unscrewed the misshapen lid and rinsed out the interior, wrinkling her nose at the smell of rotting vegetation. Then she arranged her flowers, wondering how long the pink carnations would last in the wind that blasted around the granite headstones and threatened to carry the stones of the ruined kirk with it. The evergreens were a better choice. She fumbled in her bag for a tissue and rubbed at the sand and mud on the stone. 'Cairistiona,' it said, with 'Kirsty' beneath.

She didn't linger long here. If Kirsty was anywhere it wasn't in this sad place, although India could imagine other windy hillsides that might draw her. She clambered gratefully back into the warmth of the car and set the heater as high as it would go. Then she drove on towards Dunshee.

The lower parts of the track were almost obliterated by furrows of chocolate-brown mud. Higher up, long neglected ruts played havoc with her tyres. The little Jazz wasn't designed for this terrain. Over to her left, she caught glimpses of the sea as she drove and she could tell that it was already 'blowing smoke' out there as her great grandfather would have said, the wind whipping up spume from distant waves. Freezing rain was storming in from the west, horizontal rain that blinded her, and she almost drove into the ditch, stopping herself from veering off the track just in time.

'Why am I doing this?' she thought. 'Why?'

He took a long time to come to the door. She had to hammer on the oak with her fists. And then he wrenched it open, standing in the doorway, staring down at her and blinking in the light. Her first bizarre thought was that he might crumble into dust, there on the threshold. He had never run to fat but she had always thought of him as being very fit and muscular. Now his clothes hung off him and his thinness made him seem even taller. His hair was grey, and his face was stony. She had a nightmare about him afterwards. In her dreams, he was slowly turning into one of the ancient monoliths that walked the fields below the farm. It struck her that if she had met him down in the village she might not have known who he was.

'India. How are you?' he asked, and his tongue seemed thick in his mouth, though she couldn't tell whether it was because of the drink or because he so seldom spoke to anyone these days. He had always been taciturn, but now the power of speech seemed to be deserting him altogether.

He seemed reluctant to move, but he stood to one side and motioned her in, grudgingly.

She found herself remembering their last meeting. She could feel the constriction in her throat. She set about trying to fill the silence, telling him about her recent tour, the recording contract and the television show.

'I still play Alasdair's old fiddle you know. The one he taught you to play.'

He stirred at that. 'Oh yes. But I was never … I could never …' His voice trailed off into silence. She could almost see his thoughts scattering like dried leaves in the wind.

He made her some tea. The mug was chipped and dirty, but she drank it anyway because she was afraid of upsetting him. He looked ill and he stank of stale whisky. There was such misery about him. It spilled out and filled the whole house. India found that she could hardly breathe in there. Besides, the place stank of cats.

Her mother had loved cats. India loved them herself, but she realised that Finn had just started to let them come and go as they pleased, and they had bred unchecked, tabby with ginger, feral with domestic. When she looked around the room she saw hostile yellow eyes in all the dark corners. The fire in the kitchen range was burning but it was so choked that there seemed to be no heat in it. It gave her a pang of despair. The fire at Dunshee had always blazed bright and warm, no matter what else might be going wrong with their lives. Now the house was smothered in dust, and the fire was a weary smoulder of smoke and ash.

'I have something for you,' he said. 'Now that you're here. There's something you ought to have.'

He got to his feet and shambled up the stairs. She could hear them creaking beneath his feet. Left alone, she poured the tea down the sink and rinsed away the evidence, though it was so grimy, so clogged with grease and tea leaves, that nobody would have noticed, least of all Finn.

She sat down again and stared out of the window, listening to the heightened whine of the wind in the chimney. She ought to be going. She knew from bitter experience that if the weather deteriorated any further, the next ferry might be the last of the day. The island harbour was sheltered enough, but docking at the mainland side was another matter and would already be fraught with difficulty. She could be stuck here for days. She heard faint footsteps moving over the floor above. Then nothing. Where was he? A thin ginger cat, more daring than the rest, emerged from its hiding place and batted at her foot with a tentative paw.

'Where is he then?' she asked but the creature only gazed back at her with inscrutable golden eyes.

Eventually, she got up and climbed the stairs in search of him. She knew where he would be and went straight into her mother's bedroom, where she found him, crouching in the shelter of the old box bed.

'I was looking for these. I thought you should have them.'

He was holding a green cardboard folio, tied up with black tape.

'What are they?'

He thrust the folder at her. 'Your mother's. Some of the last things she did.'

'Watercolours?'

'Drawings. She would have wanted you to have them. Take them.'

She started to open the folio but he shook his head. 'No. Take them away. Don't you be opening them here. I don't want to look at them. But *you* should look at them.'

'All right. But are you sure you want me to have them?'

'Who else if not you, India?'

'Fair enough.'

'I always thought she would leave me. I was always afraid.' His fists were clenched on his knees. His face had an awful blankness. It was as though the struggle not to give in to despair had left him unable to manage any expression but this dreadful mask.

'She didn't want to.'

'What difference does that make? She left me all the same.'

'None of us wanted her to leave,' she said, gently. 'I miss her all the time.'

'Do you?' For the first time he looked directly at her.

'Oh, Finn!'

He shook his head, looking away again.

'Don't pity me. I don't want pity. Least of all yours. She was my salvation. Now, I have to try not to think about her. I have to make a space in my day when I don't think about her. I'm not very good at it. The whisky helps.'

'Come downstairs now. She isn't here.'

'How could she leave me, India? Me of all people?'

'I don't know.'

'And if they were right, all those years ago. If there *is* something afterwards, some place they go to, some kind of heaven, why won't she come back for me?'

'The dead don't obey our rules, do they? I sometimes think that maybe they are here, all the time. Only we're so sad that we're blind and dumb to them. Our own need obscures everything.'

'Do you think that could be true?'

'Maybe.'

She went to the door of the room and saw to her relief that he was following her. 'I have to go soon, Finn. There's a gig tonight. I'm playing. And you can see what the weather's doing. I have to get off the island.'

'You'll be playing Alasdair's fiddle.'

'That's right.'

'He would have liked that.'

'He would.'

Compassion for him brought tears to her eyes, but she knew that there was nothing she could do about it. He didn't care whether she stayed or not. He wouldn't care if he never saw her again.

As she gathered herself together to leave, tucking the folio inside her jacket to protect it from the rain, fumbling in pockets for her car keys, he said, 'I saw a funeral procession, you know.'

'What?'

'It was down there on the shore.'

'A funeral procession?' She felt the ground shift beneath her feet. Even for Finn, this was bizarre. She moved towards the door.

He grinned at her but, if anything, she found this more alarming than his despondency. 'I'm not going mad, India. Or no more mad than usual. I'm telling you the simple truth. I saw a funeral procession. Men in black overcoats, carrying a wooden coffin, and they were down on the seashore there. It was twilight. A few days ago. I'd gone down to check on the boat. They crossed my path, and one of them looked back at me. I don't think it can have been real, though? Do you?'

'No, Finn. I don't think it can have been real.'

At the door, she reached out her hand to shake his, but at the last minute she changed her mind and stood on tiptoe to kiss him on the cheek. Then she headed back to her car. Her last image of him, as she turned around to wave, was of him raising his fingers to his cheek and touching the place where her lips had just brushed the sallow skin. Without looking back again, she got into her car and drove away.

Safe in her mainland hotel, with the smell of cats and whisky lingering in her nostrils, she ordered a pot of tea and some sandwiches and tugged at the knots on the folio. The tapes had been pulled tight, and she had to tease them apart with a pin. Inside was a sheaf of sketches, mostly in charcoal, although a few were in pen and ink. India drew them out, one at a time, and laid them on the bed. She thought she had seen most of Kirsty's work: all those landscapes, all those studies of the island flora and fauna that seemed to capture the very essence of the plant, the bird, the animal. When Kirsty had painted the island in spring, when primrose, violet and bluebell vied for space, or when the lanes were dazzling corridors of golden gorse – whins, they were called on the island – there was something savage about the resulting pictures, nothing like the genteel watercolours on display in most Highland galleries.

Most of Kirsty's paintings were full of light, as vibrant as she had once been herself. But these were stark studies in black and white, light and shade, Gothic in their intensity. They were more like illustrations for a book, but what book could that possibly be? Staring at them, one after another, India had to suppress a shudder. There was something terrible about them.

There was a knock on the door and Max came in. He had showered and his hair was a damp, blonde cascade. He looked relieved to see her.

'Thank God you're back!'

'I told you I wouldn't be long.'

'I thought you might get stranded. How was your island?'

'Cold and wet and windy.'

'And …?'

'Finn?' She shook her head. 'Don't ask.'

'You should have let me come with you.' His gaze alighted suddenly on the pictures. 'Wow!'

'I know.'

'Whose are they?'

'My mum did them.'

'Christ!' He came over and slipped his arm around her shoulders. They stared at the pictures together.

They couldn't be called portraits because they were largely unrecognisable, although there was one very bold sketch of a man, head and shoulders, with a background of dark cross-hatching, and the face just angles and planes of light. India recognised Finn. It was a much younger Finn, to be sure, but there was a haunted, haunting quality about the face, as though the artist had foreseen his solitary future with horrible clarity. Or perhaps known something of his past.

One of the sheets showed two figures, so closely intertwined that it was almost impossible to tell where one ended and another began, or to say which limb belonged to which person, and it was so full of a dark, heavy sensuality that India found herself blushing. In one sketch, a woman seemed to be stabbing her partner in the thigh with a dagger, or was she pulling the knife from the wound? Another had the suggestion of a great mass of roots and rocks in the foreground with human bodies somehow emerging from the landscape or perhaps becoming a part of it: hands, torsos, legs, all with a sense of movement, struggle, striving to escape. Or was it a striving to be absorbed?

There were also simpler studies of two children, swiftly drawn lines, just an impression of hair and arms and long legs.

'That one looks a bit like you!' said Max. 'You must have been on her mind, India.'

She had thought the same thing. Only when you looked more closely, you began to wonder if these were not children after all, but birds, long legged herons perhaps. In another, the same two figures seemed to have impossibly long arms that were forming an arch across something that was surely ...

'Christ, that's a gravestone,' said Max. 'These are very strange drawings, India.'

'You're not kidding.'

'When did your mother do them, do you think?'

'I don't know. Maybe in those last years. I've certainly never seen them before.'

'And look at this one.'

It was a kiss, but there was something savage about it, the lips and indeed the two heads so fused that, once again, it was difficult to say where one ended and the other began. A thought entered her head, but it seemed so crazy that she couldn't voice it. Were they kissing or feasting off each other?

'Did you know about these?'

'Not a thing. Finn gave them to me. Now I'm beginning to wish he hadn't. But look, there's a bird down in the grasses. Here. And here, on this one as well.' She sifted through the pictures. 'And here too.'

'Are they signed?'

'Some of them. Just a letter C. That was all she did most of the time. Her initial.'

'I thought your mum's name was Kirsty.'

'Her proper name was Cairistiona. It's the Gaelic form of Christine. Most people called her Kirsty.'

Max smiled. 'I can see why.'

'But these don't look anything like her usual stuff.'

'They're very disturbing, aren't they?'

India began to gather them together. 'They are.'

'What will you do with them?'

'Right now, I'm going to put them away and try to forget about them.'

'Easier said than done.'

'I know. But I've got more important things to worry about.' She glanced at her watch. 'I'm going to have a shower, get changed.'

'Will you show them to your dad?'

India shook her head. 'No way. These are mine. Finn gave them to me. Dad's fine. He's happy now. I don't want to go dragging up all that stuff again. It's history. Over and done with. Well, it is as far as he's concerned.'

'Yeah,' said Max and bent to kiss her on the forehead. 'Yes, Indie, I do know. I'll keep my mouth shut. But …'

'But what?'

'That.' He nodded at the folio. 'Bit like carrying Pandora's box around with you, isn't it?'

'Not if nobody else knows I've opened it.'

He left her to get ready for the show. Even then, India found herself staring at the green card cover of the folio, its contents indelibly imprinted on her mind's eye. Later, when she was playing, she was still seeing them and the sensuousness of those dark embraces somehow translated itself into her music. Never had she played so magically. Never had she played with such passion.

Chapter One

THERE WAS TOO much space and too much light. It dazzled Finn's eyes and made them water. He couldn't stop blinking and he dashed the tears away with the back of his hand, afraid that the men might think he was weeping. Out on deck, breathing in the salty air, he felt disorientated. He had a sudden sensation of queasiness. The spit came up into his mouth and he had to swallow hard. He wanted to yawn all the time. His clothing was too thin for the day and he found himself shivering.

The gaffer, Micky Terrans, told him to fix his eyes on the horizon.

'Whatever you do, don't look down at the sea!' Micky was lean and balding with a tonsure of wispy, fair hair, and he always wore a shabby tweed cap to keep his scalp warm. Rumour had it he even wore it in bed. 'If you look down at the sea, you'll lose your breakfast for sure.'

Not that there had been much breakfast: just the heel of a loaf and a scraping of red jam with a mouthful of cold tea, strong and bitter, and that hadn't helped the sickness at all.

He gazed towards the horizon, but everything was in motion. Even the big white birds were never still. Gannets, Micky had called them, although Finn didn't remember that he had ever seen such creatures before or, if he had seen them, nobody had given him their name. If you had no name for a thing or even a person, you could not hold that thing in your mind. You could never really know it properly. Who had told him that? It must have been his mother. He watched the birds riding the wind and then plummeting into the water, disappearing for what seemed like minutes, bobbing to the surface again in a flurry of droplets and thrashing fish that caught the light. Watching them made him uneasy, worried that they might not reappear. But the sight of them took his mind away from his sickness.

Finn could not swim and he was afraid of the water. He had never so much as set a toe in the sea. Even when he had been living in Dublin he had never spent any time at the shore. And afterwards, he had been far inland. He gazed at the gannets and wondered what it must be like to dive in like that, to plunge down below the waves in search of your dinner. He wondered what strange creatures swam down there. But that too made him feel queasy and he clutched at the railing, feeling the rust flake off under his fingers. They were between two countries, between Ireland and Scotland, and neither was visible. On a clear day, so his companions had told him, it would be different and you could see the slices of land, one behind the other, with the cake-shaped Craig, its cliffs, its shining white lighthouse in between. And then they would be steaming north, passing the Cloch lighthouse and the Tail of the Bank.

He had made sure he knew what to look out for, persisting with his questions in the face of their good natured protests that he would soon see where he was bound. And then he might well wish himself back on the Holy Ground once more. That was what Micky had said, laughing, lighting his cigarette, cupping his hand round the match to shelter it from the wind. Knowing all this made Finn feel less insecure, even though it was so strange and new and he had little idea what to expect. This was his first trip to the tatties, to the potato harvest, and it had never occurred to him that he might be homesick. If the truth be told, he wasn't really homesick at all, but the unfamiliarity of these new surroundings and new companions bothered him and he was fearful. Perhaps he wouldn't be up to the work. He had been warned that it would be back-breaking. Worse, perhaps they would send him home again. And that would be a thing too terrible to contemplate.

'Finn? Finn?'

He turned. Francis O'Brien stood behind him, shivering, his teeth chattering. He was clutching his arms around himself, hugging himself as though that might make a difference. As always, Finn felt the contrary emotions of irritation and pity. There was nothing he could do to help his friend and yet he felt that he ought to be able to think of something. His very helplessness in the face of the other boy's vulnerability made him angry.

'Are you cold?' he asked, more sharply than he had intended.

'Just a bit.'

'Well, jump up and down then!'

Francis jumped up and down on his spindly legs, his feet in the loose boots slapping against the wooden deck, his palms clapping frantically against his upper arms, but the effort seemed to make him colder still and his movements were half-hearted at best.

'Will we go below, Finn? Will we?'

'I think we'll be sick for sure if we go below decks, Francie. It's bad enough up here. But there's an awful smell of shite down there.'

Francis giggled at the rude word. The almost transparent skin of his cheeks flamed crimson. 'Sure it does, you're right, Finn.'

Francis was a slender, fair-haired boy with a face like a flower. This was his misfortune. Finn thought that you could have put him in a dress and a bonnet, and he would have made a passable girl. It was much better to be like Finn himself, a scowling, ugly, dark-skinned lad with nothing at all girlish about him. Black Irish he had heard himself called. He had asked Micky Terrans what that meant, and the gaffer had said something about the Armada and shipwrecked Spaniards that made no sense at all to Finn. But Francis was as white as an angel. Even now, when the cold air had raised livid patches on cheeks, chin and forehead, even now, there was something soft and vulnerable and girlish about that face.

'Will we be there soon?' asked Francis. 'What do you think, Finn?'

Finn shrugged. 'I don't know. How would I know? Micky Terrans says not. He says we've a long journey ahead of us at the other side. And it'll rain later on for sure. He says he can smell it in the wind and he's never wrong.'

'What do you do if you need to have a wee, Finn? '

'Don't tell me you've been holding it in all this time, Francie?'

'I haven't wanted to go till now.'

'Jesus, Francie. You'll do yourself a mischief, so you will. You have to go over the side. Stand here and go over the side. But make sure the wind's blowing away from you.'

Francis grinned. Finn wasn't aware that he was saying anything funny, but Francis laughed all the same. Francis seemed to think like your man in the bible who said that a soft answer turneth away wrath. Except that Finn didn't think it did. Finn inclined to the belief that once you were big enough and strong enough, a punch on the nose might be a better bet at turning away the wrath. But the trouble was that neither of them was big enough or strong enough. Not yet.

'Will you stand there and make sure nobody's passing, Finn?'

'I will so. Go on then. And you can watch out for me after.'

'How do you know we're to go over the side, Finn.'

'Because I asked. I have a tongue in my head and I asked Micky Terrans, didn't I?'

'I'd be scared to ask him, so I would.'

'Jesus, Francie, you'd be scared to ask your own mammy, never mind Micky the Gaffer.'

Micky Terrans had been brusquely kind to the two lads in his care. He hadn't wanted them on this trip at all, suspecting they were much younger than he had been told. They were supposed to be fifteen, but he was dismayed to see that they could be no more than twelve or thirteen. He had been promised good workers and an extra cut of their wages and he had agreed to take them on the understanding that they would be no trouble, would keep their heads down and do whatever was required of them in the potato fields. Finn seemed strong enough and might do all right, but Micky had almost sent the other lad straight back where he had come from. What could they have been thinking, to pass off this long thin drink of water as a good worker? But the man who had made the arrangements had been insistent, the boys needed to get away, and who was Micky Terrans to quarrel with a man of the cloth? So he would grin and bear it, get whatever work he could out of them and hope that Finn, young as he was, might cover for his friend.

Micky Terrans had been right about the weather. The rain did come later, torrents of it, from a slate sky. The squad of tattie howkers was tucked into the back of an open lorry, although Micky himself drove up front in the warm cab. The men and a handful of women covered themselves as best they could, crouching under tarpaulins that smelled of potatoes as the truck bounced along for hours, but it was a miserable business. They were all weary, sick and chilled to the bone by the time they made the short sea crossing to the island and climbed aboard another lorry for the journey to the farm. The rain stopped and a thin sunlight filtered through the clouds. It was warmer here. Finn could smell the damp green of the land, laid over the scent of the sea. Beyond his confusion and fatigue, he felt a certain relief. Maybe it wouldn't be so bad after all.

Here and there they saw people working in the fields or an old man stooped over his vegetable patch. On the road, two small children, no more than four or five years old, pulled a reluctant puppy in their wake. They hauled their little prisoner onto the verge to let the lorry pass by and waved. In a cottage garden, a young woman, taking advantage of the late sunshine and a stiff breeze, was pegging out a row of nappies and shirts. She wore a blue and white gingham pinafore. His mother had worn just such a pinafore. Finn had a memory of taking wooden pegs out of her pocket and handing them to her while she put out the washing on the back green of the house where they lodged. *That's my good boy. That's my good Finny.*

The woman paused in her work, pushing her hair out of her eyes, watching the tattie howkers drive past, but she neither smiled nor waved at the incomers. They were a necessary encumbrance. Nobody welcomed them except the farmer and the island children who were too young to know better.

The farm was called Dunshee. The house was an ancient, slate-roofed building with dormer windows on the upper floors. It was set on a plateau of high land, slightly at angles to the sea, to take advantage of the shelter afforded by an uneven ridge behind. There was a clean courtyard with byres and barns and stables. It wasn't many years since the islanders had used horses to work the land.

The men were to sleep in the byre, the women in a stone-floored building that had been a dairy. The accommodation was spartan enough, but Micky Terrans remarked that it was better than it had once been, now that the government had got involved. And the sleeping arrangements at Dunshee were always better than most other places. This was one of the reasons why Micky preferred to keep his squad there as long as possible, paying the farmer for the privilege and ferrying them about to other farms as necessary. Micky liked to keep his squad dry and reasonably well fed. The stalls were fitted out with low timber ramps and decent mattresses stuffed with oat straw. Each bed had two or three serviceable blankets. They were to sleep two to a stall, Francis and Finn together. There was a makeshift kitchen in an outhouse, with a chipped Belfast sink and an old copper boiler for washing the clothes, a tap in the yard and even a proper flushing lavatory with a wooden seat. The little cubicle was whitewashed and smelled pleasantly of bleach.

'I mind when you had to sew the tattie sacks together to make a quilt for yourself,' said a stocky little man from Donegal, Jimsy Murtagh. He said it as though he half regretted the loss of that time. Jimsy never looked at you straight. Finn couldn't work out whether he had a squint or was just shifty. He had a filthy tongue, although when Micky was around he had to keep it under control. 'And you would have the feckin' rats running over you in the night. And nibbling away at your bedding and your toes too if you weren't careful. But this place is clean enough. And Galbreath does as much as any farmer can to keep the rats down. You boys don't know you're born, neither you do.'

'We know all about rats, don't we, Francie?' muttered Finn when he had gone, leaving them to make up their beds.

'We do so. But this is great, Finn! Do you not think this is a great place?'

'Let's wait and see, eh?'

Later on, there was a feast of boiled potatoes and tea, with plenty of bread and jam, while they sat on long benches on either side of a big wooden table. The table was full of saw marks and paint rings but the food was plentiful. Afterwards, some of the men filled their pipes and went outside for a smoke. They weren't supposed to smoke in the byre for fear of fires. The breeze had dropped with evening and the air was still and cool, the sea a mirror. They leaned against the wall and puffed away, gazing towards the mainland, content to be resting after the exertions of the journey. When it grew darker, they came indoors and somebody passed around a bottle of whisky. Micky Terrans would have disapproved, but he had gone away to his own lodgings in the village by then. Jimsy brought out a battered squeezebox, and played Danny Boy and one of the men sang along, the rest of them joining in the chorus. When they asked who else could carry a tune, Finn nudged Francis. Francis coloured up, and shook his head, but Jimsy had seen the exchange.

'Come on lad. Don't be shy. Are you a singer?'

Francis nodded.

'Then give us a song! What can you sing?'

'He can sing the Curragh of Kildare,' said Finn. 'Go on, Francie!'

Jimsy struck up the first few notes, and Francis stood up and sang, his voice wavery at first, but growing in confidence.

'The winter it is past, and the summer's come at last,
and the small birds sing on every tree.
Their little hearts are glad, but mine is very sad,
for my true love is parted from me ...'

It was his one talent. He had a sweet voice and he sang well, his voice dipping under and over the notes, embellishing them in a dozen ways. The men and women fell silent. There could not be one of them who had not heard it before, many times. It was a song that told of youth and heartbreak and hurts that could never be repaired. After-wards, Francis sat down, blushing even more fiercely at the praise for his singing. Finn nudged him in the ribs.

'They liked that!' he whispered to his friend. 'Do you know any others?'

'A few. I'll need to think.'

Francis was sometimes called upon to sing in the church but he was seldom asked to sing the old songs he had learned from his grandmother. He had once sung the Salley Gardens at a Christmas concert, but that was about the sum of it and besides, it had not turned out well. He had drawn attention to himself, and that was not a good thing. But perhaps it would be different here, among these people.

'I'll see what I can remember.'

The boys had begun to yawn widely and the yawning proved

infectious. Soon after this, they went to their beds, the women to their own quarters, the men to their stalls. The blankets smelled musty, as though they had been stored away for a long time. Finn fell asleep almost immediately. He woke up in the night, woke from a dream of buzz-saws, alarmed by the extreme dark and the unfamiliar surroundings, but especially by the chorus of snores from the older men. But the day had exhausted him, so he snuggled back down and drifted off to sleep. He dreamed again and this time, the dream was familiar. It came to him often in the cold school dormitory where the boys sighed and shivered in their sleep and the rats scurried in the walls and sometimes came closer than that.

He was a little boy again, back in Dublin with his mother. It was a light summer night, and they were in the warm room at the top of the lodging house, with the window open. They were in bed. Snug as two bugs in a rug, his mammy said. She was in behind him, her two arms around him, her body moulded against his back. She held him close, even though it was warm, and they were sweating gently. He could feel her breath against his neck and he could smell her apple blossom talcum powder.

In the dream, he climbed out of bed and went walking down the stairs with their brown lino, down past half a dozen closed doors, towards the front hallway that smelled of boiled cabbage and bacon. And although he was quite alone, he didn't feel afraid. It was dark now, but the moonlight filtered into the hallway through the green and red stained-glass panels in the door. He could find his way easily enough and so he carried on, down towards the cellars. He had never been here before, but doors opened as he approached them, his feet floated down the stairs without touching them and it was a pleasant sensation.

The dream cellars were light and bright. He wondered why his mother had told him never to come down here when they were so beautiful. He had never known there was such magic down here, the glowing coals of a comfortable fire, soft rugs and springy couches. Although he had left her in bed, in the way of dreams his mother was waiting for him, her legs tucked up beneath her on one of the couches. She held out her arms to him and said, 'Come here, my

Finny, and give your mammy a kiss.' He clambered up beside her, snuggling in, and saw that his mother's friend Phissie was sitting at a table. Her name was Phyllis, really, but he couldn't say it properly. He called her Phissie, and she didn't seem to mind. He could see that she was doing a jigsaw puzzle. Phissie was fond of jigsaws and whenever they went to visit her Finn liked to help her, although he wasn't very good at it, his fingers too clumsy to arrange the fiddly pieces. He liked the big round puzzle of scenes from Alice in Wonderland best of all, although it was hard to do. She would do the edge first, to start him off, and hand him pieces to fill in, telling him where to put them, correcting him gently when he tried to force something into the wrong space.

'Come here to me, Finny, and give us a hand,' said Phissie. 'You have to finish the puzzle, you know.'

Suddenly, he was beside her, staring down at the scattered pieces on the polished table. But she hadn't done the edges for him, and he was confused by the miscellany of shapes and colours.

'I don't think I can,' he said.

He looked behind him for his mammy, hoping she would help, but he couldn't see her. She wasn't curled up on the couch any more and he didn't know where she was and then, just as he felt the panic rising inside him, like steam inside a kettle, he woke up.

For a moment, he didn't know where he was.

Outside, there came the rasping call of some night bird flying over the farm. He felt the tension leave his body. Just the dream. The same old dream. He settled down again. He was aware of Francie's quiet presence beside him. He was warm and comfortable with a full belly. He had a sudden, piercing sense of something else. What could it be?

Safety.

He felt safe here. He sighed, pulled the scratchy blanket up close under his chin and drifted back to sleep.

Chapter Two

ALL DAY LONG, Finn and Francis had been labouring in the sandy fields, working on the early crop. They had been well warned that these delicate earlies could easily be damaged. Mostly, the two lads would have to follow the plough along the drills, gathering up the potatoes into baskets, but with the earlies Finn wielded the *graip* or fork, digging carefully to make sure that all the tubers were lifted one by one. Kirsty Galbreath had overheard her grandfather saying, 'he works like a grown man, that one.' She was nine years old and an only child, living with her widowed mother and her grandfather on this ancient farm, perched high up on the windy spine of the island with its fields sweeping down to the sea.

She had come running up the hill from school, in her red summer sandals with her leather satchel on her back, and had seen her grandfather, leaning on the field gate, staring down at the workers with a frown on his face. She distracted him by running to him, and he swung her up in the air, her pigtails flying. She loved to feel his big hands birling her round and round. Fields and sky blurred around her and then she was on her feet, holding onto his legs to steady herself. It frustrated her that there were no other children on the farm and only a handful in the village. There was so much to tell and so few people to listen.

'Kirsty, my darling!' he said. 'Did you have a good day?' He lifted his cap and replaced it more comfortably on his head, a habitual gesture.

It was almost holiday time but they never went away. There was too much to do about the farm at this time of year, and her grandfather seldom left the island except to go to the cattle market on the mainland. Once or twice, her mother had taken her to stay with relatives in Glasgow, in October, but summer holidays were invariably spent at home.

Alasdair singled Finn out from the others and called him over.

'You there! Come here to me!' he shouted.

The boy shambled up to the gate, wiping the sweat from his face with a grimy hand.

'Yes, mister?' he said.

'What's your name?'

'Finn, mister. My name's Finn.'

He looked ready to shy away, as though expecting a blow.

'Slow down, lad,' said Alasdair abruptly, almost angrily. 'Take a rest for God's sake! I've been watching you. You've been going at it like a mad man.'

Finn looked back along the drills, wondering whether he should obey the farmer or whether he might catch it from Micky Terrans if he did. But Micky was elsewhere in the field, deep in conversation with one of the Scottish workers. Behind Finn, Francis looked up from his own, slower work. He could not bend over for long. The pain in his back half killed him. So he preferred to kneel down, shuffling along in the mud. He almost spoke, but caught Alasdair's eye, thought better of it and turned his attention to his work again. Kirsty watched the slender boy stagger to his feet and haul on his basket, lugging the potatoes over to the big containers at the side of the field. She wondered that his arms could hold the basket and its contents without snapping in two. It was uncomfortable to watch him. Instead, she turned back to Finn who was stretching out his arms, loosening the tight muscles.

'What age are you?' said Alasdair. 'Both of you. You and your pal over there …' Then he smiled. 'No. Don't answer that. I don't want to know. But take a rest. And tell your friend to do the same when he comes back. Take a drink of water and ten minutes rest. This isn't a chain gang, lad, and you're not slaves.'

'I don't think we're allowed.'

'This is *my* farm, and I say what is and isn't allowed here. Don't worry. I'll speak to your gaffer. In fact I'll do it now.' He strode off along the side of the field. Young as she was, Kirsty knew that look. You didn't cross her grandad when he was in this mood.

She stared at Finn, unashamedly curious. He gazed back and blushed, his cheeks flushing scarlet. Francis came over, carrying the empty basket. He looked scared.

'What are we to do, Finn? What was he so angry about?'

'I don't know. But I don't think he's angry with us. And we're to have a breather. He said so and he's the boss.'

'He thinks you're working too hard,' said Kirsty. 'He's my grandad. And he *is* the boss. So you'd better do as you're told.'

She skipped away, following in her grandfather's footsteps, caking her red sandals with mud. Francis stretched out on the lush grass at the side of the field, glad of the rest. But Finn watched her go, watched her swinging fearlessly from her grandfather's arm, even while the man seemed to be having some kind of altercation with Micky Terrans. She was not shaken off. Instead, the farmer slipped his big arm around her, and pulled her in close, hugging her gently.

In the summer, when the nights were light, Kirsty was allowed to stay up late and wander where she pleased on the farm, so long as she stayed away from dangerous machinery, (they had drummed the danger of tractors into her so thoroughly that she couldn't see the old red Ferguson without a thrill of horror) and the precipitous cliffs on the far western side of the island. While Kirsty was still a baby, her father had been crushed when a tractor rolled on top of him. They had rushed him to hospital by boat, but it had been too late to save him. Although she didn't remember him, she knew what he looked like. There was a black and white photo of him in the living room. It was taken at some farm show or other. He was standing beside a prize ewe: a smiling young man in overalls and a flat cap like the one her grandad wore.

She had no-one on the island to play with. There were only half a dozen children at the primary school, and most were much older or younger. Kirsty had collected a family of dolls and she would take them down to the shore or to the burn that ran at the back of the house. There, she would kneel on the big flagstone that served as a bridge and toss them into the water, seeing which of them emerged first, pretending that they were having a race. In truth, they looked more as if they were drowning than swimming, with their rigid arms raised in supplication. The peaty water did them no good at all. They were a worn and haggard bunch, but she loved them.

Annabel Laurence, who sometimes stayed at the big house, was just a little older than Kirsty, a year maybe, but she already went to boarding school on the mainland. She spent most of her holidays in London and only visited the island occasionally. Even then, she hardly acknowledged Kirsty's existence, but once she had sat in church and pulled faces at Kirsty during the whole long sermon. Kirsty had responded in kind, indignant but enthralled, until her mother noticed and shook her by the shoulder.

'Will you stop that nonsense!'

Not long after the arrival of the tattie howkers, Kirsty climbed up the rocky slopes behind the farmhouse, scrambling through heather and bracken almost as high as herself, scratching her bare knees, raising clouds of crane flies that blundered unpleasantly about her head. She flapped her hands to beat them off until she reached the summit where the breeze deterred them. Up there was a wide saucer of land sloping gently to a tumble of rocks in the middle. From the furthest lip of this saucer, she could see the great, blue-grey expanse of the western sea, pied here and there with patches of wind. Her grandfather called this place Hill Top Town. That's what she called it herself, though sometimes she wondered why, when there was no town here at all; there was only this shallow bowl of land with jagged rocks, a thin covering of lumpy turf and drifts of purple thyme papering the crevices. It was her secret place. Her palace, her fortress, her sanctuary.

Except that tonight there was an intruder. The Irish boy, Finn, was sitting on a rock, looking out at the sea, shading his eyes against the setting sun. She was not dismayed by his presence, only curious. His shoulders were hunched and even from behind he looked dejected. Not yet shy of boys, she went and plumped herself down beside him.

'Hello!' she said. 'What are you doing here?'

He turned to look at her. 'Just sitting,' he said. 'Why? Am I not allowed?'

'Why should you not be allowed?'

He didn't reply. He had learned very quickly that there were a great many things the visiting Irish were not allowed to do, a whole catalogue of rules. Micky Terrans had hammered them home. The men and women, not the boys, were allowed in the public bar of the hotel, but not in the lounge. They were not made welcome in the shop although they were tolerated, two at a time. They were not supposed to light bonfires or stray too far from the farms where they were working. If anything went missing, however small, they would be blamed. Jimsy Murtagh had declared that the most that had ever gone missing on the island was a clutch of eggs or the odd turnip out of the fields, but the tattie howkers were blamed anyway.

Kirsty knew it too. She remembered her grandfather saying, 'They must always be watching their step for fear of putting a foot wrong.'

'And why not?' her mother had replied. 'You know as well as I do what they are like!' But her grandfather would never agree.

'It's bigotry, nothing more. We are the same blood,' he said, strangely, and Kirsty had no idea what he meant.

She looked sideways at the boy. It didn't seem to her as though they could possibly have the same blood. He was very dark, with short sooty hair like her favourite cat and a thin face with marks like bruises under his eyes. But he had beautiful eyes, like little fishes. He seemed too old and grown-up to be a playmate. He looked very sad, and she saw that there were tears on his eyelashes and her own eyes filled up with sympathetic moisture.

'Oh don't cry,' she said and watched as he rubbed his eyes fiercely with a grubby hand, leaving sandy smudges around them.

'I'm not cryin',' he said, angrily. 'Why would I be cryin'? The wind's in me eyes. That's all.'

Surreptitiously she lifted the hem of her skirt and pulled a faded blue handkerchief out of her navy knickers. 'Here,' she said. 'You can have my hankie anyway.'

'I don't want it.'

'But look at you, you're all muddy.' She licked her hankie and wiped briskly at his cheeks, the way her mother sometimes cleaned her own face and hands when there was no soap and water to hand.

He started to laugh. 'I'm all right, sure. I'm fine. Leave me alone will you?' he said, pushing her away. His accent was funny. He took the hankie from her and rubbed his eyes. When he handed it back to her, it was streaked with sandy marks of soil from his face and fingers.

'What do you do with your handkerchiefs?' her mother would say when she was sorting them out for the weekly wash.

'Where's your friend?' she asked him. 'Where's the other lad?'

He looked round, uneasily. 'How should I know? Down in the byre maybe. Sleeping. I don't have to spend all my time with him, do I?'

'I was just asking.'

The truth was that Francis had wanted to come but he had given him the slip, desperate to spend some time on his own for once.

'What's your name?' she asked him. 'Finn what?'

She was a great one for names.

'You have to know the names of things, Kirsty: trees, plants, birds, flowers.' That's what her grandfather always told her. 'Names are important. It's no good being careless about such things.'

Her grandad knew the names of all the wild flowers that grew on the island and she liked to file the words away in her mind. Bogbean and ladies tresses. Speedwell and celandine. She liked the sounds that they made on her tongue. It was almost as though she could taste the words themselves like the luscious bramble that grew in such profusion and the glossy but bland crowberry. In her mind, the words themselves had colours, colours that had nothing to do with the objects they described. But even more than saying them, she liked to draw and paint them.

Ever since she could first hold a pencil, Kirsty had loved to draw. When she ran out of drawing paper she had simply drawn on the endpapers of books or in the farm account books or sometimes on the wallpaper in her bedroom. Eventually her grandfather had persuaded Mrs McGregor at the village shop to stock large pads of coarse cartridge paper, paints, paint brushes and soft pencils, and kept Kirsty well supplied with them. She liked to make pictures of flowers, birds and animals. The kitchen wall was full of them, all sellotaped together, because her mother could never bear to throw any of them away.

'My name's Finn O'Malley,' he said.

'Finn O'Malley,' she repeated. 'Are you from Ireland like the rest of them?'

He pointed to the south west where the sea glittered in the light of the setting sun.

'Somewhere over there.'

'Are you homesick?'

He considered this for a moment. 'Maybe. But I don't know why.'

'Why don't you know why?' She was a persistent child. She would follow a question to the bitter end and beyond.

'Because I don't live at home.'

You wouldn't call that place home. But then, where would he call home? His memories were a series of vivid pictures like the comic books they had once been given at Christmas. Visitors had come to the school and brought Beano Annuals with them. The boys had looked at them for a day or two but then the books had disappeared. His memories of home were like comic books with some of the pages torn out. He couldn't always make sense of them.

'Oh.' Kirsty nodded sagely. He must know what he was talking about. But she didn't really know what he meant.

'Is your mammy not here with you?' she asked.

'No. She's not with me.'

'You must miss your mammy though,' she said, after a pause.

'Yes, I miss her. But I don't live with her.'

'Do you not?'

'No.' He was reluctant to elaborate, ashamed of the truth. What would she think of him if she knew? 'I'm away at school. With a lot of other boys. Francis as well.'

'Is that his name? Your friend? He's very thin, isn't he?'

A brief smile hovered over his lips. 'We call him Francie. He's thin, for sure. He's at the school with me. There's nobody fat at the school. Well, not the boys, anyway.'

'Is he homesick as well?'

'I think he's just glad to get beyond the school wall for once. We both are.'

'We go away to school as well. When we're older. We all have to go and stay on the mainland during the week. Is that what you have to do? Do you live on an island?'

He shook his head but didn't choose to reply.

'Is it nice?' she asked. 'Your school?'

'No.'

'Why not? What's wrong with it?'

He hesitated. 'They won't let me go and see my mammy.'

She wondered who 'they' were and how they could be so cruel.

'But you can see her in the holidays, can't you?' she asked. 'Oh but you're here, of course.'

'That's right. I'm here. Diggin' your tatties.'

'That's a shame. Well, I'm glad you're here. But I'm sorry you won't see your mammy.'

He was silent again, staring at the sea. He had not asked her name but she ventured the information anyway.

'I'm Kirsty.'

'I know it. I heard the ould man calling you that.'

'Well, my proper name is Cairistiona but everyone calls me Kirsty just. Kirsty Galbreath.'

He nodded, but volunteered nothing more about himself, just sat there staring out to sea and picking at the purple thyme flowers and the small grasses, with grubby fingers.

'It's nice up here, isn't it?' she offered, after a while.

'It's all right.' He looked around as though seeing it properly for the first time.

'This is the best place on the whole island. This is Hill Top Town.'

'I thought it was Dunshee.'

'No,' she said, 'Not the farm. That *is* Dunshee. I mean this bit. Up here. Hill Top Town. That's what my grandad calls it. That's what everyone calls it, though there's no town here that I can see.'

'There is no town. You're right.'

'I asked my grandad and he said there might once have been one, a long time ago.'

'Maybe so. You mean down there?' Interested in spite of himself, he turned to look into the shallow bowl of land with its scattering of grey rocks that formed the summit of the hill.

'That's right. And do you see the part where the flags grow, the yellow irises there? That usually means water. A spring maybe. And that means a village.'

'Is that so?'

'My grandad said so.'

'And he's always right, your grandad?'

'Of course,' she said, unaware of the edge of mockery in his tone, and he didn't have the heart to laugh at her.

'This is your first time over here. At the tatties.'

'It is.'

'And how long will you be staying?'

He shrugged. 'A few months. We've only just started with the earlies. We'll be working on the other farms, and maybe going to some of the other islands, but we're to live here at Dunshee mostly. The gaffer likes Dunshee. He says you know where you are with Dunshee.'

'That's good.' She stood up, levering herself off the ground with her hand on his shoulder.

'Why is it good?'

'Because I don't have many people to play with and you can come out with me so long as you're here.'

He stood up. His corduroy trousers, already solid with mud from the fields, were too small for him. He was self conscious, looking down at his naked ankles.

'They won't let me do that, will they? And not with a girl!'

She saw that his boots were very worn, each sole parting company with the top in a gaping grin. His feet must be wet all the time.

'They will so. My grandad will. He'll let you if I ask him. You don't work on Sundays, do you?'

She could twist her grandad around her little finger.

'Leave the child be,' he often said to her mother, Isabel. 'Let the child do what she wants.'

'You spoil her!'

'And why not? What else would I be doing with my one and only grandchild? How can you spoil someone by loving them?'

'Do you like fishing?' Kirsty asked.

'Maybe.'

'I've got a rod. We can go fishing. There's a loch with trout. It belongs to the estate but my grandad's allowed to fish there.'

'I don't know ...' Finn hesitated. 'I'm here to work. I have to work. I can't just be going off at your say so.'

'You'll get a bit of time off to go fishing though. I'll ask my grandad if you can come with us.'

He would say yes. She was the apple of his eye. When he was just a boy himself, Kirsty's grandad had spoken only Gaelic. He had learned his first English at school. Now there was hardly anyone on the island except for some of the older people who remembered the old tongue. But sometimes he would call Kirsty '*a'ghraidh*'. Darling. She was his darling and he would do whatever she asked.

'Listen, we'll take you fishing. Me and my grandad. Francis can come too if you like. I don't mind. And there's the beach down there. We can go to the beach some days. Make sandcastles. Swim. It'll be good. You'll see.'

As an adult, Finn often found himself rehearsing this first conversation in his mind, polishing the story like a beach pebble, making it perfect in his memory. What was it about her, he wondered, that had so drawn him to her? Or her to him for that matter. He had never been instantly popular, not with anyone except his mother and she didn't count. Was it pity for his loneliness? Curiosity about the stranger, for it was clear that there were few visitors to the island? Or just a childish perception of his need. Was it the same instinct that made her so anxious to bottle feed the orphan lambs for her grandad? Finn O'Malley looked up at her as she stood over him, small and ingenuous, her red hair in two fat plaits hanging on either side of her freckled face, and he grinned at her.

'All right,' he said. 'If you like. I don't mind if I do. '

Chapter Three

KIRSTY ASKED HER grandfather about the fishing and he agreed. 'Aye, if you like. Tell him to bring the other lad as well. What's his name?'

'The dark one's Finn. The fair one's Francis.'

'They can both come. That Francis looks as though he could do with a good feed. If I had a beast that was looking like that, I would be giving it extra rations and calling in the vet.'

'Is this wise?' asked Isabel.

'Why not? They're only young lads. They need a holiday now and then. The work's back breaking. They're young to be over here. God knows why they were even sent. Or where they come from. I asked the gaffer, but he wasn't very forthcoming. They have a strange look about them, that pair.'

'What kind of look?'

'I can't quite put my finger on it. There's something in their eyes. Do you mind that dog we had one time? Came from that big farm on the mainland. Never could do anything with him. I always wondered what had happened to that dog before we got him.'

'I don't know what you're talking about, dad.' Isabel always called her father-in-law 'dad'. She had lost her own father not long before she herself was widowed, but she had never been close to him. He had been a straight-laced man, good and God-fearing, but humourless. Alasdair was a benign soul by comparison, although you wouldn't want to cross him.

'I mind the dog well. It had to be put down in the end. But what has a rogue sheepdog to do with the tattie howkers?'

'The money, I suppose. It could only be the money. That must be why they send them. They come from a boarding school, you know. Some big place run by the Christian Brothers. That's what Terrans told me. But why they're there, I have no idea, and I couldn't get anything more out of him. Does that mean they're orphans or what? Perhaps he doesn't know himself.'

'Heavens above! Why are you so worried about them? They're just a pair of daft lads. Maybe they misbehaved themselves. Maybe it's a borstal or something.'

'I don't think so. That Francis looks as though he wouldn't say boo to a goose. He's no delinquent.'

Isabel sighed. She couldn't see what all the fuss was about. Sometimes her father-in-law's conscience exasperated her, although she would have been the first to admit that it was what distinguished him from her own father, who had been content to pay lip-service to the concept of 'loving thy neighbour as thyself' without ever demonstrating it in real life.

'You wouldn't like to see our wee Kirsty in the same situation.'

'That's a different matter altogether and well you know it. But taking these lads fishing now, making favourites of them, I just think…'

'What?'

'Is it quite suitable?'

'Don't be so po-faced woman!'

It was the mildest of rebukes but Isabel knew when she was beaten. Alasdair only ever bothered to argue with his daughter-in-law about points of principle but then he was unmoveable.

Alasdair often took Kirsty fly fishing to the loch at the back of Ealachan House. He was on reasonably friendly terms with Malcolm Laurence who practically owned half the island and had stocked the loch with trout. Alasdair was casually deferential. He would have preferred it if he were not a tenant farmer. But what couldn't be cured must be endured, and permission to fish was one of the perks of the tenancy. He was teaching Kirsty to cast. The rod was long and too heavy for her but she managed.

Sometimes they met Malcolm Laurence's son, Nicolas. Like his siste, he was away at school during term time, but he spent at least part of his summer holidays on the island. The family had a house in London, but twelve year old Nicolas was said to be 'chesty', and they sent him north for his health. Kirsty and her grandad often saw him walking the island paths with his black Labrador at his heels, looking like a youthful version of his father. He wore the same tweedy clothes, the same polished brogues. His appearance always exasperated Alasdair.

He whistled his over-exuberant dog to heel and wished them a polite good evening, although he looked faintly surprised by their companions.

'Spot of fishing, eh?' he said.

'Just a spot,' said Alasdair and walked on.

'Nice evening for it.'

'It is indeed.'

'Would you look at that?' said Alasdair to Finn when he had gone past. 'He'll be my landlord one day! May the good lord keep Malcolm Laurence safe and sound and give him a long life.'

Finn just grinned, and whistled through his teeth, faintly embarrassed by the outburst. Francis blushed as though the slight had been aimed at himself.

'Don't you like Nicolas?' asked Kirsty. 'I think he's a nice boy. Much nicer than his horrible sister.' She screwed up her nose at the thought of Annabel.

'Oh he's fine,' said Alasdair, patting her on the head. 'Don't you waste your time worrying about Nicolas Laurence, my wee lamb. He doesn't need *your* sympathy.'

At the loch, Kirsty practised her casting for a while and then lent Finn her rod, very willingly. It was her great-grandfather's old rod, in smooth greenheart with brass fittings. It was too heavy for her to handle but fine for Finn who, so her grandad said, was quite big for his age and surprisingly strong. Francis seemed content to lean his back against a tree and watch them. When Alasdair offered to show him how to cast, he shook his head.

'I'm all right here, mister,' was all he would say. 'I don't mind if I watch.'

Kirsty sat in the shade among the creamy meadowsweet, and

watched Finn too. She noticed that he was left-handed like her grandfather.

Alasdair was being quietly kind to the boy.

'Come on, lad,' he said. 'Let's see what you can do.'

It was very warm beside the loch. When you breathed in, you could feel the heat in your mouth, a sense of suffocation. Kirsty judged, with some satisfaction, that Finn wasn't quite as competent as she. There were tiny green spiders among the meadowsweet and they scuttled over her hands and legs, tickling her as they went. She lifted her hand and watched as one of them dived into space, swinging from its own silk, trapezing from her finger. Carefully she lowered it to the ground, making sure that it landed in a hollow below a stone, not wanting to squash it when she got to her feet. The smell of cut grass drifted across from the gardens at Ealachan and mingled with the musky scent of meadowsweet.

She raised her eyes, and saw that Francis was watching Finn too. Finn was a dark silhouette, obliterating the sun. Her grandad had been showing him how to cast properly. 'Tick Tock,' he said, to time the cast. She was already proud of having a big boy for a friend. She heard the plop as the float hit the surface and saw the widening rings out on the water as fish rose to flies, but not to her grandad's bait. Or Finn's either, for that matter. She felt the nip of the midges on her arms and legs and slapped at them, but they were persistent. She was afraid that they would have to go home before they had caught anything. Over in the woods beside Ealachan house, she could hear the immense din of rooks beginning to circle, intent on roosting, jostling for position.

Seeing that they hadn't caught anything, Alasdair used ground bait, something he wasn't supposed to do, and they caught two fat trout in a matter of minutes. He dispatched each fish with a single blow from his wooden 'priest', the weighted cosh that he kept in his fishing bag . Kirsty noticed how Francis flinched when her grandfather hit the fishes. Then they took them home to Dunshee where her mother gutted them and cooked them in a frying pan on the top of the stove.

Finn gazed around in wonder. The house was warm and cluttered.

The kitchen was home to an old Scots dresser with a row of small spice drawers along the top and a row of deeper drawers set over the base. The surface was crammed with pottery cows and horses and a collection of lustre jugs, several of them containing bunches of wild flowers in varying stages of freshness. Kirsty loved to pick flowers. There was an ancient spinning wheel in one corner of the room. Even now, in the middle of summer, the fire in the kitchen range was burning brightly. The wireless was playing Scottish dance music. It was a big, boxy affair with exotic names like Hilversum and Luxemburg on the dial. In use, it grew very warm, and the cat liked to sit on top of it with the music spilling out of his soft body.

'We should likely be getting back to the barn now,' Finn said, uncertainly. 'They'll be wondering where we are.'

Francis, who was looking equally uncomfortable with his surroundings, nodded. 'I think we should go, sir.'

'Not at all!' Alasdair told them, pulling out chairs for them both and motioning them to sit down. 'What's the point of catching the fish if you don't get to eat them afterwards?'

Kirsty saw that when her mother looked at timid Francis, her expression softened. Both boys stayed to eat with them: fried trout and boiled potatoes with scones mixed with buttermilk and baked in the oven at one side of the kitchen fire. All the bread and cakes were baked in this oven. Kirsty liked to help, liked to watch her mother putting her thumb-print into each of the big bread cakes or throwing flour into the bottom of the oven. If it burned, the oven was too hot. If it stayed white, the oven was too cool. If it went pale golden brown, the oven was just right. There was something infinitely satisfying to Kirsty about this simple formula although she couldn't explain why. Sometimes she lay in bed at night, imagining herself as a grown-up woman, in charge of the house, tossing flour into the oven. Trying to get the temperature exactly right.

Finn and Francis sat side by side at the kitchen table. Francis picked at his food, too shy to eat in company. He kept looking over at Isabel who smiled at him encouragingly.

'On you go, son,' she said. 'On you go!'

Finn, on the other hand, ate ravenously, glancing over his shoulder from time to time. He held his arms protectively around his plate and forked the buttery fish and potatoes into his mouth, hardly pausing to chew between mouthfuls, burning his tongue on the delicious flesh.

'Steady, lad,' said Alasdair, watching him, his brow furrowed into a frown. 'Steady on. You'll need a wee pause between mouthfuls. You'll not be wanting to choke yourself.'

Finn looked up, and Kirsty thought that he reminded her of the farm dogs when they hunched protectively over a bone, casting dangerous, white eyed glances in all directions. Or perhaps he was more like the lonely crows that lurked about the farm, waiting to scavenge dead meat. But she said nothing. She found herself blushing for him.

Francis dug him in the ribs. Finn looked up and saw them watching him. He coloured up as well, moved his arms away from his plate and slowed down.

Isabel spooned out more potatoes for him but she snatched the spoon away quickly, as though she were feeding a wild animal.

'Thanks,' he said. 'Thanks very much, missus.' He looked up and flashed his sudden, disconcerting smile at her, but she turned away in disgust.

'Have some more potatoes, Francis. You look as if you could do with a good meal inside you.'

'Are they your only trousers?' asked Alasdair, when the meal was finished. He had been deep in thought for most of it.

Finn nodded.

'I think I might have a better pair than that up the stairs. Isabel, you'll maybe fetch the old woollen trews from the bottom of my wardrobe. He'll have to roll them up, but they'll be warmer than what he has on.'

Isabel looked daggers across the table. 'Those were James's trousers.'

'Aye. And he has no further use of them where he is. There's a couple of tweed jackets as well. They'll be a wee thing threadbare but there's a lot of wear in them still. The lads can make use of them, I'm sure.'

'If you say so.'

'I do.'

'Thanks, mister.' Finn raised his head and looked directly at Alasdair, then dropped his eyes to his plate again.

Alasdair reached out and patted him on the shoulder.

'Good lad,' he said. 'Good lad.'

For the first time, Kirsty felt something that she would always feel in Finn's company. She felt a sudden sense of proprietary pride in him, as though praise of Finn was praise of herself, but it was compounded, as it always would be, by a sharp pang of jealousy. She wanted him all to herself. But she wanted her grandad all to herself as well.

'Am I not good?' she asked her grandfather, plaintively.

'Of course you are. You're my Cairistiona. My little lass!' he said, turning from his plate to tug at her pigtails, tying them into a loose knot at the back of her neck. Kirsty was ticklish. She hunched her shoulders and shivered, but still she liked it when he teased her in this way. She caught Francis watching Finn as he ate, and Finn glancing from her to her grandfather and back again. He looked hungry. That's what she thought. But how could he be hungry when he was in the middle of eating? When he had eaten so much already?

'Just eat your tea and stop your nonsense, Kirsty,' said her mother. 'And then Finn and Francis had better get back to their friends in the barn.'

Chapter Four

WHEN SCHOOL WAS over for the summer, Kirsty was never very far from the tattie fields, and even the swimming dolls lay forgotten in her bedroom cupboard. She swung on the gate, watching the work. Often, when the weather was fine, she went into the fields and helped out, gathering up the miniature potatoes that were left behind, the 'pig potatoes' that were much too good for the pigs. She and her mother and grandad liked to eat them fried up in butter in a cast iron pan until they were crispy. Occasionally, Finn and Francis would be invited to share the meal.

When the rain came driving in from the west, Alasdair sent her home, although if it was up to her she would have soldiered on through the mud. Finn couldn't help but admire the bossiness of her, the way she laid down the law to everyone, even her grandfather. Finn found Alasdair unnerving. He was always kind to the boys but there was something uncompromising about him.

'A better friend than an enemy,' said Jimsy, and Finn could see that he was right.

Kirsty was not a steady worker. She was too easily distracted by the heron's long legs trailing behind him as he flew past or the sight of a boat in the bay. And she sang all the time.

'Do you know this one?' she asked Finn:

'If I were a blackbird I'd whistle and sing,
and follow the ship that my true love sails in.'

Kirsty had a high, clear voice and the lines made him shiver.

'Go on,' he muttered. 'Sing it all.'

'I don't know all the words.'

His mother had sung the same song. But she had smoked all the time, and it made her hoarse. You could hear it in her voice. It brought back into his mind other songs his mother had sung to him: I Wish I Was In Carrickfergus and You are My Heart's Delight. The sound of Kirsty's voice brought an unexpected lump to his throat. He had to cough to make it go away. Odds and ends of memory thronged his mind. The least little thing, like a daft song, could bring them tumbling in, distracting him, hurting the heart of him, like the sharp pain when somebody kicked you in the chest, bits and pieces of memory that were neither use nor ornament because he could not make sense of them. He wished they would go away.

'What are you like?' said Alasdair, interrupting his grand-daughter in the middle of her song. 'You're a distraction to honest working folk, that's what you are, Kirsty Galbreath! You're worse than the midgies, always nipping at people's ears!'

The older Irish indulged her.

'Come here to me,' they said when she sat among them as they took their mid-day meal. They gave her bits of bread and cheese or Victory V lozenges, that she always tried to eat, wishing she could like them. But the pungent sweets made her want to retch and she spat them out secretly into the long grass, so as not to seem impolite.

One day, when they were sitting at the edge of the field, Francis shyly plaited a whip out of reeds for her. Finn wished he had thought to do that, for he could make a whip as well as the next man.

'I could do that,' he said to her when the whip was finished. 'I could make you one of those, Kirsty.'

'Why didn't you, then?'

'Well I will so, next time.'

Finn was filling out, growing stronger, the outdoor work and plentiful food suiting him, but Francis still looked a bit like a reed himself, as though the merest breath of wind would blow him away. He would hardly ever speak unless spoken to. He was always dropping things and he still worked more slowly than Micky Terrans would have liked. A weakling. Finn helped him out whenever he could, sometimes doing the work of two to cover up for his friend, but the older men would grow impatient with him and cuff him round the head, casually, if he was too slow. 'Get that feckin' basket over here, would ya?' they would say. Once, when a blow caught him unawares, he fell over and lay stunned on the ground for a moment or two. Micky Terrans came running over, furious.

'Who the feck did that? Did you see who did that, Finn?'

Finn shook his head. He thought it had probably been Jimsy Murtagh who was very ready with the flat of his hand and his fist too if you didn't look out, but the blow had been as casual as the punishment a bitch will mete out to her pups, and just as lacking in malice. Besides, Francie was used to it. They both were. You didn't interfere. And you certainly didn't tell.

'I didn't see, Micky.'

The older men looked at each other, faintly embarrassed.

Micky helped Francis up and dusted him down. 'Are you all right, son?'

'Aye, I'm fine, mister. It was nothing at all. Nothing at all.'

But for an hour afterwards, there was the crimson print of a hand across his cheek with little bits of dirt from the tatties sticking to it.

Francis had few real friends among the tattie howkers, other than Finn. But over the weeks that the tattie howkers had been at Dunshee, Isabel seemed to have developed a rough partiality for the boy, although she had never taken to Finn in the same way. If she came down to the fields with a bit of left over baking, stale scones or maybe a fruit cake, she would make sure that Francis had the first pick from the tin.

'Take another piece,' she would tell him. 'Take one for later. Put it in your pocket, lad!'

If Alasdair took Finn and Kirsty fly fishing at Ealachan, she would always make sure that Francis went too.

'Don't you be sneaking off without that poor boy!'

She even came back from the kirk jumble sale with a suit and a pair of nearly new shoes that she thought might do very well for him since, so she said, they had belonged to an islander who was almost as skinny as Francis himself. Francis responded to these small gestures with a mixture of embarrassment and gratitude. He couldn't understand them but they seemed like blessings, and he basked in the thin light of Isabel's regard as though it were the blazing sun of real affection.

Almost every Sunday during his first summer on the island, Finn would contrive to spend time with Kirsty, often with Francis tagging along behind them. The days always seemed to follow much the same pattern. Kirsty would go down to the kirk with her mother and grandfather, all three of them dressed in their best clothes. After the service, there might be tea and biscuits and a little gossip in the village hall, while a few of the men lingered in the doorway, smoking and chatting about fishing and farming matters.

Occasionally, Malcolm Laurence would put in an appearance, expansive and charming in his Sunday suit, drinking tea, eating a scone or two with butter and raspberry jam slathered on top, passing the time of day with his tenants. His light brown hair was thinning, his face long and patrician, and he swallowed his consonants so that you had to listen hard to know what he was saying. But his self confidence was attractive. He could be surprisingly flirtatious. When he laughed, he would throw back his head and fill the room with sound. Isabel, who had worked in the kitchen at Ealachan House before her marriage, always merited a special smile and a few kind words. Alasdair would watch these exchanges from a distance, wondering how such small attentions could please his daughter-in-law so much when she was so thoroughly sensible in every other way.

Later, when Isabel could tear herself away, they would come back to Dunshee and eat their Sunday dinner, accompanied by Family Favourites on the wireless. Dinner was usually a joint of lamb or beef that had been cooking slowly in their absence. There was always a steamed pudding on Sundays as well: ginger or chocolate or apple sponge with custard. Then Kirsty was allowed to change into her old clothes so that she, Finn and Francis could go down to the beach or climb up the hill behind the farm. There was an unspoken pact between them at this time that they would not go down to the village where there would be disapproval of the friendship between Kirsty and the two young tattie howkers, no matter how much it was sanctioned by Alasdair. But they would sometimes walk beyond the confines of Dunshee, taking the tracks along the western side of the island, where there were the remains of half a dozen settlements, ruined cottages abandoned at the time of the clearances.

One warm Sunday, Alasdair walked down to the beach below Dunshee. The two boys were sitting on a rock, watching a single swan as she paddled smoothly along the shallows, while Kirsty drew pictures on the flat sand. She loved this smooth canvas that refreshed itself each day, loved how the sea sometimes left her a mysterious picture of its own, a scattering of shells, a few strands of seaweed arranged like so many question marks. Alasdair sat beside them, watching his grand-daughter fondly.

'Can you handle a boat?' He addressed the question to all of them, but his eyes were on Finn.

Kirsty looked up. 'I can row, can't I grandad? I'm a good rower!'

'I know fine you can row. But I meant the lads here.'

Francis said nothing. Finn shook his head. 'I'd never even been in a boat, mister, till the day I came to Scotland. That was the first time.'

'Would you like to learn?'

Finn glanced behind Alasdair to where the wooden rowing boat rested on the sand, tied up to an iron stanchion in the rock. He saw Alasdair going out to his creels each day and wondered what it would feel like to be in charge of the little vessel.

'I would so,' he said.

'What about you, Francis?'

'I don't think so.' Francis frowned, screwing his eyes up against the sun, and Alasdair thought for a moment that he might be going to cry. Anything new seemed to terrify him.

He hastened to reassure the boy. 'Maybe next year, eh? If you come back here?'

Francis brightened. 'Maybe next year.'

Alasdair got to his feet. 'Come on, Finn. You can help me get her into the water.'

'Can I come too?' asked Kirsty, standing up and brushing the sand from her fingers.

'No, no, no. Not the first time. I know you all too well, my Kirsty. You'd be queening it over him, and telling him everything he was doing wrong. You stay here and keep Francis company. I'll show Finn what he has to do.'

Finn helped Alasdair drag the boat towards the water. He could see the few floats that marked Alasdair's creels bobbing about and a line of waves, further out, where the sheltered waters of the bay gave place to the open waters of the sound.

'Now,' said Alasdair gently. 'First things first. You must never turn a boat against the sun. Always clockwise, lad. Always with the sun.'

'Why would that be?'

'For luck, I suppose. I don't know for sure. But it was what my own father always did, and so it's good enough for me. Once I'm in, you can step in too, but mind you step into the middle of the boat. And quickly with the other leg. We want no disasters, do we?'

Once Finn was settled, Alasdair seized the oars and pulled strongly away from the shore.

'Were you sick on the ferry?' he asked.

'No. But I felt sick.'

'Aye well, not surprising for your first time. It's a lucky man who doesn't have a touch of the mal de mer. I'm no great shakes myself on a rough day.' He chuckled and shipped the oars. The boat slopped about gently, but there was little movement on this fine day. The water was clear beneath them. Finn could see great fronds of seaweed down there, an underwater forest. On Alasdair's instructions, they changed places, and soon Finn was rowing, clumsily at first, with a good deal of splashing, but with growing confidence. When a grey head popped up only a few yards away from them, he was so surprised that he almost dropped an oar.

'Steady,' said Alasdair. 'No disasters mind.'

'What is it?'

Alasdair turned around. 'It's just a seal. Do you not know a seal when you see one? One of the selkie folk come to check if we might be doing any fishing today.'

Finn shook his head. 'I've never seen one. I thought it was a man, so.'

'Well, they do have a kind of human look about them. You've never seen one?'

'I've never been so close to the water.'

'And do you like it? Being in a boat.'

'I like it fine.'

'I can never tell with you, Finn. It's hard to tell whether you like something or not.'

Finn didn't know how to reply. What was he expected to say? You had to say and do what was expected of you. That was the trick.

'Well, once you get the hang of the rowing you can maybe help me lift my creels. Do you think you could do that? Help me haul them in and bait them again?'

'I could try. But I'm not supposed …'

'Ach don't be telling me what you're not supposed to do, Finn. I'm sick and tired of supposed. I'll have a word with your gaffer. Might as well teach you to be useful, eh, Finn? Might as well teach you some useful skills while you're here. That way, if you come back again we might manage to find a better job for you.'

Finn stared at the horizon but said nothing.

'Would you like to come back here?'

'I would like it fine.'

'You might show a bit of enthusiasm, wee man.'

'But I don't know if it'll happen.'

'How come you're over here this year? You and your pal?'

'I don't know, mister. One of the Brothers said he would arrange it.'

'The brothers?'

'One of the teachers at the school. He was from Enniskillen. Brother Patrick. I think he was sorry for us. I think that must have been it. He said he would see what he could do. See if they would send us to the tatties. He knew Micky Terrans from before. I think his da must have been a farmer.'

Alasdair sat quietly, listening. This was the most he had ever heard Finn say.

'I don't think Micky wanted to take us, but Brother Patrick persuaded him an' all. He's a great one for persuading folk is Brother Patrick.'

Finn thought about Brother Patrick, bull neck, hands like two hams. A gentle giant. The son of a farmer. Good with the beasts, they said. The Brothers ran a farm as well as the school, and they always sent for him if there were any problems. He had smiled all the time when he first came to the school, but didn't smile so much now.

'Why you two?'

Finn shrugged. 'I don't know. Well, I think he might have been sorry for Francie. You know, Francie has a hard time at the school, mister.'

'I'm sure he does. And what about you? Do you have a hard time?'

'It's kind of bad for all of us. But Francie has it worse. I think Brother Patrick could see that, but he was looking for somebody to go with Francie. He couldn't just send him on his own, could he? I mean he knew fine Francie couldn't lift a *graip* to save himself.'

'So he sent you too.'

'Aye. He sent me too. I'm strong. He said they would be glad of the money at any rate. Micky Terrans keeps back most of our pay and sends it to the school. He just gives us something to buy sweets in the shop.'

'He does, does he?'

'He says that was the arrangement. With the Brothers.'

'And are you glad, Finn? Are you glad to be here?'

'Yeah. I think so. I think I'm glad, mister. It's better than the school. And I hope they send us back here again next year, so I do.'

Chapter Five

EACH YEAR, THE swallows returned to Dunshee from wherever they chose to spend their winter months. Kirsty always looked out for the first pair of them in late April or early May. One evening, they would come swooping over the house in long curves, inspecting the rows of old nests under the eaves. Kirsty liked to imagine these early visitors deciding which would be the most suitable for their needs. She pictured the nests, comfortably lined with strands of her own hair. Whenever Isabel trimmed the ends, she always deposited the hairs on the windowsill for the birds. One winter's day, when Kirsty was five years old, her grandad had come home carrying a robin's nest that he had found tucked into one of the field hedges. It was lined with a fabric of closely interwoven red hairs. She had taken it down to the school where it sat on the nature table for years. New infants would look at it and say, 'That's Kirsty Galbreath's hair!'

'You couldn't make one of those, however hard you tried!' said the teacher. Kirsty knew that she was right, because she had tried and it was impossible. She had assembled the materials, sure that she could do it, but everything just fell to pieces beneath her fingers.

In May, Kirsty heard the sad song of the curlew over the farm by night as well as by day. Her grandad told her that curlews were residents, not summer visitors like the martins and swallows and the mysterious corncrake with his strange, sawing cry that Kirsty often heard when she was in bed on summer nights.

'Where do they go in the winter?' she asked him, and he said, 'Oh they lie low, Kirsty. They just lie low.'

She waited anxiously for Finn to return, wondering if he had been lying low as well. The island climate was very mild and the potato harvest started early, but she worried. Perhaps he wouldn't come back. Perhaps 'they', whoever they were, wouldn't let him.

Isabel brushed her daughter's long hair every night. She was very gentle, holding it twisted in her left hand and combing it carefully with her right to get the tangles out first so that it didn't tug too much.

'You have lovely hair, God bless it!' she would say.

'Mum?' said Kirsty, watching her mother's reflection in the mirror. 'Do you think the Irish boys will come to the tatties this year?' She felt her mother's grip on the thick strands of hair tighten and then relax.

'I have no notion. Why do you ask?'

'I thought you liked Francie,' said Kirsty, cunningly. 'He's a nice lad, isn't he?'

Isabel sighed. 'He's a poor soul right enough. And I was sorry for him last year. But there was nothing I could do about him.'

'You used to try to feed him up a bit.'

'Aye, I did. But maybe they'll not come this year.'

'You mean Finn, don't you?' she said. 'You wouldn't mind if Francie came back, but not if it means Finn comes too.'

'I wish you wouldn't go on like this, Kirsty!'

'You're tugging!'

'I'm sorry.'

'I like Finn. He's a nice boy. Why didn't you like him?'

'I didn't dislike him.'

'Grandad says he's a good worker. He says he has plans for him. If he comes back that is.'

'Well I hope he doesn't.'

'Why not?'

'It's not fair on him, treating him like one of the family. When all's said and done, even if he does come back to the tatties this year, he'll only be here for a few months and then he'll be gone, back to wherever he spends the winter. Back to that school. It's not fair to do that. To give people a taste of something different. Better. And then just take it away from them. It only makes things worse.'

Kirsty gazed at her mother in the mirror. 'You didn't mind treating Francie like one of the family.'

'What did I ever do but give him the odd piece of cake and a few clothes for himself? What was the harm in that? And besides, that boy would never, ever take advantage. He would just take what he was given and be grateful.'

'So would Finn.'

'Leave it be, Kirsty. Leave it be and get into bed!'

One morning, when Kirsty was sitting in the schoolroom and struggling with arithmetic, she glanced briefly out of the window, saw the truck come lumbering up the road and knew that the tattie howkers had arrived. It was raining heavily and the windows were misted with droplets. She couldn't see whether Finn and Francis were among them or not. She could hardly contain her excitement and fidgeted for the rest of the day.

'What's wrong with you, Kirsty Galbreath?' her teacher asked.

But she just shook her head, sat on her hands and said, ' Nothing, Miss.'

When she came home from school, the weather had improved, as it so often did after a morning of rain. Dog roses were unfurling in all the hedgerows and a late, hot sun was conjuring steam from the fields. The Irish had arrived early and were already at work. Kirsty came running up the hill and paused on the brink of one of the tattie fields, shading her eyes, scanning the bent figures. There he was, wielding the big fork with a will, though the sandy soil was wet and welded itself to the tines in heavy clumps. She felt another churning of excitement in her stomach. She stood up on the lower bar of the gate and shouted his name.

'Finn! Hey! Finn O'Malley!'

He looked over at her but didn't move, so she waved frantically, balancing on the gate. It left a line of rust along the front of her powder blue school dress.

'Finn! Come here!'

He rested his fork on one of the carts and came over, clumsily negotiating the edge of the field in his boots that were better than last year's, but much too big for him, and then standing still, a few paces away from her. He didn't know what to do with his hands, so he thrust them into his pockets.

'You came back!' she said.

'I did so.'

He had grown taller. And he seemed to have grown shy again in the intervening months. But she was so obviously pleased to see him that he found himself smiling at her.

'It's nice to be back,' he said.

To his surprise, she clambered over the gate, her sandals scrabbling on the rusted metal, rushed over to him, reached up and hugged him. He hardly knew where to put himself. And yet he liked it. She had been eating fruit gums and her mouth was red. She smelled of raspberry jam.

'I have to get back to work,' he said.

'Is Francie with you?'

'He's here.'

'My mammy will be glad!'

Micky agreed to bring both of us again. But I don't know how he'll do this year.'

'Why not?'

'He's not so well.'

'What's wrong with him?'

She saw his expression change, a shutter closing over a window. He shrugged. 'I don't know.'

'My mum likes Francie.'

'Aye she does. She doesn't like me much, but she likes Francie. I don't mind.'

'She likes you well enough. I'll see you later then. After tea.' It was a command rather than a request, and he wasn't inclined to argue with her.

'Where?'

'Hill Top Town, of course.'

She flew back to the gate, swarming up and over, skipping up the track towards the house. 'He's back, he's back, he's back!' she was chanting to herself as she went.

Later on that evening, she told her mother that she was going out to play.

'There's a skylark's nest up at Hill Top Town that I want a sight of.'

'Well don't be disturbing the bird on her eggs,' said her grandfather.
'I won't.'

She and Finn sat together, watching the sun sink towards the furthermost islands. Finn had given Francis the slip after their evening meal. It had not been difficult. Francis had been so tired out by the journey and the afternoon's work that he had given himself a sketchy wash and tumbled into bed practically as soon as Finn had made it up, spreading the blankets over the straw mattress. Finn had watched him anxiously for a few moments, watched the long lashes fluttering on thin cheeks, and then, satisfied that the boy was sleeping, had taken himself up to Hill Top Town where he knew that Kirsty would be waiting for him.

Far, far away they could see a couple of ring netters, like toy boats, red and green, working together on the flat waters.

'I've missed this place,' said Finn. 'I kept wishing I was here. Sometimes it was only the thought of it that kept me going.'

'I'm sure I don't know why,' said Kirsty, 'For they work you so hard.'

'They work me hard back there, as well.'

'What have you been doing? Have they let you see your mammy yet?'

'Not yet, no.'

He didn't want to talk about it, but it was only natural that she should ask. He had never explained things to her. How could he, when he didn't really understand them himself?

'Does she not write to you?'

'No. She's not allowed.'

Kirsty wanted to ask why, what his mother had done to be so punished, but she bit her tongue, suddenly shy of pressing the point. If he wanted her to know, he would tell her.

'And do you write to her?'

'How would I ever do that?'

'I could give you some paper. I have plenty. And pens. You could write her a letter from here, Finn, and I could post it for you down in the village.'

He shook his head. 'I'm no hand with a pen, Kirsty.'

'Why not?'

'I'm just not.'

'But you told me you were at the school.'

'So I am.'

'And you're a big boy now. Do they not teach you to read and write there?'

'A bit. But I wanted to write with my left hand and they won't let me do it. They say it's the devil's work.'

He pronounced it 'divil', which made her smile.

'What do you mean?'

'I have to pray for the devil to go out of me.'

'What devil?'

'I don't know, do I? For writing left handed.'

He was afraid of the pen now. That was the long and short of it. Every time he took it up in his left hand, he had a vision of Brother Bernard, his face purple with rage, his fists flying like a boxer's and just as deadly. But when Finn tried to make the letters with his right hand, they sloped backwards and, although reasonably neat, were practically illegible, a fact that seemed to throw Brother Bernard into even more of a passion. 'You're ... doing ... that ... on ... purpose!' he had bellowed, punctuating the sentence with blows. 'Take ... your ... pen ... and ... *write* as I tell you! Write! Write! Write!'

Mercifully, Kirsty interrupted his train of thought. 'Like me with my red hair do you mean?'

'What about your red hair?'

When Kirsty had first started school, she had met an old fisherman going down to his boat. She had been walking that road since she could toddle and she knew everyone along the way, so her mother just took her down to the Dunshee road end and sent her off by herself each morning. She would pass the man and say, 'Good morning,' politely, as her grandad had told her. She was surprised to see that he just grunted at her in return, crossed himself, turned right round and went back the way he had come. Then, a few days later, a letter came through the door. It was from this same old man, except that his sister had written it for him, and it asked if wee Kirsty Galbreath could please leave for school fifteen minutes earlier or perhaps fifteen minutes later, so as not to be passing him by on the road to his boat, because not a day's luck had he had with his fishing, when he could get to his boat, since the start of term. Her grandad had read the letter and laughed out loud. Isabel had been very indignant, but Alasdair had just carried on laughing.

'Silly old bugger!' he said. 'You leave it to me.'

'What will you do?' asked her mother.

'I'll write back to him.'

'And what will you say?'

'I will just tell him that he can leave earlier or later himself if he wants, so that he can avoid the terror of seeing our red headed monster on the road!'

'What's wrong with your hair?' asked Finn.

'There are people on this island who don't like my red hair. They think it's unlucky. So maybe it's the same for you if you're left handed.'

'They beat me for it. But I can't do it. I can't write properly. Not with my right hand.'

'That's so unfair. Our teacher doesn't much like it when folk write with their left hand either, but she doesn't beat them for it.'

'They're lucky.'

'You should hit them back,' she declared, robustly.

'That'll be the day! Will you come and fight them for me, Kirsty?' He started to laugh, imagining her confronting Brother Bernard, arms akimbo, or flying at him in a rage, her red hair streaming out behind her. And then the thought of brave Kirsty, only a little girl, rushing in where the angels themselves would fear to tread, gave him a strange, queasy feeling.

'I would too. I'd fight them all for you!' She looked at him, and gave a sigh of pleasure. In her eyes at least he was a hero, even now, when it seemed to her that his laughter was very close to tears. But big boys weren't supposed to cry, were they?

Chapter Six

IN LATE JULY of that year, Finn and Francis worked elsewhere on the island all day, but came back to Dunshee at nights. Sometimes, Alasdair would borrow Finn for the day to do this or that job about the farm, slipping a little money to Micky Terrans to keep him sweet. Often he would take Finn out on the water to help him with his creels, and now that the boy could handle the boat competently, he was allowed to take Kirsty out fishing as well. They took mackerel flies and sometimes they caught a box full of striped fish and sometimes they caught nothing at all. That was always the way of it with mackerel: none or a dozen. Alasdair had rigged up a miniature smokehouse in one of the outhouses where he could smoke mackerel and trout and the occasional salmon for their own use.

Isabel was anxious, all the time they were gone.

'I'm surprised you let her go with him!' she said, gazing down towards the bay where the boat was just visible, unmoving on the turquoise water, two heads in silhouette.

'It's flat calm out there. And the lad knows fine how to handle a boat now. You don't think I would have let them go otherwise, do you?'

'All I know is, if it was up to our Kirsty, they would be off to Eilean Ronan, looking for the brownie.'

Eilean Ronan was a nearby island, little more than a rock, with a ruined chieftain's house and a chapel and not much else. The brownie was a magical creature who was said to live there. He would do all your housework for you, so long as you didn't attempt to pay him. But once you offered him money, he would leave and never come back.

'He'll not take her to Ronan, no matter how much she nags him. I told him not to go so far, in case the weather changes, and whatever else you think about the lad, he always does as he's told.'

'Well I'm pleased to hear it!'

In the bay, Finn had shipped the oars, and they put out the mackerel lines, slopping about in the evening sunlight. They still couldn't persuade Francis to come out in the boat. He always made excuses. This time, he had chosen to walk into the village with a group of the older men.

'This school of yours, is it up in the hills then?' Kirsty asked Finn. She had been reading the Chalet School books and had conceived a romantic notion of Finn's school as a sort of Irish equivalent.

Finn sighed. He wished she wouldn't keep asking. He didn't want to talk about the school at all. He preferred to forget about it when he was in Scotland.

'No. You can see the hills in the distance but that's all. It's very flat round about, and that's all it is. No hills, no sea. There's a stream. The cattle drink from it.'

'And is the school nice? What about your dormitories? Do you share with Francis?'

'We all share. Lots of us, rows of beds, all in the one room.'

Saying the words evoked the smell of unwashed bodies, the smell of sweat and piss, the smell of fear. The byre was sweet by comparison. He tried to change the subject. It was what he always did when she mentioned his school. 'Look,' he said. 'Look at the seal, Kirsty!'

Kirsty loved the grey seals that popped their heads up to watch them and the shearwater skimming low with straight wings. She loved to watch Finn bending over the oars, his hair a glossy tangle, his bare brown feet planted firmly on either side of her sandshoes, and the way he looked at her, solemnly, from under dark brows.

Afterwards, they took their fish ashore, and she helped him to haul the boat high up onto the beach below Dunshee and tie it to the stanchion. They sat together on a boulder, watching the light draining gently out of the sky. She picked up a swatch of dry bladderwrack and started cracking the little capsules, each one making a satisfying 'pop'.

'I wish you were here all year round,' she said. 'You and Francie both.'

'You'd soon get tired of us.'

'No I wouldn't. I always wanted a big brother.'

'Did you?'

'I did!'

'Well, you'd soon get tired of Francie trailing along behind us.'

She looked round, as though expecting to see the boy wandering down the track to the shore, a combination of hope and timidity on his face at the sight of them.

'He was going to the village,' said Finn, reading her mind. 'He's afraid of the water. You know that.'

'He's afraid of everything.'

'He can't help it.'

Finn was always staunch in defence of his friend. Kirsty threw away her seaweed. 'Do you know any stories?' she asked.

'What kind of stories?'

'Oh any kind. All kinds. What do you read? What's your best book?'

Kirsty loved stories, especially stories with pictures. She had a bookcase in her room with a whole shelf of Enid Blyton stories and a heap of old 'Wonder Books' that someone had given her mother when she was a girl. Kirsty pored over the words and pictures: the Wild Swans, the Tinder Box, the King of the Golden River. She knew and loved them all. When she was younger, her mother or her grandad would read to her, but now she read the stories for herself. She liked to read her favourites again and again but more than that, she liked to draw pictures to go with them.

Finn was looking down at the sand. 'I don't read much,' he said. 'I told you before. I don't write much and I don't read much.'

He was wearing a faded grey jumper that was too big for him. All his clothes seemed to be too big or too small, as though none of them really belonged to him. It was unravelling at the sleeves and he picked, compulsively, at the threads. His nails were bitten to the quick and the tips of his fingers looked red and sore.

'Can you still not do it?' she asked him, candidly.

'Well, I'm not the best scholar in the world, but I can get by,' he admitted. 'I'm better than Francie at any rate, but that's not saying much. He's as thick as two short planks, God love him. We don't have any books in the school to speak of. The teachers write things up on the blackboard, and we copy them out. We don't learn very much. We once had a teacher who read to us, right enough. He wasn't our usual teacher. He was just there because the real teacher was off sick. He read something called The Wind in the Willows and it was such a gas. But he never came back to finish it.'

'That's one of my best books as well.'

'We were doubled up laughing. He put on all the different voices.'

'Which bit did he read?'

'He got through half of it before our proper teacher came back. He told us that we shouldn't laugh out loud though. Brother Michael heard us laughing once and came in to find out what was happening, and there was hell to pay.

'Is that why you don't laugh much, Finn?'

'I do so laugh. Sometimes.'

'Well, not much.'

'They don't like us laughing. We're not supposed to make too much noise in the school. The one that read to us, he never hit us. I think he couldn't stand it, couldn't stand to see it happening and him not able to do anything about it, so he took himself off. He was a bit like Brother Patrick. He never hits us either.'

'Do they really beat you?' she asked, distracted by the repetition of something he had told her earlier. 'I mean really?'

He pulled a face. 'All the time. Don't they beat the children here?'

'Well. The boys sometimes,' she admitted. 'The teacher keeps a tawse in her desk. She calls it her Lochgelly. That's the name of the place where they make them. I hate it. It's this brown belt with a split at the end, so it hurts more.'

'That's nothing at all. Brother Michael uses a piece of a car tyre with the metal still in it.'

'He doesn't!'

'He does. Have you never caught it, Kirsty?'

'Not me. My grandad won't have it. He said if our teacher ever belted me, he would go straight down there and give her a good smack with her own Lochgelly. See how she liked it! But a car tyre, Finn? A car tyre!'

'Would he do that?' asked Finn, in wonder. 'Give her a smack?'

'I think he might. I behave myself anyway, so it doesn't matter. But they don't hit the wee ones do they, Finn?'

He frowned. 'How do you mean?'

'The wee ones in the primary? They don't ever belt the wee ones here.'

He gazed at her in silence for a moment. 'I don't remember,' he said, at last.

'What do you mean, you don't remember? You must remember whether they hit the wee ones?'

'I tell you I don't remember! Jesus, Kirsty, you're enough to try the patience of a saint.'

He stood up and began to walk back up the hill towards the farm, hauling the bag of mackerel with him.

She ran after him, trying to keep up. 'So what did you like best about the Wind in the Willows?'

Finn hesitated. 'I liked that whole thing. The picnics. I always wanted to be rowing home in the sunshine like that.'

'Well now you can be.'

'What?'

'Rowing home in the sunshine like that,' she said, triumphantly, 'And you can be doing it with me.' Kirsty always liked to live her literature.

Just as they got back to the farmyard, carrying the bag of mackerel between them, a big car pulled up in front of the farmhouse. Malcolm Laurence leapt out and slammed the door behind him, the sound of it echoing round the old buildings, causing the swallows to rise into the air in alarm. Isabel came running out of the front door.

'Malcolm!' she said, her face breaking into the kind of smile that Finn had never seen there before. 'What brings you here?'

'Issie, there's been a bit of an incident in the village. One of your workers got himself into a spot of bother. I thought I'd better bring the lad back. See for yourself.'

He opened the back door of the car like a taxi driver, and Francis slid out, staggering, a white handkerchief splattered with crimson clutched to his nose.

'Oh dear God!' said Isabel. 'What happened?'

'I think some of the village lads had a go at him. They'd been in the hotel after work, and there was some kind of altercation going on between the tattie howkers and the local lads. You know how it is?'

'But not Francis.'

'Ah well ...' Malcolm glanced at Francis who had made his way to the stone bench outside the house door and was sitting there forlornly, the bloody hankie still clutched to his nose. Kirsty went and sat beside him, offering silent sympathy. Finn hovered in the background, unsure whether to run away or to stay.

'I think they went for a soft target. They wouldn't want to take on some of those older men, would they now? The ones that can handle themselves. But there was a skirmish and I think your poor lad here just got in the way. Or didn't get out of the way quickly enough.'

'Oh, Francie!' Kirsty slipped her arm around his shoulders.

'Somebody landed a lucky punch, I'd say. He went down like a pair of breeks. Lucky I arrived on the scene. They were so fired up they might have given him a kicking while he was down.'

'Lucky you did,' said Isabel. She seemed torn between the impulse to help Francis and the pleasure of Malcolm's attention.

'Well, they slunk off as soon as I put in an appearance. As expected. His friends had all disappeared by that stage. Left him to it.'

'It's so kind of you to take the trouble to bring him back!' Isabel moved a little closer to Malcolm and whispered, 'He's a poor soul, you know. I sometimes think he's a wee bit simple. Lights on, nobody home. I don't know why he's here, to be honest with you. He's nothing more than a liability. Oh, but your handkerchief.'

Malcolm seemed embarrassed both by the confidence and by the mention of his handkerchief. 'Don't worry about it. Plenty more where that came from.'

'I'll make sure it's washed. I'll make sure you get it back.'

'No need. It really doesn't matter.'

He was already on his way back to the car. 'I'm pretty sure he hasn't bled on my seat.'

'You wouldn't like to come in for a cup of tea, would you?'

'No, no. Thank-you very much but I'd best be getting home. Things to do, you know. Busy, busy, busy.'

Isabel watched the car until it disappeared around the bend in the track and then, galvanised into action, turned her attention to Finn.

'Where were you, when all this was going on?' she asked, furiously. 'Why did you leave him alone? I thought you were his friend.'

Kirsty leapt to her feet. 'Mum! He was with me. On the boat. You know where we were. We were fishing for mackerel. And Francie didn't want to come. We asked him but he wanted to go to the village instead.'

'Oh you!' said Isabel. 'You're always defending him!'

'But he hasn't *done* anything. The village lads hate the tattie howkers. That's why they only go down there in groups. You can't blame Finn.'

Alasdair had come to the door by this time and overheard the tail end of the exchange. He pushed past his daughter-in-law and bent over Francis.

'Let me see,' he said, pulling the boy's hand away from his nose. The handkerchief was sodden with blood, but the flow seemed to be easing. 'How are you feeling?'

'Dizzy.'

Francis was trembling and swaying a little, even though he was sitting down. He looked as though he might be going to faint.

'I think it's Francie here who needs the cup of tea,' said Alasdair, mildly. 'Never mind Malcolm Laurence. Go and make a pot, Isabel, strong and sweet. And put a wee dash of whisky in it as well. And a key to put down his back for the nosebleed. Never had you down for a bonnie fighter,' he teased. 'Kirsty, come back and sit beside him, and you too, Finn. I think he needs a bit of support. Pity it wasn't Finn here who was down in the village. You might have given them a run for their money, eh?'

'I might yet,' said Finn, mutinously.

'No, no. We'll have no feuds here. They're a bunch of idiots and you don't rise to the bait. Do you hear me now?'

'I hear you,' said Finn, although he still looked rebellious.

Isabel brought the tea and a clean rag out of the kitchen, taking away Malcolm Laurence's bloody handkerchief. 'I'll put this to soak in some bicarb. Otherwise I'll never get the marks out.'

Alasdair watched her go and pulled a face. 'Malcolm's hankie,' he said, shaking his head and grinning. Then, suddenly serious, he turned his attention back to Francis.

'What happened?'

'There was a group of lads and they saw us coming out of the shop and started swearing at us and calling us dirty, thieving left footers. Why do they call us left footers, mister? One or two of them picked up stones. Jimsy and the others rushed at them but I didn't know which way to go. I thought I should help them, but I was frightened, to tell you the truth, and then one of the Scots lads said, "Here's scabby heid," and the next thing I knew I was on the ground, and this big car pulled up and everyone ran off.'

Francis sipped his tea. His face was a mass of pink scars this year, the skin blotched and peeling. Isabel had given him ointment to put on it but it didn't make much difference. She worried that Kirsty might catch something from him, but Alasdair said it wasn't infectious. It was down to nerves. Whatever the cause, the cold winds that blew over the island exaggerated the condition. And there were bald patches on his head where the hair had come out in tufts.

'Just as well Malcolm was on the scene.' Alasdair nodded to Finn. 'They'd be scared of him, at any rate, seeing as how he's landlord to most of them. Wet that rag at the tap and wipe his face for him, Finn. When he's had his tea, make sure he's put to bed. He'll have a nice pair of black eyes in the morning. And I'll be having words with the other men. They should never have left him behind. Wipe your eyes, Kirsty, my wee lass. There's no harm done. I've seen much worse when I was a young man. You wouldn't believe the fights we used to have on a Saturday night. Fists flying. Black eyes and bloody noses. Something and nothing. Wipe your eyes, and come inside and give your mammy a hand to wash the holy handkerchief.'

Chapter Seven

FOR THE REST of that summer, Finn and Kirsty made sure they kept Francis close beside them. Sometimes, she and Finn went out in the boat and left him sitting down on the beach. Sometimes, Kirsty wandered about by herself while Finn and Francis, glad to be resting, watched her as she searched for treasures, things that she would take home and maybe draw later: a banded agate, a chunk of rose quartz, a curly shell.

When the weather was very fine, there were parts of the beach that became infested with pink algae that stank in the sun. It only improved when the rain came down and washed it away. But the rain made the tattie howking a misery, so nobody welcomed it.

Once they found an old green bottle with a piece of paper inside, but the water had got in and the message, whatever it might have been, disintegrated in their fingers.

'It could have been a treasure map,' she said, disappointed.

'It could have been a message from somebody stranded on a desert island,' said Francis, suddenly. 'Maybe he was looking for his relatives. Trying to get word to them so that they could come and rescue him.'

'So it could.' Kirsty looked at him in surprise. It was so seldom that he said anything interesting. 'Maybe he threw it into the sea years ago. And now it's washed up here, but we can't read the message.'

'So he'll just have to stay put,' said Finn. 'On his desert island. I would like that fine myself.'

'Like what?'

'To be cast away on a desert island.'

She frowned. 'I don't think I'd like to be all on my own.'

'There are worse things than being all on your own.'

'You'd be like Robinson Crusoe.'

'Who's Robinson Crusoe?' asked Francis

'Just a man who got cast away on a desert island.'

'When?'

'How should I know? He's in a book.'

'Have you read that as well?' asked Finn.

'No. But my grandad told me about him. And he said that there really was a man like that, once upon a time.'

'So maybe this was his last message.'

'Maybe it was. His last will and testament. And now his forgotten bones are whitening on the sand!

'Don't say that,' said Francis, with a shiver.

'Why not? It's just a story.'

'I don't like to think of it, that's all. I like to think of nice things.'

'What nice things do you have to think about?' asked Finn, brusquely.

Kirsty nudged him. 'Don't be rude.'

'It was nice before my mammy died,' said Francis, thoughtfully. 'We had porridge in the mornings. She always lit the fire before we got up so that it would be warm for us. I think about that sometimes. But that was when I had the other name.'

'What other name?' Kirsty asked, intrigued. 'How could you have another name? I thought you were Francis O'Brien. Only ladies change their names, when they get married.'

'No, my name was Michael back then. But when I went to the orphanage at first, they said they had two more boys called Michael, so I had to be Francis to save confusion. That was my confirmation name.'

'What's confirmation?'

'You go into the church and there's a bishop comes to do it and you take another name. A saint's name.' Finn was impatient with her lack of knowledge. 'Do you not have that in your church?'

'I never heard that we did. Maybe we do. I don't know.'

Francis joined in, eager to explain. 'And then, when I went to the school from the orphanage, they said I'd better just keep that name. Francis O'Brien. Because everyone was used to it.' He smiled at them. There was a gap where one of his front teeth had fallen out.

Kirsty looked at Finn again, raising her eyebrows. Finn nodded.

'It's true.'

'I still don't feel like Francis. I feel like Michael. Besides …'

'What?'

'What if my sister comes looking for me? What if she does? She won't know who I am.'

'I didn't know you had a sister.'

'I have three sisters. They are all older than me.'

'And your mother died?'

'She got very sick. They took her to hospital and they said she'd died. I went to the orphanage with the nuns, but my sisters had to go to a different place.'

'And your name was really Michael?'

He nodded. She turned to Finn. 'What about you? Is Finn your real name?'

'Tis.'

'So if anyone comes looking for you, they'll be able to find you.'

'Nobody will ever come looking for me.'

'How can you be sure.'

'I just know, that's all.'

The next wet Sunday, Kirsty got out her copy of The Wind in the Willows and took it into one of the barns. She had brought her grandad's old plaid, a long piece of black and white wool, darned in many places. She and Finn and Francis wrapped it around them and made themselves snug on a bale of hay, with the wind making music in the rafters, and she read aloud to the two boys.

'He's always going on about joy and contentment,' said Finn.

'So he is. That's why I like it.'

'You said you liked disasters.'

'Well I do. But I like people being happy as well.' She struggled to explain. 'When Moley's in the wild wood, it's terrible, but when they find Badger's house and everything's all right, it's even nicer because he's had such a bad time.'

Francis was tucked in between them. He had been listening, snuggling down into the plaid. He was drowsy, soothed by her words. There was a smell of unwashed clothes off both boys, but Kirsty had got used to it and hardly noticed it. She looked over his head at Finn.

'Which one would you be, Finn ?'

'What do you mean?'

'If you were somebody in the book. Who would you be?'

'I don't know. Who would you be?'

'Maybe Ratty, because he can do things. I want to be able to do things. You know? Or Otter. I might be Otter. Because he's not afraid of anything.'

'I'm not afraid of anything.'

'Are you not?'

'There's nothing else for me to be afraid of, is there?'

Later on that evening, she related this conversation to her grandfather when she was sitting cross legged on the rug, drawing pictures of Ratty and Mole in their boat, rowing along the river.

'Why wouldn't Finn be afraid of anything?' she asked.

Her grandfather shook his head. 'I don't know, my lamb. Maybe so many bad things have happened to him already that he knows he can put up with whatever else they throw at him.'

'What about Francie?'

Alasdair sighed. 'I'm not sure. He's not as strong as your friend Finn. Finn has a wee wall built around him. He's a tough one. Francie looks as though he could do with a few more layers of skin in more ways than one.'

Afterwards, she pondered this conversation. She was afraid of a great many things including hell and, to a lesser extent, heaven, which she didn't think would suit her at all. She found the idea of sitting at the right hand of God, singing his praises, faintly alarming. 'But I can't play the harp' she had protested anxiously, when she first attended Sunday school.

That wet Sunday marked the start of a long spell of rain that lasted almost to the end of the potato harvest and the fields were awash with mud. The boys' boots were caked with it. Worse, their hands and all their clothes were permanently dirty. The sandy earth was so engrained in their fingers that when they washed them in cold water they bled profusely. Kirsty wanted to invite them in to use the proper bathroom with warm water and scented soap instead of carbolic, but Isabel wouldn't hear of it.

'It's bad enough trying to clean it up after you've been in there, without inviting all and sundry in to use it!'

'It isn't all and sundry,' said Kirsty. 'It's only Finn and Francis.'

But her mother was adamant, so the boys had to make do with the cold tap in the outhouse. Kirsty wondered if, had it just been Francis, her mother might have relented. But she couldn't invite Francis in without inviting Finn as well, so neither was allowed.

Later that summer, just before the tattie howkers were due to leave, Kirsty wrapped up her copy of The Wind in the Willows in a sheet of fancy paper from the Post Office. She presented it to Finn, one evening, when Francis was asleep.

'What's this?' he asked, surprised.

'It's a present for you. Don't open it till you get back.'

'I'll keep it for my birthday.'

'When's that?'

'October, I think. The tenth.'

'What do you mean, you think. Do you not know your own birthday?'

'Not if it was up to the Brothers. Who would tell us things like that?'

But Finn did remember his birthday. He remembered it from his first school, what he always thought of as his real school, when he had been in Dublin with his mother. Sister Rosalie used to bring in a cake when it was your birthday and everyone would have a little piece of it. And he could remember the date from her. She had written it up on the blackboard for him. She had said it was a big race track with a finishing post to one side, and that was the number ten, and Finn had remembered it ever since.

'I'll have to try to find a hiding place for your present though or they'll have it off me!' he said.

'Why would they do that?'

'We don't get to keep things, Kirsty. Not presents. Not even sweets.

We sometimes get sweets at Christmas but they're always taken off us. We got oranges once, and we never got a suck of them.'

'Who gets to eat them then?'

'How should I know? The Brothers, I suppose.'

'What brothers? I didn't know you had any brothers.'

He sighed. 'I don't. Not my brothers. *The* Brothers.' It was all too difficult to explain.

'But what about your own things?' she persisted. 'What do you do with them?'

'What things?'

'Don't you have stuff of your own?'

He shook his head. 'Not really. I have a rosary just. They leave me that.' He fumbled in his pocket and brought out a string of brown wooden beads with a little cross on the end. 'I had a teddy bear when I first went to the school, when I was little, but they took it off me.'

'Who did?'

'The people at the school. They said, "A great strong boy like you has no need of a teddy bear." I suppose they were right.'

'Oh, Finn!' She was still not sure who these people were, and why Finn lived with them and not with his mother. She was still shy of asking. She had asked her grandfather, but he hadn't been able to explain it either.

'I found it on the muck heap, a few weeks later, but it was all torn apart and the mice had got to the stuffing.'

'Could someone not have stitched it for you?'

'Kirsty, will you stop this? I don't want to talk about it. D'you hear me? I'm saying nothing else. It was just a daft old bear anyway.'

'But will you be able to find a safe place for the book?' she asked, anxiously, not wanting to see the gift wasted. There was a strong streak of prudence in Kirsty. She took good care of all her possessions and hated to see anything broken or ill used.

'I will. I'll look after it all right. There's a farm at the school. And there's an old dresser in one of the sheds. I keep a few things at the back of one of the drawers there. Nobody looks. I'd catch it right enough if they knew about it, but nobody does, not even the other boys.'

Years later, she remembered her gift, and wondered if the book was still there, with 'to Finn with love from Kirsty xxx' on the flyleaf, mouldering at the back of a drawer in an old worm-eaten dresser, somewhere in a barn in Ireland.

Chapter Eight

KIRSTY'S BODY WAS growing and filling out, embarrassing her when she had to change for games with the younger children at school. At the start of the summer, her mother took her on a trip to Glasgow. They stayed with Aunty Beatie and the Glasgow cousins in their bungalow in Newton Mearns. They went to the big Marks and Spencer's in the city centre and bought two white nylon bras that Kirsty found desperately uncomfortable. She got a suspender belt and some American Tan stockings as well, but although she was excited by the idea of these grown up things, in reality they were fiddly and awkward. The plastic buttons dug into her legs. Sometimes they popped out at embarrassing moments, and the nylons wrinkled around her ankles. It was a miserable business and she refused to wear them anywhere, except for going to the kirk on Sundays.

She found herself waking up in the early hours of the morning and staring out of her window, watching the moon over the sea. She kept a notebook beside her bed and had taken to writing wildly lyrical poems or melodramatic stories in which she was the heroine, rescued from some fate worse than death (though what that might be, she couldn't imagine) by a tall, dark, handsome hero. But she still liked drawing best, still liked pictures far better than words.

Because Finn and Francis had managed to come to the tattie harvest for two years running, she had fully expected to see them for a third time. In fact, she had been counting on it. So when she ran down to the field to welcome them, she was relieved to find Finn, head down, working hard, but surprised that there was no sign of Francis.

'Hello again, Finn!'

She didn't rush to hug him as she had the previous year. Something had changed, in herself and in him, too.

'Hello, yourself.'

Where's Francie?' she asked. 'Is he up in the byre?'

Finn shook his head, but he wouldn't stop for her.

'I have work to do.'

'Can't you at least say hello to me?'

'I thought I just did.'

He looked thinner and more gaunt and there were the remains of what might have been bruises on his face, that strange, yellowish colour that always follows on from the black and blue. He wouldn't meet her eyes.

'What's happened to you? Have you been fighting already?'

'No.'

'Is Francis not here this year?'

'No.'

'Where is he?'

'He couldn't come. He went away.'

'Where? Did his sister come for him after all?'

'Don't talk daft. Nobody comes for you. It doesn't happen. He would be sixteen now.'

'So?'

'So, we all go away when we're sixteen. We have to go away.'

'I didn't realise Francis was older than you. My mum will be sad. She's been saving up clothes and things for him.'

'I can't help that, can I?'

'Are you not glad to be back?'

He stuck the fork in the soft ground, leaning on it with his foot, pushing the tines through the earth. She started to cry.

'Ah now, don't do that, for God's sake! Don't cry!'

'I've been waiting for you all winter! Hoping you would come back!'

He let the *graip* fall and clutched at her fingers so hard that she gasped with pain, but she didn't pull away.

'At least you're here.'

'Bad penny, that's me.'

She wondered how she was going to tell her mother about Francis, but when she got into the kitchen, Isabel was baking bread, furiously pummelling the dough, as though it were some nameless enemy. She pushed the hair from her eyes with a floury hand, leaving a smear of white on her forehead.

'You don't have to tell me because I know. Your grandad told me!'

'It's a shame, isn't it?' said Kirsty, uncertainly.

'It's a shame, right enough, but it was only to be expected. And I suppose Finn's happy about it.'

'Why would he be happy?'

'Well, he was always the favourite with your grandfather and now there's nobody to steal his limelight.'

'I don't think he's happy at all.' Kirsty picked up a box of raisins and began to eat them, tossing them into the air and catching them in her mouth. 'I think he misses Francie. We all do.'

Isabel said nothing, but punched the soft dough more vigorously than ever.

Finn did much more than dig the tatties that third summer. Alasdair had come to some arrangement with the gaffer again, cash had changed hands, and Finn was often free to help about the farm, especially once the Dunshee earlies were finished. Isabel didn't approve but Alasdair wouldn't talk about it at home, and Finn always steered the conversation away from the subject, even when he was with Kirsty.

'I'm learning,' was all he would say.

This year, there was something unsettling about him, some quality that seemed to have intensified over the winter. His natural reserve had grown into a chilly indifference towards everyone except Kirsty and her grandfather. There was something awkward and inept about his interactions with other people. Kirsty was reminded again of Alasdair's remark about the ill-treated dog that he could do nothing with. Even when Finn was injured or exhausted, he would never complain. Only a week or two after his arrival, he put a fork right through his boot and made a gash in his foot. They had to get the island nurse to come up to the farm to clean and stitch the wound and give him a tetanus injection, but he hardly even cried out.

'You'd have been bawling the house down, wouldn't you, Kirsty?' said her grandfather.

'Of course she would,' said her mother. 'There's something inhuman about that boy. I can't think why you and Kirsty like him so much. It's always Finn this and Finn that!'

But like the grey mullet that swam about the harbour, Alasdair would never rise to the bait.

One July evening, Finn had been out to the creels with Alasdair, while Kirsty had been waiting for them to come in. Alasdair was still tinkering with his boat when Finn made himself comfortable on a flat rock, Kirsty at his feet. She took up a stick and drew a face in the sand.

'This time last year, we were down here with Francis.'

Finn said nothing.

'Do you ever hear from him?' she persisted. 'Has he got a job now?'

'I don't know. They're mostly sent to work on farms.'

Kirsty couldn't imagine that Francis would be much use anywhere, never mind on a farm. He had no practical skills whatsoever.

'Do you miss him?'

'Like a nail in my boot.'

'Don't be mean. He was no farmer, that's for sure. But he could sing like an angel.'

'He could do that all right.'

Having made sure that his boat was safely tied up, Alasdair came over, sat beside them and took his pipe out of his pocket. He mostly smoked matches, but he liked the feel of the old briar in his mouth.

'Tell us a story!' It was what Kirsty had always said to her grandfather when she was a little girl, sitting on the rag rug at his feet, picking at the bright flaps of cloth, counting the colours.

'What story do you want?' asked Alasdair.

Kirsty looked beyond him, towards the hill that rose above Dunshee, with its vague suggestion of ramparts and earthworks.

'Tell us about Dermot and Grania.'

Finn stirred. 'Grania? That's an Irish story.'

'No it's not.'

'Yes it is. An Irish name and an Irish story.'

'How do you know?' she asked him.

He hesitated. 'I heard it told once when I was at the tatties. Not this year but our first time here. One of the older men, he told about this man called Dermot and this woman called Grania, and she was engaged to this other man, but she fell for Dermot instead and she ran away with him. He had this little mark on his face, a love spot the man called it. Anyway, she got a sight of it and she was mad for him and then they ran off together.'

Kirsty looked over at her grandfather who was smiling quietly to himself.

'Is he right, grandad? Is it an Irish tale?'

'That's about the long and short of it.'

'But what about Hill Top Town? You told me they lived up there.'

'Not in the story I heard,' said Finn.

'Who asked you?' said Kirsty, turning on him, irritably.

'Shush,' said her grandad. 'Leave the lad alone.'

'Well ... Anyone would think ...'

'What?'

'That he knew more about story-telling than you do.'

'But he's allowed to tell his own story, Kirsty. Everyone has his own tale to tell.'

'He doesn't have very much to say for himself at all, this summer!'

'Can I not answer for myself?' asked Finn.

'Apparently not,' said Alasdair, with a chuckle. 'You should know by now. You have to get in quick or Kirsty will always answer for you.'

Kirsty started to giggle, stole another sidelong look at Finn and saw that his lips were twitching. It was the first time he had smiled in weeks.

'Go on then,' he said. 'Tell me about Dermot and Grania.'

Alasdair made himself comfortable, puffed briefly at his pipe and began his tale.

'Well, you had it right. There was this girl called Grania, and she was in love with Dermot, so she was, madly in love with him, because it was an enchanted love, and there was nothing that could break the spell, no matter what. Dermot was a great hero. It was said that he was never weary, that his step was as light at the end of the longest battle as it was at the beginning of the day. But he had this wee spot on his face, it's true, and once any woman saw it she was enchanted by him. So Grania caught a sight of his beauty spot and there was nothing for her but that they must run away together. Now he was an honourable man, and besides, he had been a good friend to Finn, and this Finn was the man that Grania was supposed to marry.'

'Finn!' Kirsty dug her companion in the ribs. 'That's you!'

'I know.'

'So who was Finn then?'

'Oh, he was a great hero, Kirsty. A great hero. There was not his like in the whole of Ireland.'

'Ireland?'

'Yes. Finn's right. This is an Irish tale, but it is a Scottish tale as well. I've told you before, *a'ghraidh*, we are the same people. Anyway, to get back to Dermot, although he went away with her right enough, they lived apart and not as man and wife, which was what she would have liked with the enchantment full on her. But they travelled all over the place, even sailing over the sea to Scotland, sleeping here and there, at hill forts or in the wilderness, on beds made of heather, just as the fancy took them. Her man Finn McCool was after them both by this time and threatening that if he found them he would kill Dermot and punish Grania.'

Alasdair pulled on his pipe, discovered that it had gone out, lit it again and blew out a stream of blue, vanilla-scented smoke. 'So at last they came to the island, and up to the old fortress at Hill Top Town there, which was called *Dun Sidhe*, or the Hill of the Fairies.

'Why the hill of the fairies?' asked Finn.

Kirsty nudged his knee. 'Just listen, will you?'

Alasdair winked at Finn and resumed his story.

'There was a lord who lived up at *Dun Sidhe*, an earl of fairyland. And that was why the place was called the hill of the fairies, and that is what our own house, down below, is called to this very day. Dunshee is the same name.'

'See,' said Kirsty, nudging Finn. 'Now go on with the story, grandad, for those that want to hear it.'

'The earl was a wealthy man for those times and he set out to charm Grania. Like many of the fairy folk, he played the fiddle and he played it well, a fairy tune that filled her head with dreams. And because poor Dermot was paying her scant attention, she took a liking to this other man, this earl of fairyland, partly to make Dermot jealous, and partly because he was kind to her. He would bring her gulls' eggs to eat, and fish from the sea, and blaeberries from the moors.'

'I love blaeberries,' said Kirsty.

Finn scowled at her. 'Now who's interrupting?'

'And he would make her a bed of feathers to lie on, the feathers of the curlew and the corncrake, soft feathers and much more comfortable than any heather bed. And he would play to her, so that she slept deeply and well, and her dreams were sweet because of the feathers and the music. But soon, this man, the earl of fairyland, came to Grania with a plot that they might kill Dermot, and then she would marry the earl and live with him up at *Dun Sidhe* where old Finn would never find them. So they made a plan that Dermot and the earl would play at a game of dice together, and whenever the earl saw his chance, he would kill Dermot, and Grania vowed to help him.'

Finn moved restlessly. 'I don't understand,' he said.

'What's wrong now?' asked Kirsty.

'Why would she kill Dermot when she was in love with him? You said she was mad in love with him!'

'You have to listen properly!' Kirsty exclaimed. 'The other man was good to her. He fed her and made her a feather bed and he played music for her.'

Alasdair paused to relight his pipe and then continued. 'Well, they were playing at the dice, all fine and nice, and the earl saw his chance and laid his hands upon poor Dermot. But Dermot was younger and stronger, and they began wrestling together. Dermot got him down on the ground. The earl called out to Grania to save him. She took up Dermot's own knife and stabbed him in the thigh with it.'

'She stabbed Dermot?' asked Finn.

'She did.'

'I still don't see why she would do that,' said Finn, mutinously.

'Because she loved him more than he loved her. Isn't that clear to you?' said Kirsty.

'But …' He saw her face and stopped. 'All right. Go on then.'

'Thank-you,' said Alasdair. 'So when Dermot saw what she had done, and he saw the blood running down, he took himself off, more dead than alive, and if they thought anything about him at all, they thought that he was dead.'

'But a long time later, Dermot came back to the Dun, and he brought a fine fat salmon with him, and neither of them recognised him, he was so changed. He asked them if he could have leave to roast the fish on their fire, and Grania brought him a wee bowl of water so that he could wash his fingers. Now there was another magic thing about Dermot: anything he might touch would have the scent of honey upon it. He cooked the fish, and then he said to Grania, would she like a morsel, and it smelled so good that she took up a piece of it and put it in her mouth. She thought it had a strange taste for a fish. She took up the bowl of water where he had dipped his fingers and put it to her nose. As soon as she did that, she could smell the powerful honey in it, and she knew that the stranger was Dermot. By then, she was tired of the earl, who had not been by any means what she had thought he might be, so she went to Dermot and threw her two arms around him and kissed him.'

'The earl of fairyland leapt up with a roar and attacked Dermot, but Dermot killed him, and he went away from the Dun. Grania followed him, all the way down to the seashore, and she called to him and called to him, but he would not turn round. The corncrake was calling in the reeds, *crek crek* he was calling. And the heron was flying over the water. And there was Dermot, sitting on a big rock. And Grania said "Are you hungry Dermot? I will feed you. I have food and drink enough for both of us."'

'Dermot said "Give me a piece of your bread, Grania."'

'She said "Where is a knife, that will cut it?"'

'Then he said to her "Why will you not search for it in the place where you sheathed it last," meaning the wound that she had given him in the leg, and at that she was overcome with shame. She went to him and she drew the knife out and gave it back to him, and that was the greatest shame that any woman ever had, when she realised how she had betrayed this man and wounded him, and now wanted him back again.'

There was a moment's silence. It was always like this, thought Kirsty. It was as though her grandfather had conjured up images from the sea and the land around them. It was a kind of magic; he took the memories of the island, the sticks and stones, the shells and feathers and water, like some old magician, and transformed them into words. It was an ancient skill and few could manage it like Alasdair.

After a while, Finn said 'That tune …'

'What tune?' asked Kirsty.

'The tune that the earl played. Are there really tunes like that?'

'A melody to enchant a woman? Of course,' said Alasdair. 'There are all kinds of fiddle tunes that are as old as the hills and some of them have been passed down from the fairies themselves. I'll let you hear it, if you like.'

Back at Dunshee, Alasdair invited Finn into the kitchen. Isabel was away on a shopping trip to the mainland with the minister's wife and the ladies of the Guild, so there was nobody to object. Alasdair got the old fiddle down from its nail, tuned it up and played a plaintive melody that he said was a fairy song .

'I would like …' Finn began, and then hesitated.

'What would you like?' asked Alasdair.

'Nothing. No.' He turned to Kirsty. 'Can you play that?'

'The fiddle?' She shook her head.

Alasdair laughed. 'Not for lack of encouragement. I always hoped she would try, but she has no patience with it. None at all. She sings sweetly enough but she is no musician. Why? Would you like to learn, Finn? My wee Kirsty will do nothing but make pictures.'

Finn coloured and looked down at the floor. 'I couldn't do it.'

'Why couldn't you do it?'

'I've no brains, mister.'

'Who told you you'd no brains?'

'They tell me at the school. Plug ugly and pig ignorant. That's me.'

There was a sudden silence in the room. Alasdair gazed at Finn. Kirsty could see that he looked very angry. But not with Finn.

'Why would you say that?'

'Because it's true.'

That's what they always told him. And he was glad of it. It was safer that way. Nobody looked twice at you if you were plug ugly and pig ignorant. One of the herd. That was the trick of it. That was the way you survived. Look what happened if you were different. Look what had happened to Francie. But he mustn't think about Francie. Or any of that. Keep your mind on your work. Keep quiet. Survive.

'Nonsense!' Alasdair interrupted his thoughts. 'You've brains enough for two in that head of yours. Do you want to learn?'

'Am I not too old?'

'Aye, you are a bit. But I can teach you to busk a tune as well as the next man.'

Which was why Alasdair began to teach Finn the rudiments of playing the fiddle. He would never be particularly good at it, but he enjoyed the process of learning. He seldom played for anyone except Kirsty and Alasdair. After a while, he found that he could coax a simple tune out of the instrument and when, some years later, he mastered the fairy melody, nobody was more delighted with his pupil's success than Alasdair, except perhaps for Kirsty herself.

Chapter Nine

THAT SUMMER, KIRSTY left the island primary school and in late August she started school on the mainland. Finn was still on the farm, although even the late tattie harvest was nearly done and it was almost time for the visiting Irish to leave too.

'I'm looking forward to going to the mainland,' she told him. 'Looking forward to the company.' There was a hostel for everyone who had too far to travel each day.

'Am I not company?' he asked.

'When you're here you are. But you're away all winter.'

'And you come home at weekends?'

'That's right.'

'Aren't you scared?'

'Why would I be scared?'

On the first day of term, when Alasdair and Isabel took her to the ferry, Finn rose early and walked down to the harbour to see her off. He needed to see her leave, needed to be able to watch until she was out of sight. He couldn't have explained this to anyone but it seemed essential to do it. It hadn't occurred to him that she would be gone to what she called 'the big school' before he had to go back to Ireland, that he wouldn't be able to spend his few remaining evenings after work in her company, that he must wait for the weekend to see her again, one last weekend before the tattie howkers went away. And he was all too aware that he might not be coming back. Nothing was certain. Nothing predictable. Nothing was ever safe.

It was a fine August morning with just a hint of a chill in the air, an intimation of things to come. The year had turned. He lurked behind the fuel store, sitting on a pile of old fishing nets with bits of dried weed and crab claws entangled in them, until he saw the farm jeep come rattling down the hill. Kirsty got out and Alasdair shouldered her bag and carried it aboard for her. She looked smart and small, dressed in her new school uniform, the blazer several sizes too big for her. Isabel got out of the jeep, gave her daughter a hug and a kiss and then stood on the jetty, hands in the pockets of her navy blue cardigan. Kirsty turned back and waved, and Isabel raised her hand and blew a kiss. Finn had a sudden pang of some indefinable emotion. Nobody ever waved him off. Nor had they. Not since his mother, all those years ago, when he had first started at the school in Dublin. He thought about Sister Rosalie with her pink cheeks and the funny white winged head-dress of the Sisters of Charity. He remembered Sister Rosalie saying, 'Come along now, Finn!' and his mother standing at the railing, smiling and waving, with a hankie clutched in her other hand. Wiping her eyes. 'Just a bit of dust in my eye. I'll be here at home time, Finny!'

Not since then.

Alasdair got back in the jeep and backed up to the turning place. The ferry was already moving away from the jetty. Kirsty was on deck with a handful of other children, all older than herself. Only when the jeep was well up the road did Finn emerge cautiously from behind the fuel store. He walked down onto the jetty and stood there for a while, watching. Then, when he was sure that nobody could see him, he raised his hand and waved, sketchily, self consciously. Did he imagine it, or did Kirsty detach herself from the huddle of children and wave back at him? Had it really happened? He couldn't be sure, and the ferry was too far off now, leaving a trail of foam in its wake. He watched until it was a silhouette, heading for the mainland, and then he turned and jogged back to the farm, taking shortcuts over the muddy fields, mindful of unfriendly dogs and barbed wire and other hazards. He would be late, but he didn't think that Alasdair would mind too much, and for the next week or so it was Alasdair he was working for rather than Micky Terrans.

After the one-roomed island school, the size of the big school bewildered Kirsty. So many people. So much noise. Some of the children were miserably homesick and cried themselves to sleep in the hostel every night, although the rooms were comfortable and cheerfully painted, four beds to a room, with a bedside locker, a desk and wardrobe for each girl. There was a matron if you were feeling ill or even sad. The food was plain but plentiful. And there was always bread and jam or peanut butter, fresh milk and cups of tea and cocoa for those that wanted them. All in all, it was bearable. Kirsty was homesick too but she would have died rather than let anybody see her distress. She was afraid of being bullied, had heard tales of newcomers being beaten or having their heads forced into lavatories. But alongside Finn's infrequent references to his own school, these worries seemed insignificant. Besides, none of them proved to be true and perhaps because of her red hair the other children credited her with a fiery temper.

'See that Kirsty Galbreath!' they said. 'She's mad!'

She made a few new friends but, as far as Kirsty was concerned, the best thing about her new school was Miss Wilson. Jane Wilson taught art, was not long out of college herself and was still enthusiastic about her subject and her pupils. She was slender and striking and she wore fashionable clothes. She stood out like a tropical bird among the other teachers.

'They didn't make teachers like that in our day,' said the fathers, on parents' night, remembering fierce, middle-aged ladies in lisle stockings.

'They don't even make them like that nowadays,' said the mothers, eyeing up the other female staff members in their grey pleated skirts and neat blouses.

Miss Wilson wore her dark hair long and smooth and straight. In winter she dressed in short skirts and patterned tights and brightly coloured polo necks, but when she waited for her bus outside the school gates, she wore a long black coat with a fur collar and fur around the hem. She called it her 'Zhivago Coat'. Julie Christie, as Lara, had worn one like it in the film. Kirsty found it immensely romantic and wanted one for herself.

The following weekend, Kirsty was so full of the school and the hostel and her new experiences that it was Sunday afternoon before she realised that Finn would be going away so soon. They were in their usual spot, up at Hill Top Town, when he said, suddenly, 'I hope I'll see you next year.'

She gazed at him in utter dismay. 'Is it this week? Is it this week you're going, Finn?'

'I've been trying to tell you.'

'I wasn't paying attention. Oh, Finn, I'm so sorry. I hate it that you have to go away. Why can't you just stay on the farm?'

'How can I? I have to go!'

'Why?'

'Because I do. Because that's the way it is.'

'But you'll be back next spring, won't you?'

'Maybe.' He was knocking a pebble against a granite boulder, striking sparks. A faint acrid whiff of sulphur came off it.

'What do you mean, maybe?'

'I can't say for sure. I have to go where I'm sent. Where the work is.'

'Oh.'

She didn't want to have to think about this right now. She wanted everything to go on just as before, with Finn coming back, like the swallows, every spring.

'Listen, I'll write to you,' she said. 'I can write to you from the school.'

'I don't have an address. Besides, you can't,' he said. 'You mustn't write to me.' There was panic in his voice.

'Why on earth not? Our English teacher said that we should have a pen pal. He said it would improve our English, writing letters. Nobody's going to mind.'

'They wouldn't mind here. But they would mind in Ireland.'

'Why? Is it because you would have a girl writing to you?'

'Well, that too.'

'Can't you tell them I'm your cousin?'

He started to laugh. 'You have no idea, do you? No notion at all!'

'Because you don't tell me anything. I know nothing about your school, Finn!'

'They know fine I have no cousin over here. And it wouldn't make any difference if you were a cousin. It wouldn't matter if you were a girl or a boy. It would just be the fact of my getting letters from here. And they would certainly stop me coming.'

'Would they?'

'I don't talk about you or about your grandfather or the farm or anything. Don't you understand? I say as little as possible. And you mustn't ever write to me. Do you hear me now?'

'I hear you, but I can't see the sense in it. And I'll hate it. I have so much I want to tell you!'

'Then write away, but don't post the letters. Just let me see them when I come back. If I come back.'

Kirsty felt her heart contract in fear. 'What do you mean, *if* you come back?'

'I'll be sixteen later on this year, Kirsty. It depends where they send me. I expect I'll be put to work on a farm somewhere. If I am, then I may just be able to get to the tatties next summer. But it may not be here and I may not even be sent to a farm. I could be put into a factory or something.'

'But could you not come anyway? Once you're sixteen?'

'I don't know,' he said, helplessly. 'I don't know what I'll be able to do until the time comes. We go where we're sent. We have to.'

'You mean like Francie. Or Michael. Maybe he'll be able to call himself Michael, now. That would be good, wouldn't it?'

'Maybe.'

'Though I must admit I'll always think of him as Francie. Won't you?'

Finn wouldn't meet her eyes. He looked beyond her, over the sea.

'Do you know where he is, Finn? How is he getting on? Will you maybe go and see him when you finish school?'

'I won't be able to see him.'

'I didn't think I'd miss him, but I have. Haven't you? You must miss him!'

He nodded, miserably.

'I really think you ought to see if you can get in touch with him. Then you could tell my mum where he is and she could write to him. Wherever he is, they can't mind him getting letters. Not now he's older. She could send him something at Christmas.'

'I can't do that. I can't find him, Kirsty.'

'I'm sure you could, if you tried.'

'No, I couldn't.'

'How can you be so sure?'

'Because he isn't anywhere.'

'What do you mean, he isn't anywhere? He has to be somewhere.'

'I mean what I say.'

'So where is he?'

'Nowhere.'

'You mean he's still at the school?'

'No, you feckin' idiot. I mean he's dead and buried. He should have left the school, but he died.'

'Died? ' She rolled the word around in her mouth, tasting it, the finality of it. The impossibility of it. 'But he was young. Young people don't die.'

'Sometimes they do. Your father died.'

'But he wasn't so young. He was all grown up, at least. Not like Francie. So what happened? Was he ill? What did he die of?'

'He wasn't ill. Or no more ill than usual. There was an accident, Kirsty.'

'What kind of accident?'

He was reluctant to continue. He should never have started this, never have told her. But when she persisted, he said, 'He had a fall.'

'A fall?'

'Down the stairs. He fell down these big stone stairs at the school. There's a stairwell in the middle of the building and he fell down it in the night.'

'I don't understand how that could happen!'

'He was always a bit unsteady. A bit wobbly. You know that.'

She stared at him, shaking her head.

'Not that wobbly. What was he doing? Where was he going? Was he trying to run away? Was that it?'

She understood nothing about it. And he wasn't going to be the one to tell her. How could he tell her about the night times? The darkness? The things that went on under cover of night? He could hardly bear to think of it, let alone speak about it, it gave him such a terrible sense of shame. The chosen boys would be summoned out of the dormitories in the dark, roughly shaken awake, dragged out of bed, half asleep sometimes, confused, sickly and not able to defend themselves. How could they defend themselves? Finn was never chosen. His good fortune. Plug ugly, that was why. If he was ever woken and dragged out, it was only for a beating. And that was bad enough. Nightshirts rolled up. Naked from the waist down, with your bits dangling. Bend over! A line of them sometimes. The brother, rolling up his sleeve. Practically jumping up and down in his excitement. The cane, thrashing away, swishing through the air, and the sting of it, the heavy breathing.

But it was worse for the others. Especially boys like Francie. That soft face. Beautiful, like a girl. The way it had been when Finn had first met him. Although not later. Not the sad, shambling creature he had become. Night times. The darkness. The things that went on under cover of night. Beatings and whippings and much worse. The cries and groans. The way Francis would crawl back into bed when it was all over, hunched in pain, coughing and retching, his hands covering himself. Not speaking. Not saying anything about it to anyone. Because it was a sin. You mustn't speak about it, because it was a terrible sin. Not even in confession. It was unforgiveable.

'My fault,' he said to Finn. 'My fault.'

'How can it be your fault?' Finn had whispered in the dark.

'Because I'm an occasion of sin.'

And then, the night they had heard it. The single, high pitched cry and the terrible silence, followed by a muted thud. The stairwell in the middle of the building was deep and broad. The dormitories high up, at the top of the house. The boys had huddled in the doorway, listening, listening, while outside they heard running footsteps, the swish of robes on stone floors, whispers, a dozen urgent whispers, back and forth, question and answer. Ah God, ah God. Francis O'Brien.

In the morning, Brother Michael, his face grim, had gathered them together, told them that there had been a terrible accident. One of the boys had fallen from the upper floor, fallen into the stairwell. He had been walking about in the night, perhaps in search of a glass of water. Perhaps he hadn't been feeling well. They all knew that he was a sickly soul. Poor Francis O'Brien, God rest his soul. He had been taken to hospital, but he was pronounced dead on arrival. It was a sad day for all of them. And they would say a prayer for the repose of his soul. They would say it now. All together. O God, the Creator and Redeemer of all the faithful, grant to the souls of Thy servants departed, the remission of all their sins, that, by our help and pious supplications, they may obtain that pardon which they have always desired; who livest and reignest, world without end ...

Finn didn't believe any of it. He mouthed the words of the prayer, but he didn't believe that either. Give them, O Lord, eternal rest. And let perpetual light shine upon them. May they rest in peace.

Francis was at peace, that much was true, and no prayers from the likes of Brother Michael would make a blind bit of difference. But no matter how much Finn thought about the accident, he didn't know how it had happened. Francis never left the dormitory at night unless summoned. He would have been much too frightened to go wandering about in the dark.

'I don't know what happened to him,' he told Kirsty. 'The Brothers said it was an accident. But he's dead, sure enough. And buried. There's a cemetery at the school and he's somewhere in there. There's a wooden cross and that's all there is.'

'Finn, why on earth didn't you tell me sooner?'

'I didn't want to upset you.'

'Mum thinks he's still alive.'

'Tell your grandad. He can pass it on. I'm not going to be the one to tell her.'

'Don't you care?'

'You know nothing about it. Nothing. He was going to leave. He was going to get away. He'll never get away now.'

'Finn, do you really have to go back there?'

'I do. For now. But I'll be sixteen myself in October. And I'll do my best to come back here next year.'

'I'll worry about you, all the time.'

'I can take care of myself. I'm a big boy now.' He tried to smile but it was more of a grimace. 'And I'm not Francis. I'm nothing like Francis. I'll be safe enough. I'd fight them.'

'How do you mean you'd fight them?'

'Nothing. It's nothing.'

'Promise me you'll come, if you can. Promise me you'll come back to the island, just as soon as you're able. And if you can't come, you have to find a way of writing to me. A way to let me know you're safe. Will you do that?'

'I'll try.'

Chapter Ten

THE DAY BEFORE his sixteenth birthday, Finn was told to make himself ready and pack up his few belongings in a brown cardboard suitcase. He didn't have much to show for all his years in the school. Even in the sad little suitcase they rattled about a bit.

'Where am I to go?' he asked. Questions were normally frowned upon. You did as you were told and that was that. But Brother Michael was more forthcoming than usual.

'We've found a place for you on a farm in Donegal. A good place. An excellent opportunity for a boy like you with nothing to recommend him. If you work hard, you could do well there. Brother John will drive you to the bus station in the morning and put you on the bus. He'll tell the driver where to let you off. You're expected. You'll be met.'

And that was that. All these years, finished and done with, packed into a battered suitcase that one of the brothers had probably brought in with him. And Finn himself, disposed of in much the same way. Afterwards, he wondered why on earth he hadn't simply got off the bus in some one street town, somewhere between the school and his final destination, and disappeared. He had almost no money, it was true, but he was a strong boy, he might have found farm work here and there and made his own way to Belfast and the ferry. But like a long-caged animal, he saw no way out, even when the door was left ajar.

The 'good place in Donegal' was a remote, untidy and run-down smallholding. The farmer ran a few sheep on the high hills. It might have been like Dunshee, but instead it seemed deliberately chosen for its discomfort and isolation. He slept in a chilly outhouse, with inadequate bedding and insufficient food, and he worked like a dog. Actually, the dog slept in the house, in the ashes on the hearth, and in more comfort than Finn. Probably better fed as well, he thought, considering his diet of thin porridge and boiled potatoes. The views from the house were beautiful and the wintry landscape, with grey dawns and fierce sunsets, was the only thing that sustained him through those first miserable months. The school had been a dark huddle of low lying buildings. At least the light and air up here reminded him of Dunshee.

He was working for a taciturn, middle-aged couple, who seemed to have some connection to one of the Brothers, an uncle and aunt perhaps, although they were never very forthcoming. He spent the early spring in the lambing shed, cold and bloody and weak with exhaustion. Up to his armpits in wool and shit, he felt nothing but hunger and a certain indomitable hope that forced him to get up each day and soldier on. The hope had all to do with getting away to the tatties, with returning to Dunshee. There was the promise of payday, but it never seemed to come. The farmer was always having 'a few problems' and putting Finn's pay 'on the long finger' as the woman of the house put it.

For a while, Finn almost despaired of escaping, even for the summer. Desperation lent him courage. He still had Micky Terrans's home phone number. It was scrawled on a precious piece of paper that he kept screwed up in the pocket of his jacket, but he had memorised it anyway. Over Easter, he managed to walk down to the village on the pretext of wanting to go to confession. Once there, he called Micky from the phone box with a few coins he had hoarded for the purpose.

'Galbreath was asking for you,' Micky said. 'I didn't know where you were and they weren't too keen to tell me, so it's a good job you phoned.'

With Micky on his side, things were easier. He was going to be in Donegal on some business of his own and he agreed to meet up with the farmer in a bar down in Letterkenny and talk him round, with promises of the good money that would be sent back, as it had once been sent to the school. The farmer's credulity about this surprised

Finn, but he supposed previous labourers supplied by the school had been as cowed as he himself might have been, without the potential sanctuary that Dunshee had become. Finn also wondered if Alasdair had paid Micky for the favour. The gaffer wasn't a bad man, but he was shrewd where money was concerned. Whatever the truth of it, Finn found himself on the ferry to Scotland with the first squad of the year.

Kirsty was overjoyed to see him but puzzled to the point of irritation by his acquiescence. She couldn't understand it at all. Why did he have to go where he was sent? If it was a job, why wasn't he being paid? Nobody worked without pay unless it was for their own family. What was the matter with him?

'It's not what I would have chosen for myself,' he told her. 'I hate the place!'

'Then why don't you just get up and leave? I don't understand you. What's wrong with you? What age are you now?'

'I'm almost seventeen.'

'Then why don't you go and find yourself another job. Go somewhere else!'

'I don't think I can do that.'

'Why not?'

'They found me the place. I have to stay there. The guards will come and get me.'

'Guards?' she asked, puzzled by the word.

'The *Gardai*. The Irish police.'

'Why? What have you done? You're not a criminal, are you?'

'I don't know. I don't know what I did. But if I try to get away, they'll come and get me, and God knows what will become of me then.'

How do you know they will?'

'Because that's what they told me. And they're always right.'

'But there must be some way out!'

'Well …' He hesitated.

'Go on!'

'I was wondering … do you think your grandfather would have me here? All the time, I mean.'

'You mean to live here?'

'I mean to live and work here. You're right. I don't know why I can't do what I want. There's nothing for me in Ireland. Well, there's my mother, but I don't know where she is. I can't find her, can I? Can't help her. Maybe later. Maybe if I get a job. Get some money together.'

'Did she go away, Finn? Maybe she came over to Scotland.'

He shook his head. 'No. I don't think she did that.'

She would never have left him. There were few certainties in his mind. His memories of his life before the school slid and collided, an avalanche of disjointed images. But he knew that his mother would never willingly have left him. He could close his eyes and he was back there, lying in bed, listening to the noises in the street below. He could feel his mother's arms, tight around him. Safe.

'Go to sleep now, my lamb!' She would push the hair gently back from his face. 'Go to sleep now, my little soldier.'

'But I'm afraid,' he told Kirsty. He didn't want to tell her about his mother. 'And I'm so ignorant. They tell me I have to stay put, with the farmer, but I don't even know if that's the truth. Your grandad seems to think it's all nonsense.'

'Have you talked to him about this?'

'Only last year. He asked me what I was planning to do. I didn't know. Didn't have any plans. Now I just stay on that farm because I have nowhere else to go. But I would like it if I could be here.'

'Oh Finn, I'd like it too' she said. 'I'd love it!'

'Would you?' He looked at her doubtfully. 'I had it in my mind that your grandad might be able to give me a job here.'

'Well, he could certainly do with the help. He's always saying the farm's getting too much for him. I don't know if he could pay you very much.'

'It would be more than I'm getting now.'

'It would be that, all right.'

'But your mother doesn't like me.'

'My grandad does what he pleases where the farm's concerned. But you'll have to ask him yourself, you know, Finn. '

'I will so. But I thought if you ...'

'If I mention it first, he might be more ready to agree. Yes. I'll talk to him about it tonight.'

Kirsty spoke to her grandfather, although it struck her that very little persuasion was needed. At the end of that summer, Finn stayed on. Alasdair was delighted to have him. He barely consulted Kirsty's mother about it, and when she complained about his thoughtlessness, he told her in no uncertain terms that he couldn't go on working at this pace for the rest of his life. Did she want him to drop dead of a heart attack? Besides, she knew fine that he had no son to help out. Finn was no stranger, came cheap, was trustworthy and, above all, was familiar with the farm. What could she possibly have to complain about? Isabel had plenty to complain about, but there was no point in arguing with her father-in-law about this. She knew she would never win. So Finn stayed.

Micky Terrans wasn't best pleased about the permanence of the arrangement, declaring that he would be blamed back in Ireland, but admitting that he had seen it coming. Alasdair invited him into the house, opened a bottle of malt and threw the top into the hearth. By the end of the evening, Micky had mellowed.

'After all,' he said, 'What the hell can they do, eh? Not a thing!'

Which was true, as far as he was concerned.

Finn, however, was not going to be allowed to get off so lightly. At first, they tried intimidation. The farmer from Donegal wrote a threatening letter, because he had lost a good, unpaid hand, but Alasdair sent a brief reply. Nobody knew what he said, because he wouldn't show any of them the letter, but nothing more was heard from that quarter. Finn assumed that a replacement had been supplied from the school. After all, there was no shortage of boys. Sooner or later, most of them reached the milestone of sixteen and had to be sent away from the school, sent to do whatever work the Brothers might find for them. For a while, Finn fully expected the Irish police to come off every ferry, arrest him, and drag him back to Donegal, but when nobody arrived, he relaxed and started to enjoy working for Alasdair, a capable and willing hand.

'They have no hold over you!' Alasdair told him, when he confided some of his fears. 'And if you hear anything, if there is sight or sound of them on this island, you let me deal with it, son. Do you hear me now? Don't worry your head about it. You just let me deal with it!'

One Saturday morning, a smart, black-clad priest disembarked from the ferry, got into his green Morris Minor that had been winched ashore and, having asked for directions in the village, drove up the rutted track to Dunshee. Kirsty and her mother were in the kitchen when he knocked on their door, and Isabel, taken aback by the unexpected visitation, invited him in and offered him tea and biscuits.

He accepted these offerings very graciously and sat at their kitchen table, passing the time of day with them, chatting easily about Finn, wondering how the boy was, was he working hard now, because there had been no high hopes of him in the past.

Alasdair had been in the barn, working on the tractor, and might not even have known about the unexpected visitor, but for the fact that an elderly friend and conspirator, Angus McNeill, cycled furiously up from the village in the wake of the green car and stopped, panting and sweating, in the doorway.

'Jesus, I'm too old for this. That person you were worried might come, Alasdair. I think you'll find he's in your house right now. Well, it's one of them, for sure. Black suit and hat and a white collar. Shoes you could see your face in!'

'Bugger!' said Alasdair, wiping his hands on an oily rag. 'Bugger me. They don't give up, do they? Where's the lad? I had him working in the bottom field, clearing out a ditch down there.'

'Aye, I caught a glimpse of him on the way up. I think he saw the car and made himself scarce. He was right down in the ditch.'

'He'll be bloody terrified. Damn them to hell. Just when he was settling down and giving me a grand day's work as well. Do me a favour, Angus. Will you go back down the hill, when you've got your breath back, and see if you can find him? Tell him to keep out of the way while I sort this. Tell him to go into the old dairy and not to venture out till I send Kirsty for him.'

'D'you need any help, Alasdair?'

'I don't think so. This is one thing I want to handle on my own. In fact I've been looking forward to it.'

The priest was a handsome man with a great deal of wavy grey hair. He was well upholstered and smooth shaven, in his black suit and shoes. Afterwards, Kirsty particularly remembered his shoes, because they were so very much more shiny than any shoes she had ever seen before, especially on the island, where almost all footwear, even Sunday best, tended to be quickly covered in a fine film of mud in winter, dust in summer. The priest introduced himself as Father Connolly. He shook hands genially enough with Alasdair and sat down again at the table where Isabel was just pouring him a second cup of tea. Using the best china, Alasdair noticed.

Kirsty, home for the weekend and sitting with her book, watched him covertly. She had already decided that she didn't like him much. Quite apart from the shiny shoes, she didn't like the way he grinned, showing a great many teeth, nor the way the grin didn't seem to stretch to his eyes at all. There was something of the shark about it. Or the crocodile with gently smiling jaws. And besides, she was well aware that he had been damning Finn with every remark, hinting that the boy was not to be trusted. That they had done what they could with him, but with boys like this, boys who, as he put it, had been 'committed', there was no telling what they might get up to in the future. And wasn't it good, or a trifle foolhardy, of people like Isabel and Alasdair, to take such a boy into their midst, take him on trust, especially when – here he glanced across at Kirsty herself – there was a child in the house?

Father Connolly sipped at his tea and smiled across at Alasdair. 'I thought I would come in person. I had business in Scotland this week, so I thought we could settle this, man to man, amicably.'

'Did you now?' Alasdair took his china mug of tea from Isabel, his own pint pot, set it on the table, spooned sweetened, condensed milk into it and stirred it vigorously, but his gaze never left the priest's face. 'And how will we do that do you think?'

'The boy, ah the boy.' Father Connolly sat back in his chair and steepled his fingers together as though in prayer. 'It's very kind of you to take him in like this. Very kind indeed. But he can't work for you. Not possibly. He already has a job in Donegal. It's a good Catholic home, a farm, and he's contracted to work there for the next five years at least. So you see he has to come back with me. That's the law. And I've come to fetch him. So if you would be so good as to get him for me, I'll take him off your hands.'

Kirsty, glancing from her mother to her grandfather, saw how Isabel looked frightened, but her grandfather was smiling. Much like Father Connolly, the smile did not extend to his eyes. Kirsty knew that look and was wary of it, although it had never once been directed at herself. People thought of her grandfather as a good-natured, easygoing soul, and most of the time, he was. But you didn't cross him. Kirsty had heard people saying as much. People who had taken a bit too much to drink, maybe. And she knew what they meant. You wouldn't cross Ally Galbreath, they said. Not if you knew what was good for you. Even when she was a little girl, she had known that. He indulged her in every possible way, but when he said 'enough' he meant it. She looked at the priest and saw, young as she was, that the man was very much mistaken in her grandfather. He had thought the older man a soft touch, a simple islandman, easily intimidated. But Alasdair was going to say 'enough'. And what would happen then?

'Contracted, is he?' Alasdair took his time drinking his tea before replying. 'Well, leaving aside the fact that this is hardly a den of paganism, I'm not aware that Finn signed anything, and neither is he. We've had a little chat about it, you see. Why would a young lad like that tie himself into such a position for five years? It would be madness. He's not in the army!'

'Well, maybe there was no formal contract.' The priest looked faintly flustered. He was clearly a man used to getting his way. He laid down the law and people capitulated. That was how it always was. Still, he mustered his forces. 'But the Brothers found him a place at the school out of the goodness of their hearts, you know. I can show you the official documents.'

He drew out a sheet of paper, yellow with age, and scanned it, reading aloud. 'Whereas the court is satisfied that it is expedient to deal with the said child by sending him to a certified industrial school … He was a charity case. And a reformatory boy, I might add, committed there by the courts, no less. A young criminal.'

Kirsty saw Isabel blench at this. She would have to say something, tell her mother that it wasn't true, couldn't possibly be true. She made a convulsive movement and her book slid to the floor with a thump. Momentarily distracted, her grandfather caught her eye and frowned at her, shaking his head slightly.

'It's all right, lass,' he said. 'Nothing to worry about.'

Feeling that the interruption had gained him an advantage, Father Connolly continued, directing his remarks towards Isabel. 'Not the kind of lad, with all due respect, that you would want to take into your home. A regular cuckoo in the nest. A big strong lad with criminal tendencies. These boys have to be carefully controlled.'

Alasdair was holding out his hand. 'May I?' He nodded at the document. Reluctantly, the priest handed it over. Alasdair took his time, finding his glasses, reading it closely and with obvious interest. It was partly printed and partly annotated in a thin scrawl.

He threw the priest's own words back at him, with a tinge of irony. 'With all due respect to you, this says nothing about criminal tendencies. It says only that Finn has been found having a guardian who does not exercise proper guardianship, whatever that means. And given that Finn must have been no more than seven years old when this was signed, I can't see that he can ever have been a reformatory boy.'

'Well, well. It's a moot point. The child was obviously beyond care and control when he was admitted. A bad boy from a bad home. And believe me, sir, you'll have the guards at your door soon enough. In fact I'm surprised they haven't been here before this.'

Isabel still looked worried, albeit puzzled, but Kirsty saw, to her surprise, that Alasdair's smile had broadened. 'The guards?' He actually chuckled. 'He means the Irish police, Isabel. But I wonder what the Irish *Gardai* would be doing in Scotland. And I wonder how or why they would be concerning themselves with a young man who has finished his schooling, such as it was, and is no longer their legitimate concern. Or, I might add, yours.'

Father Connolly looked affronted. 'I think you overstep the mark, Mr Galbreath.'

'No, sir. You do. The boy is in my employ. It is all legal and above board. I have consulted my family solicitor on the matter. I cannot even begin to unpick the unholy tissue of illegality that must have lead to his committal in the first place. A wee lad, hardly seven years old! What was his crime? Where were his rights in all this? Did he drop a sweetie paper on the street? Oh but he has told me some tales, sir, and they do not bear repeating here, in this company.'

'Lies. Lies and exaggerations.'

'Aye, likely. For it is very hard for me to believe such horrors, and yet what young boy could invent them? But leaving all that aside, the fact remains that he is seventeen now, a grown man, and since any crime was committed against him rather than by him, neither your church, nor the Irish Courts have any legitimate hold over him. So I'll thank you to finish your tea, get back in your car, and leave this island, where you are most certainly not welcome!'

The priest left, maintaining his politeness, but it was, so Kirsty thought, a chilly and strained goodbye.

'You haven't heard the end of this!' was his parting shot.

When the green car had disappeared round the bend in the track, Alasdair sent her to fetch Finn.

'I need a word with your mother,' he said. 'But you, Kirsty, be nice to the lad. He's had a bit of a shock today.'

'I'm always nice to him.'

'Aye. You are.'

Out in the dairy, she found Finn crouching under a table, curled into a ball. There was no way he could efface himself, the size of him, but he was having a good try, like a dog terrified of thunder. She crawled in beside him.

'Is he taking me back?'

She slipped her arms around him and pulled him close, rubbing at his back to warm him.

'Course not. You should have heard my grandad giving him what for!'

'The priest?' He looked momentarily horrified, as though Alasdair might have brought a curse down upon his head.

'Aye. I didn't understand the half of what he said. The priest was trying to make out you were a criminal or something. He had this bit of paper. He said it was from a court. It talked about your guardian. A guardian who does not exercise proper guardianship, it said. Did it mean your mum?'

'I don't know. I never saw it before in my life.'

'But you'll not be going back there, Finn. "The boy is in my employ. It is legal and above board." That's what my grandad said. You're to stay here, and that's all there is to it!'

'He won't give up so easily.'

'He'll have to. You don't know my grandad.'

Father Connolly didn't give up so easily and the following morning, he was back at the farm.

'One last attempt to make you see sense,' he said.

Alasdair, who had been expecting something of the sort, was waiting for him in the yard. This time, there was no invitation to step inside, no tea and biscuits. Isabel had gone shopping to the village, and Alasdair had sent Finn off to a remote part of the farm to mend fences. But Kirsty was lurking at the back of the door, listening.

'Mr Galbreath, I've made it abundantly clear to you,' said the priest, 'what kind of a boy you have on your hands here. The potential problems. If he stays, then you have to understand that we wash our hands of him completely. You won't be able to send him back. We have no further responsibility for him.'

'That's fine by me. But tell me something, before you go. These boys, these wee lads you have committed to these damned Dickensian hellholes you call industrial schools ...'

'Places of charity. Who else would care for them?'

'I don't believe it.'

'What?'

'Well, apart from anything else, the state must surely be paying for these children. The state commits them, the state must be paying for them.'

'Not really.'

'Do you take me for a fool?'

'Well...'

'I thought so.'

'There is a small capitation payment. But not enough. It is never enough.'

'I'm not convinced. And by God, you have them out the door fast enough when they hit sixteen. I assume that's because the payments cease from that date. But you don't free them. Even then. Oh no! You send them off to do whatever work you choose for them. And threaten them with the police if they don't stay. It's iniquitous.' Kirsty could hear that her grandfather was working himself up into a rage. 'Iniquitous. It's a form of slavery. Nothing less than a form of legalised slavery!'

The priest seemed taken aback by his vehemence. Perhaps he wasn't accustomed to this kind of head-on challenge to his authority.

He began to bluster. 'They need supervision. These children have become institutionalised.'

'I don't doubt it. We had another boy here. Francis O'Brien. He came here for a couple of years, to the tatties.'

'Aye. And you're glad enough to exploit the boys in your potato fields!'

'A fair point. A very fair point. But the conditions here are better than most. And let me tell you, the lad in question always seemed happy to be here. But sadly, he never came back. We looked for him a third time, but he never came back.'

'He must have been sixteen. He would have been sent out, found work.'

'Aye. As I said. The day they hit sixteen. Out of the door faster than you can say knife. But I don't think Francis did find work you know. He was a poor soul and I don't think he would have been fit for any sort of work, except to carry a tune in the church choir now and then. But he didn't come back. And Finn tells me that was because he died.'

'I know nothing about that.'

'Francis had a fall and he died. Finn told me all about it.'

'Ah, you mean you had this from the boy. These boys can't be trusted. You can't believe anything they tell you. They invent things.'

'They heard it, the other boys. They were listening at the door and they heard it. The next day, they were told about it. This so-called accident. I always wondered why poor Francis had that look about him. Like a beaten dog. I always wondered what went on. Were you teaching at the school at that time, Father Connolly?'

Connolly's face had turned a strange colour. Like no colour at all. Kirsty was watching him from her hiding place behind the door. Like crowdie cheese, she thought.

'No.' He had the car door open, and was stumbling in his hurry to get inside. 'No indeed. I'm the parish priest and the chaplain. I go into the school now and then. Conduct masses. But I don't teach there.' He looked at his watch. 'The ferry,' he said. 'I'll miss my ferry. I must go.'

'I think you must.'

The priest paused. Looked back at Alasdair. There was a strange moment between them. A small silence. An acknowledgement of something. As though at another time and in another place, the relationship between the two of them might have been different.

'Good luck to you with the boy.'

'Thank-you. But I think I've made the right decision, don't you?'

The priest paused and then nodded briefly and got into his car, slamming the door behind him.

Alasdair watched until the car and its occupant had disappeared. Only then did he relax.

'Kirsty, my wee lamb,' he called. 'You shouldn't be listening at keyholes.'

She came out from behind the door. 'I wasn't listening at the keyhole. I was just listening. Will he come back again, do you think?'

'Not a chance. Get your boots and your coat on now and find Finn. Tell him everything's sorted. Nothing to worry about. Just as I said. This is his home now for as long as he wants.'

Chapter Eleven

FOR THE FIRST time in his life, Finn knew the luxury of his own room, even though it was only the sparsely furnished loft above the kitchen, accessed by a precarious ladder. It was a clean and private space that he could call his own. He kept his few books here, mostly gifts from Kirsty, his clothes and the plain wooden rosary beads his mother had given him. He had managed to carry them with him for years. This was the single possession from his early childhood that nobody had ever taken away from him and it had gone with him to the farm in Donegal, tucked into the brown suitcase.

The loft was warm, since one of the walls retained the heat from the kitchen fire. At Alasdair's insistence, he always ate his evening meal with the family, but when he climbed up the ladder, often bringing a mug of tea or coffee with him, he had a sensation of contentment. Nobody disturbed him, nobody beat him, nobody so much as shouted at him.

When he slept, it was without the deep current of fear that had dogged his nights at the school. Isabel did his laundry for him but she wouldn't venture up the ladder. Every week or so, she would get him to throw his sheets and pillowcases down, and give him a pile of clean linen to take up with him. Kirsty would often clamber up to his room when her mother was safely out of the house, at her Women's Guild meetings or her church choir. She would come bearing gifts of books and biscuits, or her old board games: Ludo and Snakes and Ladders, games that she would make him play whether he wanted to or not. From time to time, she would try to sketch him, to capture him on paper, but she found it almost impossible. There was some elusive quality about him that she could never pin down to her own satisfaction, no matter what material she used: pencil, pen, paint, charcoal. Her skills did not seem adequate at that time and she was frustrated by the gap between what she saw in her head and what she produced on the page.

In winter, they went to her bedroom instead, where there was usually a fire burning in the grate. They would play records on the Dansette, a Christmas present from her grandfather. Kirsty was intensely curious about Finn's past, but her grandfather had cautioned her not to press him for too much information.

'I think he has had a terrible time, and when we have a bad time, we tend to forget things. It's self preservation, Kirsty. It sometimes happens to soldiers after a war. It happened to my own father. Let him tell you what he wants, when he wants.'

Still, Kirsty found it hard to contain herself.

'Why did they make you go to that school?' she asked Finn at last, her natural candour overcoming her discretion. 'Why won't you talk to me about it? You didn't do something bad, did you? That priest was wrong, wasn't he?'

'I'm ashamed to talk about it!'

'Ashamed?' she said, wonderingly.

'The courts sent me. We were charged with being destitute.'

'What's destitute?'

'Penniless. They said we had no money. Which was right enough, I suppose. They said my mother couldn't cope. But we weren't destitute. Not really.'

She took his hand and he didn't object. His fingers were long and brown with calluses on them. The mud was caked into his nails as usual. She could feel his fingers flexing against hers, as though he were clenching and unclenching a fist.

'So what happened to your mother, Finn? Why did she leave you?'

'She never left me. They made her give me up. They said she wasn't fit to look after me, so they put me in the school. They committed me and I couldn't leave. Your grandad saw the court papers that day when the priest came. None of us could leave.'

'Who said she wasn't fit?'

'A priest. Not the one who came here. It was the parish priest I think. And Mrs Maguire. Mrs Maguire in her horrible blue hat. They were hand in glove, that pair. I don't even remember his name.'

Who was Mrs Maguire? And what was her hat like?' Kirsty could have laughed, it sounded so comical.

'Mrs Maguire, from the Legion.'

'What Legion?'

'The Legion of Mary, what else?'

He was speaking in riddles again.

'I've never heard of them.'

'Have you not? Do you not have the Legion here?'

'I've never heard anyone speak of it. We have the Guild. Is it like the Guild?'

He shrugged. 'Maybe so.'

Finn thought about Mrs Maguire from the Legion of Mary. She had worn a dark suit and a hat like a wig, with blue flowers all over it. The gauzy petals made her look as if she had bright blue hair. He had been afraid of that hat. She looked like something out the horror comics his mother wouldn't let him see. And she carried a handbag over her arm, a bag so black, so shiny, that you could see your face in it. It reminded Finn of a big black beetle. Black and shiny, like the priest's shoes.

'I can see her now. She had a red notebook in her bag and sweets, a poke of boiled sweets. Sherbet lemons, I think. They were all stuck together. She broke one off and she gave me a sweet.'

She had popped it into his mouth before he could tell her that he wasn't supposed to have sherbet lemons because they made his mouth sore.

'She asked me a lot of questions about my mother and she made notes in the book. She wrote down the things I said. I wish I hadn't said anything. It was my fault. She made me get into a car.'

He remembered the leathery smell of the seats in the car and the lemony taste of the sweet and the way it made his mouth sore afterwards. His mammy would be cross with Mrs Maguire for giving him the sweet without asking her first. She would make him rinse his mouth with warm water with a bit of salt in it, to soothe it. But he didn't remember much else about that day. They had driven for a long time. He had never been in a car before. It had made him feel sick. He and his mother always travelled by bus or on foot. Each morning, she would walk him to school. He loved that walk, holding her hand, talking to her, swinging from her arm.

Every day, on the way to school, they passed a warehouse with a yard in front, and in the yard were half a dozen fat, friendly cats, black and white, ginger, tabby. He and his mother always stopped for five minutes to pet them and stroke them, scratching the sweet spot under the chin or behind the ears. He could see them now, their fat, jowly faces with bristling whiskers, their arched backs and soft fur. He could see himself petting the cats, and his mother saying, 'Careful now, Finny. Gently. You have to be gentle.' And the purring. The miracle of the purring, as though each cat had a small engine inside and the more he stroked and scratched, the louder the purring grew, the more he could feel that vibration through his fingers. But he didn't want to talk about that. It was private. Not for sharing.

In the car that day, Finn had fallen asleep, leaning against Mrs Maguire. She had smelled of mothballs and peppermint. When he woke up, it was to gathering darkness and a driveway that seemed to go on for ever, with a big grey building, like you would imagine a prison, at the end of it. He could tell Kirsty about that. He could speak about that.

'I remember getting to the school. That first day. The smell. Boiled cabbage and bleach. The sound of footsteps, running footsteps. They shaved my head. They said I was a dirty boy. But I don't think I was. I had a bath when I could, and my mother made me wash every day.'

Another picture came into his mind. Himself, standing in front of the sink, in his vest and underpants. There was soapy water in the sink, and his mother had a pink flannel and she was helping him to wash. She said 'you have to wash up as far as possible and down as far as possible, Finny,' and he said 'What about possible?' She started to giggle and he started giggling too, although he hadn't the faintest idea what they were laughing about, but when she was happy, he felt happy as well.

'All the time, I was wondering where my mother was.'

Kirsty was dismayed. This sort of thing was quite beyond her understanding.

'What was wrong with her? Why did they send you away from her?'

'There was nothing wrong with her. But she wasn't allowed to be there. With me, I mean. I think they sent her somewhere else.'

'What about your daddy? Couldn't he have you?'

'I don't remember him. I remember my mother a lot better than I remember my father.'

Finn hadn't thought about him in years. His name was Ronnie O'Malley, and he was a singer. At least that was what his mother had told him. But now, he didn't know what was true and what was made up, what he really remembered and what was only another story.

'What was your mother called?'

'Mary, Mary Flynn. Then she married my dad. She isn't dead, Kirsty. Just somewhere else.'

'Where?'

'I don't know. They would never tell me.'

'Did she leave you?'

'I don't believe she would have done that. She used to say that she was from a town called Ballyhaunis in County Mayo, but I've never been there and I have no notion of what it was like.'

'So why do you not remember your father?'

'He was the one that left. He went off to work in England. He could sing. My mother said he sang like John McCormack, Count John McCormack, she always said, but I couldn't tell you who he was, at all. My father would sing in bars and make a bit of money that way. My mother ran away with him. Her parents didn't approve, but they went to Dublin and then they got married.'

His mother had been at pains to tell Finn how happy she had been and what a fine man his father was. She told Finn that when he was a baby, Ronnie would sit him on his knee and dance him up and down and sing to him. And she would do a bit of the singing herself, to show him.

'Dum dum diddly do, dum dum diddly day …'

Sometimes Finn thought he could remember feeling safe, with

two arms around him, and the cheerful voice singing in his ear, but mostly he knew that he was only remembering his mother's version of the tale.

'Do you look like him?' asked Kirsty.

'I never saw a picture.'

'Did your mother not talk to you about him?'

In spite of the fact that he had died when she was so young, Kirsty's father was a very real presence in the house. There was a photograph in a silver frame on Isabel's bedside table, a wedding picture of James and Isabel, looking uncomfortable in their fancy clothes. The photograph was black and white, but you could see that Isabel had fat dark curls, while James looked just like Alasdair, so he had been the sandy one, the one who gave Kirsty her red hair. On the sideboard, were trophies that James had won for ploughing, and there was a pair of his working boots with the mud still caked on their soles in the wooden blanket chest in the upstairs hallway.

'I used to ask about him, and she would answer me. But it made her sad when she talked about him, so after a while I just stopped asking.'

His mother was sitting at the window and sewing. It was summer, the window was open and the creamy net curtain was billowing inwards. There was the clack, clack of the old treadle machine as her foot went up and down, up and down. Where had the machine come from? A man had brought it into the house, hauling it up the stairs. Had that man been his father? He didn't think so. He had a fleeting impression of somebody coming into the room with a heavy, wooden case. There was a smell of wax polish off it, a nice smell. His mother would use the machine to make cross-over pinafores for herself in blue or red gingham, and shirts for Finn, for going to church on Sundays.

He had liked going to church on Sundays, even though he got a bit bored. He liked the smell of incense and the candles that you could light for your 'special intention', if you put a penny in the box, and the confessionals that looked like miniature wooden churches. He imagined them peopled with tiny congregations. He liked to watch the priest in his green dress with white lace beneath and the altar boys with their lacy dresses, although he was never very sure why all these boys had to wear dresses like girls, but maybe they were just made that way. He even enjoyed listening to the priest's wavery voice, singing the mass in a foreign language that Sister Rosalie told them was called Latin, a dead language, she said, but he didn't know who had killed it. His mother would nudge him and he would look up at her and she would pull a face at him and make him giggle. The church was warm and comforting. Sometimes he would even fall asleep in there, leaning against his mammy's side, her arm around him, his head tucked in close to her soft chest, his cheek against the prickliness of her grey wool costume.

'But didn't you have grandparents? Didn't your mother have her own family?'

'I told you. They lived near Ballyhaunis. But I never met them.'

'So where did you live? When you were a wee boy? You must remember that, surely.'

'I remember the room we had. It was in Dublin. Just the two of us. The woman downstairs looked after me while my mammy went out to work.'

His mother had a job in a factory and she had to go out very early to get the bus. She used to wrap Finn up in a blanket and carry him downstairs to the neighbour who looked after him. The whole house smelled of smoke and cabbage and a dusty smell, like old feathers. He could see it in his mind's eye, as well as smell it. Their room was right at the top of the house. It got very hot in summer and very cold in winter. He could close his eyes and he was back there, lying in bed, in summer, listening to the noises in the street below. If he closed his eyes he could feel his mother's arms. She had soft arms with little freckles on them. And he could smell her: a mixture of cigarettes and perfume and face powder.

'Go to sleep now, my lamb!' That's what she always said to him. She would push the hair back from his face. 'Go to sleep now, my little soldier.'

'You look sad,' said Kirsty, breaking into his thoughts.

'No. I'm all right.'

'You're away from that place now. That school. You don't need to go back there, ever. You're safe.'

'I know.'

'I suppose you wonder where your mother is.'

'Wouldn't you? If you were in my shoes?'

'You've never heard from her since?'

'No. But it wasn't unusual, Kirsty. Nobody did. We were supposed to forget.'

'How could you forget something like that?'

Finn said nothing. Just stared out to sea. But Kirsty was right. How could you ever forget something like that? And yet there was something he had forgotten. Something he had done, or not done. Something terrible that was all his fault. And about that, he could remember nothing at all.

Chapter Twelve

ONE SUNDAY AFTERNOON in early May, when Finn had been living and working at Dunshee for a couple of years, Kirsty carried him off on an expedition to find the well of the winds, an ancient site in the north of the island. Alasdair was fond of telling tales about it.

'In the old days, when my grandfather's grandfather was a boy,' he said, 'the sea captains who might be becalmed on the island would go to the well and ask for a wind to carry them away. There were two old women who were guardians and they would uncover it if you paid them a little money, and then they would clear the water with a clam shell and mutter their spells over it, and the wind would blow. But they were always careful to cover the well when they had finished, for if they didn't, the waters would overflow and flood the whole world.'

Kirsty had never been there before, but her grandfather had given her directions. They cycled the miles to the north end of the island, Finn borrowing Alasdair's old bone shaker, left their bikes in a ditch and walked along the boundary wall between one farm and the next, as far as the lower slopes of a hill called *Carn Na Faire* or the Watch Cairn. The well was supposed to be situated low down on the hill. When she was little, Kirsty had imagined a circular stone structure, like the pictures in her book of nursery rhymes, 'Pussy's in the well.' But Alasdair had described a spring, a trickle of fresh water emerging from below a big boulder.

The lower slopes of the hill were hard going, threaded with gorse and willows, tangled with brambles, just coming into leaf. Soon they would be white with blossom but they were armed with a million thorns. The spaces between were scattered with celandines and blue-bells, with buttery primroses and dark violets, good enough to eat, patches, drifts, hillocks of them. Kirsty sat down for a momentary rest and it looked to Finn as though she were drowning in yellow and purple flowers.

'Isn't this glorious!' she said, running her hands over them. 'Isn't this just glorious?'

Finn had his fishing knife with him and cut down some of the willows so that they could pass. They scoured the lower slopes of the hill, listening for the sound of running water. There were plenty of stones and damp places but they could see nothing that looked as though it might be the Well of the Winds. And then, Kirsty noticed a patch of hillside where the willows seemed to be growing in a rudimentary circle. Stumbling over tussocks, she struggled between the branches. Finn followed, finding the going harder because he was so much bigger. The wind dropped and they found themselves in a sheltered place, warm and quiet.

Dropping into the silence came the faint sound of running water. Ahead of them, a large boulder, embroidered with livid green moss, was tucked into the hillside, and below it they could see a line of muddy patches. Finn crouched down and began to scoop out the mud and grass at the base of the boulder. Soon, he had uncovered a flat stone. A trickle of water bubbled out from beneath it and even as he cleared away the accumulation of leaves and moss a pool formed miraculously beneath his hands. The bottom was clean and sandy.

'Is it fresh?' asked Kirsty.

He looked up at her. 'I don't know. '

'Well, drink some and see.'

'Do you think I should?'

'Course you should. I'm going to.'

She was down beside him, steadying herself on his shoulder, kneeling down to scoop up a handful of the water. He saw the silvery droplets fall from her fingers as she carried them to her mouth.

'Well?' he asked.

'It's lovely. Try it.'

He did as he was told. She was right. The water was very cold but fresh and good.

'Do you suppose it is magical?' she asked.

'What's it supposed to do?'

'It's a cure-all. Whatever's wrong with you, it'll heal you. That's what they believed in the olden days.

'I don't feel any different.'

'You have to give it time. And you'd better put the capstone back on or it'll flood the whole world.'

'Not likely,' he said, grinning, but he did as he was told and slid the stone back into place. Nevertheless, the water still oozed in a thin trickle from beneath it.

Finn was a quiet lodger and a willing worker, but the more Alasdair and Kirsty sang his praises, the more Isabel set her lips in a thin line and endured his presence. Always polite, he did whatever she told him without complaint. He offered to carry her shopping up from the village for her whenever he saw her on the road. He cut cabbages or dug carrots or brought a boiling of potatoes from the fields and washed them under the tap in the yard, but there was nothing he could do to endear himself to her, and eventually he just stopped trying.

Isabel would have found it very hard to define exactly what she disliked about him, but she knew that in every way that mattered to her, Finn did not come up to the mark. She pitied his past, but she could not love this changeling who had invaded her home. He was too self contained. There was nothing remotely sweet about him, nothing vulnerable or loveable, as there had been about Francis. She had been drawn to the other boy's helplessness as she never would be to Finn. She could have mothered Francis, but Finn neither wanted nor needed mothering, and Isabel sensed a certain resentment, simmering below his deferential surface. He was in the habit of obedience, that was all. But it did not come naturally to him. He was like a dog, beaten into submission, but with retaliation on his mind and in the curl of his lip.

Although she would have admitted it to nobody, not even herself, Isabel was dissatisfied with her life. Sometimes, she would wake at three or four in the morning to a sense of futility, a downward spiral of days, from which there was no escape. She had been widowed for many years now and for a long while, she had wanted nothing more than to live in peace and quiet. The shock of the accident, the adjustments that had to be made, all this upheaval had taken time and emotional energy. Now, a change had come over her. It was not that she was consciously searching for a new husband. But she was increasingly aware of her own isolation. Sooner or later, Kirsty would fly the nest. Isabel felt trapped in the circumscribed world of the island, where everyone knew her history and her business, and she knew everyone else's. Sometimes she longed for the relief of anonymity, for the opportunity to make a fresh start, to re-fashion herself in some way, go to new places, do new things, meet new people.

I'm still a young woman, she thought. And look at me! Hair like a haystack. Baggy cardigans. Tweed skirts and wellington boots. I've nothing nice and if I had, there would be nowhere to wear it.

Her infrequent trips to her cousins in Glasgow disturbed her even more. She would wander around clothes shops, touching the fine fabrics, sometimes trying on a coat or a dress. During her most recent visit, she had gone to a hairdresser, asking for a new style. Then, her cousin had taken her into a department store where a young woman with plum coloured lips and nails to match, had done her make-up. She had stared back at this strange, new face in the mirror, half delighted, half horrified by the blue eyeshadow, the kohl liner, the long lashes, all framed by a sleek bob. But as soon as she got back to the island, the wind and rain transformed her hair into a mass of frizz again. She often wished she could move away and start afresh, but the thought of the upheaval frightened her. How could she do such a thing to Alasdair? He had no sense of her dissatisfaction. Perhaps she hid it too well.

Her only close friend was an older woman called Agnes who cooked for the Laurences at Ealachan.

'Time you found yourself a new man!' Agnes said, as they sat over a pot of tea in the kitchen of the big house, in the quiet spell between lunch and dinner. 'You've been stuck up there are Dunshee for too long. There's no reason why you shouldn't marry again. Plenty of people do, Issie.'

But Isabel didn't know where or how she would find a man in

this place, where everyone seemed either too young or too old, too married or too eccentric. She had worked at Ealachan herself, before her marriage to James, and there had been a time, quite a long time, when she had thought herself madly in love with Malcolm Laurence. It was a crush, really, but the thought of him still gave her a small quiver of desire in the pit of her stomach. Once, he had patted her backside as he passed her on the stairs, a casual caress, so light that she could hardly believe he had done it, not knowing whether to be flattered or outraged. But she knew that none of it meant anything. His wife, Viola, was a formidable woman, stick thin and stylish, with fine blonde hair, a long straight nose and skin like a piece of porcelain. Isabel always found her just a little inhuman. She kept Malcolm on a very tight rein indeed. No matter what her dreams and fantasies might be, Isabel knew that Malcolm had never seen her as more than a pretty face or a nice soft body.

Now, seeing Kirsty grow into a young woman, Isabel found herself bitterly regretting the loss of that little red-headed girl who had once toddled so joyfully about the farm. She couldn't help it. It just came upon her sometimes, swept over her like a bereavement. It was both a pleasure and a pain in her heart, the way her baby had grown and was now slipping away from her. She had invested so much love in this only child. But once her darling bird had flown, there would be nobody to fill the gap in her life. Certainly not Finn.

At school Kirsty had chosen art as one of her subjects and, on the advice of Miss Wilson, had applied to study Fine Art at Edinburgh University. She would have preferred to try for the Glasgow School of Art, but her mother wouldn't hear of it.

'You read such things in the papers about art students!' she said, disapprovingly.

To Kirsty, it seemed marvellous that she should be able to study something she adored and get a grant to do it as well. On the whole, her grandfather agreed with Miss Wilson. He had begun to take a passionate interest in Kirsty's future. He was fairly bursting with pride in her.

'There will be no prouder man than me on the day you graduate,' he said.

'Grandad, I haven't even got there yet!'

'What about Finn?' said Isabel, slyly. 'You'll be leaving him far behind, won't you? He'll miss you!'

It was a low blow and unworthy of her, but she couldn't resist using a weapon that she had unexpectedly discovered in her armoury.

Kirsty hesitated. 'I'll miss him too. But then I'm away half the time as it is. He'll be here when I come home. You all will. I'll be back before you know it.'

In September of that year, one of the Glasgow cousins came to the island in his white van to take Kirsty to Edinburgh. All that day, Finn had been noticeable only by his absence. Even when Kirsty's belongings were packed, and they were eating their evening meal, there was no sign of him.

'Skiving!' Isabel was furious.

'Leave him alone' said Alasdair. 'You know what's wrong with him.'

'What?'

'You know.' Alasdair nodded in Kirsty's direction.

'Och, well, he'll just have to get used to it, won't he? We will, so he'll have to.'

Kirsty said nothing. Leaving the island was one thing. She had been ready to spread her wings for some time now. But leaving Finn was quite another. Sadness at their imminent parting flooded through her. As soon as she could decently do so, she left the table and went in search of him.

It was a warm evening. The last of the swallows were assembling on the wires but the nights were already drawing in and soon it would be dark. She wandered through the outbuildings, calling his name and at last climbed up to Hill Top Town. Sure enough, she found him standing on the very rim of the saucer of land, staring out to sea, as she had found him that first evening, all those years ago.

'I was wondering where you'd got to.'

She tried to slip her hand into his, but he shrugged it off, thrusting his hands into his pockets. During this last summer, she had changed, physically as well as mentally. She had a broad, pale face almost disfigured by freckles. Her eyes were dark green and whenever she smiled she displayed white, slightly uneven teeth. Her face was handsome rather than pretty, and it was her hair that was her chief beauty. She still had her dense red curtain of hair, long and glorious: far prettier than the rest of her. Sometimes when he looked at her now, Finn hardly knew her. Had she but known it, he and Isabel were sharing something of the same regret for the Kirsty they had lost.

'You're upset.'

'I'm all right. I'll miss you, but I know you have to go. I've always known it. Always known this would happen.'

'You can't miss me more than I'll miss you, Finn. '

'Well, maybe so, but you'll have plenty to keep you busy.'

'So will you. It'll be Christmas and I'll be back home before you know it.'

'Maybe.'

'I will, honestly.'

'It doesn't matter. At least I'll know where you are.'

'Will you write to me?'

'I'm not much of a hand at the letter writing, Kirsty. You know that.'

'You could try. I'll write to you. Oh Finn, what will I do without you?'

'You'll manage fine.'

He was right of course. She would. But would he manage without her?

'Let's say goodbye here. I'd rather say it here, where it's just the two of us.'

'Goodbye then.' He stepped away from her a pace. 'There. It's said. Away you go and make sure you have everything ready.'

She rushed at him and hugged him, circling his unresponsive body with her two arms, reaching up to plant a kiss on his prickly cheek.

'Finn …'

'I hate goodbyes.'

'It isn't goodbye. I'll be home soon.'

He gazed down at her in the twilight, his face grave. 'I just don't like change very much. It frightens me. Enjoy yourself, Kirsty. But don't forget about me.'

'How could I ever do that? Never in a million years.'

Chapter Thirteen

THE EDINBURGH HALLS of residence were on the south side of the city, below Salisbury Crags and Arthur's Seat. Each floor had eight single bedrooms and a large shared kitchen. Kirsty's room was a clean but shabby cell, with a desk, a wardrobe, a sink and a narrow single bed. On her first afternoon, she decorated it with a hand-crocheted throw and cushions, with her threadbare teddy nestling among them. She tacked up a couple of posters of richly coloured mediaeval paintings, bought an electric kettle and some mugs and felt ready to turn her attention to her fellow residents.

In the kitchen, she found a small blonde girl, peering into one of the cupboards, trying to decide which shelf to commandeer.

'I think you're in the next room to me. I heard you come in. Have your mum and dad gone then?'

The girl nodded. 'Molly. My name's Molly.'

'I'm Kirsty. Want a coffee?'

The girl nodded again. She seemed to be a little choked with tears.

'Where are you from?'

'Leeds.'

'Come on then. I've got a kettle in my room. And some mugs. Bring the milk with you.'

'You're well organised.'

'Ah but I'm used to it.'

'Were you at boarding school?'

'Not what you might call boarding school, but I live on an island. I had to stay in a hostel during term time.'

'That must have been hard.'

'I got used to it. We all did.'

She made Nescafe, brought out a tin and lifted the lid to reveal a large fruit cake, white with almonds, sticky with cherries. 'My mum thinks I'll starve if I don't have supplies!'

She cut two large slices and handed one to her new friend.

'What are you going to study?'

'English and Fine Art.'

'Me too. Well, Fine Art's my main subject. Do you know Edinburgh well?'

'Not really.'

'We'll find our way around together then.'

'I've never met anyone from the Western Isles before,' said Molly.

'That's because there aren't many of us left. People drift away from the islands all the time.'

'Like you?'

'Ah but I might go back.' Kirsty was suddenly serious. 'Although perhaps not for good. I don't know. I can't make up my mind.

'Do you have a boyfriend at home?'

'A boyfriend? No! But I have my family. Well, my mum and my grandad. My dad's dead.'

'I'm sorry.'

'You don't have to be. It was a long time ago.'

'Is it a nice place?'

'It's the most beautiful place on earth. I'm going to miss it all the time. But I want to do this. Don't you?

In the middle of her first term, Kirsty met Nicolas Laurence in the library cafeteria. She had heard he was at the university but she hadn't seen him for years. He had been spending his summers away from the island, and she was disconcerted to find that she hardly recognised him. He looked much more like a lecturer than a student and an affluent one at that. He was perched on one of the low stools, dressed in jeans, a very white shirt and a sports jacket. Everything about him looked expensive, from the gold watch at his wrist to the soft leather desert boots on his feet. He looked wholly at ease with himself, in the way that wealthy people so often do.

'I wouldn't have known you,' she said, hugging him and then

turning to introduce Molly. 'Nicolas is the big cheese on our island. Aren't you, Nick?'

'Not at all!' He was faintly embarrassed.

'Well, his dad is, and Nick will be, eventually.'

Molly looked puzzled, so she added, 'He's our landlord. He owns us all, body and soul. Don't you, Nick?'

'She's joking.'

'Only partly.' She turned to Molly. 'He pays the occasional flying visit so that he can check out what the lower orders are up to, seeing as how he's the gentry.'

'I wish you wouldn't,' he said mildly.

'Wouldn't what?'

'Wind him up maybe?' said Molly, always the peacemaker.

'I'm not winding him up. It's true. He's our landlord. And he's loaded, aren't you, Nick?'

'My father's your landlord, Christine, not me.'

'It will amount to the same thing. Eventually. We'll all have to do what you tell us.'

'You'll always do whatever you like. You damn well know that.'

She relented and patted his knee. 'I know. Don't take me so seriously! I'd forgotten you were here. Although now I come to think of it, your father mentioned it to my mum when I got my acceptance. What are you doing here?'

'Geography. Third year.'

'And then?'

'I'll probably go into the family firm.'

'How could you not?'

He went away, bought coffees for them and sat down beside Kirsty.

'Shove along,' he said. 'What about you? What are you doing?'

'Fine Art.'

'I might have guessed. God but you've changed.'

'Not really. I'm the same old Cairistiona.'

'Well, you don't look it. I always think of you as a little girl with plaits and ankle socks. And now look at you!'

'You've changed quite a bit yourself.' She grinned at him.

'Are you going home this term?'

'I'll probably just wait for Christmas. It's such a trek. And I can't really afford the fare.'

'We'll be there for Christmas. And Hogmanay. My parents are planning a big party. Will you come?'

'If I'm asked.'

'I'm asking you now. They must be missing you at Dunshee.'

'I write to them and I phone my mum every week. But they're used to me being away.'

'And whatever will Finn McCool do without you? Faithful Finn!'

'Don't talk about him like that. You know nothing about him.'

'Why are you still fighting his battles? You've outgrown him and you know it.'

Kirsty looked at her watch. 'Don't you have a lecture or something?'

Nicolas stood up. 'I do indeed. Best get on. We must have a meal some time, Christine.'

'That would be nice. Give me a ring.'

'I will.' He bent down and would have kissed her on the lips but she turned her head to one side, so he found himself clumsily brushing her cheek instead.

She watched him go. 'Get me another coffee, Molly. I'll pay you when I've been to the bank.'

'I think I can stand you a coffee. But only if you tell me all about him.'

Molly brought the coffee back and sat down in Nicolas's place.

'Why didn't you mention him before?'

'Because he hardly ever crosses my mind. I haven't seen him for ages.'

'You've got this rich, good looking friend in Edinburgh and he hardly ever crosses your mind?'

'His father owns half the island. Well, a big chunk of it, anyway. He's our landlord. They divide their time between the island and London. Nick used to be sent up to Scotland for his health.'

'He doesn't exactly look fragile.'

'No. Well it must have done him some good, mustn't it?'

'I think he fancies you.'

'No he doesn't. Apart from the fact that I've known him since we were kids, I don't have the right sort of bank balance.'

'Why does he keep calling you Christine?'

'He always has done. He could never manage Cairistiona, and he doesn't much like the name Kirsty.'

'Who's Finn McCool then?'

Kirsty smiled. 'It isn't Finn McCool. That's just Nick, trying to be funny and not succeeding. It's Finn O'Malley. And will you stop the inquisition? He's just somebody on the island. He works on our farm. Another person I've known forever.'

'Your Nicolas doesn't seem to like him.'

'He isn't my Nicolas. And believe me, Nicolas never gives Finn a second thought. He only said it to wind me up.'

The truth was that Finn was private. She didn't want to talk about him at all, even to her closest friends, Molly and Anne, a history student from Devon, who lived down the same corridor. The girls had become a threesome. Winter Sundays were very quiet in Edinburgh and the girls were often forced to spend time studying, from sheer lack of anything more entertaining to do. Most Sunday afternoons, Kirsty, Anne and Molly would take a break from their books and trudge down the Royal Mile to the Fudge House, where they would sit and drink hot chocolate and nibble home made fudge.

'So come on,' said Anne, on one of these long, chocolate-soaked Sundays. 'Tell us all about this Finn person.'

'He's just my friend.' Kirsty was eating whipped cream off the top of her chocolate with a spoon. 'We used to go about together all the time. Do kids' stuff. We're not cousins, but that's what we're like.'

Anne rummaged in her bag of fudge. 'This place is almost as bad as home on a Sunday, but at least it's only one day a week. God knows what you found to do on your island, Kirsty. Aren't you supposed to go to church for hours and hours on Sundays and do nothing else?'

'You're thinking of the Wee Frees.'

'The wee what?'

Kirsty giggled. 'The Free Church of Scotland. But it's not so strict where I live. Besides, there are a million things to do. We just ran wild.'

'I didn't think your island was that big.'

'No, but there's only a couple of villages and a handful of farms and crofts. The rest of it is moorland. Peat bog. White sandy beaches. You can walk for miles if you want to.'

'Exciting stuff,' said Anne. 'So what else do you find to do there?'

Kirsty gazed at her friends across the table. How could she ever explain?

'Oh, we go out in my grandad's rowing boat. Sometimes we go and lift his creels for him. Or we go fishing.'

The thought that Finn was there on the island, waiting faithfully for her return, was obscurely comforting. But talking about these simple pleasures reduced them, made them seem humdrum and stupid.

Kirsty kept a tiny black and white snapshot of Finn in her desk drawer. But she hadn't showed it to anybody else. Just occasionally, she would take it out and look at it. She had taken the picture herself, had caught him looking down at her, smiling his rare smile, from the top of a drystone wall, his hair blowing into his eyes. She had borrowed her grandfather's camera because she had wanted to take photographs so that she could sketch things later. She had been afraid of breaking the camera, which was one of her grandad's prize possessions, so she had put it back into her rucksack and then clambered up after Finn. She remembered his cold hand reaching down for her, hauling her up beside him. The summer was almost done. There was the astringent scent of leaf mould, the sudden stink of fungus. They had been feasting on the plump brambles that jewelled the island hedgerows, but she had been stung by a wasp. The pain had brought tears to her eyes, but he had sucked the wound clean and then sweetened her tears with fruit.

'Don't cry,' he had said. 'Don't cry, Kirsty,' and she had said 'I'm not crying. I never cry. Not for an old wasp sting.'

She remembered clambering onto the wall, thorny stalks thrashing about her knees. She remembered grazing her legs on granite and wild rose whips. And then they were on top of the wall, clutching each other, balancing as stones skittered about them while the wind blew bitter flurries of rain in from the west.

But once she had left the island, everything had changed. Nothing would ever be the same again. And now, whenever she looked at the snapshot, she had a fleeting but powerful sense of regret, wishing just for a moment that she was back there, balancing on that wall, Finn's hand in hers. My friend, she thought. My big brother.

Chapter Fourteen

KIRSTY WENT HOME for Christmas, travelling most of the way by bus. On the ferry, she swung on the rail like a child, trying to make the little vessel move faster. As they neared the harbour, she began to look out for Finn, running from side to side to get a better view, craning her neck, unable to control her excitement. At last, as the ferry moved closer to the jetty, she caught sight of him. He was leaning against the jeep, arms folded, long legs stretched in front of him. Almost as soon as Finn was staying permanently on the farm, Alasdair had paid for driving lessons for him. To his surprise, he had passed first time. He wore a black wool jacket and filthy blue overalls and his boots were caked in mud. He pushed himself into an upright position and walked slowly towards the boat, his eyes searching among the passengers.

She leaned precariously over the side and waved madly. 'Finn! I'm here!'

He looked up at her. His face was grimy, his hair uncombed. Ashore, she ran to him and hugged him. For a moment, she held him close, setting her cheek hard against his chest, listening to his heartbeat, with the wool of his coat prickling her skin. His long arms went round her and they stood very still, his lips just touching the top of her head. When she stepped back from him, holding him at arm's length, it wasn't his muddy overalls that distracted her. It was as though this sudden proximity had made them both shy, recollecting them to some sense of a reality that, just for a moment, had been transcended by both of them.

Finn carried her bags up to the jeep. Kirsty clung to his arm, hindering his progress with questions, but she was in control now, her conversation friendly, with nothing of the intensity of that first embrace. On the way up to Dunshee, he said, 'I thought you might come home for a visit in the autumn. You said you might.'

'It's a long way, Finn.' She threaded her arm through his as he drove.

'Don't,' he said, changing gear. 'What's that smell, Kirsty?'

'It's my perfume. Patchouli. Don't you like it?'

He wrinkled his nose. 'Not much. Smells like fly spray to me.'

'How are they?' she asked him, after a pause.

'They'll be all the better for seeing you,' he said, gruffly. There was the mildest of reproaches in his tone.

Kirsty felt a pang of irritation. She had expected an unconditional welcome.

'Did they expect me home sooner?'

He looked straight ahead, concentrating on the road.

Kirsty frowned and bit her lip.

'I had things to do, Finn. I couldn't help it.'

'I know.'

'I'm here now, that's the main thing.'

'Yes,' he said. 'You're here. That's the main thing.'

At Dunshee, Isabel embraced her daughter.

'You've turned into a hippy,' she said, with grudging admiration.

In the kitchen, the table was already laid with blue and white plates and a loaf of crusty bread. Soon they would be joined by the big two-handled pan of stew, a dish of floury potatoes and another of mashed carrots and turnip with plenty of butter and pepper.

Finn went off to wash his hands. When he returned, Kirsty was touched to see that he had made a rudimentary attempt to comb his hair. He had discarded his shabby overalls to reveal equally shabby, but rather less grubby jeans and a blue cotton shirt, threadbare and faded from too many washes.

'It's lovely to have you back,' said Alasdair, heaping her plate with stew. But even while they ate, Kirsty could see that all her mother's body language still spoke of disapproval or, worse, a deep seated dislike where Finn was concerned. When the meal was over, he left the kitchen without a word, while Kirsty went upstairs to unpack her bag. She plumped herself down among the creamy woollen blankets. She had forgotten how comfortable her old box bed was, especially in winter. Night had fallen and her grandad had lit a fire for her. One of the house cats had come in with her, a lovely creature with silvery stripes and great green eyes. Once, the cat had had a real name, but Kirsty had called him Fish Face for so long that everyone had forgotten it. He wasn't a very sociable cat, but he liked Kirsty. Tonight, he rolled over and bit, gently but firmly, at her hand when she tried to stroke him, but he was content to burrow among the blankets. Then he righted himself and folded his paws under him, making himself into a neat rectangle, dozing, with the triangles of his ears still alert. She buried her face in his fur, inhaling the warm, sweet smell of him. She was glad to be home.

Christmas passed quietly enough. Kirsty had brought gifts from Edinburgh: a warm Aran sweater for Finn, a silver necklace and some tulip bulbs for her mother, a bottle of malt whisky for her grandad. For Kirsty herself, there was an embarrassment of parcels under the threadbare artificial Christmas tree: new clothes of all kinds, make-up and perfume, as well as books, paints and brushes, paper and canvas. It was as though her mother and her grandfather wanted to show her what she was missing. Finn's gift was a sketch pad and good pencils. He had bought them on one of his infrequent trips to the mainland.

The Laurence family always spent Christmas in London, but came back to Ealachan for New Year. Kirsty was walking past the iron gates of the house, when a big, black car headed up from the ferry. It drew to a halt and the window slid noiselessly down. Nicolas Laurence, looking very handsome, stuck his head out.

'Hi there, Christine! Did you have a good Christmas?'

'It's nice to be back. Are your mum and dad here yet?'

'They came over yesterday. I don't see much of you in Edinburgh.' He sounded disappointed.

'It's a big place.'

'Are you coming to the party? Hogmanay. We've got people coming down from London and a few from Edinburgh as well. You will come, won't you? Your grandfather and your mother too.'

'Not sure you'll ever prise my grandad out of the house on Hogmanay, but mum might come. Is Annabel here?'

'No. She's in Paris. With a man, I think. You know what she's like. Eight o'clock on New Year's Eve,' he called out of the window as the car pulled away. 'Don't bring anything but yourselves. There'll be lots to eat.'

'And lots to drink as well, if I know Nicolas,' said Kirsty, when she told her mother about the invitation. 'Will you come?'

'I'd like to.'

'Well do. You don't have to stay cooped up here and I certainly want to go.'

'Your Grandad won't go, though, will he? He'd rather stay here with Finn.'

'I never thought about that. No invitation for Finn.'

'Why would there be?'

'They've never been the best of friends. We used to catch him just watching us sometimes. Poor Nicolas. But we'd never let him join in.'

'Which was very unkind of you, Kirsty.'

'Nicolas wasn't part of it, mum. We didn't want him. We didn't need anybody else back then. I know you've never liked Finn much, but he was a good friend to me.'

'I liked that other lad, Francis. I just couldn't see why you were so fond of Finn. I still can't.'

'We were like brother and sister. That's what it always felt like.'

'But he isn't your brother. He's an incomer. Oh Kirsty, I should have remarried, shouldn't I?'

'Don't be daft. Who would you have married, mum?'

'Well, I suppose I might have found somebody!' Isabel started to laugh.

'But getting a brother for me wouldn't have been a good enough reason to get married again.'

'Maybe we should have moved to the mainland.'

'Did you want to?' Kirsty found herself slightly disturbed by the thought. 'I mean later. When you got over losing my dad. Did you want to marry again?'

'You never do get over losing somebody. You get through it, but not over it. It's different for you, I know. You don't remember him. But yes, if I'd met the right man, maybe I would have remarried.'

'I suppose you still could. You're not old, mum.'

'Maybe we could even have moved away. But your grandad would never have left Dunshee and I couldn't just leave, could I? Besides, this was a good place to bring up a child. It was a good place for you.'

'We were so free.' Kirsty sighed at the memory. 'We could do what we wanted, go where we liked. As long as we were together, it was fine. I felt safe. And it *was* like having a brother. A big brother, who would always look out for me.'

And yet, she thought, it had been as fragile as a cobweb. An outsider could have brought the whole thing crashing down round their ears in a moment. Back then, mentioning it to anybody else, even Nick, would have been like telling her dreams. It was the same with her work, with ideas for pictures. If she talked about them too much or to the wrong people, they just evaporated. Her friendship with Finn was a fragile arrangement. Not to be pinned down. And once destroyed, it would be as difficult to rebuild as a robin's nest.

'We're off to a party at Ealachan on Hogmanay. Me and my mum.'

Kirsty made the announcement to the table in general, but Alasdair already knew, so really, it was for Finn's benefit.

'And I'm looking forward to it,' added Isabel.

'Do you want to go to a party with that crowd, Kirsty?' asked Finn.

'I don't see why not!' Isabel's reply was quick and sharp.

Finn had stopped eating and set his knife and fork neatly on his plate, although he hadn't quite finished his meal. 'I notice he didn't invite me.'

Alasdair let out a great guffaw of laughter.

'That'll be the day!' he said. 'That will be the bloody day!'

'Alasdair!' said Isabel.

'Well, it will be the day!'

'Why shouldn't he invite Finn?' asked Kirsty.

'Because he wouldn't go, would you, lad?'

'I don't know. I might.'

'And because there's all the difference in the world between being a tenant farmer and being a hired hand,' said Isabel.

'But you were a hired hand as well, mum.'

'I worked for them. Nothing wrong with that. It was a pleasure to work for Malcolm Laurence. He's a perfect gentleman. And so is his son.'

'I'll be off,' Finn said, suddenly, pushing his chair noisily backwards over the stone floor. 'I've things to do before dark.'

Kirsty's appetite had deserted her. She left most of her pudding and excused herself from the table. She put on her coat and found Finn lurking in one of the outbuildings, pretending to polish a piece of old tack with an oily rag.

'For God's sake, Finn! Come back inside. It's freezing out here. You know I don't give a damn about Nicolas. But mum wants to go. In fact, she needs to go. She doesn't get much of a chance to get out of the house, and I'm going with her whether you like it or not and that's that.'

'You'll be away back to Edinburgh soon.'

'And that's exactly why I want to make things nice for mum while I'm here.'

'Do you not want to make things nice for me?'

'I thought I did make things nice. Honestly, Finn, you don't have to be jealous. It'll be good for mum to go to the party and there's no reason why she shouldn't.'

'Everything's changed.'

'Nothing's changed. Well, not between you and me. But I can't always be here, Finn, and I can't always be worrying about your feelings.' She rounded on him in sudden exasperation. 'I could spend a lifetime trying to reassure you, couldn't I? And it still wouldn't be enough.'

Finn looked sheepish, kicking at the wall. 'I'm sorry,' he said finally. 'I can't help it but I'm sorry.'

'Are you coming back in?'

'Maybe later.'

'All right. Be like that.'

Kirsty hadn't been inside Ealachan House very often, although once or twice, when they were children, Nicolas had invited her in for juice and biscuits. It had always seemed a gloomy place, and she had imagined Nicolas as a lonely little boy, trailing through its chilly rooms. There were two or three enormous reception rooms with fancy marble fireplaces, gilded mirrors and chandeliers. The staircase was an elegant sweep. There was a conservatory, a library lined from floor to ceiling with books, and a panelled billiard room with a carved observation gallery above.

Some previous owner had planted shelter belts for the benefit of his garden. Now, the trees grew so thickly that, even in winter, once you were in the house or even on the lawns in front of the house, the sense of being on an island disappeared. Beautiful as the gardens were, Kirsty always found herself half suffocated by trees and wanting to escape from them. To find the sea again, you had to go clambering up a path that traversed a steep bank behind one of the walled gardens. A breathless climb through dense vegetation brought you at last to the heathery spine of the island from where you could see the silhouettes of other islands and breathe salty air again.

Kirsty and her mother arrived late. Isabel had been fussing over her appearance, changing her dress, her shoes and her hairstyle until Kirsty grew impatient with her.

'You look lovely,' she said at last. 'And if you don't come now, I'm going without you!'

The other party guests had arrived from the mainland in a selection of sports cars and brightly painted Citroen 2CVs. Kirsty didn't move in these circles in Edinburgh. None of her close friends even owned a car. The girls were tall and slender in Biba and Mary Quant. The young men were smartly tousled, in white shirts and dark trousers, and they all drank champagne as though it were going out of fashion, swallowed their final consonants and narrowed their vowels so that it was hard to figure out exactly what they were saying.

Nicolas came up behind them. 'Don't you look wonderful, Christine?'

Kirsty was wearing a sea green Indian cotton dress with a high waist and little bells that jingled as she walked. She was flattered by his obvious admiration. Finn had pretended not to notice anything different about her.

'How the other half do live,' she said, as she and Isabel stood outside the downstairs lavatory together, waiting their turn. 'Mind you, they could do with a new loo.' The lavatory, which she remembered from childhood visits, was a bleak room of immense and icy proportions with sheets of slippery toilet paper, a worn wooden seat and a broken chain.

'I used to clean this place,' Isabel said, starting to laugh.

Kirsty danced with a succession of charming but not particularly handsome young men. Sometimes, in the intervals between dances, she would see her mother, standing with a glass of champagne in her hand, chatting to Malcolm. He didn't dance, although his wife was visible from time to time, whirling through the Dashing White Sergeant and Strip the Willow with a string of partners. Isabel seemed to be enjoying his company immensely. Occasionally, Nicolas would rescue Kirsty and dance with her himself. When the bells rang out at midnight, he was beside her. They embraced, briefly, and he gave her a chaste kiss on the cheek. She noticed that her mother was beside Malcolm and, since his wife was nowhere to be seen, she too was the recipient of an embrace and a peck on the cheek.

In the early hours of the morning, with the party growing raucous, Nicolas offered to drive them back to the farm, but he had been drinking so much that they refused and set off to walk home by themselves. It was no more than a couple of miles but the ground was white with frost and by the time they were struggling up the last few hundred yards of the track to Dunshee, they were both exhausted. Kirsty had swathed herself in a woolly coat and tucked her dress up, so that she could walk more comfortably, and she and her mother were going arm in arm, trying to keep to the grass at the side of the track to save their shoes.

Just before the farm gate, a tall figure uncoiled itself from a rock and barred their way.

'Finn!' Kirsty had been expecting this. 'What are you doing out here?'

'Waiting for you. I was worried about you. Down among the Hooray Henries.'

'You should have known we'd be all right.'

'So Nicolas didn't bring you home then?'

'He offered, but we thought we'd be safer walking.'

'Thank God for that.'

She took Finn's arm and slipped her hand inside his pocket. On his other side, Isabel struggled under her own steam for a while, but at last she gave in to her fatigue and took his arm as well.

'We've had a lovely time, haven't we, mum?'

Isabel, a little drunk with champagne and the happiness of Malcolm's attention, agreed. 'It was a nice party.'

'But our feet are killing us. I wish you hadn't waited up though. You'll be so tired in the morning.' Kirsty looked up at him in the gloom. 'We can sleep in but you can't.'

'It doesn't matter.'

'Honestly,' she told him, lightly. 'You'll be better off when I'm back in Edinburgh.

'Don't say that!'

'Well it's true.' She spoke in a low voice, not wanting her mother to hear. But Isabel was in a world of her own.

Kirsty leaned in close. 'You'll soon get back to normal again. I just seem to upset you.'

'You don't really believe that, do you? If I thought you really believed that ...'

They were outside the front door. The house was in darkness. Alasdair had waited for the Hogmanay bells and then taken himself off to bed.

Isabel let go of Finn's arm. 'I'm dead on my feet. Make sure you put the lights off, Kirsty.'

Kirsty and Finn lingered in the doorway, their combined breath making patterns in the cold air. She reached up and kissed him quickly on the lips.

'You're drunk, Kirsty!' He held her at arm's length, embarrassed.

'I think I must be! But do go to bed. Please. You know I worry about you.'

'Happy New Year, my darling Kirsty. Sleep well.'

'You too, Finn. You too. And may all your dreams come true!'

Chapter Fifteen

IN THE SUMMER term of that first year at university, Kirsty discovered that she had a talent for finding and adapting vintage velvet skirts, and Edwardian blouses and shawls that suited her looks. She would ferret about Edinburgh's second hand shops in search of bargains, long before it became fashionable to do so. She hadn't realised that she looked Pre-Raphaelite until one of her tutors told her so, showing her pictures of Lizzie Siddal. After that, she used the pictures as inspiration for her own idiosyncratic style. She wore beads and bells around her neck and jangly bangles. She drifted around in a cloud of patchouli. She was self consciously arty.

Every afternoon, Kirsty's Director of Studies, Dr Sharansky, held court in his room. Though it was frowned upon by the authorities, he did not let this deter him. There was home-made beer and wine and only certain favoured individuals, Kirsty included, were invited to these gatherings. They would sit around his big table, that was littered with books, pictures and manuscripts of all kinds. There were always more men than women in the room, postgraduates some of them or junior lecturers. Sometimes there were foreign visitors: young poets and playwrights and artists.

One afternoon, Kirsty was perched among these smoky and self conscious young academics like some bright bird, when the door was suddenly flung open and a man strode into the room. He was tall and slim and seemed to inhabit every inch of his body in a way that Kirsty had never seen before. Like her, he was revelling in his own persona, and she recognised a kindred spirit but one who was older and much more practiced.

'Ash!' said Sharansky, leaping to his feet, delighted with his new guest.

He turned around, beaming at the rest of them. 'This, my friends, is Duncan Ashley. Otherwise known as Ash.'

He was a painter, exhibiting in the capital's galleries, already making a name for himself. Kirsty had never heard of him, and never seen any of his work but Sharansky was clearly impressed by him. The conversation ebbed and flowed as she sat there, watching him, wondering why all the air seemed to have been sucked from the room. She fidgeted on the hard chair, struggling to breathe, aware of a flush rising from her neck to her cheeks.

Ash turned his gaze on her, raising his eyebrows.

Dr Sharansky hurried to introduce her. 'Ash, this is Kirsty Galbreath.'

'Pleased to meet you!' he leaned over and shook her hand. His own hands were strong and freckled. She found herself smiling inanely at him, tongue tied for once.

'Are you another fine artist then?' he asked, with a hint of sarcasm and a malicious glance at Sharansky.

'Sort of.'

'Our Kirsty has real talent!'

'I'm glad to hear it.' He smiled, distant, unattainable, more physically attractive than anyone she had ever met.

He stayed for an hour, drank several glasses of wine in quick succession, then got to his feet and, without so much as a stumble, said 'goodbye all!' and left. As he passed her chair, he ran his hand across her back, a mere touch. She didn't know whether it was deliberate or accidental but her body's instant response surprised her. Again, the air left the room. Later, walking home through the hop-scented Edinburgh evening, she thought, I'll probably never see him again. But she was rather sorry about that.

In their second year, Kirsty elected to share a top floor flat in the New Town with her friends, Molly and Anne. It was spartan and poorly furnished, it was chilly, even in summer, but it was theirs and they loved it. Much to Finn's disappointment, Kirsty spent only a couple of weeks on the island that summer and he was busy about the farm for most of that time. Then she went back to Edinburgh where Molly, with a couple of resits, was studying madly. That first morning in their new flat, Kirsty walked up to Henderson's for wholemeal bread, through the New Town streets that smelled faintly of Gauloises. When they sat down to eat their warm bread and jam at the heavy utility table in the living room window, she had a sudden intimation of pure happiness. Anything could happen and all of it seemed exciting.

That same day, she started a part-time job in a tiny art gallery on Rose Street. Dr Sharansky had 'put in a word' for her. For a few hours each week, Kirsty would sit behind a desk, fielding enquiries about the pictures. During the whole time she worked there, nobody ever bought anything from her, although a handful of sales were made at the private views that opened each exhibition.

One Saturday, in late summer, with the city in its usual Festival turmoil, she found that the new exhibition consisted of a series of huge canvases, near-pornographic paintings in thick layers of muted oils, all depicting naked women and muscular (although fully clothed) men in attitudes of extraordinary violence. The canvases were scrawled with the name 'Ash' in large black letters. Kirsty saw him at the private view, but he was surrounded by adoring acolytes and she couldn't get near. Later that week, however, he came into the gallery on his own.

'How's it going?' he asked. The answer was not very well, which was hardly surprising, thought Kirsty. She might appreciate his work, but she couldn't imagine anyone wanting to live with it.

He rocked back on his heels, hands in pockets. 'Don't I know you from somewhere?'

'I'm one of Peter Sharansky's students.'

'Oh yes, I remember, You were at one of those gatherings of his.'

'I was.'

'He's a bit of an idiot, isn't he?'

She was taken aback. 'I like him.'

'Yeah, well.' He strode off into the other room.

'Do you want a coffee?' she asked. They kept a filter machine on the go for artists and favoured customers.

'I wouldn't say no.'

After that, Kirsty found herself hoping that Ash would come into the gallery while she was there, and he did seem to visit more often than was strictly necessary. Whenever he arrived, she would offer him coffee, with her tongue tying itself in knots. Everything she said to him seemed foolishly naïve. She would ask him questions about his work and let him talk about himself and his ambitions, which he seemed more than happy to do.

One afternoon, he came in just before closing time, when the Rose Street shops were putting up their shutters. She switched off the lights and locked the door, and they went out into the hot August evening together. Their footsteps echoed off the old stones as he tucked her arm through his. She could feel the warmth of him, his firm, wiry body, striding along beside her.

'Do you fancy a drink?' he asked.

'Why not?'

They went to the Abbotsford, its ornate interior full of BBC producers and tourists. Ash had to shout to make himself heard. He drank beer and she drank cider and after two half pints, she felt lightheaded, because she hadn't eaten anything since breakfast time.

They talked and talked. She told him about her own painting and he said, 'Why didn't you go to Art School?'

She explained how difficult it had been to get away from the island at all.

'But Fine Art!' he said. 'That's not what you want, surely?'

'I don't know what I want yet. And it's certainly giving me all kinds of ideas about what I might want to paint.'

'Well, good for you. I'm hungry, aren't you?'

They went to an Italian restaurant where they ate spicy pasta, laughing over the gigantic pepper mill and the way the waiter brandished it over their plates. On the street outside, her hand found his little finger and then, as if it were something quite new in the world, they were holding hands. He walked her home to the New Town flat and when they got to the door, she wanted him to come in, but he said 'Better not. Maybe next time.'

At the last possible moment, he kissed her, his tongue dipping into her mouth, a sudden and shocking intrusion, leaving her full of the sweet taste of him. She floated up the stairs with a foolish grin on her face.

Even after his exhibition had finished, Ash and Kirsty saw each other often. Sometimes she would go out for drinks or meals with him, late lunches or early dinners, and she would come in a bit tipsy and very happy, but he still seemed reluctant to begin a proper affair. For a while, he asked for nothing but her company. Once he bought her a big bunch of roses and she walked home through the Edinburgh streets carrying an armful of blooms, aware of how striking she looked, with her long red hair and the pink roses.

'Girl with a Bouquet,' she thought, happily self-conscious.

The problem was that he was married. His wife was living in London and he said that they were estranged, that he didn't see much of her, but they had a daughter, a little girl called Hannah. He made no secret of the fact and was adamant that he loved his daughter but not his wife. Whatever the truth of that, Kirsty knew that she couldn't compete with a child, nor was she willing to try.

Soon after the start of the autumn term, Nicolas Laurence got in touch with her again. He was in his final year and working hard, but sometimes he would invite her out to the theatre or the cinema. Once he brought a picnic in a willow basket and took her for lunch in the Meadows behind George Square. They drank champagne and ate late strawberries under the trees. Her friends and flatmates couldn't understand why she wasn't madly in love with him. Nicolas saw her with Ash on a couple of occasions and tried to question her about him, but Kirsty was deft at keeping the different compartments of her life separate and would only say that Ash was a friend and that he was helping her with her art. This was true. Ash was giving her lessons, although her friends were sceptical about his motives. But Kirsty could have told them that the caution was all on his side.

Just before Christmas, the girls decided to throw a party. They pooled their finances and bought wine and cider from the off licence round the corner, cold meats and chocolate covered plums from the nearby Polish deli, bread and cheese from Henderson's. Kirsty found herself wondering which of the men in her life to invite, but Nicolas settled the matter by going off to London for the weekend which probably meant that Annabel had got herself embroiled in some kind of misery again. She was always having what Nicolas called 'man trouble' and demanding that her brother come and sort it out for her.

Kirsty went to Marks and Spencer's and found an empire-line nightie with a low neck and little sleeves that emphasised her breasts. It was in some pale, diaphanous fabric and she intended to wear it for the party, even though the flat was too cold for comfort. Isabel had crocheted a shawl for her the previous summer, and she wrapped it around herself. Anne had managed to bring a record player on the bus all the way from Devon and they were playing Joni Mitchell and Leonard Cohen at full volume. In later years, Kirsty could never hear Cactus Tree or Suzanne, without remembering that magical time in the New Town flat.

Most of the guests left in the early hours of the morning. The other girls went to bed, but Ash lingered, helped with the washing up, made a pot of tea. He was unexpectedly fond of tea. He brought the mugs into the bedroom; she sat on the floor at his feet, loosened her hair, and began to brush it out.

'Christ,' he said. 'Don't do that, Kirsty!'

'Why not?'

'Because I won't be responsible for my actions, if you do!'

She blushed. 'I'm sorry.'

'God's sake, woman, don't apologise! I suppose I'd better go as soon as I've finished this.'

'Do you have to?'

'Do you really want me to stay?'

'I do.'

'Are you sure about this?'

'I'm sure.'

'Then, come to bed, Kirsty.'

After that, even when he was away, he would stay in touch, writing her ten page letters, ornamenting them with tiny pen-and-ink sketches, making them for her on trains, in offices, in his hotel room, late into the night.

'I feel like a character in a Victorian novel. I'm distracted by love for you.' He wrote as he spoke, with great emphasis and exaggeration.

When she thought about him afterwards, she would remember chiefly that fine tapestry of words and images, woven just for her. He seemed profligate with his affection at that time, and she loved him for his generosity. His letters were full of boyish intensity. 'What do I have to offer you?' he would say, and she would rush to reassure him, not realising that this was the literal truth. He had very little to offer her.

In his Edinburgh flat he would insist that she work, insist that he teach her whatever he could and she was, and would remain, eternally grateful to him for that. The flat was at the top of a big house on the Newington Road. He had his studio there, high up in the building. It was full of his painting things: canvases propped against walls, jars spiky with brushes, the smell of paint and thinner. It was what she aspired to and she adored it and him in about equal measure. Patiently, he showed her what he knew of drawing and painting, and she would work assiduously until she was almost faint with desire for him. He would send her to bed to wait for him and then get lost in some piece of work of his own. She would lie awake, desperate with longing, and when he came through, at last, would make love to her with a passion that seemed all the more intense for his ability to defer the pleasure. They talked and touched and their words flew from one to the other, a tangle of words and fierce images that caught and held them together.

'My red headed, shiny girl, whose face collapses with love when she looks at me,' he called her.

Afterwards though, it struck her that there had been a kind of cruelty about all this. They were never an equal partnership. She had always been early for their meetings however hard she tried not to be; he had always been late. The fact remained that, whatever he said, whatever stories he concocted to explain everything, his wife was still a significant presence in his life.

Her things were everywhere in the flat. Kirsty couldn't ignore them. Joanna. That was her name. Ash called her Jo. Jo was everywhere. Everywhere and nowhere. And she was not the villain he had painted her. Ash had been lying. Ash lied as the skylark sings and believed implicitly in his own fantasies. There was little evidence of the child beyond a couple of teddies perched on a window seat and a yellow baby cup in the kitchen cupboard, but there was a pink toothbrush and a woman's dressing gown in the bathroom, tubes of make-up and a bottle of Rive Gauche in the bedroom, even, on one occasion, a carefully arranged platter of fruits and vegetables on the kitchen table that may well have been placed there by Ash himself. But for some reason, Kirsty associated it with Joanna. She began to wonder just how real their separation was. She and Ash bickered about it. She tried to force some kind of declaration out of him but he clammed up. Maybe Joanna was his safety net, his insurance against making a commitment to anyone else.

One day, when Kirsty had been in the flat painting for an hour or so, Ash took a phonecall and came rushing into the studio in a panic, taking the brush out of her hand, hustling her out of the room and out of the flat, gabbling about 'a sudden emergency' and how he had to go away, now, immediately. It was like a scene from a farce. At the time, she left meekly enough, but in retrospect, she thought that Joanna had probably been on her way from the station.

When she tried to discuss these things with him, tried to have some kind of debate, his voice took on the whining, haranguing tone of somebody who has been storing up points in his head and is now intent on making them.

'You're so bloody needy,' he said.

She saw that this was how it always would be. She shed a great many tears and her university work suffered, but self preservation finally took over and she ended the affair, refusing to have any more to do with him.

She had come to the realisation that, while she had been wounded by his lies, she only really cared about her work. If she truly loved anything, apart from her family, it was that. But her work itself was all tied up with the island: the plants, the stones, the sea and sky, even the small things, the way a leaf lay over another leaf, the way the light sat on the water. If she could put it into words, then she probably wouldn't have to paint it. The transitory nature of everything fascinated and saddened her. It had something to do with Ash, with her attraction to him and with all he had taught her, but it had much more to do with her childhood and her friendship with Finn, the way he had come and gone from her life, come and gone from the island. Nothing held. Not for a minute. You might grasp something and it was gone. You might try to transfix something and it would die, like a butterfly on a pin. You might capture something on canvas, but you were capturing only change itself.

Chapter Sixteen

In the summer after her second year, Kirsty took a break from the gallery and went home to the island, intending to stay for a couple of weeks before returning to Edinburgh. But almost as soon as she got back, she realised that her mother was ill, seriously ill in a way that made Kirsty breathless with panic. Over the past year, Isabel had found it increasingly hard to swallow anything but the softest food. Now, she seemed to be living on soup and porridge and she had lost a tremendous amount of weight. In the warm summer weather, Kirsty was alarmed to see how thin her mother's arms and legs had grown, although she seemed to be trying to disguise it, wearing loose clothes and cardigans. She looked like a skeleton in a dress.

'Why didn't you tell me?' she asked. 'Why didn't you say what was going on?'

'You seemed to be having such a good time in Edinburgh. We didn't want to worry you. It'll be all right. Once they find out what's causing it, they'll sort it out, never fear.'

But they didn't seem able to sort it out and her mother's illness tinged the remains of the summer with its own peculiar misery. Meals became an agony of suspense, while Isabel tried to swallow. Soon, anything other than the most bland puree made her cough, then choke. Kirsty came to dread the hunted look that accompanied every mouthful. There were trips to a mainland hospital for tests, procedures, treatments that seemed to work but only for a little while.

'I feel much better,' said Isabel after each change of medication.

She was always hopeful, always positive, but Kirsty didn't think she was getting any better. Soon there were spells of devastating fatigue, when all she could do was lie on the couch, listening to the radio or reading while Kirsty kept her company. One of her doctors told her that she ought to get more exercise, so Kirsty persuaded her to walk down to the village. But only a few hundred yards down the track, she stopped.

'I'm sorry, Kirsty' she said. 'I just don't know if I can. I feel so weak.'

'Come on, mum!' Kirsty chivvied her along. 'You have to build up your strength, you know.'

'I'm trying. I'm really trying.'

Isabel struggled on for a few hundred yards, but before they reached the main road, she collapsed onto the muddy bank. Eventually, Finn came by in the jeep, and he and Kirsty helped Isabel inside. For once in her life, Isabel seemed glad that she had Finn to lean on.

'Thank-you,' she said, and smiled at him, although in her exhausted state it seemed more like a grimace.

'I'll be better soon,' she kept saying.

It made Kirsty's heart ache to hear her, but she conspired in the fiction. She so much wanted it to be true that she clutched at any sign of hope, however faint. Afterwards it seemed to her as though her mother's doctors had entered into this conspiracy as well, endlessly prevaricating.

'Oh we'll get to the bottom of it sooner or later, Mrs Galbreath,' they kept telling her.

Kirsty wondered if it was because doctors were as fearful of death as their patients. Incurable illness was such a defeat for them that they couldn't bear to contemplate it either.

She kept having to ask her grandfather for money. Though he gave it, gladly, she was always aware that he had no cash to spare either. The farm was barely profitable, and rent must be paid to the estate. She racked her brains for ways to earn some money for herself, but there was little work to be had on the island. Besides, most of her time was taken up with helping her mother to and from hospital, doing the housework, cooking meals that Isabel couldn't eat, (though Finn and her grandfather made short work of them) or catching up on the farm paperwork, the letters and accounts that Alasdair had long neglected.

'What did we do without Kirsty?' he said, over another plentiful breakfast.

Finn glanced across at her but his sympathy was more than she could bear and she got up to clear the plates. When he came over to help her, he touched her hand in a gesture of solidarity. She squeezed his fingers in return and then busied herself at the sink. Later, when Alasdair and her mother were in bed, he came into the kitchen again and threw himself into a chair, tugging off his boots.

'It's a bugger,' he said, and she knew he wasn't only talking about the mud clinging to the soles.

'What am I to do, Finn? I can't go back, can I? I can't leave you and my grandad to cope with this.'

'You can't give up half way through your course.'

She came and sat beside him and leaned on his shoulder. She felt profoundly weary, too tired even to think. 'I can't go back right now, that's for sure.'

'Can't you take a year off? Isn't that allowed?'

'I could always ask. Explain the situation.'

'Once they get to the bottom of it, once they find out what's happening, and she's better, you could go back. Even if you've missed a year, you could just pick up where you left off, couldn't you?'

'I could try.'

She requested and was given a deferral of her course for a year. Dr Sharansky was very understanding.

'These things happen,' he wrote. 'Take whatever time you need, keep reading, keep painting, and come back when you're ready.'

Nevertheless, Kirsty felt as though her ambition and her creativity had been put on hold, although she still painted in the quiet of her own room or outside, with a folding easel. Finn framed up the landscapes, and the village shop and the hotel displayed them. The more conventional views sold quickly, although the ones she liked best, those that were more experimental and abstract, weren't so popular. She wondered if she could apply to the Arts Council in Edinburgh for a bursary. It might buy her some time. But would the time be available when so much of it had to be devoted to Isabel?

During one of those autumnal warm spells that often come like a late blessing to the west of Scotland, Kirsty was lying in the stuffy box bed with the weight of the cat on her legs. He divided his favours about equally between Kirsty and her mother. She had been asleep for an hour or so, but something had wakened her from a peculiarly unpleasant dream, the details of which slid away from her almost immediately, leaving only a sensation of misery. She lay there, straining to hear, but the house was quiet. Fish Face stretched and burrowed into the coverlet, flexing his claws. She closed her eyes and had a sudden sense of things spiralling out of control. The walls of the bed were closing in on her. Panic seized her. There was a ringing in her ears and a tingling sensation in her fingers. She felt unreal. If she were to look at herself in a mirror, she wouldn't recognise what she saw there. She opened her eyes, got up on wobbly legs and went to the window. On the bed, the cat shifted, yawned widely, and settled down again in the warm space that she had vacated.

Outside, the moon was suspended massively over the island. A giant orange, she thought, gazing at it, distracted by its strangeness for a moment. Her bed looked rumpled and uninviting. She went quietly out of the room, past her grandfather's bedroom door (he was snoring) and past her mother's room, where she paused for a moment, listening. There was no light showing round the door, and she could hear Isabel's even breathing. She pictured her for a moment with the heavy curtains pulled against the alien moonlight, propped up on three or four pillows, because this was the only way she could sleep without being overcome by the coughing that choked her.

Kirsty moved through the upper landing. The old lino was cold and gritty on the soles of her feet and she wished that she had put her slippers on. She went downstairs quietly, walking to the wall side of the creaking fifth stair, and then paused for a moment in the hallway, wondering if she should go outside and sit in the garden for a while, with the moon for company. But this big orange stranger was too bizarre and she was afraid. Without putting on the light, she stole though the kitchen, comforted by the hum and whirr of the fridge and the settling of ashes in the range. She went through the oak door at the other side of the kitchen and stood in the lobby, at the foot of the ladder, staring upwards. There was a faint light burning in the room above.

'Finn?' she said. It was the merest whisper, but she heard the creak of floorboards as he came towards the open trapdoor. She saw his dark head silhouetted against the lamplight.

'Kirsty? What's the matter? Is it your mother?'

'No. I just need some company.'

'Are you coming up?'

'Can I?'

'You don't have to ask.'

She climbed up the steep ladder. It was a long time since she had been in his room, although it had been a wet weather den and a refuge for them both when they were younger. He was waiting at the top, where he took her elbow and pulled her into the room. The roof was at such a pitch here that Finn had to be careful, otherwise he would bang his head off the sloping sides. There were skylight windows to front and back, and the light of the now risen moon flooded the room with silver. To one side, if you stood up and peered through the sloping, salt-smeared glass, you could see the shoreline and the glittering sea; to the other was the outline of Hill Top Town, just behind the farm. Finn had been reading by the light of a lamp that Kirsty recognised as her old red anglepoise, the one she had got rid of because it kept keeling over, fainting onto the desk when she was trying to work. She looked at his book but it was nothing exciting: something to do with animal husbandry.

'Why are you reading this stuff at three in the morning?' she asked him. 'In fact why are you reading at all?'

'I couldn't sleep. I thought it might send me off.'

'Maybe it's what I need as well.'

She sat down on his bed. It had a lumpy mattress, a heap of woollen blankets and a shabby crochet coverlet made years before by her grandmother. She ran her fingers over its shapeless, bobbly surface and was ashamed of herself for allowing her mother to discriminate against her friend in this way.

'This used to be mine.'

'I know,' he said. 'That's why I like it.'

'I thought it was my mum. Putting you in your place.'

'No. I wanted it. It reminded me of you when you were away. She put it out for the kirk jumble sale, but I brought it up here.'

'Finn, you're as bad as the cat. He likes my stuff when I'm away as well!'

'I know.'

It was some time since she had been in his room, and now she was seeing it through adult eyes. She was looking at a dilapidated garret with worn out furniture and few personal possessions. Still, he had arranged everything very neatly: his table with a few papers spread out and an old transistor radio, his chair with its faded cushion, a bedside cabinet with a pile of books, most of which had been gifts from Kirsty herself. There was a cooling mug of tea sitting on a raffia mat, a farming calendar with pictures of agricultural machinery hanging on the whitewashed wall.

'Oh, Finn!' she said, involuntarily.

'What?' He looked at her gravely but she shook her head. She had no words for what she wanted to say. She smiled at him, but he didn't smile back. She realised that she had hardly paid any attention to him for all these months of summer. She had been too busy with her mother. He had just been there, going quietly about his work, and she had been glad of his calm presence.

She watched him as he closed the trapdoor. He was wearing a pair of navy shorts. His legs were long and muscular. His arms and shoulders were brown but his thighs were white in the lamplight. Suddenly self conscious, he got into bed and pulled the covers up over himself, leaning back against the pillows so that his face was in shadow. The room smelled a little of his perspiration, but not unpleasantly so. He always took a shower after his day's work, and his hair was still damp and scented with shampoo. Kirsty felt shy of him. He was as strange as the moon. She crossed her arms, perching uneasily on the edge of his bed, rocking backwards and forwards to comfort herself.

'What's the matter, Kirsty?'

'I woke up and I couldn't get back to sleep. I'm so worried about my mum. I don't know what to do, Finn. I hate not knowing what to do.'

'What more can you do? She's having treatment.'

'I don't think it's the right treatment. I think it's more serious than they're telling us.'

'You could speak to the doctor.'

'He's never there when I visit.' Her mother's consultant seemed to make a point of being absent during visiting hours. Once she had found herself trotting along corridors in pursuit of him, but he had been called away to an emergency before she could speak to him. Afterwards she had been very angry with herself for her timidity. Her mother's illness seemed to have reduced her to a kind of infantile subordination, quite out of character.

'Is she sleeping just now?'

'They're both asleep. '

'But you can't?'

'No.'

There was a pause. He was running his finger over the stitched edge of the blanket. 'It's nice having you back,' he said at last.

'It would be nice to be back, if …'

'If it wasn't for your mother.'

'She's been no friend to you, Finn. Why should you care about her now?'

'She's your mother. I couldn't wish ill to her even if I wanted to.'

'Sometimes I've even thought about going up to the Well of the Winds and getting some of that water. You never know.'

'It's good spring water, Kirsty, but that's all it is.'

'I know. But I'd try anything right now. Anything at all.'

He stared at her, and she saw her own desperation reflected in his eyes. 'I am so sorry,' he said.

'Finn …' she hesitated.

'What?'

'What are you planning to do?'

'I was just about to go to sleep.'

'No. What are you planning to do with your life?'

He was disconcerted by the question. 'How do you mean?'

'I've practically ignored you this summer and I'm sorry for it. '

'It doesn't matter.'

'It does. But you're in my mind you know. You're always in my mind, in one way and another. I just feel you're so ... so wasted here.'

'Your grandfather couldn't manage without me.'

'Maybe not. But he doesn't pay you very much for what you do.'

'He pays me more than I was getting in Ireland. He couldn't afford to pay me more. And I don't need very much.'

'That's beside the point, Finn. You're worth more than that.'

She had never really thought about his wages before. Now, because she had been doing the farm accounts, she had realised just how little Finn earned for all his hard work. 'I feel as though we're exploiting you. And you can't just ...' She hesitated.

'What can't I do?'

'You can't spend your whole life up here being general dogsbody to the Galbreath family. It's not fair. It's not right. You're like the brownie over there!' She nodded in the direction of Eilean Ronan, in the bay.

'I don't work for nothing.'

'Well, next to it.'

'You know what happens when you offer to pay a brownie ...?'

'Yes. He goes away. And maybe you should too. You could really make something of yourself.'

'Am I not something now?'

'Of course you are.'

'Where would I go?'

'You could go to college. Find something you want to study.'

'With what? Who would foot the bill?'

'You could go to the mainland. Go to Oban or Fort William. Or even Glasgow. Get a job. Do some part time studying. Learn a trade.'

'Oh come on, Kirsty,' he said. 'I have no qualifications. I can do the work on the farm but I barely finished school. And when I was at the school, I didn't learn very much. You know that as well as I do. We were taught nothing but how to avoid the blows. How to do as we were told. How to keep our heads down.'

'I do know it, but I still think you're worth more than just being the hired hand at Dunshee. You were always better at figures than me, and I'm doing the accounts. There's no future in this place for you. No future in these little island farms either.'

'You really think I ought to leave the island?'

'I don't want you to leave. I can't bear the thought of Dunshee without you in it. I only thought ...'

She shivered. What would she do if he took her at her word and went? But he would never do that. She knew it in her bones. He might go with her, but he would never willingly leave her behind.

He turned back the blankets. 'Get in if you're cold.'

She remembered the heather bed up at Hill Top Town, and how they had clambered into it together, giggling, scratching their legs on the stalks. She had been little more than a child. And although he had been older, too old really, and her mother would have disapproved, still, their mutual innocence had protected them. He held out his hand and she climbed into bed beside him, into the welcome circle of his arm, tucking her head into his shoulder. With his free hand he switched off the light. She rubbed her feet against his warm thighs.

'Jesus, Kirsty, your feet are freezing.'

'I forgot my slippers. I was too warm in bed and now I'm cold.'

'So you think I should go away and better myself, do you?' He said it ironically, his chin on the top of her head. Now he was smiling. She could sense it in the dark.

She pressed her cheek against his body and slid her arm around him. She could feel his heart beating. A flutter of desire took her by surprise. 'I could kiss him on the lips,' she thought. 'I could just turn my head and kiss him.' She knew everything about him but the taste of him.

It would be only one more complication.

'My little sister,' he said.

'Do you remember Hill Top Town?'

'And the heather bed?'

'I knew you'd remember.'

'I remember everything. It was Grania who lay in the heather bed. In the story. Wasn't it? I like that name, Grania.'

They lay together quietly, and for the first time in months, Kirsty felt the dreadful tangle of hope and despair slide away from her. It didn't go completely, just subsided. She breathed in the familiar scent of Finn and held onto his little finger, and his proximity soothed her. She closed her eyes. After a while, she drifted into sleep. Her dreams were full of his grave, watchful presence. He seemed to have the ability to take all her troubles to himself for that space of time, and when she woke a couple of hours later, she found that he had not moved, but was still there, wide awake, looking down at her in the pale light.

'Oh Lord,' she said, sitting up. 'Finn. Your arm!'

'It doesn't matter.' He flexed it, restoring circulation.

'I should go. If my grandad finds me up here ...'

'He wouldn't approve.'

'I can cope with that but he'll tell my mum and she'll get all worked up.'

'You'd better go then.' He held her at arm's length, looking into her face. 'You off to the hospital again today?'

'She's got a follow-up appointment. Nicolas is giving us a lift.'

His arms stiffened at the mention of the name.

'You didn't say.'

'I knew you'd go all huffy on me.'

'I could take you.'

'I know you could, but the journey half kills her, Finn. It helps that he's here on the island and he's got such a comfortable car. And he volunteered. It was my mum who said yes, not me.'

'I thought he'd be back in London by now.'

'So did I.'

She knew now that Nicolas was not returning to London or to Edinburgh. He had graduated and he planned to stay on at Ealachan House. Soon he would be taking over the management of the estate as well as working for the family firm. Finn would hate the very idea of it. She couldn't bring herself to tell him yet. She didn't know which was worse, telling him or deceiving him.

'I'm sorry. If I didn't have to go, I wouldn't.'

'You'd better get down that ladder. Your grandad's an early riser.'

She got back to her room just in time. She heard her grandfather's door open, and his heavy shuffle as he went to the lavatory and then clumped downstairs to make the tea. He always brought her a mug of strong tea and left it beside her bed. She lay there, waiting for him, pretending to be asleep, thinking about Finn, his eyes, his lips, all the planes and angles of his face. She thought about his grace when they were together and his other self, the person the world saw, a big, sullen, clumsy young man with nothing to recommend him.

'What will I do about him?' she thought.

Finn wouldn't leave the island, not while she was here, and she couldn't go while her mother was so ill. As she drank her tea, she pictured herself living at Dunshee for the rest of her life, cooking meals, doing the washing, doing the accounts, helping with all the dirty, muddy, heavy work of the farm. She pictured herself trapped here, growing old and spinsterish, unable to leave. She thought of Edinburgh. In her mind's eye it was always springtime with George Square full of blossom and fat yellow tulips in Princes Street Gardens. She thought of Ash. What had all that been about? That frantic desire which, if she allowed herself, she could still summon, a sharp sense of arousal at the thought of his body. It had been good while it lasted, but it hadn't been real. They had bandied the word love about as if it meant something. Now, she felt the world closing in on her as surely as the walls of her box bed. There must be some other way. Some way of helping herself as well as everyone else. But for the moment she didn't know what it could possibly be.

Chapter Seventeen

AFTER CHRISTMAS, ISABEL spent six weeks in a mainland hospital. She lay there, attached to a drip and a feeding tube, getting steadily worse, while Kirsty and Alasdair tried to persuade her consultant to transfer her to a specialist unit for a second opinion. They kept saying they were 'trying to expedite her transfer'.

'No they aren't!' said Kirsty in despair. She was at Ealachan, having coffee with Nicolas who had been in London over Christmas.

'She's wasting away while they keep doing one test after another and saying they aren't sure what's wrong. Even the nurses know it's serious. I'm desperate, Nick. I've actually thought about discharging her, driving her to Glasgow and leaving her at the other hospital. But my mum won't have it, of course. She says they're doing their best.'

'Do you want me to see what I can do, Kirsty?'

'What can you do?'

'I have contacts. Well, dad does. And he's asking after your mother all the time. He was very fond of her when she worked down at Ealachan you know!'

'I know. She had an almighty crush on him!'

'Did she?'

'Don't tell him. It would embarrass the life out of her if he knew.'

'The doctors might listen to me, where they won't listen to you.'

'If there's anything you can do, I'll be grateful.'

After that, Nicolas took charge, became assertive in that confident, low key way he had. He got the estate secretary to phone up and make him an appointment with the consultant. He set up a meeting, but he wouldn't let Kirsty come. Soon after, Isabel was moved to a hospital outside Glasgow and the specialist there diagnosed her within a day or two. She had a massive tumour. They thought that the cancer might be too advanced for treatment, but the surgeon suggested an operation to make her more comfortable, to help her eat again.

Alasdair and Finn turned the downstairs sitting room into a bedroom for her because the stairs had become too much for her to manage. She moved between her bed and the kitchen, which was where she sat all day, dozing beside the warm range, talking to Kirsty as she did the housework in the morning; listening to the radio or reading in the daytime; watching TV in the evening.

As she had grown more seriously ill, Isabel had started to look more youthful. Contrary to expectations, the years had fallen away from her, as though stripped by some invisible force. Illness had softened the sharp edges of her personality. She was thin and pale, but oddly beautiful, her skin almost translucent.

One day, sitting gazing out of the window, while Kirsty sliced vegetables for the evening meal, she said, 'Nicolas looks like a man in love to me.'

'Who with?'

'You. Has been for years hasn't he?'

'Maybe.'

'You could do worse, you know!'

'I still kind of want to go back to Edinburgh.'

'Well, there's that too. But what about Ealachan? Who wouldn't want to say yes to a place like that? I'd have given anything for ...' she trailed off.

'I don't want to play at houses. I want to paint.' Kirsty spoke more sharply than she had intended. 'That's all I really want to do.'

'You could always do both. Has he asked you to marry him yet?'

'No! Of course not.'

'It wouldn't surprise me if he does, Kirsty. What would you say?'

'I can't think about anything until you're sorted, mum.'

'You'd be mad to turn him down.' It would have been her dream, thought Isabel, imagining a proposal from Malcolm.

'I'd be mad to say yes if I didn't love him.'

'You just look right together. You're good friends and that's what matters in the long run. Besides, who else are you going to find in this place?'

'I don't intend to stay in this place.' Kirsty faltered. 'Mum, I want to paint. I want to do more than get married and have babies. But I can't think about anything except you, right now, and then there's grandad. He isn't getting any younger either.'

'Finn. There's always Finn. He'll help with the farm.'

'That's not fair. It isn't his responsibility.'

'But he wouldn't walk out on your grandad, would he? Listen Kirsty, if I'd had someone as rich and lovely as Nicolas Laurence who wanted to marry me, and I liked him the way you so obviously like him, I'd have bitten his hand off!'

'I wonder what Finn would say?'

'This has nothing to do with Finn. It's none of his business. He's had a good home here all these years. Better than he deserved, I'm sure. But you've outgrown him.'

'You don't outgrow your real friends, mum.'

'However close you think you are, he's still the hired hand. Not a bean to his name. And no prospects either. I know it shouldn't matter, but there's a world of difference between the two of you now.'

'I don't want to talk about this any more.'

'And it isn't as if your grandad could leave him the farm. That belongs to Nicolas.'

'You sound as if I've thought about marrying Finn. I never have. Why would I?'

'I'm relieved to hear it.'

Sometimes, Kirsty felt as if she wanted to pack a bag, get on the first ferry of the day and never look back. She would go to Italy or France and paint, make a new life for herself, forget about all of them. She couldn't do it, of course. But the prospect of leaning on Nicolas instead seemed very attractive. He was making himself indispensable, and she loved him for his kindness, his gentleness, his concern for her. It seemed churlish not to return such affection.

Isabel had been right. When Nicolas asked Kirsty to marry him, he didn't exactly get down on one knee. They were in the conservatory at Ealachan, sitting in green Lloyd Loom chairs. He leant over, took her hand and said, 'Christine, my darling, you will marry me, won't you? '

She looked at him in dismay. 'Nicolas, I can't possibly make up my mind while my mother is so ill.'

He was crestfallen. 'I do realise that, and maybe I shouldn't have asked you just yet. But I want you to know my feelings.'

'I do know your feelings. You've made them quite clear.'

'Have I?'

'Of course you have.'

He looked so uncertain that she leant over and kissed him. She suddenly felt very fond of him and very sorry for him.

'Well, just so long as you know. And please, take all the time you want. But I think we could be very happy. I adore you, Christine, always have done.'

'As soon as I can think about something other than my mum, we'll talk about it.'

He seemed satisfied with that. Perhaps he thought that it was a foregone conclusion. Of course she would marry him. She would be crazy to turn him down, wouldn't she? Perhaps that was what he was thinking.

To all intents and purposes, the operation had been a success. Isabel could eat again with some semblance of normality, but the doctor had told Kirsty and her grandfather that the tumour itself was inoperable. Isabel knew the truth about her illness, but never acknowledged it. She sat outside in the garden, watching things grow and blossom. She kept talking about what she was going to do in the future, 'when I'm better' but they could see that she was getting weaker by the day. She complained of aches and pains in her legs and in her shoulders. The district nurse came along and said it could be rheumatism, but Kirsty and her grandfather knew it wasn't rheumatism. Kirsty was very frightened. She had to be brave for all of them: herself, her mother, her grandfather who seemed bewildered by imminent tragedy.

Which was why Ealachan House was such a refuge. And Nicolas was so kind to her when she was there. Nothing was too good for her. He gave her flowers from the gardens and he sent baskets of fruit to tempt her mother's appetite: apricots from the greenhouse; strawberries and raspberries from the fruit cages. When he went to the mainland, he always fetched a gift of some sort: scent and jewellery but also good drawing paper and canvases, expensive brushes, packs of charcoal.

Finn carried Isabel about like a child, wherever she wanted to go, and sometimes she said, 'Thank-you Finn. You're a good lad you know.'

The first time this happened, he looked so surprised that Kirsty almost burst out laughing, but Isabel's change of heart was disturbing. He had always been a cuckoo in her nest. Kirsty would have been happier with the old abrasive Isabel.

One evening, Finn came into the kitchen and put a glass lemonade bottle down on the table.

'What's that?'

'Spring water. From the Well of the Winds. I managed to find the place again. I nearly got lost, and it was getting dark, but I found it.' He had been racking his brains for anything that might lessen the burden on Kirsty.

'Oh Finn.'

'Well, it's worth a try, isn't it? Anything's worth a try.'

'How do you think I should give it to her? Do you think I should boil it up and make tea with it?'

Finn shrugged. 'Mightn't that ...'

'Spoil it? Maybe I'll just make it up into orange squash for her. She'll never know.'

Isabel never knew. But the water didn't help. Afterwards, Kirsty and Finn wondered if they should have told Isabel what they were giving her. Perhaps that would have made all the difference. Perhaps knowing that she was drinking the water of the Well of the Winds would have helped. Or perhaps not.

Nicolas's sister Annabel and a couple of his old school friends came visiting. Annabel was tall, slender and elegant as her mother, with sleek blonde hair. She wore sunglasses perched on top of her head, even on the island, and chiffon scarves that streamed out in the wind. Nicolas took the visitors down to the hotel for a meal. He had invited Kirsty too, but she had cancelled at the last minute because her mother was having a bad day. The newcomers were in the bar afterwards, and Finn was there as well, just sitting by himself, having a quiet beer.

'Take a break!' Kirsty had said to him, forgetting that Nicolas and Annabel would be in the hotel. 'Go for a walk. Have a drink. No point in all of us taking the strain at once.'

Finn could only muster a little compassion for Isabel. She had never been kind to him but he found the change in her disturbing. He knew how he ought to feel, saw the people around him feeling love and sympathy, but he couldn't identify those feelings in himself, and that alarmed him. He was truly sorry for Kirsty. If he could have taken her pain upon himself, he would have done it without a moment's hesitation. But he found himself struggling to give her words of comfort. Instead he would work quietly and diligently, as he always had, hoping that his actions would speak louder than Nicolas's words. He was jealous of Nicolas, jealous of his easy manner, his money, his influence, jealous of all the ways in which he could be of help to Kirsty.

His mood wasn't improved when Nicola, Annabel and the London visitors started whispering and glancing over at him.

He heard one of them say, 'The natives certainly are revolting tonight!'

Even when they were trying to be quiet, they had voices that would cut through glass. And tact was never their strong suit. It didn't seem to cross their minds that Finn might be hurt by their comments. Or perhaps they didn't care.

He tried to ignore them but then he heard Annabel say, 'What in God's name does your lovely Christine see in that moron, Nick?' Finn was more upset by the way she said 'your Christine' than by the word moron. He had been called worse. Much worse.

'Oh well, I don't suppose she sees much in him at all,' Nicolas replied. 'But my Christine isn't one to ignore her old obligations when she's going up in the world.'

Afterwards, Finn didn't remember how he got there, but he

suddenly found himself squaring up to Nicolas. He'd have knocked him down if he'd had the chance. Nicolas was fit, but Finn was bigger and stronger and full of rage. He could feel it vibrating through every molecule of his body. The barman was quick off the mark though. Helped by a couple of trawlermen who were drinking at the bar he grabbed Finn and held him back. Nicolas and his friends left, but not before one of them had called him an 'illiterate Paddy bastard'.

Back at Dunshee, he told Kirsty all about it, but he didn't get the sympathy he expected. In the old days, she would always have taken his side in any dispute, especially with the Laurence family. But there had been some subtle change in her allegiance.

'You shouldn't get involved,' she said, furiously. 'I hate it when they have a go at you like that. But you shouldn't have given them the opportunity. You should just have left.'

'Oh aye,' said Finn. 'That's right. Take his side!'

'I'm not taking anybody's side. I just can't be doing with this kind of hassle. Not right now anyway.'

A few days later, when the visitors had left, Nicolas came up to the farm. 'You really ought to have a word with that tinker who works for you, Christine,' he said, casually. 'Otherwise I might be obliged to give him a good kicking one of these days.'

All the tensions of the past few months boiled up inside her.

'You and whose army?' she said. 'You and whose army, Nicolas? What did you expect him to do when you were so horrible to him? He's my good friend, but you treat him like some kind of pariah. And I wouldn't go bragging about giving anybody a good kicking if I were you! He could knock you flat with one punch.'

Nicolas was dismayed. She looked as though she wanted to punch him herself.

'I hate you!' she shouted. 'Sometimes I really hate you, Nicolas Laurence!'

He backed down and tried to dismiss it as a joke. He could see that she was genuinely upset, so he had the good grace to apologise to her, if not to Finn. But he put it all down to her fragile state of mind. He kept saying 'Sorry, sorry, Christine, I'm so sorry.' And he seemed to mean it.

Finn was sulking. If Kirsty went near him, he just shrugged her off. He wouldn't even let her sit near him. He sprawled on the lumpy kitchen sofa next to the range, reading the newspaper, slumped there with his long legs stretched out so that she had to step over them every time she walked past. Isabel and Alasdair had gone to bed and they were alone in the kitchen together. She finished the washing up without his help and tried to sit down next to him but he was having none of it. He stood up.

'Where are you going?'

'I've got stuff to do outside.'

'I don't believe you.'

He shrugged. 'Do you know, I don't give a fuck whether you believe me or not, Kirsty.'

She was very shocked. He never swore, or not when she was around anyway.

'What do you mean by that?'

'I'm fucking sick of it, if you must know. Sick of the way you treat me!'

'How do I treat you?' she asked. 'And you don't have to swear at me.'

'There you go again. Ordering me about.'

'When did I *ever* order you about?'

The frustration and rage boiled up inside him all over again.

'I think you treat me like shite!' he said, viciously. 'You use me. When you want a bit of comfort or a bit of company, you think I'll always be waiting for you with open arms. And you seem to think I'll be grateful for any crumb of affection you throw my way. Well not any more – Christine!'

He tried to go out of the kitchen but she barred his way.

'Will you move?' he said.

'Or you'll what?'

He didn't answer.

'Or you'll what? Oh don't be so bloody stupid, Finn!'

'That's right. I'm a thick Irish bastard. A moron. That's what they used to tell us we were. Thickos. Charity cases. And it seems to me that I still am. I've just exchanged one form of slavery for another.'

He took her by the shoulders and put her out of his way so hard that he bruised her arms. She could feel the marks of his fingers. She went up to bed, and wept into her pillow. She thought he might come up and apologise, but he didn't. She cried herself to sleep, very quietly so that neither her mother nor her grandfather would be able to hear her.

The next morning, however, he intercepted her in the yard. He could hardly look at her.

'I'm sorry.' He stretched out his hand and she saw that he was holding something out to her. It was a tiny piece of flint, beautifully shaped.

'An arrow head!'

He had found it up at Hill Top Town, one of his few treasured possessions. People on the island used to call these things Elf Shot, believing that they were made by the fairy folk, the *daoine sidhe*. Finn had spent half the night making a little hole in one end so that he could put it on a fine leather thong and make it into a pendant for her. He took it from her and put it carefully over her head, his long fingers brushing her hair. She felt the static raising the strands of hair, a small tremor against her scalp.

The last week of her mother's life was surprisingly quiet. The inevitability of the ending calmed them all. The very last thing Isabel said was, 'Do you want a cup of tea, Kirsty?' She slipped into a coma after that and only stirred when the pain broke through the morphine. The nurses kept her pretty much drugged so she didn't suffer acutely. She just lingered on. Kirsty could hear her breathing, rasping. That sound would stay with Kirsty for ever. She kept waiting for it to stop or change in some way.

Kirsty stayed beside her mother's bed. After a while, she found herself whispering into the pale pink shell of her mother's ear, 'You can go now mum. You can go if you want to. I'm ready for you to go.' But still Isabel lingered. Kirsty wondered if it was she herself who was keeping her mother there. Maybe Isabel knew that Kirsty couldn't bear to lose her. Maybe that was why she was reluctant to go, even though her body was worn out. Alasdair came in and out of the room, but kept starting to cry, saying it's unnatural, saying it should be him, laid there, dying.

She wouldn't let Nicolas or Malcolm into her mother's bedroom, although Malcolm came up to the house with his son, his face grave and strained. Not at the end. She didn't want either of them to see her like that, but especially not Malcolm. It seemed like an insult to her dignity. Isabel looked so sad. Not awful, just sad. Kirsty kept remembering Shakespeare's line about the dying Falstaff: 'His nose was as sharp as a pen and he babbled of green fields.' Her mother's nose had gone strange and sharp and fine, exactly like an old fashioned pen nib. It was very odd to be sitting there and thinking of Shakespeare getting his images right, while her mother lay dying.

Finn sat with her whenever he could, and the fact that he was there was enough. Sometimes an image came to her of Finn, holding her in his strong hands, holding her steady. Sometimes she imagined what it might be like if he were to let go of her altogether, let her fall. She knew that she might go tumbling down forever. She wanted to say to him, 'Don't ever let me fall, Finn. Don't leave me. Don't ever let me go.' But it seemed daft, so she never did.

He wasn't very sad about Isabel and he didn't pretend to be. Kirsty admired him for that. She had never been a mother to him. He had lost his mother and no replacement would do. He sat at the opposite side of the bed, and when Isabel died, he held Kirsty's hand, and Kirsty held Isabel's hand, and it was all right. It was like pushing somebody onwards and outwards.

The difference between life and death was amazing. Somebody could be literally 'at death's door' but when they had gone, it really was as though they had stepped through a door. Her mother was simply not there. Kirsty felt surprised as well as sad. It was surprising.

They had to delay the service for a week, since there were so many people who wanted to come from the mainland: all the Glasgow relatives, and one or two cousins from Canada as well. Kirsty wished that a few more of them had come to see Isabel while she was alive and not now, to watch a box being put into the ground.

Chapter Eighteen

IT WAS THE empty time between the death and the funeral. No man's land. A grey space of a week, a blank page in a diary. The closed coffin with her mother's body in it sat in the room where she had died, surrounded by flowers. The scent of lilies was overpowering. Nicolas had sent them up from the Ealachan gardens. Isabel had loved lilies, but Kirsty disliked them. She would have preferred her mother to be surrounded by the wild flowers of the island. Only Finn understood and she knew that other people would find it strange. He had brought her a posy for herself: late honeysuckle and heather, a bizarre combination that smelled very sweet. She had had a terrible, terrifying impulse to sketch her mother in those last few weeks, the way emotions seemed to flit across her thin face, distantly, weather seen from space, and then the ultimate tranquillity of death, the complete absence of expression, of the person she had once been, utterly and irretrievably gone. Her courage had deserted her and instead she had found herself sketching the honeysuckle and the heather, over and over again.

The room had stopped being a sickroom and was now a chapel of rest. The coffin had been placed on a wheeled metal stand with the easy chairs and polished furniture and her mother's favourite ornaments, the Doulton ladies, arranged around it. Kirsty had already cleared out most of the medicine. There was so much morphine. She reckoned she could have taken it to Edinburgh and made a fortune selling it on the streets of the capital. She wasn't quite sure what to do with it, but the district nurse had reluctantly taken it away for safe disposal when Kirsty, all out of patience, had threatened to throw it on the midden at the back of the farm.

Kirsty seldom went into the room where the coffin rested, although she showed a succession of relatives, friends and neighbours in there, to 'pay their respects' – whatever that meant. She handed in trays of tea, bottles of whisky and plates of shortbread biscuits while they sat around, talking quietly about the past, with the occasional outburst of nervous hilarity, quickly silenced. She wished they would just carry on laughing. Her mother wouldn't have minded.

Aunty Beatie, on the other hand, couldn't stop weeping. She had worked her way through several boxes of tissues and industrial quantities of tea, presumably to replace lost fluids. Kirsty used the floral wedding china that Isabel had inherited from her own mother and kept for special occasions. She supposed this must be special enough. One of the Canadian cousins, a smart and courteous elderly man, broke a cup. He put it down on the floor beside him and then, to his own mortification, trod on it, but Kirsty reassured him.

'There are another thirty five pieces,' she said. 'Not counting the milk and sugar, the teapot and the two cake plates.'

He looked at her as though she had gone mad, and indeed she did feel slightly hysterical. She had to suppress a dreadful desire to giggle at inappropriate moments.

The visitors watched the coffin. Her grandfather got down his fiddle and played a lament. He played at all the island occasions: ceilidhs and weddings and christenings, but it was a sad thing to be playing for his own daughter-in-law's wake. They wanted Kirsty to sing but she refused. 'I couldn't do it,' she said. Instead, somebody else sang a sad song, a lament, in Gaelic. Kirsty heard them and thought about Francis singing The Curragh of Kildare, all those years ago.

'And straight I will repair to the Curragh of Kildare and it's there I'll find tidings of my love.'

There were always people in the room, day and night, keeping the coffin company. She wondered what they were waiting for. The room was so empty that she wanted to tell them to stop keeping vigil over a wooden box. Wherever her mother was, she wasn't here. She wanted them all to go away and leave her in peace but it would be churlish to tell them so. She clattered the wedding china in the sink, hoping to break more of it, but it was robust and didn't even chip.

About the middle of the week, Nicolas took her to the mainland to buy some new clothes for the funeral. She got a black wool suit and some smart black shoes and a hat. The only hats she had ever worn had been bright woolly hats in Edinburgh winters, with her hair streaming out from under them.

Nicolas insisted on paying.

'I know you're a bit strapped for cash' he remarked, diffidently.

She was embarrassed by his generosity, but he brushed her objections aside. 'I'd do the same for any friend. This doesn't place any obligations on you. You know that, don't you?' And because he was such a gentleman, she believed him.

He took her for lunch in a hotel with tartan carpets and heavy brown furniture, and insisted that she drink a double Lagavulin. The pungent, peaty spirit brought tears to her eyes, but it also spread warmth through her cold bones and she was glad of it. It softened the edges of the hard knot of pain that she felt in her heart and in her head.

'A suit might come in handy, anyway,' said Nicolas. He probably had visions of her welcoming his business guests to Ealachan, wearing her funeral suit, but she knew that she would never wear it again. It would sit in the back of her wardrobe until the moths reduced it to irregular black lace. If it were left to her, she would have worn something bright. But the other mourners would have been shocked and even Kirsty didn't have the nerve to go against tradition in this way.

'Oh, Kirsty, you do look like a hippy, but such a pretty one!' her mother had said, seeing her wearing her long Indian cottons on the island, amazed and charmed by this strange, eccentric daughter. It suddenly occurred to Kirsty that her mother might have been a little envious. She had been such a pretty woman herself but ever since her husband's death, there had been a touch of austerity about her. There were old black and white photographs of Isabel when she and James were courting. Isabel had worn floral print dresses and high heeled shoes, her hair falling in soft waves. Again, Kirsty found herself wondering why. Why had her mother found no other lover? A week ago she might have asked, but now it was too late.

The week dragged on. The weather was warm and golden with

that immanent stillness peculiar to September. The apples and plums and pears were ripening in the Ealachan orchards. The hedges were all jewelled with blackberries and festooned with dewy spider's webs every morning. Up at Dunshee, the old grey horse, the last of the real working horses that would ever be housed there, cropped his field and stood looking out to sea, dreaming in the sunshine. The potato harvest was done. The day before the funeral, Finn burned the last of the leaves in heaps along the margins of the sandy fields where they grew. The acrid scent of the bonfires drifted in at her bedroom window. Only Kirsty was cold. Her hands were icy. She shivered as though it were the middle of winter and her mouth was dry. Later on, when Finn came in for his supper, the smell of smoke was still clinging to his clothes. For Kirsty, time was standing still. There was no past, no future. There was only the now of this polished September day where time hung as heavy on her cold hands as the biggest, shiniest apple, on the oldest tree.

Finn had cut his hand on barbed wire and went to rinse his fingers under the kitchen tap.

Kirsty had been making a blackberry and apple pie for the visitors. The table was white with flour, littered with apple peel and cores. There was a bowl of glossy berries waiting to join the sliced apples in the big stoneware pie dish.

'How did you do that?' she asked him. Her tongue felt thick and numb in her mouth. 'You'll get blood poisoning!'

'It's nothing much. I stumbled and reached out to the fence.'

'You should be wearing gloves if you're working with wire.'

'I wasn't working with wire. Just beside it. I didn't mean to touch it.'

'I'll get you a plaster.'

'It's all right. I'm fine.'

Nevertheless, she made him stand still while she disinfected the ragged cut and stemmed the bleeding with gauze and elastoplast. She bent over his hand to finish the dressing but then found that she couldn't let go of his fingers. She raised her eyes to meet his. The kitchen was empty for once and the house was quiet, the only sounds the whisper of voices from the other room and the simmering of a pan of soup on the hob. The build-up of steam kept pushing the lid off the pan with a knocking sound.

The feeling was so sudden and intense that it took her breath away, leaving her gasping for air. He held her gaze, then pulled her towards him and kissed her on the lips. Or she kissed him. Afterwards she couldn't say who made the first move. They kissed long and hard, their bodies pressed close. Everything about him, the clumsiness, the smoky scent of him, the taste of him, was at once familiar and yet absolutely strange. The kitchen tilted around her. Her whole world had moved on its axis and then righted itself. But everything was different. Nothing would ever be the same. Before they could kiss again, they heard the rattle of the back door opening and they sprang apart. She gave a cry of regret and rage at the space between them.

'Shsh.' Finn frowned at her. 'Later?' he asked, tentatively.

'Where? When?' She was desperate. She would die for lack of him. She would die of the ice inside her.

'Wherever you like,' he whispered.

'My room. Tonight.'

'Are you sure?'

The kitchen door opened and Kirsty's grandfather came in. He had been down to the kirk, making arrangements for the funeral service.

She turned away, busying herself with setting the table for supper.

'Yes,' she said, over her shoulder. 'I'm sure.' She turned and smiled at her grandfather. 'How did that go? Everything sorted?'

'Aye,' said the old man. He sighed and threw himself into a chair. He looked grey and exhausted. 'Aye, lass. That's everything sorted.'

She thought that they would never go away or go to bed. It was the night before the funeral and they seemed determined to extend the wake as long as possible, these relatives and friends who had seldom visited Isabel during her last illness.

'Where were you all,' she thought, 'when I was struggling to get her moved to the right hospital? Where were you in her last week, when I was sitting beside her bed, watching her fade away?'

Nicolas had phoned her earlier that day. 'Just try to get a good night's sleep.'

'I'll do my best. But we've got a lot of guests.'

'You'll have to be firm with them. Can't you get Finn to throw them out? Send them packing to their digs and tell the ones that are staying with you to get off to bed. Tomorrow will be a long, hard day.'

'I'll be fine.'

'Well just you look after yourself.'

She wished all of them would go away, but she smiled at them until her face ached and refilled their glasses, hoping to tire them out. At last her grandfather staggered up to bed, and that was her cue to stand up and yawn and shoo them all away. Beatie and her daughters were sleeping in Isabel's old bedroom, two in the bed and one on cushions on the floor. Fish Face was already ensconced on the bed, waiting resentfully for Isabel to come back. He was missing her and would miss her even more when Beatie pushed him off the bed, and one of her daughters put him outside the room, closing the door on him.

A couple of the younger cousins had brought sleeping bags and were planning to bed down in the kitchen. The two Canadians took a flashlight and headed off down the track. They were staying in one of the estate cottages. Kirsty went upstairs, washed, and got ready for bed. Her head was just starting to ache. She crept out into the hallway and stood there listening. The house had fallen very quiet. There was no movement from below. Maybe he had changed his mind. Then it struck her that Finn, coming down from his room, wouldn't be able to go through the kitchen without disturbing the sleeping relatives.

He was equal to the challenge. A little while later, leaning out of her window, she heard the lonely, sawing call of the corncrake down by the shore, and then the eerie, high pitched whoop of owls, calling to each other. She heard the gentle lifting of a latch. He had come out of the back door and in at the front. Now he was quietly climbing the stairs. She felt her heart thudding beneath her nightdress.

Before he could even tap on the door, she had opened it for him, and he was inside. He was wearing shabby jeans and a faded tee-shirt and he was barefoot. He stooped to brush the dirt from the soles of his feet and she stood there in the lamplight, watching him, watching the light glisten on his hair, like the thick pelt of some animal.

'I almost forgot about that pair sleeping in the kitchen!' he whispered.

'I wondered what you would do.'

'Thank God nobody put the bolt on the front door. I thought I might not be able to get in.'

She was trembling with a mixture of fear and excitement.

'I'm cold,' she said. 'I've been cold all week.'

She had brushed her hair and it was streaming around her shoulders in thick, bright red ripples He reached out and touched the soft mass of it.

'The house is so full of people. We mustn't make any noise.'

'I know.'

She could hear a sound from outside her room. It was Aunty Beatie, going to the bathroom, padding along the hallway in her plastic rollers, her quilted nylon housecoat and furry slippers.

'She won't come in here?' he asked.

'No. I don't think so. '

They stood, frozen, listening, trying not to laugh, while Beatie flushed the lavatory twice and then went back to bed. The house fell quiet again.

The interruption had broken the mood, made them nervous, shy of each other.

'Are we crazy?' she asked him.

'I don't know.'

'How's your hand?'

'OK. Bit sore.' The plaster was already grubby. Everything Finn did covered him in mud or dust or worse. No matter how much he scrubbed his hands, the ingrained grime never quite went away. He seemed to have had dirty hands for as long as she could remember, to have grown up with them. She thought about Nicolas's slender hands, soft, white, well manicured. Finn sat down on the bed and looked up at her. He was so tall that he made the bed look small. He folded his long arms around himself, not knowing what to do with them, shutting her out, keeping her away.

He said 'I don't know,' and she said 'I'm not sure,' simultaneously. 'You first,' he said.

'I'm not sure if we should be doing this.'

'No. Maybe not.'

He was not going to help her. He couldn't. He was so afraid of rejection. She turned to the window, crossing her own arms in unconscious imitation of his, but there was nothing to be seen outside. Her body seemed strange and unwieldy to her. Ever since her mother had become ill, it had been as though she were living only in her head. She had forgotten about her body and its demands. Now, she came into herself with a flicker of sensation.

'Oh, Finn, help me!' she said. 'I'm so cold.'

He stood up and opened his arms to her, and she rushed at him, almost butting her head against him in her eagerness to be close to him. He caught her and they were falling onto the bed, into the shelter of her bed, into the cocoon that the box bed had become, and he was kissing her clumsily, but as though he would never be able to stop, kissing her cheeks, her eyes, her throat, biting fiercely at her lips, and he was saying 'Kirsty, oh Kirsty!' At last, he braced himself above her, looking down at her, trying to breathe. He saw that she was wearing the pendant. The elf shot. The arrow head as old as *Dun Sidhe* itself.

'Wait,' she said. 'Wait a minute.'

She reached down and slid the nightdress up, crossing her arms to tug it over her head, and he helped her, and the air struck cool on her skin. He sat on the edge of the bed and pulled his tee-shirt off, tugging at his jeans in a frenzy, hurting his poor hand all over again and swearing under his breath, and it seemed comical to her. She almost found herself laughing, until at last he turned towards her and covered her sad, cold flesh with his lovely, long, warm body, and slid inside her. She gave a little cry at the acute sensation, but she was warm and wet and there was no space, no space between them at all.

'Oh,' she said. 'How strange!'

He paused for a moment, looking down at her. 'It feels …'

'Right' she said. 'It feels so … oh Finn … it feels so right …'

He moved inside her, never quite leaving her, and she pushed herself towards him. She forgot all about the last terrible year. Love was stronger than death, she thought. And life was stronger than death. Life would always have its way.

And then they ceased to think in words at all because they were moving together, moving like the incessant wind at Hill Top Town, and there was nothing but their awareness of each other. Their mouths were fused, their bodies were fused, and they thought they would die with the pleasure of it, they couldn't tell where one ended and the other began. And for the first time in a long time they were warm and whole and wholly alive.

Did they cry out together? The house gathered its silence round them, and they found themselves wondering who heard? Did anybody hear them? Perhaps not. Finn lay his finger lightly on her lips. Shook his head. Let out his breath in a long, quivering sigh. 'Oof,' he said.

'I know.'

He moved away from her, and she hated the space between them. He pulled the coverlet over them, then turned and slid his arm under her so that he could hold her close, resting his lips on her forehead. She had taken the ice out of his heart. All the images of all the stories that they had ever told each other were winding in procession through his head. It seemed as though all the words of all their tales had been aimed at this one end. Even if some of them had been sad.

Early in the morning, they slid out of bed, dressed, crept quietly down the stairs so as not to wake the others, and went into the garden, which was drenched with autumn dew, the chilly precursor of frost. The fields below the farm were bathed in mist. They could hear the short, sharp calls of oystercatchers down on the shore. Together they climbed the rocks behind Dunshee and sat among the clefts and crags of Hill Top Town. West, the sea and sky were one grey meld. To the east, the sun was rising over the mainland. They sat side by side, hand in hand, their bodies touching, but they didn't talk. Their lips were swollen with kissing but they were quiet and contented in each other's company. Time passed and they knew that they must go back and face the day of the funeral. They embraced and it crossed Kirsty's mind, in those last few moments, that nothing could part them.

'Who could possibly separate us?' she thought. 'Who in the whole wide world could ever tear us apart now?'

Chapter Nineteen

THE FUNERAL SERVICE was held in the kirk with its stained glass window of St Columba, standing up precariously in a brown cockle-shell boat. The minister said nice things about Isabel and seemed genuinely sad. Kirsty sat in the front row with her grandfather and her Aunty Beatie. The rest of the relatives were in a huddle behind them, and then came Finn, wearing an ill-fitting suit that he had borrowed for the occasion, poised in a sort of no-man's-land in the middle with the other islanders crowded at the back.

Malcolm, seated in his own family's pew, was openly moved and blew his nose into a large white handkerchief from time to time. Kirsty looked neither right not left, staring at the minister with her head held high and her face stony. She had wanted her grandfather on one side and Finn on the other, but Beatie had bustled in and the rest of the relatives had filed into the pews behind. Finn had waited until they were settled before taking his place.

Contrary to the Scottish custom at that time, the younger women went to the cemetery, where Isabel was laid to rest beside Kirsty's father, though the older ones stayed at the hotel, drinking sweet sherry and discussing the shortcomings of the service. This was a typical Scottish burial with eight cords allotted to friends and relatives who lowered the coffin into the grave. It was normally seen as man's work but Kirsty had insisted that she would take the cord at the foot while her grandfather took the one at the head of the coffin, and nobody dared to disagree. Neither did they argue with her when she called over Finn on her left and Nicolas on her right. There were some dark looks and murmurs of complaint among the assembled friends and relatives. Kirsty ignored them all. The weather was fine and mild and there were late roses blooming on the adjacent graves.

Afterwards there were sandwiches, sausage rolls and shortbread in the hotel function room with tea and coffee and a generous measure of whisky for everyone, courtesy of Malcolm. Beatie and her car-load would be going back to Glasgow in the morning with the Canadian cousins who had already exchanged their funeral suits for brightly coloured golfing sweaters and grey slacks. The friends and relatives all went back to Dunshee to drink tea and whisky and nibble at the remains of the funeral buffet. Kirsty saw that they were well provided and then slipped on a jacket and a scarf that had the scent of her mother on it and walked up to Hill Top Town. Finn was waiting for her. She sat down beside him on the damp ground. He slipped his arm around her and she leaned in to him. They sat in silence for a while but it was Kirsty who spoke first.

'I was talking to Malcolm today. About the estate and their plans for the future. It kind of worried me.'

'What plans?'

'He didn't say it in so many words. Well he wouldn't at the funeral, would he? He was genuinely fond of my mum, you know. But I think the family would like my grandad to retire. Then they could take over Dunshee, do it up and market it as – oh I don't know. A self-catering holiday development. Something commercial anyway.'

'But what about the farm?'

'None of the farms are very profitable for them. Holiday lets would be better. And I've heard him say it before. This isn't a social project. It's a business. When push comes to shove, they don't care.'

'Can they do that?' Finn looked shocked, as well he might. He had never anticipated this kind of change.

'They can do what they like. We're very reliant on their goodwill. We have no security. You know fine that we're all on short tenancies on this estate.'

'What about your grandad? They couldn't just turn him out, could they?'

'Oh they would certainly have to give him somewhere else to live. But he would have to take what he was given, wouldn't he?'

'He isn't that old. I didn't think this would be an issue. Or at least not till later.'

'He's sixty eight. He doesn't have the strength or stamina he once had.'

'But I do.'

'I know you do. And I think it would kill him to move away. He belongs at Dunshee. He's built in with the stones. Him and his father before him. He should be able to live here until the day he dies. If my dad was still around, things would be different. Grandad could retire. The Laurences wouldn't find it so easy to take over.'

'And what about me?' asked Finn, quietly. 'Do I not count?'

'You count with me and my grandad. But not with the Laurences.'

'That's for sure.'

She sighed. 'I shouldn't have mentioned this. Not tonight. There's no immediate problem. But it worried me a bit. We'll have to find some kind of solution. You and me and grandad. We'll have to find some way round this.'

'Your mother wanted you to marry Nicolas, didn't she?'

'How do you know that?'

'She told me.'

'Well, I wish she hadn't.'

'I don't know if she even knew who she was talking to by that time, Kirsty. The morphine was making her very vague by then. But she was desperate for you to marry him. She thought he would take care of you.'

'I don't need anyone to take care of me!'

Kirsty had been thinking about Finn all day, aware of him in the church, stuck in the middle, with no friends to speak of except herself and her grandfather. But then Finn was his own worst enemy. He didn't mix with the other young men of the island, or only on the most superficial level. His social skills were practically non-existent and always had been. There was something about him that made people uncomfortable.

'The best thing for you, you know, would be to leave the island and get an education for yourself. You just sort of fell into farming, didn't you? It was a way out for you.'

Her knowledge of his life was a sketchy patchwork of painful fragments that he had let slip over the years. From these, she had constructed some of his story. He had never yet assembled the whole picture for her, She thought it was because he couldn't bear to do it. Not for her. Not for himself, either.

'Maybe you could do something else. You're brilliant with boats. And you can fix anything.'

He grinned. 'Of necessity.'

'My point is, even you don't know what you're capable of. You're stranded here. Washed up. And I'm beginning to wonder if you should be staying here at all.'

'It's not such a bad place.'

'It's a wonderful place!' she said. 'We belong here. I think we both feel exactly the same about it. And that would be just fine if you could take over the farm after my grandad's dead and gone. But you have no rights, no family except us. So you're stuck and I can't bear the thought of it.'

'So what am I to do, Kirsty? You tell me that!'

'I don't know. I just think that maybe you could find yourself a better job if you were prepared to leave me behind.'

'Is that what you want me to do? Leave you behind?'

'No. No, I'm not saying that. It's just that our friendship, our love, what we have together…' Kirsty was floundering now, hunting for the right words, wishing she had never started this. 'What we've always had, it's above and beyond everything else. More important than *anything*. But we have to face the fact that Malcolm will hand over the running of the whole estate to Nick. He already has done, more or less. And Nick will never give the tenancy to you, so we'll have to do something else, won't we? We'll have to think of something else!'

'We could go to the mainland together. I suppose we could do that.'

'It's a possibility. We could even go to Edinburgh. I could finish my degree. But I'll be leaving my grandad and I know what will happen then. Nick will give him notice and move him into one of those nasty little prefabs down in the village, and he'll be so miserable he'll probably drink himself to death within the year. I've seen it happen to other people. The estate owns our lives here, and we do as we're told.'

Finn was silent for so long that she thought he had fallen asleep. She nudged him and he got to his feet, pulling her with him. 'You're exhausted,' he said 'Let's go home. We can talk about all this later.'

She followed him meekly down the hill. It was a dark and moonless night and the grass was damp around their ankles. Practical as ever, Finn had brought a flashlight. He took her hand, and concentrated on shining the torch ahead of them, illuminating the ridges and tussocks of grass. He was still very quiet.

'Are you all right, Finn?'

'Just tired. And you?'

'I'm tired too. In fact I'm beyond tired.'

Back at Dunshee, he told her that he had one or two things to do about the farm. He had forgotten to shut up the hens for the night. The fox might be on the prowl. She offered to help but he shook his head.

'No, Kirsty. You get off to your bed.'

'All right. I'm dead on my feet anyway. Will you come up later?'

'If I can. But you need your sleep. Don't try to stay awake. You just go to sleep now, Kirsty.'

She reached up and kissed him. 'Goodnight, Finn. '

He put his arms around her and pulled her close, so close that she could hardly breathe, a brief, intense embrace. 'Goodnight my Cairistiona, my darling,' he said, and went off into the darkness. She watched the thin beam of the torch wavering in front of him for a moment or two, and then went inside to bed.

One job lead to another and it was very late when Finn came in. Everyone seemed to be asleep. He saw that even Kirsty's room was in darkness now, so he went up to his loft and lay on the bed for a while. He didn't fall asleep immediately but drifted on a sea of memories, his head full of thoughts of Dublin and his mother.

They were walking down Grafton Street, past Bewleys. He could smell the powerful scents of coffee and baking. They passed Bewleys often and whenever they did, his mother said 'When our ship comes in, we'll go in there, and have a feast. Would you like that, Finn?'

Then, one day, they did go in. They had their own table and there were ladies at the other tables, many of them in fancy hats. There was coloured glass in the windows. Finn liked that very much, the pictures in the glass and the way the sunshine filtered through them and cast red, green and blue shadows on tables and faces. He gazed at them in wonder. They sat down at a table, he and his mother, and no sooner had they settled themselves into their seats than a strange man came by and raised his hat to Finn's mother. She seemed to know him. She told Finn that he was a friend and his name was Johnny. The man shook him by the hand and sat down at their table.

'Fancy meeting you here!' he said, and winked at Finn's mother and then at Finn as well, for good measure.

The man was nice. Finn remembered how kind he was. The waitress came over and he ordered a pot of tea for Finn and his mother and a cup of coffee for himself, and a plateful of buns for all of them. There were serviettes on the table and Johnny folded one up into a paper boat for Finn. 'Is this our ship, coming in?' Finn asked, and Johnny and his mother laughed. Then, Johnny showed Finn how to do it and when the boat was made, he perched it on Finn's head and said it would make a fine hat too.

Finn could still make paper boats out of bits of paper. He had made them for Kirsty when she was a little girl, and they had sailed a whole fleet of them down the burn, where once she had thrown her swimming dolls. Finn remembered his mother shaking her head at Johnny and saying 'what are you like?' and the curls bouncing around her face. The buns had cherries in them and sugar crystals on top and they were shiny and sticky, the nicest thing he had ever tasted in his life. It amazed Finn that there was as much butter as they could eat. The best butter. His mother ate even more than he did. Johnny too. They cleared the whole plate between the three of them, and he and his mother had two pots of tea.

Johnny drank another cup of strong coffee with plenty of sugar. Then he paid the bill and held up Mary's coat for her to slide her arms into.

'Thank-you, kind sir,' she said. But Johnny left before them, which seemed strange to Finn. His mother didn't mind. She swung Finn's arm as they walked, laughing and talking all the way down Grafton Street.

He couldn't remember when he had first begun to make sense of that meeting. It had been so gradual that there was no definite moment of realisation, just a slowly dawning awareness in later years that Johnny must have been a special friend to his mother. It had only happened once, the visit to Bewleys. He had seen Johnny again a few times. The man would come to the house and bring sweets with him, bars of chocolate, Fry's Chocolate Cream for his mother and Five Boys chocolate for Finn, thin and warm from the heat of his pocket.

'Better eat it up quickly, Finn!' he said. 'There's more where that came from.'

And for a while there had been more: chocolate and sweets and a red clockwork engine made of tin, with sharp edges. 'Mind your fingers, Finn,' his mother said. Finn had called it 'the train that goes itself' because you wound it up with a little key, But it had stopped, all of it, and not just the engine. As far as he could remember, it had stopped before that day when Mrs Maguire from the Legion of Mary came calling in her blue petal hat, but how long before, he didn't know. Was it before or after he had started at his first school? Time was a jigsaw puzzle but nobody had done the edges.

Finn thought about that school. It had been a small school, run by the nuns. His teacher was called Sister Rosalie, and it was clear that she liked all the children, but if she had any favourites, Finn was one of them. She would say 'come along now my little hero!'

The children were supposed to bring in dinner money and a few pennies for the black babies as well. You got a stamp to stick on a card. A girl called Assumpta burst out crying because she thought she would get a black baby all to herself when her card was full. She was distraught when she found out that she couldn't have one and Sister Rosalie tried to distract her with coloured crayons, but she wouldn't be consoled for a long time and heaved with sobs for an hour after. Finn never had any money for the black babies, and sometimes his mother forgot to give him his dinner money as well. Now, he could see that the reason why she 'forgot' so often was that she didn't have it to give, but Sister Rosalie would come to the dinner hall with them and she would always make sure Finn had something to eat, a bit of meat pie and lots of potatoes, with a big bowl of jam sponge and custard to follow.

'Can't let a growing boy starve, can we?' she said, smiling at the dinner lady. 'Fill his plate, so! There's always plenty of pudding.'

It had been a very nice school. He had been happy there, until the day when he stayed at home, the day when Mrs Maguire came to call. He should never have answered the door, never have let her in. But he thought they knew Mrs Maguire. He had seen her in church and thought that she was one of the people he was allowed to let in. She had asked him lots of questions, fierce questions, too hard for a little lad to answer, most of them. He had started to cry with the fierceness of them all. What was he doing here? And how could a child be left here because it was a scandal? He shouldn't, he couldn't, he mustn't. What was it that he mustn't do? She seemed enraged about something, her anger filling the room. He didn't understand what he had done wrong but just thinking about it made him feel guilty. He tried to clear his mind. But the harder he tried to remember, the more blurred and confused the memories became, the pieces a jumble of colours and shapes. All he knew was that he should never have let her in. He had made a mistake. It was all his fault.

It was after that that they took him away from the nice school and away from his mother. Mrs Maguire had given him a sour sweet and taken him away in a car. He had never seen his mother again. Somebody at the new school, one of the big, frightening boys, had told him that his mother would have been sent to a place where the nuns were in charge. For a while, when he was still young, he imagined that the nuns must have been like Sister Rosalie and he envied her. But later, he realised that not all nuns were like Sister Rosalie. Later still, he heard about the Magdalene Laundries, from other pupils whose mothers and sisters had been taken to such places, and wondered if that was where his mother might be, but nobody would tell him for sure. Nobody would give him any information. If you asked questions, you were beaten for it. He had soon learned to keep his head down.

A letter had come for him. Only one letter, in all the time he had been at the new school. One of the Brothers had to read it out to him because he couldn't read very well. The letter was neat and short, on flimsy blue paper. It said that his mother was in a fine place now, working hard and saying her prayers. She was very happy and he was to be a good boy and make himself useful. They took the letter away from him afterwards and said they would put it in a safe place so that he could have it later, but he had never seen it again. He didn't think that his mother could have been in a fine place at all. He wanted to go and see her, but whenever he asked about visiting her, the responses had ranged from shocked surprise to a cuff round the ear.

He made a plan. He was going to earn a lot of money and save it all up, and then he was going to take his mother out of that place and bring her home. Even the nuns wouldn't be able to say no to him when he turned up in his flash car. In some versions of the plan, he roared up on a big motorbike and his mother clambered onto the back of it and they rode away together. But how could he ever do that, when he had no idea where she was?

He must have fallen into a doze, lying fully clothed on his bed at Dunshee, overwhelmed by memories, but somewhere between sleeping and waking, between dream and reality, panic seized him. They were coming in the night. They were coming for him. Still half asleep, he sat up on the bed, his mouth dry, his heart hammering in his chest.

Listening. Listening.

The silence was absolute. But he felt as though he might be going to die. There was something he had done wrong. He had made a mistake. Something his mother had warned him about and he had got things wrong and that was why Mrs Maguire had come. It was all his fault. But he couldn't remember what it was, only that it was important. A matter of life and death. He woke properly and took deep breaths, trying to calm himself. For weeks now, everything had seemed strange and unreal, even his own face in the mirror. It was all too much. Everything was too much for him. He couldn't cope with any of it. He drank a mouthful of water from the glass beside his bed and then he stood up. He knew what he had to do. He was certain of it. Other feelings tried to struggle to the surface, nipping at him, reminding him of other allegiances, other powerful emotions, but he suppressed them all. It was what he had learned to do, ruthlessly. It was a matter of priorities. Of survival. He knew what he had to do.

Chapter Twenty

THE FOLLOWING MORNING, Kirsty slept later than usual. She had been dreaming about her mother, and had found herself weeping in the dream, but she couldn't rouse herself. When she woke, she felt exhausted, her eyes as heavy as though she really had been crying. She went downstairs to find the Glasgow cousins all packed up and ready to go. They were eating toast, and bacon and had put the kettle on for more tea.

'We thought we'd let you sleep,' said Beatie.

Alasdair came into the kitchen, bringing a gust of sharp air with him. He had been out and about on the farm.

Kirsty said, 'I think I'll do Finn a couple of eggs. Who else wants an egg?'

Alasdair sat down at the kitchen table and pulled off his boots. 'Well you'll have to wake him up first. You're not the only one to sleep in.'

'Why? Is he still in bed then?'

Alasdair shrugged. 'I think so. Any other morning, I would have thought he'd gone fishing or something. But there's no sign of him about the farm.'

Kirsty went into the lobby by the back door. She climbed up the ladder and through the hatch, but Finn's room was empty, the bed neat, its covers straightened. She came back down the ladder so quickly that she almost fell, and her grandfather had to catch hold of her to steady her.

'Careful, lass. You'll break your leg.'

'He's not there! He's not up there and he's made his bed!'

Beatie was pouring tea into china mugs. Kirsty saw, with a stab of irrational resentment, that one of them was her mother's mug. 'What on earth's the matter, Kirsty? He'll have skived off for the morning.'

'Maybe he just went out for a walk,' suggested one of the younger cousins.

'That's what I said. Skived off for the day,' said Beatie. 'Though why that should throw our Kirsty into a panic, I don't know. The sooner you marry that nice Nicolas Laurence and set yourself up at the big house the better, if you want my opinion. You need to stop gallivanting about the countryside with a good-for-nothing Irishman.'

There was, it seemed, no greater insult to be offered, but Kirsty hardly heard it. She cast one horrified look at her aunt and rushed out of the door, calling 'Finn! Finn!' at the top of her voice.

Her voice echoed about the old buildings and threw the word back at her, the name bouncing from wall to wall in a hollow cadence of sounds. She ran all the way down to the beach but the tide was out and there were no footprints except the meandering tracks of oystercatchers and dunlin. When the beach yielded no sign of him, she went the other way, climbing the slope behind the house towards Hill Top Town, slipping and slithering over heather and rocks.

She couldn't find him.

Not long before the ferry was due to leave, she arrived back at the house, breathless and upset. The cousins had already left, grumbling about her rudeness in abandoning them, and Alasdair had the engine of the farm jeep running, so she jumped in and they drove down to the terminal. All the way, she sat silent, her face white beneath her freckles, while her grandfather stood on the accelerator, not knowing what to say.

They pulled up at the terminal, and Kirsty came tumbling out. In the past year, Caledonian McBrayne had started a roll-on/roll-off ferry service that made visiting by car much less of an ordeal It was the first ferry of the morning and the cousins were all aboard, disapproving spectators, but although Alasdair called out to him, it was clear that the skipper had seen nothing of Finn.

Kirsty was helpless to control her agitation, but as the ferry moved slowly out into the bay, Alasdair managed to coax her back into the jeep.

'He'll be at home now, for sure,' he said, but although Kirsty rushed all over the house and outbuildings again, shouting his name, there was no sign of her friend.

'Where has he gone? Where can he be? We went up to Hill Top Town last night. He was so quiet on the way back down to the farm. We hadn't had a moment to ourselves all day.'

'Don't do that, my Kirsty!' Her grandfather was gazing at her with concern.

She looked down at her arms. She had been scratching at herself, compulsively, and her nails had left long red tracks on the white skin.

'I don't remember what I said to him. Maybe I upset him. I have to find him.'

'Well he can't have left the island,' said her grandfather. 'He wasn't on the ferry. He can't have disappeared into thin air, can he? We'll just go and look for the lad. I'll drive.'

They drove the length and breadth of the island, asking people if they had seen him, but nobody had. When they finally got back to Dunshee, Kirsty climbed up into Finn's loft again. That was when she realised that he had taken the old cardboard suitcase, the one he had first brought with him from Ireland, all those years ago, when he was only a summer visitor to the farm. Most of his clothes were missing as well. Sick at heart, she sat in her own bedroom, staring out of the window, willing him to come walking up the path from the shore.

Later that night, one of the island fishermen, Seamus, came up to the house. He and his crew had set out to the fishing in the early hours of the morning and Finn had been waiting for them at the harbour.

'He asked if we could put him off on the mainland, anywhere would do, he said, because he had to get away for a bit. We thought it was strange, but we didn't ask him too much. You never got much change out of Finn.'

'Was he all right? Did he look all right?'

'He looked much as he always does, Kirsty. Perhaps a bit more serious than usual, but then he's not a man who smiles very much at the best of times. We're only just in. When I went down to the pub for my pint, Sandy behind the bar asked me if I had seen Finn

O'Malley, because you had been going demented all day looking for him. I came up as quickly as I could. But we put him ashore first thing this morning. We thought he was on some errand for your grandfather.'

Seamus went away, puzzled. It was well known on the island that Kirsty and the sullen Irishman were as thick as thieves and always had been. Finn wasn't well liked. He was too taciturn, had never been one of the lads, but he was known to be a good, conscientious worker. Why would he desert the farm on the day after her mother's funeral? It made no sense at all, and would be a subject for gossip and speculation for many weeks to come.

'Perhaps he'll call,' said Alasdair.

'I don't want him to call. I want him to be here. I just want to see him!'

'Kirsty, you'll have to be patient. He knows where you are. And how much we need him here. The phone will ring in a day or so, and it'll be Finn. You'll see.'

Ever since he first started to work at Dunshee, Finn had been saving most of his pay in a Post Office account. He had the pass book in his pocket and he knew that he had enough money, if he was careful, to be able to live in cheap rented accommodation for several weeks. But he wanted to get a job as soon as possible. And he had other plans too. At first, he had thought about looking for work on one of the many mainland farms, but he rejected this plan almost as soon as it occurred to him.

Instead, he found himself heading in the direction of Glasgow. He handed the little brown case containing all his worldly possessions to the driver, to stow away in the luggage compartment, and climbed onto the bus to complete the last part of his journey. He gazed out of the grubby window, trying to put all thoughts of Kirsty out of his mind, watching as the road wound alongside mountains and sea lochs, then gradually gave place to something busier, threading through the outlying factories and the suburban clutter of the city. He had been here only a few times, years ago when he was a tattie howker and they would skirt the city on the way to the island, but he couldn't claim to know the place. Still, there was a certain comforting familiarity about it, and he supposed it must be because somewhere in his head, he remembered Dublin, the broad artery of the river running through the heart of the place.

For a few days, he took lodgings in a YMCA hostel not far from the river and walked around the city by day, eating fried food or sandwiches in small cafes and wondering how to set about finding work. The place was full of shops and offices and they were all full of people working, but he was at a loss as to how he might become one of their number. Sometimes he would see a notice advertising a job, but they were always looking for experience and he had none. Once or twice, he plucked up enough courage to make an enquiry, but it seemed that his appearance, his worn clothing and perhaps also his accent – for he was aware that he still sounded Irish – went against him in a city that had always been divided along sectarian lines.

In the evening, with the nights drawing in and the autumnal chill flooding the streets with pinkish mist from the river, he might find his way into a pub and have a couple of pints, but he was no big drinker and the ale was sour in his mouth. The other young men staying in the hostel were students, on their way back to university and college courses, as well as people coming to the city, like himself, in search of work. But they were better qualified. Better dressed. Better equipped to negotiate the hurdles. He felt very lost, and very miserable. More than once, he was on the verge of packing his bag, finding his way back to the bus station and returning to the island, but he always stopped himself. He was in the habit of this kind of self denial and it came easily to him.

He missed Kirsty constantly, with a terrible all-consuming sadness, but then he was in the habit of missing her, so it was nothing new and he could cope with it. Almost more than Kirsty, he missed the routine of the farm and Alasdair's quiet, undemanding presence. He missed working with the beasts and the sight of the sea from the hill above Dunshee, and the sound of the lonely birds flying over the farm in the evening.

On a rainy Sunday morning, he went out to buy a newspaper so that he could search through the situations vacant columns, and he found himself passing a church, a lowering brick building with a tall tower, the whole place black with the industrial grime of years. There was a patch of ground in front where thin grass struggled through the clay and dying willow herb gave forth a mass of fluffy seeds. The little precinct was bounded by a privet hedge and the sweet-sour city scent of it reminded him of his childhood. The doors were open and people were going inside, couples in their Sunday best, individual elderly women, whole families. On impulse, he followed them into the warmth, and was engulfed in familiarity: the subtle darkness, the muted organ notes, the scent of incense and lilies, the flickering candles at the side altar where Mary spread her arms wide, her blue veiled head crowned with spiky metal stars.

It was as comforting as a blanket. He realised that this was as close as he would ever come to being at home, and the thought saddened him. He slid into a pew. An old woman, wearing a furry coat and matching hat, moved her handbag along to make room for him. The coat smelled of mothballs. 'There you go, son,' she whispered. She had the yellow fringe of a lifelong smoker. He could smell the cigarette smoke off her along with the mothballs. The priest came onto the altar with his servers and the mass began, a simple, Sunday mass. In the gallery behind, a small choir sang Star of the Sea, a little raggedly to be sure.

Dark night has come down on this rough spoken world,
and the banners of darkness are boldly unfurled,
and the tempest tossed church all her eyes are on thee,
we look to thy shining, sweet star of the sea.

It had been one of his mother's favourite hymns. She had always nudged Finn, and whispered 'I like this one, don't you?' Look out for thy shining, sweet star of the sea. It made him think of being in a boat somewhere, and a dark horizon with a single bright star.

The familiar words of the mass came back into his mind and he spoke the responses with the rest of the congregation, automatically, effortlessly absorbed into the ritual. The sermon was short. The young Scottish priest seemed hesitant, as though uncertain of the value of any advice he might have to give his parishioners. This was unlike most of the sermons Finn had heard, either as a boy or at the school. There were a few announcements, an invitation to take tea and biscuits in the church hall, and then they were on to the main business, the consecration of the bread and wine.

Take and eat ye, all of this, for this is my body.

The holy wafer, the Host, was raised above them, and then the chalice with its wine. Once, in the school, a couple of the boys, more brave or perhaps just more foolhardy than the rest, had taken a good swig of the communion wine when they were briefly left alone in the sacristy and had replaced it with water. They said it was sweet and tasted of raisins but there was no kick to it at all. It had been a nine days' wonder among the boys, since none of them could imagine what might happen if the sacrilege were ever to be discovered. Hanging would be the least of it. But fortunately, the priest never found out.

Lord I am not worthy that thou shouldst enter under my roof, but only say the word and my soul shall be healed.

Finn didn't take communion. He stood up and let his neighbour squeeze past him to wait at the altar rail and again when she resumed her place, hands steepled in front of her, head bowed, mouth firmly shut. She was wearing old lady bootees to match the coat. He remembered how difficult it had been to swallow the wafer, and how the Brothers had told them that they mustn't chew it, because it was the body of Christ, but it stuck to the roof of your mouth, and what were you supposed to do? You were supposed to let it sit there till your spit moistened it and it dissolved away, and then you could swallow it.

He knelt back down and buried his face in his hands. He had seldom had occasion to visit the kirk on the island but when he did, the plainness of the place had disturbed him. 'That's what's so fine about it,' Alasdair had told him, and he couldn't disagree. There was something very reassuring about the whitewashed kirk, the only ornament the stained glass window of Saint Columba, but he couldn't dismiss his own past as easily as all that. Nor could he deny the comfort of this church and its ancient rituals, now that he was in it.

Once the final blessing was said, 'Go forth in peace', he went forth and would have headed back to the hostel, but his furry friend from the pew took his arm.

'You're new here,' she said. 'Come into the hall. Have a cup of tea. Meet Father Kevin.'

Kevin Gleason was the young priest who had seemed so reluctant to sermonise. He introduced himself, shook Finn by the hand and gestured vaguely towards the table where the ladies of the parish were serving builder's tea and weak coffee in thick white cups, with orange squash for the children. There were plates full of jammy dodgers and rich tea biscuits. Children, released from the constraints of being in church, thundered about the bare boards of the hall, chasing each other, bringing a frown to Father Kevin's brow. All the same, he seemed determinedly cheerful as he worked his way round the hall, chatting to his parishioners, drinking his tea. Finn sat alone at the end of one of the trestle tables, reluctant to leave, knowing that the hostel on a Sunday was not a pleasant place. He could only lie on his bed, read the newspaper, maybe go out for chips later.

The priest came over and sat down opposite him with a sigh and a smile. 'I'm that desperate for a cigarette. You don't have any on you, do you?'

Finn shook his head. 'I don't smoke.'

'I suppose I'll have to wait. Do me good. You're new here, aren't you?'

'I am. I'm new to the city. I didn't even know this was a Catholic church. I was passing and I thought I might as well come in.'

'Well you're very welcome. Are you over from Ireland? On holiday?'

'No.' Did he look as if he was on holiday? He very much doubted it. 'No. I've been working on a farm for several years. But one of my employers died and I thought I needed a change. I'm looking for work.'

'Any luck?'

'Not so far.'

'What can you do?'

'That's my problem. I'm a farm hand. It's not much use in the city. I'm good with machinery though. You have to be when you're living on an island. You have to be able to fix things.'

'Well, one of our St Vincent De Paul men here has a garage. I could put in a word for you, if you like.'

'That would be very kind of you.'

'Where are you staying?'

'I'm at the YMCA. I have some savings, but I do need to find some work and then maybe get a room.'

'I'll give him a ring. I know he was saying he might need to take on extra help before the winter really sets in. That's when everything breaks down. The pay won't be great though.'

'It doesn't matter. I'll take anything.'

'Come round to the presbytery tomorrow. I'll let you know.'

Which was why Finn found himself working as a trainee mechanic and general dogsbody in a cold garage in Maryhill. His boss was Hugh O'Reilly, known as Wee Shug, and so long as Finn turned up on time, kept his head down and did as he was told, he was treated well enough. The pay may have been low, but it was more than he was used to and the hours were regular. He rented himself a mildewy room in a sandstone tenement for what seemed an exorbitant rent, and he went to mass every Sunday out of a sense of gratitude to Father Kevin, more than from any real resurgence of the faith he had once known when he was very young and it had been possible to believe in almost anything.

He dimly remembered how that had felt. Now, he believed in nothing. He parroted the prayers and the responses and listened to the sermons, but most of it was automatic. The words just came into his head. He was comfortable in the church, but he didn't examine those feelings. He never went to confession and he never went to communion. But each Sunday after church, he went into the hall for tea and biscuits, and each week, Kevin would make a point of spending a few minutes at his table, asking how the job was going, was his room all right, how was he settling in? The concern seemed genuine and not just part of his duty as a parish priest. It was perhaps the closest Finn had ever come, since Francis, to making a male friend of his own age. And what a strange and unlikely choice it seemed to be.

Chapter Twenty One

In her waking moments, Kirsty felt not just sad, but angry. Surely Finn must have known what this would do to her? Why had he made love to her and then left her? Did he care about her at all? Her dreams were troubled excursions through the corridors of an unknown house, where ceilings were too low, stairs twisted and turned beneath her dragging feet and doors came off their hinges as soon as she tried to close them. It felt as though the very foundations of her world had shifted. Her mother had been so ill for so many months that she had begun to come to terms with that loss before Isabel died. In some ways, the pain of losing Finn was sharper and more unbearable. He had always been there. She had always counted on him.

Nicolas sent flowers and chocolates and bottles of wine, none of which were wanted. Kirsty refused to see him at first, but eventually she relented and let him in. They would sit and play gin rummy or board games like Cluedo and even Snakes and Ladders, Kirsty, Nicolas and Alasdair together. For Kirsty, it was a little like recovering after a long illness, although there had been no symptoms other than misery and fatigue. She felt as though the real Kirsty was standing outside herself, watching this other Kirsty, this stranger who was walking and talking and doing what had to be done to survive. Finn hadn't phoned or written. He had never so much as sent a postcard. At last, she was forced to admit that he was not coming back. She would have to adjust and make the best of it.

She didn't think about her work for a long time. Even the effort of wielding a pencil seemed too great. Nicolas went to the mainland and, as he had done while her mother was ill, bought the best that he could find: not just watercolours but oils and acrylics, and pastels.

Kirsty watched him unload a great mass of art supplies from the back of the car.

'What on earth possessed you?' she asked. 'You seem to have bought the whole shop. I don't need half of this.'

'I thought it might do you good. Give you something to think about.'

'Well, it'll do that sure enough.'

'I know winter's on the way, but I could take you out and about and you could draw.'

'I rather like winter. I like to see the bare bones of things. You can see the landscape the way it really is. The rocks beneath. And the trees, all naked and strong.'

'Then wrap up warm, my darling, and I'll take you out.'

Nicolas drove Kirsty up to the north end of the island, where she spent the short afternoons drawing the stunted rowans that grew there, a dozen studies of their bizarre shapes. She became obsessed with a ruin that stood alone, a gable end and two side walls of a big stone house. It was on the old maps, the ones that showed Dunshee as well, but nothing now remained except these three naked walls and a few anonymous lumps and bumps beneath the turf. Nicolas waited and watched as she sketched, reading a paperback, making sure that she was warm enough, feeding her with salmon sandwiches and fruit cake. He could make no sense of the drawings.

'Can't you see how it falls?' she asked. 'Everything falls in the end!'

Anxious about her, he brought her back and stayed on at Dunshee for supper. Alasdair took himself off to bed early, but Nicolas lingered in the kitchen, helping Kirsty to tidy away the dishes and set the table for morning. She gave him a glass of whisky but refused one for herself.

'The smell of it turns my stomach.'

'But you're feeling a bit better?'

'I'm better, yes.'

'You've had a terrible time.'

'It hasn't been a picnic.'

'But that … that bastard needn't have added to your troubles. I didn't like him much but I can't bear to see you hurt. I could have killed him when I saw you so upset.'

'Don't talk about it, Nick. I don't want to talk about it. I'd rather just forget all about him.'

'Well, I'm glad to hear it. All that fuss about a bloody tinker.'

She sat down at the table and gazed at him, blinking. It was a nervous tic, one she seemed to have acquired since her mother's death.

'Shut up, Nick. I don't want to hear this.'

'I don't know why you're still defending him.'

'I haven't been defending him. But I will now if you like. Maybe he thought it was all for the best. Maybe he thought he was doing the right thing.'

'Then he should have done it years ago. Gone away and got on with his own life. He never really belonged here, Christine. But all the same, he could have waited for a better time.'

'Would there ever have been a right time?'

'I've always thought there was something strange about him, you know. He couldn't interact with people at all. No social skills. I don't know why you're so loyal to him. You had nothing in common. And now you know what he's really like.'

'Yes, now I know what he's really like.'

' And you're much better off without him. Aren't you?'

'Much better.'

'It's all for the best, you know.'

She gazed beyond him, staring at the kitchen window as though half expecting to see a familiar face there.

'So, have you given any thought to my proposal?' Nicolas seemed faintly embarrassed by the word. 'You'll never find a more loving husband than me. I really do mean that. I'll look after you. Nobody could ever love you more than I do.'

'You're right.'

'So what do you think? Do you think we might make a go of it?'

'Maybe. Maybe we could. Yes.'

'You don't sound very positive.'

'What more do you want? I've said yes, haven't I? What more can you ask?'

Kirsty Galbreath's engagement to Nicolas Laurence, only a few weeks after her mother's death, was a nine days' wonder on the island, and she knew that some people, her grandfather included, were surprised and not altogether pleased by the speed and suddenness of it.

'Are you absolutely sure?' he kept asking her in the run-up to the wedding. 'It seems so sudden and so soon. I knew you were fond of him, but I could never see you *married* to the man, Kirsty.'

'Why not? Do you think he's too good for us? Too posh?'

'Not at all, and well you know it, lass. But I always thought ...' he stopped, and she saw that his face was flushed. 'Well, I'm not at all sure what I thought. But I'll say this and then I'll keep quiet. I do not think you would have agreed to this wedding if Finn were still on the island. There now. It's said and you can make of it what you wish.'

'But he isn't here, is he?'

'Och, lass, lass, he may come back.'

She shook her head. 'No. He's gone. He's not coming back. You know it as well as I do. That's the way he is. So why not marry Nicolas? Why on earth not?'

'There are other things you can do. You're not reliant on any man, Kirsty, you of all people! I thought you wanted to finish your course. Maybe go to Italy. You could do that now.'

'I have no money. And besides, who would look after you?'

'I can look after myself. My only worry was the farm and Nicolas has seen to that.'

Without Finn to help him, Alasdair had been struggling with the farm. The week after Kirsty had agreed to the engagement, Nicolas had given him full-time paid help, and it had made all the difference, though Alasdair kept complaining about the new lad and saying that he was not a patch on Finn. But would Nick have been so generous if she had not agreed to marry him?

'I'm painting here. I don't need to go to Italy.'

It was true. She was painting anyway, compulsively and to the point of exhaustion. It was the only way she could get through each day, creating images on canvas, on paper. Making lines around the light, while Nicolas wore her down with his loving concern.

Was she somehow paying Finn back for his desertion? And what would it matter, since he would never know about it? Why was she so sure that he wouldn't be coming back? She didn't know the answer to any of these questions, but she felt certain about all of them.

Nicolas's family wanted them to wait until spring so that they could bring a few hundred guests over from the mainland, take over the whole hotel and most of Ealachan and have a major celebration, with Kirsty wearing a dress like a snowball and all the men in kilts and all the flowers in Christendom and a celebration meal with a towering wedding cake for Nicolas to slice through with a sword. She knew that Nicolas would have quite liked this as well.

'I want to show you off to everybody,' he laughed, and she said, 'like a prize cow, you mean,' and he said 'no, not at all'. He was determined not to quarrel with her. He indulged her in all possible ways, so how could she not respond to him? But she drew the line at a big wedding. She felt sick at the thought of it. So she said, 'You can either marry me now, very quietly, with no guests other than the family, or not at all.'

He agreed, of course, as she had known he would.

On the weekend of the wedding, the weather was foul, the seas a heaving morass with spume blowing off the waves and gannets plummeting into them. Nobody would have been able to get to the island anyway. The ferry stopped running after one abortive attempt to dock at the mainland side. Nicolas's parents and Annabel were already there, having arrived early to 'help out' and bringing a handful of relatives with them. Annabel had made a point of being friendly. On the morning of the wedding, she came up to Dunshee and helped Kirsty into a lavender cotton Laura Ashley dress with a close fitting bodice and long, full skirt. Then she brushed her hair into a rippling mass of red waves and threaded lilac silk flowers through the length of it.

'You must really be missing your mother,' said Annabel, with unexpected sensitivity. 'You must have wanted her to be doing your hair today. I don't suppose you want me at all.'

Kirsty's eyes filled with tears.

Annabel dabbed at her face with a tissue. 'Don't do that darling. Your make-up will run.'

'It was very kind of you to come,' said Kirsty, and she meant it.

She looked at her face in the mirror. 'I look like a ghost,' she said and fumbled for the blusher.

'Good idea' said Annabel. 'Here. Let me do it for you. You are a bit pale. Only to be expected I suppose.'

Maybe I am a ghost, she thought, as Annabel brushed colour into her cheeks. Maybe I died and I don't know it. Maybe I'm a ghost at my own wedding.

Just before she left, just before the car arrived to take them down to the kirk, Annabel kissed Kirsty on the cheek.

'Thank-you for making my brother so happy.'

'I haven't done anything yet,' said Kirsty. 'I mean, tell me that in five years' time.'

'But this is what he's wanted for ages you know. He's always been in love with you. I know we haven't always seen eye to eye.'

'We were just children.'

'Let's start afresh.'

'All right.' Kirsty hugged her, thinking, as she did, how like her brother Annabel was now, fair and patrician with sharp blue eyes. 'Yes' she said. 'Let's be friends.'

She came into the church on her grandfather's arm and saw Nicolas peering anxiously down the aisle. Perhaps he had been expecting her to follow Finn's example and run away. He was wearing a kilt and he looked unexpectedly vulnerable and very handsome. Annabel and her mother wore smart suits and big hats. From somewhere, probably at great expense, the Laurences had managed to procure lilies, and the scent of them was so strong and sweet that it made her head ache. She wished they hadn't. It reminded her of the funeral. Outside, the weather was still wild. The wind went rumbling round the kirk and rattled St Columba's boat and his halo, drowning out the couple's voices, so that the congregation could hardly hear their vows. Kirsty became tongue tied, and said 'I do' in a whisper.

They had a meal in the hotel dining room afterwards, and Nicolas insisted on everyone drinking pink champagne. Kirsty wasn't very hungry, though she drank rather a lot, but the more she drank, the paler and more queasy she looked. Annabel and her mother had organised a wedding cake. It was heart shaped and heaped with delicate sugar roses and Kirsty couldn't help but be touched by it. Annabel seemed very determined to make Kirsty like her.

Afterwards they went back to Ealachan. And that was the strangest thing of all: not going back to Dunshee, to her own bed in the wall. Her stomach turned over when she thought about it in the car that was taking them to the house. Ealachan was familiar enough now, but she had only ever been there as a visitor. Her heart was pounding. It reminded her of that first day when she had had to go to the mainland to school, moving into the hostel with a bunch of strangers.

'I feel like the second wife in Rebecca.'

'But there's no first wife to haunt you, darling. And certainly no Mrs Danvers!'

Nicolas had come and picked up her suitcases and boxes the day before. When she got to Ealachan, after the wedding, she found that somebody had unpacked them and everything had been put away in a vast oak wardrobe and chest of drawers. Mrs Danvers after all, she thought. They were in a big bedroom, bigger than any room she had ever slept in before. It was a room she had never been in, because it was the one where Nicolas's mother used to sleep, with his father in the next room, with a connecting door between. For one wild moment, she thought that Nicolas intended to do the same thing, but then she saw his striped pyjamas, neatly folded on one side of the bed.

'I think it's one of the nicest bedrooms in the house, but if you don't like it, you can pick another,' he said, anxiously. 'We're not exactly short of rooms.'

There was a four-poster bed with a deep mattress and a hand-made patchwork quilt. There was intricately carved furniture, and it had its own bathroom behind a polished wooden door in one corner of the room. The big white bath crouched there, a heraldic beast on ball and claw feet and there was a blue flowered loo that Nicolas said was very old and valuable. Kirsty hardly dared to pee in it, never mind anything else. She sat down on the bed, completely exhausted.

'Oh God,' she thought. 'He'll want to make love to me. What will I do?' and then it occurred to her that this was not what a bride normally felt on her wedding night and she was ashamed of herself.

They had kissed and touched, but that was all. She had been so fragile after her mother's death that Nicolas was afraid to go any further. 'No hurry' he kept saying. 'Take your time.'

That first night, he held her close, soothed her and let her sleep. And in the morning, he was so kind, so tentative, so undemanding, that she couldn't help but love him in return. She lay in his arms, flooded with pleasure, grateful for his gentleness and his generosity.

It was the house that disturbed her. She was only familiar with the downstairs rooms, so for the first few days she kept getting lost on her way from the bedroom to the drawing room or library or wherever else she wanted to go. People found her wandering about, opening doors, looking for Nicolas. Or even a way out. Once she found herself climbing up a spiral stair that lead to the clock tower in the centre of the house. That wasn't where she wanted to be at all. It smelled musty and sour, as though nobody ever went there, and she was terrified. She relinquished Rebecca and fancied herself as poor, mad Mrs Rochester, trailing about, disorientated to the point of insanity. They had sympathised with the first Mrs Rochester, Finn and herself. Well, as usual, she had told Finn what to think. They had decided that Jane was no better than she should be; one of those small, steely women who always had a knack of getting their own way.

Nick's parents had already gone back to London, taking Annabel with them. Nick had decided to postpone their honeymoon until the spring.

'There are so many wonderful places I want to show you, but I think you need time to settle down here first!' She realised that he was right. She didn't want to go anywhere just yet.

The enormous, formal drawing room made Kirsty uncomfortable, so Nick commandeered a parlour, tucked away at one side of the house, with an old sofa, plump cushions, threadbare rugs, a television, and an open fire. For the first few weeks she spent a lot of her time there, but she still felt like a visitor in her own home.

There were two black retrievers called Mutt and Jeff, that slept so close to the fire that Nicolas had to nudge them out of the way with his foot.

'Do you smell burning dog?' she said. It became a joke between them. But there wasn't a cat in the house, which surprised Kirsty. She wondered that the whole place wasn't overrun with mice. She tried to bring Fish Face, but he wouldn't stay. He turned his back on her and wailed horribly until she opened the back door. Then he just walked all the way back to Dunshee. It took him the best part of the day and he turned up at the farmhouse that night looking scruffy and indignant, but none the worse for his expedition.

'You could try locking him in or buttering his paws,' said her grandfather.

'Buttering his paws?'

'He would lick it off and get used to the scent of his new home.'

'Maybe they should do that to me as well.'

She decided that such subterfuge wouldn't be fair, so she left the cat at Dunshee. She would just have to go up and brush him from time to time, otherwise his fur would be all knots and she couldn't rely on Alasdair to do it. Nicolas kept promising to get her a kitten but he always forgot. Perhaps he thought that Mutt and Jeff wouldn't take kindly to an alien cat.

Nicolas had installed her painting things in one of the many spare bedrooms. At first, her work came slowly, but as the winter progressed, a slow transformation began to occur. She had discovered one reason, at least, for her sense of disorientation: she was pregnant. And just at first, the realisation of her condition threw her into an utter panic. Nicolas was worried by her fragility but delighted by the news and his joy was contagious. She put all doubts out of her mind with an ease that surprised her, but perhaps the hormones flooding her body were to blame. Happiness crept up on her as her body changed and adapted to its new circumstances. In fact, she seemed to grow stronger and more creative as the pregnancy advanced, working joyfully, but in quite a different style from the way she had worked before: painting impressionistic studies of the island and the gardens that were memories of summer and full of light. She felt more contented than she would have believed possible, although she could not view the birth with equanimity. The house enfolded her too, sheltering her from all harm, though there were parts of it, attics and outhouses, that she hadn't seen yet.

'There are probably rooms that I haven't seen yet either,' said Nicolas. 'And I've lived here on and off for my whole life!'

She knew that he was saying it to make her feel at home. Buttering her paws. But it was kind of him.

She went back to Dunshee from time to time, to see her grand-father and to brush the cat. She still called it 'home' in her own mind. She could walk over the fields and be there in less than an hour. The first time she went back, the weather was cold and sunny, and when she got to the top of the track, she half expected Finn to rise up in front of her, the way he used to. There was nowhere on the whole island that didn't have memories of Finn, nowhere except Ealachan.

Finn had never been there. The closest he had been was the back door, with the occasional delivery of something from Dunshee. They would never have thought of inviting him in. But everywhere else, every stone, every pathway, every stretch of turf or sand and even the seas around the island; all of them seemed to have some past association. The heart of her ached with the loss of him, and there was nobody she could tell, certainly not Nicolas, and not even her grandfather. Even when she went to the cemetery she was not free of the memories. Roughly once a week, she would take flowers to Isabel's neat grave in the new cemetery, but there was an older grave-yard and ruined kirk nearby, with many ancient slabs and enclosures choked with weeds. She couldn't resist scrambling down into the old graveyard. She closed her eyes, remembering a time when she and Finn had gone there at twilight.

It was winter, they had been at a loose end, and he had dared Kirsty to run three times around one of the grave slabs and summon forth the dead. She had to go counterclockwise. God knows where he had got the idea from: perhaps from some tale told by the tattie howkers. The tomb belonged to a past chieftain of the island. Finn thought he was so much older and braver than she, but she wasn't going to be beaten. She had called his bluff.

When she closed her eyes, she could picture herself running round and round, with the brambles tearing at her ankles, and then jumping up on top of the slab and calling out, 'Come forth, Macdonald!' into the gathering darkness. At that moment, a white hare had erupted from the undergrowth right at their feet and scuttered away. She smiled at the memory. Finn was as white as the hare in the gloom, and Kirsty wasn't much better. He said, 'Jesus, Mary and Joseph!' Then they started laughing and couldn't stop. She remembered them holding onto each other, laughing as they stumbled about among the gravestones until they were weak with it, and then walking home, still spooked, still laughing.

She thought that if she could just reach out her hand, she would be able to touch him. It was so cold and she could almost feel his warm breath on her cheek. She wanted him to say 'Kirsty,' wanted to hear him say her name one more time. But when she opened her eyes there was nothing to be seen except the brambles effacing the old stones. There was some fruit on them still, but the frosts had nipped the berries and they were shrivelled and mean. The folk here said that they belonged to the devil now, the brambles that were left behind. She cradled her belly, only just beginning to swell, the smallest of bumps, rubbing her two hands gently up and down.

Is he dead, she wondered? No. He couldn't be. Not Finn. She would know if he were dead. She would feel it, and she felt nothing. Which was daft when she remembered how lucky she was. Queen of all she surveyed. That's what Nicolas told her. And after all, it was true. Wasn't it?

Chapter Twenty Two

ONE WINTER'S NIGHT, Finn and Kevin Gleason were sitting over a quiet beer in a corner pub, not far from the church. He and the young priest had taken to coming here occasionally. The pub was Irish. There were pictures of Celtic players on the walls, as well as banners and scarves. The music was defiantly Republican.

What's the news? What's the news? O my bold Shelmalier,
with your long barrelled gun of the sea?
Say, what wind from the sun blows his messenger here,
with a hymn of the dawn for the free.
Goodly news, goodly news do I bring, youth of Forth,
goodly news do I bring, Bargy man!
For the boys march today from the south to the north,
lead by Kelly, the boy from Killane.

'Your man Luke has a great voice on him,' said Kevin, savouring his Guinness and his cigarette, drawing in smoke like a drowning man.

'Who is it singing?'

'Do you not know the Dubliners when you hear them?'

'Not really.' He had only listened to Kirsty's records and, occasionally, the old wireless at Dunshee. At the school, they had heard nothing but hymns.

'But I don't think he can have been all of that, do you?'

'All of what?'

'Kelly the boy from Killane. He fought in the Irish Rebellion in – oh, I don't know for sure – late 1700s? Seven feet is his height with some inches to spare. Nah. I don't buy that!'

Finn laughed. 'I never knew it was like this over here.'

'You mean the whole Republican bit? The sectarianism? The divisions?'

'I was told about it. But I didn't know. I never experienced it.'

'What about where you worked?'

'There was a bit of it. They didn't much like the tattie howkers, that's for sure. Well, not the Irish, anyway. Or only for the work they could get out of us. Except for my boss. He was a good man.' And Kirsty, he thought. And my darling Kirsty.

'It's bad enough here,' said Kevin. 'But it's the same all over the central belt. They ask you what school you went to. That was the way it was when I was growing up. My parents are both Irish. And as soon as you tell them, they know. Saint this or saint that. Holy Family. Corpus Christi. Dead giveaway. You can see it, even if they don't say it. None of that changes. We've had to put bars on the church windows. You'll get the odd brick hurled through. Or graffiti. And in summer, the parades will stop outside and they'll be banging that drum, fit to burst. Papes. Left footers, they call us.'

'Why left footers?'

'Because we genuflect. Go down on one knee! Did you not know that, Finn?'

'I never did.'

Did you have none of that when you were working at the tatties?'

'Sometimes. But it was a small place. And I kept my head down.'

'Much as you do here.'

'That's right.'

Throughout that first winter in Glasgow, Finn had begun to confide in Kevin, telling him a little about his past in the industrial school, although not much about Dunshee or the island. He found the quiet diffidence of the young priest reassuring. Kevin Gleason would never ask questions or only in the most roundabout way. Instead, he told Finn about his initial uncertainties as to whether he really had a vocation, his gradual sense of assurance. These confidences seemed to invite some kind of rejoinder. Finn found himself speaking about his time at the school, although not in any great detail, because it seemed tactless to broach these things with a priest of all people. But there was no need to go into detail, because Father Gleason seemed to know things already, understanding them more clearly than Finn himself.

On the advice of the priest, he had enrolled for evening classes in Maths and English. His teachers were pleased with him, and he had begun to realise that Alasdair and Kirsty might have been right all along. He was capable of learning, and probably more intelligent than most. Besides, he was single minded. His only real friend was Kevin Gleason, and even then there was nothing effusive or intimate about the relationship

'You know …' Kevin hesitated. 'You know you mentioned your mother? And how you were wondering if you might be able to find her?'

Finn coloured up. Incautiously, he had spoken about Mary one night. He had had one pint too many and had regretted it afterwards.

'I quite understand if you don't want to talk about this.

'No. No, I do. It's just difficult. When I was at the school there, back in Ireland, the other boys said she might be in a Magdalene Laundry. I didn't even know such places existed. Not then.'

'And did you never hear from her?'

'Not a thing. In all these years.'

'Well, it happened. Women were sent to these places. It wasn't so very uncommon you know. And they are still on the go. Although there are fewer and fewer of them. But I think some of the poor souls are so used to them that it would be a cruelty to turn them out now. Women were committed to them for the most spurious of reasons. I've heard tell of poor lassies who were assaulted themselves maybe and were carted off for being a temptation.'

'An occasion of sin?' Finn thought about Francis. He had been an occasion of sin as well.

'Yes, that's right. One of the priests I studied with, it happened to his own sister. He got her out eventually, but it's a shame to the church, so it is. '

'It's all a shame,' said Finn. 'What happened to me and the other boys, that was a crying shame as well.'

Kevin didn't know how to respond. Finn hadn't told him very much, but the things he had let slip over the past few months were enough to make a grown man weep. He had wept about them in the privacy of his room, wept for the cruelty and the betrayal. And he had prayed about these things too. So far, there seemed to be few answers. He still found himself wondering if anyone was actually listening. But you had to soldier on through the doubts. It was the only way to survive. Especially when you had invested so much in your beliefs. And just occasionally, he thought that maybe it wasn't the fixed beliefs that mattered, but the stories behind them. Those were important. The kind of stories that might show a man how a life ought to be lived.

'How about I make some enquiries for you? Try to find out where your mother might be?'

'Could you do that?'

'I could try. I might have more success than you will. Give me her details as far as you have them. Her maiden name, her place of birth, all that. I can't promise anything. And what I find out may not be what you want to hear.'

'It would be good to know something.'

'It might help. But you never know, Finn. She could have come out by now. She might have remarried.'

'She would have looked for me, surely.'

'Maybe. But people don't always do what we expect them to do.'

'No, they don't.'

'That's what I mean about finding out something you don't want to hear. How old were you when you finally moved over to Scotland? Not just to the tatties.'

'I was sixteen. Almost seventeen.'

'I don't suppose many people knew where you were.'

'That's true enough. The school didn't want to give out any information.'

'And there could be other reasons. Maybe she was told that you were well settled.'

'But even if you do find her. If you find her for me, how can I ever go back?'

'You mean to Ireland? Do you not want to go back? That would be understandable.'

'I'm afraid to go back.'

'It would be nerve racking, right enough.'

'No. You don't understand. I'd be afraid they might take me back.'

'Take you? Where?'

Finn shifted in his seat. 'They might send the police after me. They sent a priest after me before, when I was sixteen. They sent a priest to fetch me from the farm, and if it hadn't been for my boss, if it hadn't been for Alasdair ...' He stopped, remembering Kirsty, her anxious face framed by fat red plaits. Kirsty hugging him while he couldn't stop trembling. For a brief moment his whole body yearned for her, for the grown-up Kirsty she had become.

'Oh, Finn, don't talk daft! You're a grown man, with a job and a home here. Nobody will be after you. In fact, you should bloody well be after them!' Kevin looked so angry that, for a moment, Finn was taken aback, but then he was reminded of Alasdair and realised that the anger wasn't directed at himself.

'Well, I'd be grateful if you could find out anything about her. If you do, I'll maybe go over and see her. After all, that was one of the reasons why I came away.'

'From your island?'

'So many unfinished things. I couldn't settle. I had to get away. Had to try to remember.'

'Remember what?'

Finn started to laugh. 'If I could remember that, I wouldn't need to find out, would I? It's hard enough to remember ordinary things from back then when I was a child. But I always had this feeling that there was something important. Something I did or didn't do. I don't know what it was. But I blame myself. I think it might help if I knew what had happened to my mother.'

'You were a wee boy. How could you be to blame for anything?'

'I only know the way I feel. And I feel guilty as sin.'

'Oh!' Kevin raised his glass briefly. 'Well, there you go. It's pretty normal, isn't it? Cradle Catholics. That's what we were born for. Guilt. Absorbed it with our mother's milk.'

When Kevin Gleason finally brought news of Finn's mother, it seemed as much of a surprise to the priest as it was to Finn himself. Finn had just come in from work and he rushed around, pulling the bed straight, clearing away his dirty breakfast things.

'Finn, Finn, it's all right. You don't need to clear up for me. You should see my place in the morning. If I didn't have Mrs Mackay coming in to sort it all out I'd never find the time.'

'But I like to keep everything straight.'

'I can see you do.'

'Sit yourself down.' Finn whisked a newspaper off a threadbare armchair with lurid green upholstery.

'Thanks, Finn. I'd have said let's go out, but I think this needs to be said in private.'

Finn perched on the bed. 'She's dead, isn't she?'

'No, no. She isn't dead.'

'No?'

'Certainly not.'

'I just had a feeling …'

'She's not dead, Finn. But the lads in your school were right. She was admitted to one of the Magdalene Laundries not far from Dublin. I'm assuming there was plenty of laundry work in the city so the place must have done rather well. You were sent to the school and she was sent to work in the laundry.'

Kevin glanced around uncomfortably. He had known that this would be a difficult conversation. He liked Finn, liked his honesty and his lack of guile. And he pitied him. The young man had been cruelly treated, mostly by those who claimed to know better, who should have known better. He needed a friend. But that didn't make dealing with him any easier. There was an electric kettle on a plastic tray, with a single mug and a packet of Tetley's teabags.

'Can I make you a cup of tea or something?'

Finn shook his head. 'There's whisky. In the cupboard there. Have one yourself.'

Kevin got up, found the half bottle with two thick tumblers, poured out a measure for Finn and one for himself. 'Here. Take a good swig.'

'Is she still there? In that laundry? How can I get her out? Will they let me go and get her do you think?'

'She isn't there. Not any more.'

'They let her out? When did they let her out? Where is she? Can I see her?'

'Finn. It's complicated. She's not dead. And yes, I think you can see her. I can arrange it. If she'll agree to see you. Which I think she will. But it will have to be done carefully. And you won't need to go back to Ireland.'

'So where is she?'

'She's in England. You'll need a long weekend maybe. A day or two off work would do it. If I can arrange a meeting, I'll ask Hugh to give you the time off. It'll be no problem. Drink your whisky and I'll tell you all about it.'

Chapter Twenty Three

KIRSTY'S PREGNANCY WAS smooth and uneventful. She even escaped with only minor queasiness instead of proper morning sickness. All her tests were clear and there was, so she was constantly assured, nothing to worry about. The baby was very active, especially at night. When she and Nicolas lay in bed, he was enchanted to feel the energetic kicks and punches against his back. 'Do you think it's a boy?' he whispered. 'It feels like a big strong rugby player to me!'

The labour was another matter. Nicolas made sure that she was taken to a mainland hospital in good time which was just as well, since the child arrived earlier than predicted. If it had been up to Kirsty, she would have preferred to stay on the island with the local midwife in attendance, but Nicolas was so solicitous and so insistent that there was no arguing with him, and the doctor agreed with him.

Kirsty had never known pain like it. Why did nobody warn me about this, she thought. Why did nobody tell me? Nevertheless, the memory of the pain soon slid away from her in her preoccupation with the baby. She remembered the sharpness of it, but time itself had contracted and instead of hours, it felt like minutes. She understood why nobody told you about the pain. It was because nobody could remember it as it truly was. Perhaps this was a biological imperative, something that happened so that you would be able do it again.

The child – a girl, and not Nicolas's rugby playing boy – was big for a first baby, big for an early baby. Kirsty didn't like to dwell on that fact. It was just as well that she was a long, strong girl, since it took forceps to drag her into the world and she spent her first night in a Special Care Unit with the other premature children. She weighed all of nine pounds, and looked like a cuckoo in a nest, with her face all bruised from the forceps and a crest of black hair peeping out from the top of the blanket.

In the middle of the night, they wheeled Kirsty down to the unit to feed her. She had been insistent about breast feeding, although the nurses came and asked her if they could give the baby a bottle 'just to start her off'. Nicolas might have agreed but Kirsty was wide awake by this time, exhausted and in pain but determined.

'No. I have to feed her myself,' she said. 'If I don't start now, I might not be able to do it. And I don't want her getting used to a bottle before she gets used to me.'

'You don't argue with my wife when she's in this mood,' said Nicolas with a certain amount of pride. 'She is a redhead, you know!' So they trundled her down in the lift, in a wheelchair, with a drip still attached to her arm. In the quietness of the Special Care Unit they put the baby to her breast. After a few false starts, the child turned towards her mother, nuzzled close, latched on.

Kirsty looked down at the dark head against the white of her skin, at the little screwed up face, suckling and suckling as though in pain. She smoothed her hand over the dark hair and felt its softness and strangeness against her palm. 'What have I done?' she thought. 'Oh dear God, what have I done to you, Finn?' She had a sudden terrible fear for the future compounded with an extreme sense of love for her daughter.

They called the child India, Nicolas's choice of name, although Kirsty didn't object. She liked its air of mystery. And it went well with the dark, exotic beauty of the little girl.

'I wonder where we got her from?' said Nicolas, happily.

'I wonder.'

'But your mother was quite dark, wasn't she?' Nicolas peered into the child's face, trying to spot resemblances.

'She was, yes. And this wee one's not going to be a redhead, that's for sure!'

'No. Well, I love your red hair, Christine, but I suppose it's one less thing to worry about. At least she won't get her leg pulled when she goes to school.'

'And nobody will think that she's unlucky to have on a boat! Or unlucky to meet on the way *to* a boat.'

Nicolas was puzzled. 'Is it? Unlucky to meet a redhead on the way to a boat?'

'I told you that story ages ago.'

'No. You've never told me.'

'I must have told you. It was old Ian McNeill. He just thought that whenever he met me on the road he had no luck at his fishing.'

It was Finn she had told. Not Nicolas. Finn, of course.

'Why would he do that?'

'It was nothing. My grandad sorted it out.'

The baby had a rosebud mouth, sallow skin and a corona of dark hair that could never be persuaded to lie flat, even weeks after she was born. But then, her baby blue eyes darkened to brown. Little brown fishes, thought Kirsty. She was a wide awake child, watching everything in the room with intense interest.

They were doomed to months of sleepless nights. Although India was alert and good humoured when she had something to distract her, she was a colicky and complaining child at night. Nicolas offered to employ a nurse, but Kirsty wouldn't hear of it. She was still feeding India herself and was reluctant to let anyone else interfere. At last, in desperation, they took the baby into bed with them. They were both so ragged from lack of sleep that they would have tried anything. And neither of them could bear to leave her to cry. Once she was fed and changed, Kirsty would put her on Nicolas's chest while he lay on his back, propped up on a pillow. The baby seemed to find the position comfortable, and they would all three of them fall asleep, Kirsty tucked in against her husband, the baby sprawled on top of him, soothed by his breathing and his heartbeat.

Annabel sent her a little sling and whenever the weather was fine, Kirsty would put the baby in it and walk up to Dunshee. Partly this was because the walking seemed to soothe the child, but mostly it was to get out of the house and visit her grandfather. Alasdair was increasingly troubled with arthritis. He ought to have retired long ago, but there was nobody else to take on the farm and he still didn't want to leave it. Kirsty was glad, because she still liked to sit up in her old bedroom, gazing towards the sea. Often she would trundle the buggy down the track to the beach, park India in the shade, and sketch the cliffs at the south end of the island, trying to capture their soaring, vertiginous quality.

Like the old ruin, these massive basalt cliffs were becoming something of an obsession with her. She would make sketches and then take them home to Ealachan where she would use ever larger canvases in an attempt to explore them. When she was sketching, all went well, but when she tried to paint them, she was seldom happy with the results. She would complain that the paint had become 'stuck' and hard to work, that everything had become too solid, too dragged down, that there was no freedom in it. The work she wanted to achieve, monumental, non-negotiable, would not take shape beneath her hands.

Kirsty would have judged that she was happy at that time. The child so filled her mind that there was little room for anything or anyone else and she missed her mother more than she missed Finn. She would gaze at India's rosy face and wish that Isabel was here, wish that there was somebody to confide in, to ask about things such as potty training. She had taken the decision to put Finn out of her thoughts and she had largely succeeded.

He's not coming back. He's gone for good, she told herself. He was my friend and I loved him, will always love him, but I can't live the rest of my life wondering if he's going to get off the next ferry.

Chapter Twenty Four

Finn perched nervously on the edge of a couch, waiting for her to come. The room where he had been asked to wait was so clean that every surface shone. The floor was wooden, with a single blue rug, the walls painted white. There was an alcove with a white marble statue of the Blessed Virgin Mary, a posy of sweet smelling pinks in front of it. The scent of them reminded him of his childhood. There had been a procession of some kind, a holy day, when the church was strewn with petals. The whole place had been full of the spicy clove perfume of pinks and stocks, their shredded petals making a kind of scented confetti. What a big part the church had played in his life back then, its rituals stitched into the fabric of his days, giving them shape and meaning. But he marvelled at how the same set of beliefs could result in such polar opposites of experience.

The room was full of sunlight, very warm and quiet. Occasionally he would be aware of distant footsteps, the muted sound of a door closing, a snatch of conversation. But these singular sounds only served to emphasise the silence. The impression was of a stillness that was not oppressive. It was so peaceful that Finn found the tension draining out of him, his eyelids drooping.

He was again aware of footsteps, but this time they grew steadily closer. He could feel his heart pounding, could hear the drum beat of it in his ears. He rose to his feet as the door swung open, but when she came into the room, her face eager and afraid, his first definite thought was, this can't be her, she's too small. She always had been small, a slim, diminutive woman. It was just that back then, he had been even smaller, and she had been everything, she had been huge, she had been his whole world.

She had a sweet face, like Sister Rosalie, how strange, all pink and white, but with many fine lines around eyes and mouth. She turned her face towards him, glistening eyes and a smiling, uncertain mouth, dwarfed by the white wimple and the dark veil. She moved smoothly, as though there were wheels beneath the habit. He didn't recognise her at all. He thought, this must be a mistake. This is a stranger. Why did they think this might be my mother?

She was reaching out to him, a tiny hand, red and rather rough. She put her hand on his. Her fingers were cool and dry. And then the hand was withdrawn, tucked safely back inside her sleeves again.

'Oh, Finn!' she said. 'Is it really you? Can this really be you, all grown up?'

He was a whirlpool of feelings: sadness, resentment, regret. He had no words. No words at all

'Mammy?'

'It is you. But I can hardly believe it. Look at you, Finn. Look at you.'

She sat down on the couch, and he sat beside her, but then moved away from her a little, old habits dying hard. You never touched a nun. Never. Was she really his mother? She didn't attempt to touch him again, didn't even take his hand. 'This is difficult. I know.'

'Difficult?' he echoed.

'Well.'

'When did you …?'

'Take my vows? Years ago. Years.' The fingers suddenly emerged from the voluminous sleeves and she counted on them. 'It must be nine years now.'

'But why?'

'Because I wanted to.'

'Why would you want to? After all they put you through? And what about me?'

It came out as a wail, the yelp of a miserable little boy. Still she didn't touch him.

'I hated it. Hated it. I could only think about getting out and getting you back.'

'I wish you had,' he said, but she didn't hear him, too intent on explaining.

'It was appalling, Finn. Just appalling. Worse than prison. But there was nothing I could do about it. Well, I did run off once. Me and another couple of girls. We got out one night, and then we got over the wall. The three of us had some idea of getting to England and I thought I would try to get you back. I might have some rights over here. But it was winter and it was foggy and the *Gardai* caught up with us before we'd gone more than a mile or two. Oh you don't want to know what it was like.'

'I do know what it was like. It was like that for me too.'

Worse, he thought. It was worse. He hated himself for his sudden resentment but he couldn't help it.

She hesitated. 'Do you remember anything about that day? The day they took you away?'

He shook his head. 'Not much. I don't like to think about it. I remember Mrs Maguire from the Legion of Mary. I remember being taken to the school. It seemed like a very long way. I fell asleep in the car and when I woke up I needed a pee. They had to stop the car and let me do it by the road.'

Where had that come from? How had he forgotten that until now? Mrs Maguire, studiously averting her gaze. The little stream of piss in the road. His embarrassment.

'I couldn't bear to think about you.'

He interrupted her. 'They said you weren't fit to look after me. That's what they told me. They said I was a bad boy, and a charity case.'

'You were never a bad boy. Never. I wasn't the best of mothers but you were such a lovely little boy.'

'There was nothing wrong with you.'

'But you've done all right, haven't you? Look at you. You've done all right!' She wanted to believe it, wanted to persuade herself of the truth of it.

'I'm all right.'

'They told me you were living in Glasgow. Is that right?'

He gave her a sketchy account of his recent history without

going into too much detail. He told her he had been doing evening classes, had just sat his exams. The results would be coming out in the summer. His teachers were pleased with him. They thought he might go far. But it felt as though he were recounting somebody else's story.

'So you're all right. Thank God for that. And this priest. The one who contacted our Mother Superior. He's helped you?'

'He's been kind, yes.'

'So it hasn't all been bad?'

'I wanted to come and find you. I wanted to get you out. But they wouldn't tell me anything. They wouldn't tell me where you were. I thought you were dead!' He almost shouted the words. She flinched at his vehemence.

There was a muted knock at the door, and a lay sister came in, wheeling a trolley with china cups, home made biscuits, a big pot of tea. There was nothing, Finn thought, so momentous that it couldn't be cured or at least alleviated by the generous application of quantities of tea. That was the way it was in the Church. And perhaps they were right.

When they were alone again, balancing cups, he asked, 'But why did you do this? Was this the only way out?'

She gazed towards the high window, drank a mouthful of tea.

'I always intended to get out. And to find you. If ever I prayed at that time, it was only to find you. To save you from wherever they had you. But years passed, and nothing changed, and then something did change. The Mother Superior, she was such a bloody ould dragon, God forgive me, Finn, but I hated her, if ever I hated anyone. Anyway, she died. Quite suddenly. Took a stroke and keeled over in her cell one night. There was a new regime, and things changed. It was gradual. But things changed. The new one was a good woman and I think she was appalled by what she found and needed to manage the change somehow. There was one day, in church, when we were singing, we did a lot a singing there, and I found myself thinking that I was happy. I was content. It was a feeling in myself that I couldn't ignore. I told Mother Anne about you and she said she would make some enquiries, but years had passed and you were gone. You were gone from that school and they said you were gone from Ireland and nobody knew where you were. Grown and gone. So I thought, well, you'd made a life for yourself, and why would you want me interfering?'

'How could you think that?'

'Because it's true. It seemed to me that if I pursued you it would have been an imposition on you. I'd have been this long-lost mother, appearing out of the blue. I couldn't do that to you. I was like somebody who has fallen asleep for a hundred years and finds everything changed when she wakes. Like those people in the old stories who are taken by the fairies, but when they come back they find that years have passed and nothing is the same.'

'But ... this?' His gesture took in the room, the statue, her habit.

'It was what I wanted to do. I looked in my heart and saw that it was what I wanted.'

'I don't believe you.'

'It doesn't matter whether you believe me or not. It's the truth. I found my vocation. I found my faith again in the strangest of places. A candle in the dark. Mother Anne was my spiritual advisor and counsellor and she put me through the mill. She didn't believe me either, just at first. She had to be sure that it wasn't false. Wasn't all some illusion. It took a long time but I took my vows at last. And then I was sent over here. There's a nursery school attached to the convent. We go out into the world from time to time. But on the whole, we stay still and people come to us. We sing. I love the singing. And we pray.'

'Did you pray for me?' It came out as a croak. An ugly sound.

'Oh Finn, all the time.'

'How can you still believe? How can you believe any of it?'

'But you go to church, don't you? I heard you went to church in Glasgow. That priest, the one who contacted me. He told me you still had the faith.'

'Kevin's been a good friend to me. But I don't believe in anything.'

He wanted to curl up and become small again and tuck himself in close to her. But he wanted his real mother, not this small stranger, her hair hidden by wimple and veil. She made him feel big and clumsy. He wanted to run away from this smooth, beeswax scented place and forget that any of it had happened. He wanted her to be dead so that he could mourn her in peace and move on with his life.

'I can't mend the past,' she said. 'None of us can. I thought I would die without you.'

'You couldn't beat them, so you joined them.'

'No. I found myself. I'm Sister Dominica now. Ah God, let me look at you. I know this is too much, too soon. You need to think about all this. Sort things out in your head. I wouldn't blame you if you wanted to go away and turn your back on me. But you can come and see me you know. If you want to. There's a guest house. You could come and stay. We could spend a little time together. There's so much to talk about. Things you should know. About that time. About what happened.' She frowned. 'There are things you don't remember, Finn.'

'I don't want to talk about it. I don't want to remember it. I've spent all these years trying to forget and I don't want to dredge it up again. There's nothing you can tell me that I want to know. Nothing!'

She gazed at him anxiously. He couldn't be angry with her but he was disappointed. He knew that she had been helpless, as helpless as he was in the face of inhuman and intractable cruelty, but she had capitulated when she should not.

He thought, I wouldn't have done that! I wouldn't have given in! I wouldn't have joined the enemy! The words came into his mind with such fierceness that they tumbled over one another and made him dizzy with the venom of them.

When he was on the bus on the way back to Glasgow, he remembered the sudden sadness that had shaded her serenity.

'There are things we should talk about, Finn. About that time. About what happened.'

But he hadn't wanted to talk about it and he didn't want to think about it any more. He had spent his life so far blaming himself for the seismic shift that had destroyed his world and his mother's world too. He was free now. He would follow Kirsty's advice and make something of himself, but he would do it alone and unaided. When he was rich and successful he would go back to Dunshee. He would go back and see Kirsty and say, 'Look. Look at what I've done. Did you think I couldn't do it? Look at what I've made of myself!'

And then she would see. They would all see. All the doubters. They would all see just what Finn O'Malley could do.

Chapter Twenty Five

THREE YEARS LATER, Kirsty gave birth to another daughter, Flora, a tiny red-headed replica of herself. During this second pregnancy, she found that she and her work had vastly outgrown the bedroom, and Nicolas made a studio for her in one of the outbuildings at the back of the house. She still liked to walk about the island, sketching, taking photographs or just observing the layers of light and colour, the subtleties of each season. Whenever she could, she would take India with her, admiring her daughter's energy as she toddled along on sturdy legs, covering three miles for her mother's every mile. Sometimes, Alasdair would come down to the beach below Dunshee with them and make sandcastles or sand boats. India could be an obstinate and fractious little girl when she chose, but she would always smile for Alasdair.

Kirsty had already exhibited in galleries in Edinburgh, including the one where she had worked as a student, and in a couple of small galleries in London, where her island studies were greeted with enthusiasm. They were vivid, original, very beautiful, but also, as one critic put it, 'curiously detached, as though the artist were an observer from another planet, seeing the place for the first time.' A journalist came to the island and wrote a piece about Kirsty's work. She was even featured in a couple of glossy, rural life magazines. She had a few sales, but she didn't much care whether she sold her pictures or not. For Kirsty, the exploration was always more important than the end product.

Flora's birth, smooth as it was, seemed to cast her into a kind of despondency. 'I just sit here and lactate,' she said to Nicolas.

'But I love to see you feeding her.'

'I know. And I love doing it. I keep looking at her and thinking,

I've done all that! It came out of me, not some bottle. But I can't seem to string two sensible words together, never mind thoughts.'

India, meanwhile, was going through a stage of saying 'no' to everything. She would do anything to oblige her grandfather, but nothing for anyone else, not Kirsty, not even Nicolas. She would stamp her foot and put her hands on her hips and defy everyone, her forehead creased in a frown. It drove Nicolas mad, but whenever he saw her standing, arms akimbo, like an outraged adult, it made him laugh so much that he would have to leave the room.

Kirsty knew that she was lucky. She had help in the house and no money worries, but she felt as though she had become mother to the whole world and found it impossible to watch films or television programmes where children were hurt or injured. It was too painful and would reduce her to tears in a moment. Just occasionally, the thought of Finn would come into her mind: what he had told her about his mother and his enforced separation from her. How could they have borne it? She felt it more acutely now that she was a mother herself. She knew that she would have killed to protect her children. But the thought of having either of them taken away from her by force was so appalling that it made her stomach churn. Poor Finn. Poor Mary.

The following year, Kirsty made an extended visit to her in-laws in London with the two children and, while she was there, had her hair cut very short. Afterwards, she gazed at herself, wondering what Nicolas would say, missing the weight and the warmth of it, running her hand tentatively over the back of her neck. She felt very strange and vulnerable without it and drew a whole page full of trembling shorn sheep in her sketch book.

'My God, what have you done?' said Nicolas, when she got back to the island.

'The kids were always tugging at it. I couldn't keep up to it.'

'I loved your hair.'

'It'll grow again.'

He looked at her critically. 'I can't say it doesn't suit you, because it does. But you're much too thin you know. You used to be such a lovely, voluptuous girl. Not that I don't like you just the way you are,' he added, hastily.

'I'm as fit as a flea.'

'It's all that walking you do. But I did love your hair, you know.'

'I just wanted a change.'

'Fair enough. But next time, ask me what I think first, eh?'

She had come back from the London trip to find that Nicolas had converted her workspace so that it filled the whole of one of the old stables. There was an upstairs studio with perfect light and plenty of storage. Downstairs there was a gallery where he had hung a selection of her work. The rooms were warm and welcoming. There was even a tiny kitchen and shower room.

'Do you think it will inspire you?' he asked her, anxiously.

'It should inspire me.' She grinned at him. 'But I'll need to rehang some of them, you know.'

'Whatever you like. It's all yours. I thought we could open it to the public for a bit in the summer. And if you're busy painting, we can pay one of the youngsters from the village to come and mind it.'

'We'd have to do that, yes. I'm no saleswoman.'

'You used to do it in Edinburgh. Do you remember that awful artist you were going out with?'

'Ash? He wasn't awful. I liked him a lot. But he sold out, right enough.'

'Is he still painting?'

'Yes, but he does magazine illustrations and greetings cards and limited edition prints of sexy ladies. I read about him sometimes.'

'Is that such a bad thing?'

'No. He's very good at it. He makes good money. And he has a family to support.'

She had seen him just once, at an arts conference of some sort. Another woman was ushering him this way and that. He was a distinguished visitor, but Kirsty was quite a notable visitor as well by that time. She noticed that the woman was fluttering a little, the way women always did when they were around him, because he had an extraordinarily potent physical presence. She wondered uneasily if she had once fluttered like that? And hadn't he always been much too fond of acolytes? Nothing had changed. Like waters stirred at the bottom of a still pool, memories bubbled to the surface. His smile.

His face. Joyful times and sad. But also, a great many lies, so many lies that love had buckled beneath the weight of them like a car in a crusher.

He had seen her and come over to speak to her.

'I'm sorry,' he had said. 'Sorry I put you through all that.'

'It doesn't matter. Not now.'

Ash had been clever and charming and she had loved him. He had taught her a great deal and helped her with the first tentative steps in her career, for which she would always be grateful. But she saw that she could have done it all without him. He had run her ragged for a year. He hadn't been worth the emotional energy. No man was. Not even Finn. He had much greater claim to her affection, but she could live well enough without him. Even him. She had proved it, hadn't she?

'Kirsty, your hair!' said her grandfather when she went up to Dunshee with India in tow.

She put her hand tentatively to her shorn head. 'I know. It's a bit strange for me as well.'

'Who cut it, lass?'

'Annabel made an appointment for me, so I told them to hack it all off and they did. Well, they did a bit more than that actually. It cost a fortune: the cut I mean. Annabel insisted on paying.'

'And where's the baby?'

'She's down at Ealachan with Nick. India and I escaped while they were taking a nap. Thought I'd bring her up to see you and show you my hair!'

'I think you look very pretty.'

'That's what Annabel keeps telling me.'

'Is she here as well?'

'No. She's off in Italy somewhere. With some man. Annabel and her men. I get quite jealous of her.'

'Do you?'

'Not really. But she's just so free to come and go. You should see what India does if I try to go out for the evening.' Kirsty looked fondly at her elder daughter who was sitting in her own old baby chair with

Fish Face on her lap. He was growing old and cantankerous, but he seemed to like India.

'That won't last for long. You should count your blessings.'

'Usually I do. And she's getting a lot less clingy. I'm easily pleased, grandad. My kids, my studio, the gallery.'

'It seems like quite a lot really, Kirsty.'

'You mean Nick spoils me?'

'He does.'

'Well, I would agree with you. But then, I work hard. I take my work seriously, even if Nicolas doesn't.'

'Of course he does!'

'I don't think so. I think he says all the right things but he sees it as a hobby. I enjoy it too much for it to count as work. And I don't make much money. He can't take me seriously. He sees it as a way of keeping me happy.'

'And isn't that what it does?'

'Yes. Of course. But I don't think he understands how driven I feel. It's more than a hobby. It's my life. I can't not do it. But I get the sense that in Nicolas's world, it's just a way of passing the time. It keeps me out of mischief. We have friends who come and stay. They say things like "Are you still painting?" As if I could ever stop. They would never ask if I was still banking? Or being an architect. But it's Christine's little hobby. That's the way they see it.'

'I'm not sure you're right about Nicolas. I think he admires what you do more than you realise.'

'Well, maybe so. But I reckon the family business comes first. It always has and it always will.'

Fish Face was twitching his tail. He had had enough of India's over-enthusiastic caresses.

'Leave him alone, India. He'll scratch you.' Kirsty came to Fish Face's rescue. She took the child onto her own knee, but India squirmed off, clambered onto a chair and got down Alasdair's old fiddle.

'Can I, grandad? I'll be careful!'

'Aye, why not? Let your mammy hear you.'

Alasdair tuned up the fiddle and India, standing between his knees so that he could help her, scraped a tune from it. Alasdair was fairly bursting with pride.

'Would you credit it?' he said. 'Isn't she just wonderful?'

'That's very good, my wee lamb!' Kirsty beamed at her daughter, genuinely impressed. 'She's a natural! Not like her mother. Do you remember the way you always used to want me to learn,' said Kirsty. 'But I was never very keen.'

'She'll be good.' He put the fiddle back on its nail. 'She wants to go fishing as well, don't you, my wee lass?'

India nodded, vigorously.

'She found your old rod in a cupboard, Kirsty, the last time she was here. You know how she likes to rummage. Much too big for her, but I could root out a smaller one. I said I would have to ask you and Nicolas first.'

'Oh I expect it will be all right. You used to take me fishing all the time.'

'Aye. You were good at the casting.'

'Tick Tock.'

'Tick Tock. You should take it up again Kirsty.'

'Maybe I will some day. She reminds me so much of myself. I get the feeling she'd far rather be up here on this hillside than down in the gardens.'

'And what about you, Kirsty? Have you got used to living down there?'

'I suppose so. But if I couldn't come up here, I don't know what I'd do.'

'And Finn. Do you ever think about him at all?'

'Oh yes. Yes, of course I do. But I try not to.'

When she thought about Finn now, it was with a sense of regret for the loss of his friendship. But when she tried to remember his face, she found that it slid away from her and she could never piece it together clearly. Once or twice over the years, she had dreamed about him, vivid dreams, full of a sort of desperate eroticism, dreams that disturbed her peace for several days afterwards. She told nobody. Who could help dreaming?

Chapter Twenty Six

WHEN INDIA WAS eight years old, much to Kirsty's dismay, Nicolas began to talk about sending her away to the mainland, to prep school.

'She's certainly not going to live in a hostel and go to the comprehensive.'

'It didn't do me any harm.'

'Maybe so, but you were exceptional, darling.'

'India seems pretty exceptional to me.'

She was willowy and pale skinned with long dark hair tied back into a ponytail. The single teacher at the island school said that she was 'a very bright child.'

'Well, well. I suppose we don't have to worry about it for a little while yet.'

Alasdair had begun teaching India to play the fiddle properly while she was very young and had found her a willing pupil. Now, she could string together a succession of reels and jigs, playing with her eyes closed and her face rapt, as she listened to the music in her head. Kirsty felt that Nicolas disapproved, ever so slightly. He had been investigating the Suzuki method of learning the violin and wondering where they could find a teacher who would be prepared to travel to the island.

'The whole principle is that it should be fun, second nature, like breathing,' he said.

'I agree. Just the way my grandad has been teaching her.'

But Nicolas wanted India to learn classical violin. He didn't think that Alasdair's traditional music was the real thing. He had been secretly sending away for prospectuses for mainland prep schools that specialised in music.

'Why does she have to go so soon?' asked Kirsty.

'Annabel and I went at eight.'

'I know you did. But I still think it's too young,' she said stubbornly. 'We never discussed boarding schools before they were born, did we?'

'I just assumed they would go away when the time came. You couldn't possibly have imagined anything else.'

'I didn't imagine anything at all. What if I don't approve?'

'How could you know? It will do her the world of good.'

'I just don't approve of having children and then sending them away from home. You gentry can't wait to get rid of your kids. Us lower orders quite like having them around.'

'It's a necessary evil,' he said, reasonably, laughing at her vehemence. 'Living where we do. If we lived in Edinburgh or Glasgow it might be different. You had to go away from home as well, didn't you?'

Sensing that she was getting nowhere, she changed tack. Nicolas was not as easily swayed by her arguments as he had once been. Much as he loved her, she could see that there were times, nowadays, when he just dug in his heels. But he always kept his temper. Sometimes she wished that he would have a proper argument with her. When she was in a temper, she wanted to fling things: cushions, vases, knives even, at his head, but she knew that he wouldn't respond. He would just go out of the room, close the door on her and leave her to cool down. It was infuriating.

'Think how much Flora would miss her,' she said. 'She needs her big sister for a while longer at least.'

Flora was just five and had started at the village primary school the previous month. When she went trotting down the driveway beside her big sister, she reminded Kirsty of herself, with her shiny red hair, her freckles, her pleated skirt, her scuffed sandals (they never stayed new for longer than a day) and ankle socks streaked with dust where she habitually rubbed one foot against the other.

Nicolas's face softened. 'Well. Maybe another year then,' he said. He loved his little Flora and would go a long way to avoid upsetting her. 'I suppose we could manage another year. But next September, India will be nine and I think she'll have to go. I was thinking about St Andrews. Annabel was very happy there.'

Although the family had lived in London where there were excellent schools if you had the money, both Annabel and Nicolas had been sent away to school at what Kirsty saw as a horrendously young age.

'I'll miss her.'

'We could always have another.' He said it blithely, and she laughed. But she knew he didn't mean it. He would hate all the disruption that a new baby would bring, and she felt strangely repelled by the thought of another pregnancy.

'Besides,' he said, 'Think of all the time you'll have for your work when she's gone.'

'I have plenty of time now.'

She could see that he was doing his best to be nice to her, now that he had won the skirmish. 'What are you working on?' he asked. He seldom came to her studio these days, although he talked about her work with great pride whenever they had visitors.

'Dunshee. A series of studies of Dunshee. The way it was in the past and the way it is now.'

The truth was that her beloved Dunshee was growing more unkempt with each month that passed. There were holes in the barn roof. The window frames were rotting slowly. There were mice in the loft. Woodlice ambled slowly about the kitchen. Ants thronged the flagstones from springtime onwards, busy with their own pursuits, and there was mould on the walls. Nature was reclaiming the house by degrees. Billy, the lad who was supposed to help about the farm, kept skiving off to the village to drink in the hotel bar or, more seriously, to his room at the top of the ladder where he kept a bottle of whisky. There was no reason why he shouldn't keep whisky in his room, but he shouldn't be drinking it during working hours. Kirsty knew that he did, because she had occasionally smelled it on his breath in the afternoon: the sudden, sour whiff of it that made her want to retch.

She hated him being in Finn 's room although there was nothing of Finn left in there except the memory of him, and even that seemed to be fading. She had packed his few remaining possessions, his books, his overalls and working boots, into a suitcase and left it up there in a cupboard under the eaves, where she supposed it still was, although perhaps the mice had got to it by now, shredding his books, gnawing holes in the overalls, nesting in the boots.

Once or twice, she had spoken to Billy about his drinking, but she didn't dare tell Nicolas. Nicolas would have dismissed him, but then who would help Alasdair? She had the uneasy feeling that if Billy went, Nicolas wouldn't replace him, but would use the crisis to institute some change, moving Alasdair down to the village. She had a deep sense of foreboding about the future of Dunshee.

On the ninth anniversary of her mother's death, she went up to the old kirkyard with a posy from the gardens: late roses and a few Michaelmas daisies. There was a stone on her mother's grave now, a granite headstone engraved with birds and flowers. 'Isabel Galbreath, a dear mum, and daughter,' it read. 'Be thou my vision, oh lord of my heart.' It had been Isabel's favourite hymn and Kirsty loved it too. There was something comforting about the ancient words, 'Be thou my high tower,' with their suggestion of round towers and hill-top strongholds. Alasdair had asked the stonemason to carve the word 'daughter' because that was how he had always thought of Isabel.

There was a vase on her mother's grave, slotted neatly into a hole in the base of the headstone. When she lifted it out, there were worms and centipedes and earwigs scuttling about beneath. The lid of the vase was hard to get off and there were always a few dead flower stalks left inside. She took a plastic bottle to the tap in the corner of the cemetery and fetched water to rinse out the vase and refill it. By the time she was ready to replace it, the denizens of the hole had disappeared. She arranged her posy carefully.

'Oh, mum!' she said aloud, and although it was so many years since her mother had died, she felt a lump in her throat and tears in her eyes. She felt tired to the point of exhaustion. She would have liked to lie down on the short turf and go to sleep, but somebody might come and see her. So she gathered together her plastic bottle and her plastic bag, with the stalks of the flowers and the few dead blooms from her last arrangement, and took them to the litter bin.

Before going home, she scrambled down into the older part of the kirkyard where she and Finn had once tried to summon the dead MacDonald from his grave. She hadn't been here for years. The place was full of clear, slanting light as the sun sank behind the island. There were brambles growing over the more unkempt graves, and she picked the ripe berries and ate a few of them. They bruised her fingers with their juice, and she knew that her tongue would be the same colour.

She found the MacDonald grave, stumbling upon it almost by chance, and began to walk around it with the brambles tugging at her jeans. Shrubs and long grasses barred her way, but she pushed them aside. Once, twice, three times.

'Come forth!' she whispered. 'Come forth!' She saw movement among the brambles but it was only a wren, hopping about among the stalks on his impossibly spindly legs, searching out insects with the needle of his beak.

She stood up straight and looked towards the mainland, scanning the darkening stretch of water. The last ferry of the day was returning to the island. She could see from here that the deck was empty. No cars. No passengers either. It was returning to its berth for the night and wouldn't leave again until morning. For no reason that she could see, she felt an irrational stab of fear. There was a nervous fluttering in her stomach. Her heart raced and the sky wheeled above her. She steadied herself on a tombstone, feeling the gritty texture of granite and lichen beneath her fingers. She breathed deeply and, after a moment or two, the sensation of panic passed. What was that, she thought? What happened then?

The children would be wondering where she had got to. She wiped her mouth with her hand, leaving a red smear of berry juice on her cheek, and headed down the hill towards Ealachan. Nothing, she thought. I am waiting for nothing.

Later on that night, she was alone in the small parlour, dozing in front of the television. Nicolas had been in his study all evening, working on some estate correspondence, but an hour ago he had gone to bed. The children were fast asleep. Kirsty had been attempting to knit a pullover for Flora who had become very interested in her own clothes. She wanted one in pink with a teddy bear on the front, but Kirsty had never been good at such things and she noticed that she had dropped a stitch, four or five rows back. She couldn't bear the thought of unpicking it all just now, so she bundled it into her knitting bag and pushed it down the side of the sofa. To console herself, she poured a large sherry, which was all there was in the room besides Nicolas's whisky. She would have liked a gin and tonic but she couldn't be bothered trekking down to the kitchen through the chilly, silent and faintly spooky house. She decided to watch the television news and go to bed.

Annabel was coming tomorrow. The girls were delighted at the prospect of a visit from their aunt. Somewhat to Kirsty's surprise, she was very patient with the girls and would sit for hours, playing board games, threading beads, colouring in pictures, making unlikely and madly collapsible structures out of Lego.

Kirsty has just taken a large gulp of her sherry when the newsreader, with suddenly assumed gravity, began to speak about a tragedy that was unfolding somewhere out on the North Sea. There had been explosions on an oil platform. A fire was raging. She saw smoke billowing. Twisted metal. She watched rescue vessels and helicopters hovering, unable to get closer because of the smoke and the flames. She saw water funnelling up into the air, a desperate attempt to combat the fire. She wished that Nicolas was awake because this was too sad to watch alone.

She drank again and the alcohol steadied her. They were attempting to assess the number of dead and injured, but nobody was sure. It could be dozens. It could be more than a hundred. There was a shot of ambulances; many of the survivors were badly burned. They were interviewing the few who were relatively unscathed, who had been picked up by boats and helicopters: haggard men with grimy faces, men wrapped in blankets, men on their way to hospital to be treated for smoke inhalation and hypothermia. What was it like? How do you feel? Stupid, unanswerable questions.

The camera focused in on a pale face. It was a face on which the full horror of the evening's events were painted as one might paint them on a canvas, the black hair damp with sea water or sweat or both, the cheeks bruised and dirty. It was a gift for any artist, this coldly beautiful face, shaded and hollowed by terror.

'How did you get off?' the young reporter was asking.

'I don't know. I must have jumped. Somebody pulled me out of the water. It shouldn't have happened. I know that. It should not have happened.' The man turned away, shaking his head, putting out a hand to shield himself from the camera's intrusive eye. 'No' he said. 'No. That's enough.'

Long after they had moved on to the next item on the schedule, she sat staring at the screen.

Had she imagined the whole thing?

Or could it be true that she had just seen Finn O'Malley turning away from his interrogator, shaking his head, pushing the empty air aside?

At last she got up, poured another large sherry, drained the glass in one gulp, and then went over to her desk where she kept her sketchbooks, newspaper clippings, catalogues. She rummaged about frantically, looking for the current Writers' and Artists' Year Book. Leafing through it, she found what she was looking for: contact details for the BBC. She phoned the switchboard and was passed on to whatever duty officer was manning the television news desk at this late hour.

'Can I help you?' asked the young woman at the other end. She sounded tired, as if she was at the end of a long shift and couldn't wait to get home.

'I hope so,' said Kirsty and then hesitated. This was preposterous.

There was a silence at the other end. The girl was waiting.

'I was watching the news, the news about the accident in the North Sea.'

'Yes, Madam.'

'Your reporter was interviewing one of the survivors.'

She sensed the girl gathering herself together to deal with the situation.

'There are believed to be survivors,' she intoned, professionally. 'The police have issued a telephone number. I think it's an Aberdeen number. Can I give it to you?'

'I just need to know. The man you were interviewing. The point is, I know him. How can I contact him? Do you have any contact details?'

There was another pregnant pause. She could almost see the

girl at the other end mouthing, 'We've got one here!' to an unseen companion.

'Was this a relative? Did you have a relative working aboard the rig, madam?'

'No. Not a relative. But as good as. An old friend. Missing. I need to know where he is.'

'Well, madam,' said the girl, and she sounded quite friendly. Humouring her. 'I'm afraid we couldn't possibly issue such details, even if we had them. Our reporter was on the scene, but we have no way of knowing the identities of the people he was talking to. Can I give you the police number? They may be able to tell you more.'

Kirsty heard the scepticism in her voice. Not a cat in hell's chance, she was thinking.

She took the number anyway and dialled it at intervals for an hour, but it was always engaged.

When at last she got through, they again asked her if she was a relative. She should have lied, of course. She realised that when it was too late. She should have said yes, he's my husband, my cousin, my long lost brother who left home years ago. But when she said 'he's an old friend', they told her politely but firmly that they could give out no information.

'Finn,' she said. 'His name's Finn O'Malley. I saw him on the television. He's been gone so long. Years. I have to know if it was him.'

'And your name?' asked the policeman.

'Kirsty Galbreath.' Why did she say that name, she wondered? Why not Kirsty Laurence?

'Well Ms Galbreath, we will be issuing a list of survivors in due course. Can I suggest that you wait until this is published at the proper time?'

'I can't wait. I have to know.'

'Then I'm sorry, but I really can't help you. May I suggest that you contact this Mr O'Malley's family.'

'You don't understand. He doesn't have a family. We're the only family he has.'

'With all due respect, Ms Galbreath, if you haven't seen him for years, how do you know?'

She hung up. He was right of course. Finn may have a wife and children by now. They may have been watching the news with the same sick sense of trepidation. They may, even now, be weeping with relief, phoning the police, speeding to the hospital with all the right in the world to embrace Finn, to give thanks that he was alive.

It was very late. The fire had gone out and she was cold. Even the dogs had gone to bed. When she went upstairs, she found the cat asleep on Nicolas's feet. New Cat they called him, even though he was not new at all, but five years old, brought home by India from a friend's house as a gift for her mother. Poor Fish Face had long gone to rest under the fuchsia hedge at Dunshee. She undressed and crept into bed but she couldn't sleep. When she closed her eyes, a thousand images of Finn leapt from the darkness. She tried to warm her cold feet on him, but he only sighed and turned away from her.

A few days after the disaster, the newspapers published a list of survivors. Over one hundred and thirty men had died and only sixty odd had survived. Among the list of survivors there was the name of Finn O'Malley.

Kirsty showed it to Nicolas, but he seemed indifferent.

'So?' he said. 'Now you know where he went. He's probably a rigger. Making himself a bit of cash. He was one of the lucky ones.'

'I think you'd rather Finn was at the bottom of the North Sea.'

'That's not fair. I don't wish any ill to the man. In fact I don't really think about him at all. Besides, I've got too much else to worry about right now.'

'What are you worried about?'

'Are you really so self absorbed that you don't know? Our company – we supplied some of the equipment on the rig. Have you no bloody idea of the implications of all this?'

'I'm sorry. I didn't think.'

'And I'm sorry too. But there could be all kinds of ramifications, mostly financial.'

'It always comes down to money, doesn't it, Nicolas?'

But once again, he wouldn't argue with her. He took himself out of the room and left her alone with her cooling coffee.

The local newspaper had reported the accident and its survivors extensively. Finn wasn't a rigger. To her surprise, she read that he was an engineer. He had just been coming off duty, which was why he wasn't in the accommodation block. Which was why he had survived. But that was as much as she could find out. Nobody would tell her anything. The persistent thought that he might be married gave her an unreasonable pang of jealousy.

She would lie awake in the early hours of the morning with a dozen scenarios playing themselves out in her head: Finn with his wife, Finn back in Ireland. But would he ever go back to Ireland? She supposed not. Although he had once confessed to her that he missed Dublin, had loved Dublin, and wished that the rest of his memories were as happy. She saw him with his children, playing in some imagined garden. She saw him in Glasgow, in Edinburgh, in London.

She did not see him at all.

Kirsty wasted many fruitless hours in the village post office, looking through whatever phone books they had, Scottish directories mostly. She found a few O'Malleys. She even dialled a few numbers. Nobody who answered knew anything about Finn. She had to face the unpalatable truth that, after his brief, disturbing resurrection, Finn had disappeared again, as surely and perhaps as deliberately as on that first occasion. He had never intended to be seen. Wherever he was now, it was obvious that he had no thought whatsoever of contacting her again.

Chapter Twenty Seven

FINN DROVE SOUTH from his rented house in Inverurie, spent the night in a guest house and went over on the car ferry from Stranraer to Belfast. He was fortunate. The sea was calm, even though it was winter, much calmer than it had been that night on the rig. The big, powerful vessel ate up the miles. He was travelling alone. He didn't want to book any hotels, so he had decided to take pot luck with accommodation. In fact, he hadn't really wanted to plan this trip at all. He had been steeling himself to make it for some time, ever since the disaster. It had seemed an inevitable next step. Something he had to do before moving on. But planning was another matter. He had told nobody he was going away, not even the woman who came in a couple of times a week to do his cleaning. He had just got up one morning, packed a small bag, left a note for her on the kitchen table and gone.

It was when they were passing Ailsa Craig that it started, images jostling for place in his mind. Francis, standing beside him watching the sea, jumping up and down to keep warm. Micky Terrans with his tweed caps and smart waistcoats. What had become of him, he wondered? And the stoical boy he himself had once been, suffering it all without complaint. How had he managed to suffer it all? How had he survived intact? Had he survived? Really? There was something irretrievably lost, and it wasn't just the gaps in his memory. Was it the capacity to love and be loved in return? Was that it? You mustn't love anything or anybody too much, because if you did, it would be taken away from you. Was that why he felt so little about anything?

It occurred to him that it might have been better to make the longer sea crossing from Holyhead. He would have had time to think, time to adjust. This was almost too swift, even though there would be a long journey at the other side. But they had always travelled to Stranraer all those years ago, so it had been the first place to come into his mind. And besides, he associated the Dublin-Holyhead crossing with his father and he didn't want to have to think about his father. Not this time. Perhaps never. This trip was about something else entirely.

He went to the onboard cafe and bought himself a mug of coffee and a Danish pastry, cramming it into his mouth without thinking. Then he went out on deck again, pulling up the collar of his coat against the cold. Nobody else had ventured out and the icy wind was a blade over his face. But he wanted to watch the horizon, wanted to see Ireland changing from a misty illusion, to see it resolving itself into solid ground. And still I live in hopes to see, the Holy Ground once more.

'Oh, Jesus,' he said under his breath, although he had given up believing in Jesus, Our Father, or the Blessed Virgin Mary, a very long time ago. He stayed out on deck until summoned below by the tannoy at the journey's end. And then he drove south, stopping briefly for a snack in a main street cafe in a small border town. The place seemed sullen and ugly, blighted by old hatreds, the air tense with suspicion. With every mile he drove further south, things seemed less dour, but he couldn't decide whether this was his own perception or some genuine lightening of the mood.

That afternoon, he reached Dublin where he checked into a small but expensive hotel near St Stephen's Green. The receptionist was disposed to be friendly, but he was politely noncommittal. Women were generally attracted to him. He was used to this, his appearance belying his lack of engagement. He couldn't be bothered with conversation. He took a shower, lay on the comfortable bed for half an hour and watched television. The programme was about antiques. An elderly woman was selling off family heirlooms so that she could pay for a trip to Disneyland for her grandchildren. He switched off the television and lay back down, listening to the muted sounds of traffic from outside.

Dublin. He was holding his mother's hand and they were going to visit somebody. His mother had few friends in the city but on this occasion, they must have been invited out. He remembered her fastening his jacket. 'Chin up,' she said. 'Chin up, Finny.' His jacket was too small for him, he was growing so fast. But she wound a scarf, round and round his neck, and over his face. It was striped because she had knitted it from odds and ends of wool.

'That'll keep out Jack Frost,' she said. 'He'll never nip your nose through that!'

They walked for what seemed like a long time, down cobbled streets. His mother was wearing her brown coat and a headscarf with a coach and horses on it. He remembered a dark staircase with steep stone stairs, and his mother holding his hand and helping him up, counting. He had always liked to count stairs. Stairs and street lights. 'Here we are, my little soldier!' she said, at the top.

They stepped into a warm room full of the gorgeous smell of cooked meat. He was very hungry and the smell made his mouth water. They didn't eat much meat, as a rule. His mother's meat and potato pie was mostly potatoes. The woman who lived here helped to unwind his scarf and take off his coat. She sat him down on a hearthrug in front of the fire and gave him some wooden building bricks to play with. He could feel the heat of the coals burning his cheeks. The soft voices talking about grown-up things soothed him, made him feel sleepy. They were smoking and the blue wisps from their cigarettes drifted towards the chimney. The colours of the blocks were all faded and the edges were worn so that you couldn't build them up properly. They tumbled down all the time, so he laid them flat and made a road with them instead. A stripey cat stalked over and looked at him, then stretched and yawned widely, arching its back and showing needle teeth and a pink mouth. The cat's breath smelled faintly fishy.

'Don't mind Frisky,' the woman said. 'He won't touch you, so.' She was comfortably fat and her clothes were too tight for her. Her chest was like two dumplings, spilling out over the top of her sweater. When she hugged him, he could smell a faint scent of coal tar soap. Her name was Phyllis, and she was his mother's friend, but he couldn't say her name. He called her Phissie. She didn't seem to mind. She gave him tea with lots of milk and sugar the way he liked it, baby tea she called it, which made him feel cross because he wasn't a baby. And then she took a big piece of corned beef out of a pan, real beef that she had cooked herself, all pink and juicy and sweet smelling, and she cut generous slices off it and put it between two thick slices of white bread and butter and set it in front of him. The heat of the meat was making the butter melt and soak into the bread.

'Eat up, Finny,' said his mother. 'Phyllis makes the best corned beef sandwiches in all Ireland, if not the whole world.'

'Will he have mustard?' asked Phyllis.

'I don't know.'

She put a little mustard on the tip of her knife and let him lick it, but he didn't like the taste of it. It nipped his tongue. So he shook his head. 'No thank-you, Phissie!' He took a mouthful of his sandwich to take away the sting of the mustard. And when he finished that, she made him another one. And he finished that too, licking the crumbs off the plate.

'I wouldn't like to have the feeding of him,' said Phyllis.

The luscious taste and the scent of the beef had lodged itself in his mind. Finny. He had forgotten that his mother called him Finny. The woman in the convent hadn't called him Finny. He had been Finn, there. Just one more thing to disturb him. He had not been back to see her again, although she wrote to him from time to time and he sent her the odd letter or postcard in return. It was easier to put things on paper than to have to deal with her at first hand. At Christmas, he sent her parcels of useful things: toiletries, sweets, books. Sometimes, when there was a woman in his life, he would delegate the task to her. But he never kept his girlfriends for very long. They soon got tired of him and went away.

'You'll go to any lengths to avoid commitment!' the last one had said, flinging clothes into her suitcase. 'If I didn't know better, I'd think you had a wife somewhere else.'

She had infiltrated some of her possessions into his house over the few months they had been lovers, but he had never invited her to move in with him, never given her any reason to suppose that the arrangement was other than casual and temporary, on both sides. He was good-looking, intelligent and reasonably affluent, so they would assume that he was some kind of rough diamond. They would be attracted by his composure but they would be baffled to find that it was only skin deep, a veneer of civility. He was never abusive, never deliberately cruel or controlling. He didn't care enough to want to control anyone. He was, in the last analysis, utterly indifferent. Why did women always expect more? He had nothing to give. Nothing whatsoever. They always thought they would change him, win him round, but they never did.

In his hotel room, he showered, dressed and went out into the city for a while, but there was almost nothing that he remembered until he walked down to Bewleys where the smell of coffee and baking, where the sight of the stained glass windows, bright jewels in the wintry street, brought his mother vividly into his mind again. He ought to go and visit her. Her letters were short and neat. She didn't have much to say to him. God bless you, she wrote at the end of each note. God bless you, Finn. Who was he to turn down blessings? He went into a bar, drank a couple of whiskeys, ate a bland lasagne and went back to his hotel where he slept fitfully, his dreams full of uneasy fragments of the past.

In the morning, he consulted his road map and drove out of the city. It took him a long time to find the place and his chief impression was of its deliberate remoteness. He understood why it had been almost impossible to escape from it. Why the older boys who had tried, had invariably been brought back by the Gardai. At first, he drove through monotonous agricultural land, past farms, new bungalows, affluent churches, villages set among fields and hedges, quiet streets with pubs, shops, signposts to the occasional tourist attraction, usually some prehistoric site or other . Sometimes a stately home, or the remains of one. But gradually this civilised countryside gave place to something fiercer, more hostile, especially now, in winter.

He was in a wilderness of peat bogs with the wind blowing un-hindered across them. He stopped, consulted his road map, drove on towards a line of low hills. A narrow road with grass sprouting down the middle wound along a valley. He could feel it swishing beneath the car. Stunted thorns fringed the road. He had not passed another car for the last half hour. It was mid-afternoon already. The sky was a uniform grey. At last, he found what he was looking for: the entrance to a driveway, twin stone pillars almost hidden from view by ivy and a dense blackthorn hedge. Sloes. They had gathered sloes where they could find them and tried to eat them to satisfy their extreme hunger but the fruits were bitter and had made them sick. If he had not had a map, he would never have recognised the place. His comings and goings had been infrequent. Once you were there, there you stayed.

He turned right and drove slowly along the uneven track, seeing almost nothing he remembered. But then, rounding a bend, he came upon what had once been the Brothers' garden, its wall crumbling so that the inside was laid bare, a jumble of shrubs, bushes and ancient fruit trees. Nature had done its work all too well, and the once-green lawns had been obliterated by a tangled mass of vegetation. Even now, in winter, it would be difficult to fight your way in. He was almost cheered by the sight of so much disorder where once there had been perfection and plenty. He drove on.

Around the next bend, he saw the house and his foot found the brake. It was in a state of advanced dilapidation that gave it the look of some mediaeval ruin, although there was no great age to the building. It was a late Victorian Anglo-Irish edifice, perhaps one of those country houses built as a status symbol with new money and then adapted haphazardly over the years to suit its changing purpose. Neglect and abandonment had given it a sinister beauty. The roofs had been stripped, deliberately, it seemed. The windows were broken, perhaps by wind and weather, perhaps by country children, throwing stones. But who would venture out so far just to vandalise this place? Well, perhaps there were some who would, he thought. There was a crucifix perched on one of the gable ends. It looked pathetic. An anomaly.

He drove on for a couple of hundred yards, parked his car some distance away from the house and got out. His hand was shaking when he tried to put the keys in his coat pocket. His feet sank into mud as he walked towards the building, found a door swinging loose on its hinges, pushed it open and went inside. His heart was in his mouth. What did he expect? Demons lurking in corners, waiting to snatch at him from the shadows? For sure, the place was disturbing. Terrifying even. The rooms were leprous with damp, paper shredded off the walls like peeling skin, the floors deep in bird droppings, plaster fragments, all of it stinking of mildew. The very air of the place seemed sickly, heavy with decay, but there were no cries, no shouts, not so much as a whisper. Nothing human. And it was human beings who had rendered this place truly terrifying. The stairs were perilous and he did not attempt them. He just stood at the bottom, his hand on the banister rail, peering up towards the faint grey light of the upper floors. Instead of demons, Francis came walking into his mind. Sweet Francis. He could almost hear him singing, the notes dipping and soaring like birdsong.

The winter it is past, and the summer's come at last, and the little birds they sing in the trees.

What had really happened to him? Had it been an accident? Over the years Finn had come to understand that memory could not be trusted. You told yourself stories in an effort to impose shape and meaning on the chaos of your life. And then somehow, those stories began to seem like true accounts. He had not seen what had happened to Francis, but he had heard and he could imagine. In one scenario, he saw Francis, blinded by his own desperation, climbing onto the polished wooden rail and jumping off. In Francis' shoes, he could just about imagine that he might have done it. But there was a much more disturbing image that came to him from time to time, like a flashback to something seen, although he knew fine he had been in bed with the thin sheet pulled over his head, because that was what they always did on these nights. And he had seen nothing. Not with his own two eyes. Nevertheless, he could see it. Could see Francis, poor, skinny Francis, vulnerable as a puppy and quite as unable to defend himself. Francis, who was due to leave the school any day now, on the point of escaping for good. Francis, his thin frame bent over the banister and then, savagely, tipped head first into the darkness below.

A sudden flurry of sound and movement from above made him jump, but it was only panic-stricken pigeons, flapping away, indignant at his intrusion. The house was wasting away and would never be resuscitated now. Who would want to? It was haunted by the memory of the evil it had once contained. You wouldn't want to live here. Wouldn't want to spend more time than you had to. There were no ghosts here. No demons. It was just a building, a shrivelled shell and like the misery it had once contained, there was a kind of banality in it. It was a sad, bad old place. But the only ghosts were in his head.

He went out again, breathing in the chilly air with relief, clearing his lungs, leaving the door to swing open behind him. He wished somebody would come along and finish the job. Burn the place down to the ground. When he got to his car, he turned and looked back at the house. Behind the ruined building was a long, low ridge, covered in trees. It had begun to rain, heavily. But the sun, emerging from a bank of dark clouds as it sank towards the western horizon, was turning the whole sky a livid shade of ochre. A strange and wonderful sound, growing in volume, distracted him. He saw a great mass of rooks, hundreds, perhaps thousands of birds, filling the yellow sky, tumbling like so many flakes of ash from some massive conflagration, soaring above and falling towards the trees behind the house. The sight and the sound, bizarre, but wholly natural, raised his spirits. He felt his heart give a leap of pleasure. Who would have thought it, in such a place? He remembered another time, another place. Watching the rooks fly back to Ealachan. The warmth. The weight of the green-heart rod. Alasdair teaching him to cast. Kirsty, watching. His darling Kirsty. Tick tock, he thought. Tick tock.

Time passed. He didn't know how long, but when he came to himself, he saw that darkness had fallen. He got into his car and drove away without a backward glance. Another night and then he would go back to Scotland and get on with the rest of his life.

Chapter Twenty Eight

DUNSHEE WAS ON the market. Eighteen months had passed since Kirsty had had that one tantalising glimpse of Finn. Two oil rig disasters, Finn's and Piper Alpha, in as many years, had affected the Laurence family business badly. The firm, which dealt in safety equipment of all kinds, had been forced to pay out a share of the compensation. Their standards had been criticised. Nicolas muttered about commercial pressures but they would have to sell off some property if they were to survive. Malcolm Laurence declared that he would sell Ealachan over his dead body but some of the farms would have to go. When a tiny bungalow, quite suitable as a retirement cottage, fell vacant in the village, Nicolas felt that the time had come to move Alasdair and sell Dunshee. What with the views and the beach, it should fetch a tidy sum. Somebody would surely pay handsomely for an island retreat.

'You do realise it will kill him, don't you?' said Kirsty, wildly.

'Don't be so melodramatic. I'll even renovate the bungalow for him. You can chose the colour scheme if you like. He's too old to be doing farm work and we can't afford to subsidise him any longer.'

People had been coming to look at the farm, but only intermittently. One man arrived by helicopter. He said he was considering it as a meditation centre but found it much too isolated. He didn't appear to notice the irony of this. Many of the potential buyers were in search of a Hebridean holiday home. They were all looking for peace and quiet. All of them found Dunshee too remote for their urban tastes.

'It isn't quite what we thought it would be,' they said, even when they saw it green and bonny in summer. God knows what they would make of it in winter.

Kirsty insisted on being there to show people around. Her

grandfather would be living there until the place was sold and entry dates agreed. The bungalow was being renovated and decorated. No expense would be spared.

'And why not?' said Kirsty to her husband. 'It'll still be your property. When he dies, you'll have one more holiday home to rent out.'

'Which won't be for a very long time, I hope,' said Nicolas evenly. She believed him, but it didn't make the proposed move any easier. Her grandfather seemed to have shrunk in the past few months. He walked through the house with her, stroking his furniture, the old dresser, the brass bedstead that he had slept on all his married life. It would be much too big for his bedroom in the bungalow.

'What will I do with all my things?' he asked querulously. 'And what about your mother's ornaments?'

She knew that they should already be sorting and packing, but she couldn't bring herself to begin. It would be better to do everything in a hurry at the last minute. That way it wouldn't be too painful for either of them.

Her own bedroom was the hardest to bear. She showed people round and had to listen to them calling her bed 'quaint' and 'sweet' and 'primitive'. Some planned to keep it just as it was. Some mused that they could turn it into a big cupboard because 'who could possibly sleep in there?'

'I did,' she said, and the woman turned to look at her as though she was some strange, outlandish creature.

'You did?'

'Yes. This was my bedroom. I used to sleep in here when I was a child. And as an adult as well. It was very comfortable in winter. Very warm.'

You can even make love in it, she thought.

Deep misery had spawned a sort of boredom in her. She couldn't bear to listen to these people, never mind enthuse about their plans for her old home. One or two of them even went to survey, but nobody made an offer, and Nicolas's visions of a closing date with eager bidders came to nothing. Perhaps the price was just too high. Then, in August, Nicolas's saviour arrived in the shape of a smart young man, driving a red Jaguar off the ferry. He had made an appointment to view. His name was John Grainger and he called at Ealachan and drove up to Dunshee with Kirsty beside him. He was a very charming young man and made polite conversation all the way up the track, although the wear and tear on his vehicle must have been colossal and she could see him wincing every time they negotiated a particularly deep rut.

At the farm, he got out of the car and pulled a brand new Barbour jacket over his suit, although it was a warm day.

"Yes, yes, I see,' he said all the time. When she asked him if he wanted to go down to the beach, he glanced at his shoes, shuddered and shook his head firmly. 'No. That won't be necessary, thank-you very much.'

He had brought a plan of the land and checked it over with her against an ordnance survey map that he produced from one of the Barbour pockets.

'There could be more land available for rent if need be. But I don't think whoever buys it will want to farm it. Do you, Mr Grainger?'

He ignored the question and traced the contours of the hill at the back of the house with his fingertip. 'So from here, behind the house, right up there and as far as the sea, all that is being sold with the farm as well? Am I right?'

'Yes it is. But there's no real beach on the other side. The only beach is the one on this side, in front of the house. There's an iron age hill fort up there and then just cliffs. There's one place where you can get down. A sort of stair in the rocks. But it's very wild over there.'

She remembered Finn scrambling down these rocks in search of the gulls' eggs her grandfather had liked to eat when he could get them. Tern eggs were 'like the best caviar' said Alasdair, although to her knowledge he had never tasted the stuff. It had been a perilous occupation since the birds would attack your unprotected head. She remembered waiting anxiously for Finn to reappear and the relief of seeing his upturned face as he clambered back up. He was holding the eggs in a leather bag, being careful not to break them. She had taken his hand and hauled him up and over the edge where he rolled onto the short turf, his long arms and legs starfished out, still keeping the eggs intact, laughing.

'Jesus,' he said. 'They're so savage. I thought they would peck my eyes out!'

'Why wouldn't they when you were raiding their nests? I would peck your eyes out as well!'

She shook the memories away with an effort. 'Do you want to go up there?' she asked the young man. 'I'll take you, if you like.'

'No, no. I'll take your word for it.'

Her grandfather had made a pot of tea. He slammed it down on the kitchen table, along with thick white mugs and a plate of shortbread from the post office. Nicolas had suggested real coffee. He had read somewhere that the scent of it encouraged buyers. Alasdair's reaction to this was unrepeatable. He only ever drank Camp coffee with Nestlé's condensed milk. When Kirsty was little she used to steal a sweet, sticky teaspoonful or two from the tin that he kept in the kitchen cupboard. She knew that Alasdair wanted to tell this smart young man to bugger off and leave him in peace. The injustice of it all rose like bile in her throat. This is his home, she thought. His home that we are selling over his head. And I'm doing this to my own grandfather!

The young man took off his jacket, sat down at the kitchen table and drank his tea.

Partly to break the silence, she said, 'Excuse me for asking, but you don't exactly seem very interested in the property.'

'Ah,' he said. 'Didn't your husband tell you? I'm acting for a client.'

'No he didn't tell me.'

Par for the course, she thought. Another southerner with more cash than sense and a wholly illusory impression of life on a small Scottish island.

'Did he say anything to you, grandad?'

Alasdair shook his head. 'When did your Nicolas ever confide in me?'

'What kind of client?' she asked, wondering if it was anybody famous.

'Just somebody looking for a countryside retreat. He saw this place advertised and thought it might fit the bill.'

'Not a farmer then.'

'I don't think so.'

'Well you can tell him from me, it won't be what he expects.'

'What makes you say that?'

'Because it never is, that's why. I can tell you right now, he'll find it too cold, too muddy, and not half civilised enough. You'll be doing him a favour if you tell him to forget all about it. Find him a nice cottage in the Cotswolds. That'll be more his style.'

Grainger looked round the kitchen and cleared his throat. 'Will you be needing all of your furniture, Mr Galbreath?'

'I can't take all of it with me, if that's what you mean,' said Alasdair. 'Not to a house that size.'

'It's just that we could perhaps negotiate a price to include whatever furniture you want to leave. If he decides to take things further, of course.'

Kirsty looked at her grandfather. 'I suppose you might be able to leave some stuff here, grandad? Better than storing it at Ealachan. Mind you, it would have to be a separate sale; the furniture doesn't belong to the estate.' She frowned at the young man. 'I know that sounds a bit odd, but I'm only here for my grandad's sake. It's been his home all his life, you know. And mine too. He doesn't really want to leave.'

'It must be quite a wrench.' He seemed taken aback by Kirsty's forthright declaration.

'Yes. It is.'

She felt sorry for him. After all, none of this was his fault.

'What's he like then, this client of yours?'

'To tell you the absolute truth, I've never met him. He dealt with my boss. I'll report back to him and, no doubt, he'll tell the prospective purchaser all about the place. But it'll only be one of a whole portfolio of properties he'll be considering. That's usually what happens.'

'Oh well.' She stood up, looking down at her grandad. Her heart ached for him. 'Do you want to see anything else?'

'No, thank-you. I've had a good tour of the house and that's all I need really.' Kirsty saw that they had made him very uncomfortable and felt a pang of guilt.

'What a lovely picture,' he said, staring at the wall behind Kirsty's head.

She looked round and saw her own painting of Dunshee with Hill Top Town behind. She had painted it in spring, exaggerating the dilapidation. The house was falling down but it looked as though it were falling into drifts of primroses and violets and bluebells, sinking slowly into swathes of yellow and purple that bruised the very land it stood on.

'My grand-daughter's work.' Alasdair nodded proudly at Kirsty.

'It's very beautiful. Quite disturbing really.' He could no longer contain himself. 'You're Kirsty Galbreath, aren't you? I mean, *the* Kirsty Galbreath.'

Kirsty used her own name on her paintings now. As always, she was faintly embarrassed by praise of her work.

'Why? Have you seen my paintings before?'

'Yes. In fact, we have one at home. It's called *Machair*. My wife loves it. Well, I love it too. I bought it for her when we got married.'

'I'm very glad you like it. I was quite fond of that one myself. I'd better take you back to Ealachan. You'll want to speak to my husband before you go.'

'Yes please.' He shook hands with Alasdair. 'Thank-you very much for your time, Mr Galbreath.'

To her considerable surprise, the sale went through. Dunshee was sold to a firm of solicitors with an address in Glasgow's West End. Nicolas knew that this was a 'back to back' arrangement. The solicitor would instantly sell the property on to his client. He found this suspicious and wondered if there might be some business rivalry involved, but couldn't fathom why any company would want to buy such a run-down farm, even as a toe-hold on the island. The planning regulations were too stringent to allow any unsuitable development. He decided that the buyer was simply obsessively secretive: a minor celebrity with delusions of grandeur. Besides, he badly needed the money. Under Scots Law, the sale became binding once the offer was made and accepted. A formal entry date in October was set, though the cash for the property was paid immediately. The new owner would be visiting in September and he had asked that Kirsty's grandfather should remain at the house, at least until after the visit.

'Very strange to buy first and view later. He must be quite mad,' said Nicolas.

'But his money's good?'

'Oh yes, his money is very, very good.'

'Then what do you have to complain about?'

'Nothing. Just so long as he doesn't have anything to complain about either. But if he's coming soon, I won't be here, you know. I'm going to be in the States. Can you manage on your own?'

'I'm sure I can. Everything's arranged. There are only a few details to finalise.'

'I hate to land you in it, but I can't avoid this trip you know.'

'It's all right, Nick. Besides, it's probably better if it's me who deals with him. It's going to be very difficult for my grandad. You know that.'

'Alasdair will be fine, once he's installed in the new place. He'll wonder why he didn't move years ago.'

'So he's not to pack anything up until after the new owner has been and had a look at it?'

'That's what he said.'

' Do you think he's going to make him an offer for the contents?'

'Oh, Christine,' said Nicolas, shaking his head in disbelief. 'There's nothing very special up at Dunshee. I can't see it. Can you?'

He was happy to have the house off his hands. The contents were really none of his business. Nor was the buyer.

Later that week, and just before Nicolas was due to leave on his trip to America, the solicitor phoned again to arrange his client's visit. He would be coming over on an early ferry and spending only one day on the island.

'Let's hope he's married with children,' said Nicolas. 'Somebody suitable for the girls to play with when they're at home.'

'They would have to be suitable, wouldn't they Nick?'

'Well. You know what I mean.'

'Let's hope he lives up to your expectations.'

Chapter Twenty Nine

IN THE CONSERVATORY at Ealachan, Kirsty was waiting for Dunshee's new owner. She was watching the clock, hearing its steady beat and the 'ting' as it struck the quarter hours, and she was visualising the ferry pulling in to the harbour. She found Nick's absence a relief, but India was away at school in St Andrews now, and Kirsty missed her all the time. She poured herself another mug of coffee. Flora had already left for the village primary school. She had become very concerned about her clothes recently, spending all her pocket money on fashion magazines, but she was always forgetting things: her sweatshirt, her gym bag, her hairslide. She was so sweet natured and apologetic that it was hard to be cross with her. Kirsty felt that she was fending off the day when Flora too would be sent away.

Before he left for the States, Nicolas had gone up to the farm, accompanied by one of the gardeners, and they had moved a couple of decrepit vehicles and several heaps of scrap metal from the yard. Most of the animals had been sold off to neighbouring farmers, although a few remained, including the old horse and a small flock of sheep. Alasdair couldn't bring himself to part with them. Jess, the arthritic collie, would go with him to his new house. There were a couple of semi-feral cats too but they would just have to stay on the farm since they had resisted all attempts to catch them. Perhaps she could persuade the new owner that they would deter vermin. Alasdair had also kept a few chickens which he intended to house in the tiny back garden of his new bungalow, though his neighbours didn't know it yet.

'If the worst comes to the worst, we could always find room for the chickens here,' said Nicolas.

Kirsty had also been up to the farm and had filled half a dozen black bin bags with old newspapers, cardboard boxes, anonymous bits of plastic, things Alasdair had been hoarding for God knows what purpose, alongside out-of-date packets and tins from the bathroom and kitchen cupboards. She had found a long forgotten cache of her mother's medicines at the back of a drawer: eleven year old tubes of ointment, bottles of sinister-looking liquid, medications that had done no good at all.

That morning, Kirsty had already phoned her grandfather to make sure that he was up and about, the house spic and span, the range lit and the kettle boiled.

'Aye,' he said, in answer to all her questions. 'And I've had a bath,' he added, finally. 'So I'll not disgrace you, my Cairistiona.'

'I'm sorry, grandad. I don't mean to go on at you.'

She didn't much care what the new owner thought, but Nicolas had been nagging her about making a good impression. It was not like him either, this generalised anxiety, but the air of secrecy surrounding the sale seemed to have affected him. The arrangement was that the new owner would come first to Ealachan. Then, Kirsty would drive him up to Dunshee. She was more certain than ever that leaving the farm would break her grandfather's heart. Sometimes she thought that it would break hers as well. India had wept over the sale and Kirsty had felt like weeping with her. She understood her daughter's distress. When she was down here among the trees the energy just drained out of her. India probably felt the same.

Kirsty was startled by the roar of an engine. A motorcycle had stopped right outside the front door on the wide gravelled space there, throwing up a little shower of pebbles as it drew to a halt. She went to the window of the drawing room. Kirsty knew next to nothing about bikes, but she realised that this was an expensive machine, a powerful trail bike, designed for the hills. She found herself running through the hallway and out of the front door, onto the wide top step, her heart hammering. There was a rushing in her ears.

The man riding the bike was wearing black leathers and a gleaming helmet. He dismounted from the bike with a sudden fluid movement and turned towards her, but she couldn't see his face. She saw herself reflected in the helmet. Somewhere, in the deepest recesses of her mind, she knew it. She put out one hand as though to push something away. Or grasp something close. He pulled off the helmet and the glossy black hair, shot through with grey, spilled out.

He said 'Kirsty?' Just her name. With a measure of uncertainty. 'Kirsty?' and finally 'Cairistiona?'

Everything started to go faint and far away. She could see a corona of stars in her field of vision, pinpricks of light that twinkled on and off. She tried to steady herself but her hands met empty air on both sides. The doorway was too wide to offer support. She saw that it really was Finn O'Malley and crumpled in a faint on the doorstep.

When she came to herself, only a few seconds later, she was conscious that Finn was kneeling beside her, holding her hand. Even in all the confusion of the moment, even while her brain struggled to latch onto reality, she felt the familiarity, the intense pleasure of Finn's fingers twined with her own. She struggled to sit up.

'It's really you!' she kept saying, 'Oh God it's really you!'

At last, Finn helped her up but still she wouldn't let go of his hand for fear that he should turn out to be a dream, a mirage, for fear that he should disappear forever.

'D'you think we could go in?' he asked, gently. 'My Kirsty?'

She swayed a little, and he slipped his other arm round her. 'You need to sit down,' he said. 'Through here?'

She nodded. They went into the conservatory and, coming to herself at last, she moved away from him with a sudden, convulsive effort and sat down.

'It's all right, Kirsty,' said Finn. 'It's all right.' He was crouching in front of her and looking directly into her eyes. He looked older, with fine lines around eyes and mouth. But not that much different. 'I'm sorry. I shouldn't have surprised you like this.'

She couldn't help herself. She put out her hand, touching the soft hair.

'You're not going, are you?'

'I'm not going anywhere. Trust me.'

'It's you, isn't it?'

'Yes. I've bought Dunshee. I'm the one you're waiting for.'

'Dear God, I knew it.'

'Don't say all that deception was for nothing.'

He smiled at her and her heart turned over. Bizarrely, she had a sense of extreme terror. She wanted to take his hand again, hold onto him and never let him out of her sight. At the same time, she wanted to thrust him away from her, to run, run for all she was worth and hide from him in the furthest recesses of the house.

'No. It worked all right. Nicolas fell for it hook, line and sinker.'

'He always underestimated me. And you?'

'I fell for it too, at first. But there was something about it, something about all those conversations about the house and the contents and my picture. It just seemed very peculiar. I hardly dared to hope but I had a feeling ...'

'But you didn't mention it to Nicolas? This feeling?'

'Of course not. He wouldn't have believed me anyway. He would have thought I had finally gone crazy. Maybe I have. And why the secrecy, anyway?'

'Because I thought Nicolas might not want to sell it to me if he knew who was buying it.'

'You don't know how strapped for cash my husband has been.'

'Family firm in trouble?'

'You know it is.'

'Good.'

'Don't say that, Finn. This family firm is mine as well.'

'I know that. And I'm sorry. He isn't here, is he?'

'No. He's in the States. But you knew that as well, didn't you? Your solicitor must have told you.'

'I cannot tell a lie. I knew it.'

'I still don't understand.'

'How could I afford it, you mean?'

'Well, that too.'

'Lot of water under the bridge, Kirsty. A lot of things have happened to me in the last eleven or twelve years and some of them have been, oh, quite lucrative. And now I've bought Dunshee off your husband. Or to be more accurate, my solicitor bought it and I bought it off him. We came to a little arrangement.'

'Is that legal?'

'Of course it's legal. I'm not stupid, although Nicolas seemed to think I was, all those years ago.

Kirsty was still gazing at him as though he might vanish if once she let him out of her sight. He looked at her, dropped his gaze, looked at her again.

'Ah, Jesus,' he said 'What have they done to your hair?'

'It was me. I had it cut.'

'So I see.'

'You don't like it?'

'You know what? I don't care, just so long as it's your face I'm seeing. Your voice I'm hearing.'

'I think I must be dreaming. Am I dreaming? How long has it been? Eleven years. Not to phone or write in eleven years!'

'I'm certain I thought about you a bit more than you ever thought of me,' he said with a touch of bitterness.

'That's not true!'

'Well, I can't say I'm sorry if I gave you a few sleepless nights.'

'And you've really bought Dunshee?'

'I have.'

'But how could you afford it?'

'Well, for one thing, I got a tidy sum in compensation for the accident.'

'I saw you. I saw you when you came off the rig. You were on the television news. I tried to contact you. But nobody would tell me where you were. It was like losing you all over again.'

It came out as a wail, querulous and childish. She controlled herself with an effort. 'And then I thought you might be married, with a family. And I didn't want to intrude.'

'No. I'm not married.' He looked into her eyes, putting the smallest of stresses on the 'I'.

'You could have died.'

'But I didn't die. I'm here. It's taken two years, but the money finally came through at the right time. Just as your husband decided to sell Dunshee over Alasdair's head. Fortuitous, eh? Mind you, I would have tried to buy it anyway and I might have scraped together enough, even without the compensation. The money just made things a whole lot easier.'

Kirsty gazed at him, seeing him properly for the first time, thinking that he was different. Physically he hadn't changed much. His face was more lined, more weather-beaten. There was the odd grey streak in the black hair. He still looked as though he would feel more at home outdoors than inside, but he had lost that shambling awkwardness that put him at such a disadvantage when it came to dealing with people like Nicolas. Now, he seemed a force to be reckoned with, the Irish accent moderated into a soft, educated burr. Finn neither looked nor behaved like a farmhand.

'It's all right,' he said again. 'I'm not going anywhere, I promise you. But do you think we could have some coffee? I could really do with a cup of coffee.'

'I'll get Heather to make some. She's in the kitchen.'

'Heather?'

'She helps out around the house.'

'Jesus, Kirsty, how times have changed. You have servants now. Other than me, I mean.'

'Not servants. No. She's a housekeeper. Nick does a lot of entertaining. And you were never a servant.'

'No, I was the brownie, wasn't I? Working for love.'

'This is a big house. Nick works from home a lot. She just helps.'

He had wrong footed her. She went into the kitchen, asked Heather to bring in a tray of coffee and went back to the conservatory, half expecting to find that he had disappeared. But he was still there, pacing up and down, gazing out of the windows at the garden. They sat down on opposite sides of the table.

'Nice room,' he said, but his eyes were focussed on hers. 'I was never in here before.'

She was fighting every hungry inclination of her body. She wanted to rush at him and embrace him. She couldn't think of anything to say to him. Or perhaps she could think of so much that she hardly knew where to begin. She just sat there, looking at him, twisting her fingers in her lap, torn between her dreadful fear of losing him again and her equal fear of what his presence might mean.

'I can't believe you're here,' she said. 'I'll wake up tomorrow and think it's all been a dream.'

'It's not a dream.'

'But you're only here for the day. That's what they told me. You're going away again.'

'For a little while. Just to sort things out. I promise I'll be back soon.'

'And the house? What are you going to do with the house?'

I'm planning to live there. What else? Maybe even farm in a small way. I've bought enough of the land to make that possible. And I've got some consultancy work.'

'What kind of consultancy?'

'Engineering. Don't look so surprised. You can change your whole life around in twelve years if you're single minded. And I *was* single minded, Kirsty. But I made a discovery about myself as well.'

'What?'

'That I'm quite bright.'

'I always told you you were.'

'You and your grandfather both.'

'Where did you go?'

'To Glasgow at first. I managed to get a job and some qualifications. And then I got a grant and a university place to do engineering. I've even worked in the USA. I saved quite a lot. I had very little to spend my money on. But now I've got the compensation money as well, I can afford to spend it on a smallholding.'

'Most of the stock has gone.'

'We'll start again. In a small way. I'm in no hurry about any of this, Kirsty.'

Her hand flew to her mouth. 'Oh my God, my grandad!' She started to laugh. 'He's waiting to meet the new owner. You didn't tell him, did you? He isn't keeping your secrets as well?'

'No. I thought he might let it slip. Do you think he'll be pleased?'

'When he gets over the shock, he will.'

'We'll go up there when we've had our coffee. But you'd better phone him and warn him who you're bringing.'

'The shock of just seeing you would kill him. It almost killed me, Finn! But what will I say to him?'

'Well, there's something else. And I want your grandfather to know before your husband does.'

'What?' she asked, but he just shook his head.

'We'll talk about it at Dunshee.'

Helplessly, she leant forward and seized his two hands again. 'Oh Finn! I can't believe you're here. I keep thinking you'll disappear.'

At that moment, Heather came in, carrying a tray of coffee and cake. If she was shocked to see Kirsty, hand in hand with the visitor, she remained remarkably composed. She was new to the island and had never met Finn before. Kirsty let go of his hands, blushing furiously.

'This is Finn O'Malley,' she said. 'He's the new owner of Dunshee, but we're old friends. I didn't know. I didn't know it was Finn who had bought it!'

'That'll have been a nice surprise for you.'

'It's a lovely surprise. We haven't seen each other for years.'

Heather smiled at Finn in a professional manner, put the tray down on the table, and left them to their coffee. But Kirsty felt as though there was something in the air of the room that certainly hadn't been there before. Finn had brought it with him, like a cold wind blowing in from the sea.

While he sat in silence, drinking strong black coffee, Kirsty phoned her grandfather.

'I thought you'd be here by now,' he said, plaintively.

'There's been a delay.'

'Did he miss the ferry?'

'No. No, he's here. And we'll be coming up soon. I don't quite know how to tell you this, grandad. It's somebody you know.'

'What are you talking about, Kirsty?'

'The person who bought Dunshee. You know him. You know him very well.'

'I don't know anyone with that amount of cash. If I did I would have touched him for a bob or two long ago.'

'You do. He just doesn't want you to get a shock when you see him.'

'Are you having me on, Kirsty?'

'No. No, I'm serious.'

'Well come on lass. Who the hell is it?'

Finn gestured to her to give him the phone. She handed it over.

'Hello there, Mr Galbreath,' said Finn. 'Alasdair. It's me.'

There was a very long pause. Then Finn said, 'Yes. Yes. I know. I'll be with you in a little while. Yes. She'll bring me up. I know. I know. I'm sorry. I'll make it up to you.' He handed the phone back to her. 'We should go.'

'What did he say?' asked Kirsty.

Finn grinned. 'He said, "Are you the bloody bum that walked out on me?" But I think he wants to see me. We'd better go.'

It was when they were up at Dunshee that Finn dropped his second bombshell. He had left the bike at Ealachan and they had driven together in near silence, Kirsty at the wheel with Finn beside her. She was acutely conscious of his proximity, wanting to reach out and touch him all the time, but restraining herself.

Like Kirsty, Alasdair couldn't hide his delight at the sight of the prodigal returned.

'Oh lad, lad,' he kept saying, 'It does my heart good to see you. I know I should be angry, but you don't know how good it is to see you again.'

Finn sat down beside the kitchen range, stretching out his long legs in front of him.

'Well,' he said, and although he was talking to Alasdair, he was looking at Kirsty. 'The thing is, I was wondering if you might just like to stay put, Alasdair.'

'Stay put?'

'Why should you move?' asked Finn. 'This was always your home. Did you really think I would come along and ask you to move out of it?'

He cast another look at Kirsty that managed to be both malicious and amused.

'Are you sure about this, Finn?' asked Kirsty.

'Of course I'm sure. We lived together for enough years. Nobody was ever as kind to me as you, Alasdair. Nobody. I'm sure we could live together again. What do you say?'

'And I don't have to move anything? Not my furniture?'

'Not a stick of it. Nor yet your few sheep, nor the chickens, nor the dog.'

'There's an old horse too,' added Kirsty.

'Oh the more the merrier.'

'Then I'll stay. But I don't know how I can ever begin to thank you, lad.'

'You don't have to thank me. I have more than enough to thank you for. I'll be in your debt till the end of my days.'

'Don't be daft.'

'That's settled then,' said Finn. He glanced at Kirsty. 'But there's one condition.'

'What's that?'

'You have to leave that picture for me, Kirsty. I love the picture. The one of the farm among the flowers.'

'Of course. I did it for my grandad anyway. But what am I going to tell Nick about all this?'

'What does it have to do with him?' asked Alasdair. 'He doesn't own this place any more. Finn does.'

'He has a house all ready for you, Grandad.'

'So you want me to move down there, do you?'

'No, of course not.'

'It won't go to waste. He can use it for something else now, can't he? Find himself another tenant. Use it as a holiday cottage.'

'But I don't know how I'm going to tell him. He'll think I knew. He's going to think I knew all about this and didn't tell him.'

'Didn't you?' asked her grandfather.

'No. I thought some publicity-shy celebrity had bought it.'

Finn was clearly enjoying her discomfiture. Sometimes, as the transaction progressed, he had wondered what the hell he was doing and why. Now, he put his hands behind his head and leant back on the familiar sofa, watching her.

'Ah God, God,' he said. 'I can't tell you how good it is to be home again!'

Nicolas was very angry. Kirsty had never before seen anyone incandescent with rage, but that's how she would have described him.

And she had been right. He was instantly and uncharacteristically suspicious of her role in the transaction.

'Did you know about this, Christine?'

'No, of course not. I'd have told you.'

'So you expect me to believe that he didn't tell you beforehand? Or your grandfather?

'I swear, it came as a complete surprise to both of us. And you needn't look so sceptical. I would have told you.'

'Would you?'

'Of course I would.'

'Then why all the secrecy? Why couldn't he have come clean?'

'I think he wanted it to be a surprise for my grandad.'

'Well, it was certainly that. And completely irresponsible. It could have killed the old man.'

'I don't think so.'

They had had arguments in plenty over the years, but none where he had accused her of breaking the trust between them.

'I think he wanted to have everything settled first. And you weren't exactly on good terms when he left, were you?'

'Can you blame me?'

'Well he's quite different now.'

'So I gather. And do you know, it was all that compensation or the knock-on effect of it that meant we had to sell in the first place.'

'There's a certain justice in it then, isn't there?'

'That's not what I would call it. This is all nonsense.' Nicolas was pacing about the room. Kirsty saw that he was still furious. Furious. 'The house is all ready and waiting for Alasdair. It's cost me a great deal of money to renovate it. I won't make the offer twice.'

'You don't need to. Finn and my grandad always got on well. There's no reason to suppose they won't get on just as well now. And you'll easily find another tenant for the bungalow, so you'll get a proper market rent for it. You can't lose, Nick. I don't really know what you're complaining about.'

The first thing Finn did was to take Kirsty's room for his own, sleeping in her old bed, in the wall. It was a good six inches too short for him, but he didn't seem to mind. Kirsty had been anxious about her grand-father for a week or two. In spite of all that she had said to Nicolas, she did wonder how they would get on, now that their positions were reversed, with Finn as the owner of the farm. But she needn't have worried. The two seemed to have resumed their old, easy relationship and Alasdair looked happier than she had seen him since Isabel's death.

Everyone else was trying hard to be civilised, Nicolas especially. It was impossible to avoid Finn altogether on an island as small as this one. He was always polite whenever they met, and Nicolas was invariably courteous. Flora was shy of Finn. On their first meeting, she stood very close to her mother and refused to shake hands with him, bunching her skirt up and sucking her thumb, a baby habit that she only resorted to in stressful situations. Afterwards, she said 'Why are you so happy mum? Is it because grandad doesn't have to move?' and Kirsty said 'Yes, it's wonderful, isn't it? He doesn't have to leave his home.'

Soon after, India came home for her half-term holiday. Flora was full of the news, and India had to pretend to be very blasé about it all. She walked up to Dunshee with her mother, but when she ran into the kitchen, there was Finn, sitting at the table and fiddling with his old fishing reel that he had found at the back of a cupboard. India seemed taken aback at finding him there, even though she had heard the whole story (several times over) from Flora. She and Finn stared at each other for a moment.

Then he stood up. 'You must be India.'

He reached out and shook her by the hand.

'How do you do?' she replied, very solemnly, and went over to kiss Alasdair. 'Can I play the fiddle, grandad? I've been learning new things at school.'

Finn stood with his arms folded, listening to her, and when she had finished he said 'You play beautifully.'

She didn't know how to respond to the compliment. Her self possession deserted her.

'You're a very clever little girl, India,' he said.

She coloured up and hung over the back of her grandad's chair, scowling at Finn as though daring him to say anything else.

Chapter Thirty

KIRSTY AND NICOLAS were planning to spend Christmas in London that year. Malcolm and Viola lived in a tall house in Maida Vale, its stonework crumbling, its paint flaking away from the walls. Kirsty was never comfortable there although her daughters liked it very much. There was an old nursery at the top of the house that was a treasury of vintage toys: a Noah's ark full of battered animals, a long legged horse on green rockers and a collection of Edwardian pond yachts. India and Flora were in their element.

Kirsty didn't want to go away for Christmas, but Nicolas argued that her grandfather would have Finn to keep him company.

'So we can go south without worrying about him,' he said and she was forced to agree.

Before they left, Kirsty drove up to Dunshee through sleety rain. She took a heap of parcels for her grandfather: pipe tobacco, a packet of strong tea, (Alasdair hated teabags), chunky milk chocolate, a new walking stick with a curly horn handle, some fishing tackle. Among the parcels, she had included a couple of gifts for Finn. One was a lavishly illustrated book of Celtic myths and legends including the story of Dermot and Grania. The other was a small photo frame in pewter. In it was a snapshot, taken years before, of Kirsty and Finn together, sitting in the old wooden boat, in shallow water. Finn's hands were on the oars while Kirsty was smiling at the photographer. Her grandfather had taken the picture. She must have been about nine, just a bit younger than India was now, and Finn thirteen, so it was before he had moved to Dunshee permanently. Kirsty was wearing shorts and a navy blue Aran sweater. Her hair was in plaits. Finn was thin and long legged and his hair was a shaggy nimbus.

He arrived each year as a shorn sheep and then it would grow as the summer progressed. Sometimes her mother had taken the shears to it, hacking off enough of it to make him decent again.

She had found the photo when she was helping her grandfather to clear out his papers. It was the only picture she had ever found of the two of them together. She'd had it copied on the mainland, wanting to keep the original for herself. She had enjoyed choosing these things for him. But now, when she was handing them over, they seemed too intimate, too personal, the kind of clandestine gifts a woman might buy for her lover.

Just before she left, he slipped his own little parcel into her coat pocket.

It was heavy for its size and solid. Not having any proper wrapping paper, he had done it up in white writing paper. He leant in at the car window.

'Enjoy your Christmas.' The wind was whipping his hair around his face. His hands, gripping the edge of the window, looked red and raw with the cold.

'I'll try!'

She turned her face up to him, tilting her cheek slightly, but he leant in, cradled the back of her head with one hand and kissed her hard on the mouth. His lips were cool and dry. The sudden stab of desire in the pit of her stomach took her by surprise. Her response to him was so immediate, so powerful, that it was as much as she could do to prevent herself from leaping out of the car and embracing him. With an effort of will, she stayed where she was.

This is impossible, she thought. Nothing's the same and you can't do it. You can't go back. It would be disastrous for everyone.

He released her, but she grasped at his fingers, anxious to maintain the contact between them for as long as possible. She looked up at him and saw the darkness behind his eyes.

I know him so well, she thought. But perhaps she hardly knew him at all. Her stomach churned in apprehension.

A squall was passing over and a sudden flurry of rain on the windscreen blinded her and drenched him. There were droplets on his eyelashes. He turned away and stumbled back inside the house. She sat there for a moment or two before she could bring herself to start the engine and drive back down to Ealachan.

It was Christmas night before she could find the time to open his gift. She had left it nestling at the bottom of her handbag. Now, when everyone else was in bed, exhausted by massive intakes of food and drink, she seized a few moments for herself. She wondered what Finn could have given her. Nowadays, if she wanted to wear the arrowhead pendant, she kept it tucked inside a sweater, but sometimes she wondered if Nicolas ever really looked at her closely enough to notice it. How had that happened? When had love become familiarity? When had he stopped gazing at her as though unable to believe his good fortune in marrying her and begun, instead, to jolly her along as though humouring a difficult child? What fault line between them had opened so gradually that she had barely noticed it?

She unwrapped the white paper and a stone tumbled into her lap. She recognised it at once; not this particular stone, but where it came from. It was an agate from the beach below Dunshee, or rather a half agate with the flat, oval face polished. It didn't have the gloss of a machine polished stone, but the matt shimmer of something the sea itself had smoothed. One summer, she and Finn had become obsessed with stones and had spent many hours looking for agates and identifying them with the help of a book from her grandfather's shelf. Finn had been reluctant at first but gradually, he too had been drawn in. They had been as enchanted by the names of the different stones as they were by the agates themselves: white chalcedony, blue chalcedony, celadonite, jasper, carnelian, moss agate, onyx agate, thunder egg.

This was a blue-grey quartz with streaks of green celadonite in it. It was a scenic agate with a landscape frozen into the quartz, a world within a world. A mass of mossy clumps at the base were seaweed clad rocks, or maybe twisted roots. Further off was a milky blue sea with white-topped waves. Some variation in the quartz gave the impression of a broad path leading to the horizon, like the reflection the moon made when it was full. There were mountains in the distance and turbulent light in the sky, the moon riding high above clouds. Mysteriously, some brownish fault in the quartz was a small boat with figures in it, just heading out to sea. There was a scrap of paper with it.

'This is a talisman,' he had written. 'I found it the first time I went back down to the beach. I think it was waiting for me. That's the two of us. In your grandad's boat. Setting out together. All my love, Finn x.'

She stared into it for a long time before she could bring herself to put it back in her bag and get into bed. She had the fleeting thought that maybe if she could find the right words, she and Finn could disappear into that enchanted landscape and stay there together, forever.

Early in the New Year, Flora was ill with influenza for several weeks. Nicolas came and went between the island and the mainland, with frequent trips further afield, fuming about some new setback to the family finances. Annabel had taken over an office beside Kirsty's gallery at Ealachan House and was spending more time on the island, although she still made frequent trips to the family home in London. At Ealachan, she devoted a great deal of her time to Flora, who had become a favourite with her.

'She's such a sweetie,' she told Kirsty. 'I love India very much but she's so ...'

'I know what you mean,' said Kirsty. India had many wonderful qualities and Kirsty loved her dearly, but you would never call her a sweetie. Flora was softer and less sure of herself, loving everyone indiscriminately and therefore, thought Kirsty, with a pang of apprehension for her daughter, vulnerable to the occasional disappointment.

When Annabel was not reading to Flora or playing games of Happy Families, she was trying to work on designs for a new jewellery collection. She had also taken to walking down to the beach at Dunshee, looking for driftwood and semi-precious stones, 'hunting for inspirational objects' she called it. Flora was too wobbly on her feet to walk far yet.

'I saw your friend Finn this morning.'

Annabel and Kirsty were sitting together in the gallery. Kirsty was trying to work, but she was listless and looking for any distraction. Annabel had made coffee.

'I asked him if he wanted to come for a walk with me but he wouldn't. Actually, I was angling for a ride on that fabulous bike. But I suppose that's out of the question. What a bird of ill omen he is, Christine!'

'No, he isn't!'

'You know what I mean. He'd be very good looking if only he would smile a bit more. What does he have to be so dismal about?'

'Oh that's just Finn!' It was the way she always fended off enquiries about him.

'Maybe you see a different side to him.'

'Maybe I do.'

'I'd like to get to know him better.'

'You didn't think much of him when we were kids.'

'That was different. Kids are little savages anyway. I was horrible back then. Such a snob.'

Kirsty found that the thought of Annabel getting to know Finn better was faintly upsetting. 'You probably wouldn't like him very much if you did get to know him,' she ventured.

'Surely there must be a nice, normal chap, buried somewhere beneath that grim exterior.'

'Must there?'

'So tell me more about him. I'm interested.'

Kirsty wished she had never started this conversation but felt forced to continue. 'I think maybe there's something lacking in him. Sympathy. Or do I mean empathy?'

'God, Christine!' said Annabel, in astonishment. 'This is your *friend* you're talking about.'

'I don't mean he's dangerous or anything like that. And I know we haven't always seen eye to eye, you and me, but I wouldn't like you to get hurt.'

Without ever growing particularly close or even understanding each other very well, they had become friends over the years. She had seen a vulnerable side to Annabel. None of her countless relationships had ever come to anything. Perhaps the men in her life were scared of her or perhaps she had just made wrong choices all the time and yet she was an attractive woman, always travelling hopefully, never quite arriving. Even her design business seemed amateurish and was only moderately successful in spite of the Laurence family connections.

'He's my good friend,' Kirsty conceded. 'He was like a brother to me when we were younger. Still is, in some ways. But he's not a very easy man to know.'

'He's been amazingly kind to Alasdair. Even Nicolas is forced to admit that. Grudgingly.'

'But then my grandfather was always very kind to him. When it really mattered. With Finn you get what you give. No more, no less. And even then, not always.'

'You mean I couldn't handle him?' Annabel asked, only half in jest.

'I think I'm trying to say that he's not like other people. He isn't just different. I think in many ways he's indifferent. He ... he had some terrible experiences as a child.'

'What experiences?'

'Even I don't know all the details. He was put in a boarding school back in Ireland. An industrial school.'

'What's that?'

'I don't know exactly. I think they used to be a bit like workhouses. All I know is, Finn was sent to this industrial school and it was a terrible place. He was very badly treated. Don't ever tell him we discussed this. But it's as if it made him switch something off. Some capacity to love and be loved. I think it's buried so deep inside him that he'll maybe never find it again. He isn't like the rest of us.'

'So what is he like?'

'What you see is exactly what you get. It isn't a pose. He won't mellow over time. Won't grow to like you when he knows you better. I think he really is indifferent to most people.'

'But he isn't like that with you, surely?'

'We go back a long way. And sometimes ... I don't think ...'

'What? Don't stop now. I'm intrigued.'

Kirsty gave a little sigh. As well be hung for a sheep as a lamb.

'I don't think I count as somebody else. Not for Finn, anyway.'

'What a very strange thing to say!'

'Well, maybe I'm just havering.'

Kirsty had a pad on her knee. As she spoke, she had been sketching little images of shells and flowers and seaweed. Annabel looked at them.

'Lovely'

'Do you think so? They're just doodles.'

'Even your doodles are more interesting than mine.'

'Your jewellery? I'll do a bit of work on the designs if you like. I didn't know whether you wanted help or not.'

'I need all the help I can get. And I suppose I'll just have to take your word for it about Finn. You think he wouldn't let me get close.'

'Feel free to try, but he lets almost nobody get close to him. Hardly even me. We were very close once upon a time. Like family. But he left here without a second thought, you know. Not a letter, not a phonecall. I know a little bit about what he is and why. I know that whatever happened to him was the kind of cruelty that makes you retreat deep inside yourself. I think Finn finds it very hard to escape.'

Annabel smiled ruefully. 'I doubt if he even notices me, and maybe that upsets my vanity a bit.'

'Haven't you got enough good-looking guys trailing around after you without adding one more scalp?'

'But we all want what we can't have. There's something so attractive about the unattainable, don't you think?'

'Maybe.'

But what do I want, thought Kirsty. She stared out of the window at the garden. There was the faintest haze of green over the shrubs and the purple and yellow of early crocuses on the grass. Up at Dunshee though, the snowdrops would still be in bloom, drifts of white against the grey stone walls. Finn was up there, a short walk away, but it might as well be a thousand miles.

Chapter Thirty One

EVEN DOWN AT sheltered Ealachan, Kirsty could hear the wind moaning about the old pitched roofs, a hostile creature stalking the inhabitants of the house. Spring might be coming, but the Atlantic lows were still rolling in from the west to buffet the island again and again. Lying beside Nicolas or alone, during his increasingly frequent absences, she imagined the magnified din of the storms up at Dunshee. She thought about Finn, wakeful in her old bed, for nobody could sleep through these gales. The noise was always monstrous up there, a relentless, deafening roar that engulfed the house and shook it to its ancient foundations. She remembered how often she had woken with a start from a restless doze, imagining that somebody or something was outside her room, tapping on the glass or rattling the door, desperate to gain access.

Since Christmas, she and Finn had met from time to time in the island shop where curious eyes observed them constantly. Gossip about them had been rife at first. 'Have you seen him? Have you seen the bike? Some change eh? What will she do? How will her husband take it?' Then things had calmed down. People had got used to seeing Finn about the place again. But the Christmas kiss had made her wary and for the past few weeks, they had talked only of trivialities, of things that didn't matter: the work at Dunshee, the weather, the prospects for the coming summer.

'He's certainly changed for the better,' admitted Nicolas.

'How do you mean, for the better?'

'Well, he seems more civilized for a start. He can hold an intelligent conversation these days.'

'Since when did you ever hold an intelligent conversation with Finn?'

'We do meet occasionally, Kirsty. In the village. In the hotel.'

'You mean you wouldn't be ashamed to introduce him to your friends?'

'I do mean that, yes.'

But Kirsty thought that this so-called civilization was only a veneer, although she didn't say as much to Nicolas. Her warning to Annabel had been no exaggeration. She knew that Finn was a stunted tree, like one of the fairy thorns behind the farm. Even she, who liked to name things, didn't have the words to describe him properly, although time and distance had given her a clearer perspective on him. Sometimes it seemed to her as though, all those years ago, a changeling had been left at Dunshee. This feeling was quite separate from her affection for him which ran, strong and true, through every inch of her.

In February, a Russian trawler, one of the large 'Klondikers' that fished these waters, ran aground on a reef at a place called Port Carrick on the western side of the island. All the able bodied islanders turned out to help.

Nicolas and Annabel were both away when the phone rang at Ealachan.

'I'm sorry to waken you, Kirsty,' said Robert Dunlop, a farmer from the north end, who was helping to co-ordinate the rescue and mustering assistance from all over the island. 'I thought Nick was at home.'

'No. He and Annabel were meant to be back yesterday but the ferry was cancelled because of the weather.'

'So it was. Never mind then.'

'I'll come though.'

'Are you sure?'

'Yes. Heather will be here for Flora. And we can put some people up at this house if necessary. We've got plenty of space.'

'That's very generous of you. But I think the hotel can probably cope.'

'Well, the offer's there. Have you phoned Dunshee yet?'

'Not yet. But I was going to. Do you think I should?'

'Finn will want to help. But do tell him not to let my grandad get involved. He's not up to it.'

'I'll do that, Kirsty.'

Daylight, if this gloomy, grey haze could be called light at all, revealed the big trawler, a stranded whale, wallowing in the heaving, green seas of the cove. The lifeboat couldn't get alongside in these conditions. They had managed to rig up a breeches buoy to take the crew from the shattered ship to the shore. Local fishermen and farmers had mustered, and Finn was in among them, lending expertise, muscle and encouragement. Watching from the shore, Kirsty felt a surge of panic, remembering that other night when she had seen him on television after the rig disaster.

The Klondiker would lie out there for months while the authorities haggled over salvage rights. The mackerel in her hold would rot and the stench would be appalling. Then, more gales would break her back and for a while, the seashore would be littered with bits of wood, metal, plastic and torn papers with mysterious Cyrillic script on them, great treasure for the island children when first discovered. A winter or so later, nothing would remain, wind and water having settled the salvage problem once and for all. The crew were all saved and the islanders took a dozen or so seamen to the hotel where they could be medicated, fed and housed, until they could be sent home.

The wreck held a great fascination for the islanders and in spite of the foul weather, people lingered on the shore for a long time after the rescue, watching the surge and swell of the waves breaking against the stranded hull. Kirsty found Finn sitting alone on a rock. She picked her way among boulders and hummocks of drenched heather.

'You did a great job there!'

He looked up and tried to smile at her but she saw, to her distress, that he was shivering. She sat down beside him and slipped her arm around him.

'People will see,' he muttered.

'Nobody's looking at us. They're all looking at that.' She nodded at the wreck. 'You can't help but look at it, can you?'

'No.'

'Are you OK?'

'Not really.'

'Have you hurt yourself?'

'No. No I'm fine. Grazed my hand on the ropes, that's all.'

They sat together in silence for a while. 'Does it bring it back?' she asked eventually. 'The rig and all that?'

'A bit.'

'I was thinking about it as well. It must have been appalling for you.'

'Sometimes I dream about it. I dream about being in the water. I'm trying to cry out, but I can't. I can't get the sounds out. And sometimes I can just be – I don't know – watching TV, cleaning my teeth, and it's like somebody switches it on. Like a movie. Like a daydream, but you can't stop yourself from thinking about it. And there I am, in the middle of it all again.'

One more thing to add to the terrible images that haunted him. His private library. Except that he had no control over what he was forced to see. The images assaulted him at random.

She tried to pull him closer, but he resisted her.

'The worst thing was …' He stopped.

'What?'

'There was a part of me that wanted to let go, stop fighting, have done with it all. Too hard, I thought. It's too hard. I'd been struggling for so many years. I just wanted to give in. Let the sea take me. And then you came into my mind, Kirsty. I had this sudden image of you, a bossy wee girl again. I was in the water and I thought I was going to die, and the idea of not seeing you one last time was unbearable. I knew then that I had to come back and see you. One way or another, I had to come back.'

'What are we going to do, Finn ?'

'How the fuck should I know? I thought things would just … I don't know what I thought.'

There was a sudden break in the weather, a patch of blue, a gleam of wintry sunshine. It would be an interval only. Already they could see the next band of clouds rolling in from the west, but Finn stood up and pulled her to her feet. 'The jeep's down on the track back there. There's a flask in it. Come on. Let's get some shelter.'

They sat in the muddy vehicle and drank milky coffee laced with whisky. Maybe the whisky loosened her tongue. Or maybe she couldn't bear not knowing.

'Why did you leave me?' she asked him, staring through the window at the driving rain. 'Why did you do that to me? And at such a moment!'

'Because I had to. You were right. You said I needed to get away. And I did. I could see that I would only hold you back if I stayed. You had enough on your plate. There were things I had to do. Things to sort out. I had to find my mother for one thing.'

'And did you find her?'

'Oh, God. Yes. I found her all right.'

'Where? Where was she, Finn?'

'Where she is still. In a convent. She's a nun.'

'Good Lord!'

'That's right.' He gave a short laugh. 'Good Lord is right. She was put to work for the nuns. In a laundry. It was virtual slavery. It happened to a lot of women. The courts committed them if they were judged to be leading immoral lives. But then, she couldn't beat them, so she joined them.'

Even as he said the words, he was aware that they were not quite true. He had come to believe that his mother's vocation was genuine. He didn't like it but whether he liked it or not didn't matter. Mary had her own path to follow. Her life had been interrupted just as his had been interrupted, and the disruption had changed her irrevocably, just as it had changed him. But he was forced to admit that she was doing what she wanted.

'She's Sister Dominica now. She seems happy enough. But she's not the person I remember. You can't trust anyone to stay the same.'

'I would have stayed the same. I would have gone to hell in a handcart with you back then!'

'Would you really?'

'You left *me*, remember!'

'I thought if I went, you would go away too. Back to university, back to your painting. I didn't want you thinking that you had to be tied to me when I had nothing to offer you. I thought your grandfather would probably persuade you to go back to Edinburgh. Once he had other help about the farm.'

'But to leave without saying a word. Without so much as a note to tell me where you'd gone!'

'I didn't know what to say. I didn't know where I was going. You don't know how often I almost came back. I planned to write to you. But time passed and then it seemed too late. I never imagined that you would marry Nicolas!'

'Why wouldn't I marry him? '

Because you loved *me*! He wanted to say it, but couldn't bring himself to speak the words aloud.

'How did you find out?' she asked.

He laughed ruefully. 'I saw it in a magazine.'

'You didn't!'

'I did.'

'Oh I'm sorry.'

He had been sitting in a dentist's waiting room in Glasgow with his tooth aching fiercely and he had been flicking through an old copy of Scottish Field to distract himself from the pain, when it had caught his eye. It was one of those typical 'society' wedding pictures with everyone grinning inanely: 'Mr and Mrs Malcolm Laurence of Ealachan House, their son Nicolas and his bride Miss Christine Galbreath.'

'I loved you so much, Finn. But you went away. What was I supposed to do with the rest of my life? I waited for you that night. I waited for you for ages and then I fell asleep because I was so exhausted. The next day, when I found that you'd gone, oh Finn, you'll never know what it did to me. I was heartbroken. Heartbroken.'

'But you went and married Nicolas anyway.'

'He was there and he was kind to me. He loved me.'

'Why so soon, Kirsty? Why did you marry him so soon?'

I thought you had gone for good. I thought, why not?'

'Jesus!'

'Nothing mattered to me after that. For a little while I hoped that you would come back, but then I realised you wouldn't, because that's the way you are, because that's how ruthless you are. It was as though somebody had switched off all the lights inside me.'

There was a long pause. Finn seemed to be steeling himself to speak. At last, he said, 'You're still not telling me the truth, are you?'

'What do you mean?'

'Kirsty! I have eyes in my head. I can see!'

'I have no idea what you're talking about.'

Fear seized her, a terror so acute and all encompassing that she could only gaze at him, rigid with apprehension.

'Maybe you shouldn't have given me that photograph for Christmas, Kirsty. If I suspected it before, I knew for sure as soon as I looked at it. India. She's the image of me, isn't she?'

'I don't know what you're talking about!'

'But Nick came to your rescue as usual, and you took the easy way out. Poor bastard. I don't suppose he knew what he was letting himself in for. I suppose he still doesn't. I suppose you're deceiving him, too.'

She gazed at him, shaking her head.

'Still lying?' he said. 'To me and to yourself! Jesus. If only I'd known …'

'Would that have made you stay? Would it have solved anything?'

'It might!'

'I don't think so. Not if you were so set on going.'

'Ah but I'm sick of it all, sick of the deceit and the misery. You've brought this on yourself, Kirsty.

'You've got it all wrong,' she repeated stubbornly. She couldn't let this happen. And to her relief, he seemed to capitulate.

'Have it your own way. Keep pretending. Even though she's a wee cuckoo in his nest.'

'Don't say that!'

'I'm surprised he doesn't see it. Your Nicolas. But I suppose we only see what we want to see. So what now, Kirsty? What now?'

'I don't know.'

'It's not too late.'

'I still want you for my friend.'

'Fuck that!' he said, furiously. 'Friendship? What good is your friendship to me?'

'But nothing's the same any more. And there are the girls to consider. I'm a wife and mother now.'

'Indeed you are.'

'It's too late. You have to see that it's too late for us to be anything but friends, Finn. '

'You mean you don't care to be around me any more.'

'I want to be with you all the time.'

'Then do something about it.'

'I can't.'

'Because you love Nicolas? Say it! Say you love Nicolas and you don't want to leave him.'

'I love my husband very much and I can't possibly leave him. It would break his heart. Like you broke mine.'

'Come home with me. Now. Come back to Dunshee.'

'I can't.'

'Why not?'

'Because too many other people would get hurt. And besides ...'

'Besides what?'

'I'm afraid.'

'Of what?'

'I'm afraid of the way you love me. Afraid of what it might do to both of us.'

He switched on the engine.

'I'll take you back to your car.'

'What are we going to do, Finn ?'

'How the fuck should I know?' he said angrily, and then didn't speak again until they reached her car, parked in a muddy lay-by at the side of the main road. He stopped, leaned over and opened the passenger door.

'Get out.'

'Finn!'

'For fuck's sake Kirsty, will you just get out and leave me alone.'

She got out and he drove away immediately, leaving her in the road. She got into her own car, turned on the engine and ran the heater to clear the misted windscreen before she could drive safely back to Ealachan.

Chapter Thirty Two

A DAY OR two later, when the winds had abated and Nicolas had managed to get home to the island, he sat her down and said, 'Darling, we have to have a serious talk.'

'Why?' she asked.

'Because things can't go on like this. It's not good news, I'm afraid. Not good at all. I think we're going to have to offload a lot more property. Certainly this place.'

'This place?'

'Well. Ealachan. We really need the money.'

She was confused. 'I don't understand.'

'Sell the place,' he said. 'Realise some capital. You know? Selling off the farm and the other places wasn't nearly enough.'

'But where will we live?'

'There's always Maida Vale. There's plenty of room. Mummy and daddy are rattling around that big house anyway.'

'Then why don't you sell that?' She thought about the tall house with its rooms stuffed with brown furniture and brown paintings.

'Couldn't do that. Need some sort of a base in London. We all do, Annabel included.'

'Couldn't it be a smaller base?'

'I can't throw my poor old father out of his home can I?'

No, but you could do it to my grandad, she thought.

'Your father always liked this place much better than London.'

'Maybe so but he's not fit to travel nowadays, is he? And in any case, he doesn't remember where he is from one day to the next.'

Malcolm had become vague and forgetful. He spent all his time up in the nursery at Maida Vale, playing with his collection of pond yachts, rigging and rerigging them, arranging them in little flotillas. He had even been known to fill up one of the cast iron baths and sail them up and down. 'Lee-oh!' he said. 'Going about!' He seemed profoundly happy. There were times when Kirsty envied him.

'We need to do something fairly drastic, and offloading this place, if we can, is the most realistic option. It was always a luxury. Now it's become one we can't afford.'

'What about me?'

'I've been thinking about that. It'll do you good, being in London. We could get you into more of the galleries down there. Annabel would help.'

'What will I paint?'

'Well, whatever you like, darling.'

'This is what I paint. This place.'

'But you could always paint something else, couldn't you?'

'No. I don't want to paint something else. This place is my inspiration. I can never have enough of it. Never come to the end of it. Never!'

She saw that he was looking at her with profound scepticism and knew that he didn't understand, would never understand what drove her.

'Nicolas?'

'Yes?'

'This is about more than selling Ealachan, isn't it? It's about your parents, too.'

'To some extent. My mother could do with a bit of help with dad. Annabel can't always be there. She has her own business to see to.'

'And what about my grandad?'

'He has Finn now, doesn't he? Worked out rather well that.'

'Will you be staying at home to help with your father? Or will you be taking off to the States at every available opportunity?'

Sometimes she suspected that it wasn't only business interests that took Nicolas over to the States so often. But how could she complain? 'Pots and kettles, Kirsty' that's what her mother would have said. 'Pots and kettles.' And yet she had done nothing wrong, nothing except renew an old friendship.

She saw him colour up. 'We do have business interests over there. In fact it's our best bet for solvency. But if you don't want to help with dad, we can always get a nurse in.'

'Christ, Nicolas, I wouldn't mind sailing his pond yachts with him, or whatever else he wants to do. It isn't that at all.'

'Well then'

She said nothing. She was trapped. One way or another, he would remove her from Finn's influence. Panic was succeeded by anger. If once she opened her mouth, the words would spill out and she wouldn't be able to stop herself. But what could she say that wouldn't sound unreasonable.

India was due home for the Easter holidays in less than a week. Nicolas had been in Edinburgh on business and was planning to make a detour to St Andrews, pick her up from school and bring her to the island with him. Flora had been back at the village school for the past month but was still looking peaky. Annabel had begged to be allowed to take her out of school a few days before the official start of the holidays and fly her off somewhere warm.

'Why not?' said Kirsty, conscious that her husband would not approve. School attendance was a point of principle with him, though Kirsty and Annabel had no such scruples. Besides, this would leave Kirsty alone at Ealachan for a blissful few days. She felt guilty at how much of a relief it was to be spared the demands of her immediate family.

Her grandfather was confined to the house with a heavy cold and consequent flare-up of his arthritis: not so bad that he needed constant attention, but too uncomfortable for him to do more than sit in front of the television with a blanket over his knees. Sensing that he wanted a little loving care, she loaded a few treats into the car and drove up to Dunshee. Finn was out and about on the farm, although a young man called Dave, much more efficient than Billy, came up from the village to help. Finn had no intention of taking on the full burden of the work again but realised that most of it was well beyond Alasdair's strength, even though it was more smallholding than farm these days.

Kirsty went into the kitchen and found her grandfather where Finn had left him that morning, huddled in a chair beside the range, with the radio and yesterday's newspaper beside him, a half drunk mug of tea and a plate of chocolate digestives on the table. A fat tabby cat, Fish Face's real successor, was asleep on a cushion on the opposite chair, its body making a perfect circle. It opened one eye but didn't raise its head as she came in. She went over and kissed the top of her grandad's head where the white hair was thinning. The shiny pink scalp beneath seemed very vulnerable. He had been such a big strong man; now he had shrunk, his limbs folding in on themselves. He had been a part of her life for so long. What would she do without him?

'How are you?' she asked him.

'Och, not so bad, lass. Not so bad.'

'I've brought you some fruit cake. It isn't like mum's but it's pretty good all the same. And whisky and honey. I know how much you like a hot toddy.'

'It's you yourself that will cheer me up. So sit down and tell me all the news.'

She shooed the cat off the cushion. It went and sat in the hearth, with its back to her, hunching its shoulders and twitching its tail indignantly. She talked to him about India and Flora, which was chiefly what he meant by 'the news.' Then she pottered about the room, singing to herself, making ham sandwiches with mustard for their lunch. It was soothing to be here again, working quietly in what she still thought of as her kitchen. She had always disliked the kitchen at Ealachan with its stone floor and banks of gloomy wooden cupboards, but Nicolas had been disinclined to change it. Besides, there had always been somebody else to do the cooking. Now, as she sliced down through the layers of brown and pink and yellow, she had a moment of pure happiness.

'Oh it's so nice to be back!'

'It's good to have you here.' She turned round to see Finn standing in the kitchen doorway, taking off his wellington boots, sliding out of a scuffed jacket. He was wearing a baggy sweater that seemed to be unravelling at neck and cuffs and a pair of faded jeans, not fashion-ably faded, just old. However else he may have changed, he still didn't care about his clothes. He kept them clean, but that was it.

'Are those for me as well?' he asked, looking at the sandwiches.

'Of course they are,' said Alasdair. 'She's made a great pile of them. You sit yourself down and get stuck in!'

They sat cater-corner at the kitchen table. Alasdair stayed where he was, with a tray on his lap.

'He's always trying to feed me up,' said Finn. 'He keeps telling me there isn't enough meat on my bones.'

'You seem fine to me.' But it was true that he had lost a bit of weight. She suspected that sometimes he just forgot to eat. She reached out and touched his arm, above the elbow, and was shocked by the dangerous flicker of sensation that passed between them. She wondered if he felt it too.

Their eyes met and again she felt a frisson of anxiety. When they were young, she had always been confident that she could banish his dark moods. Feisty Kirsty, walking in where even angels might fear to tread. Now, she was not so sure. He had left her once before. What if he left again? And then she thought that if Nicolas had his way, it was she herself who would be leaving.

'This is just like old times,' she said.

'Where are they?' he asked her abruptly. 'Your lot, down there?'

'They're all away. Nicolas and India will be back later in the week. Annabel's taken Flora off for a break.'

'How do you bear it, Kirsty? Living in the same house as that family?'

'Don't be silly. They're my family. I love them. And they're all very nice to me so I expect they love me too.' But she knew that he meant Nicolas. How could she bear living with Nicolas?

He finished his sandwiches and drank his tea in near silence. It wasn't a sullen silence. He just seemed disinclined to argue with her. Afterwards, she cleared away the dishes into the sink.

'Leave those,' he told her. 'I'll do them later.'

Alasdair was sneezing so badly by this time that when she suggested an afternoon nap, he agreed. She took him upstairs and straightened the bed for him while he got into his striped pyjamas. He was shivering and she laid a hand on his forehead.

'You're running a bit of a temperature. No point in you getting dressed again. You stay here and I'll bring you up some supper later on.'

'Are you staying?' he asked, hopefully.

'I might as well. There's nobody down at Ealachan. No need for me to go back there till later. I might see if Finn fancies a walk. Then come back and cook something for us all. Would you like that?'

'I'd like it fine. I'd like it just fine. It would be like old times.'

She made sure that he was comfortable, drew the curtains, switched off the lamp and left him in peace. He was snoring almost before she was out of the room.

In the kitchen, Finn was waiting for her, leafing impatiently through the day-old newspaper.

'Are you going?' he asked.

'No. I thought I might stay for a bit, if you don't mind.'

'Mind?' he echoed.

'Well then, do you fancy a walk?'

'Where?'

'Hill Top Town.'

'Will he be all right?' He gestured upwards.

'He'll be fine. He's fast asleep already. You could ask Dave to look in on him in an hour or so. Take him some tea.'

'I could do that. Yes.'

Chapter Thirty Three

THEY CLAMBERED UP the rocks behind the farmhouse. Above them, skylarks soared and sang. It was the best time of the year for walking, before waist-high bracken obliterated pathways and provided a breeding ground for flies. A handful of lambs in the field near the farm were playing King of the Castle on a heap of rocks and turf.

Finn soon pulled ahead of her.

'Wait for me!' she called.

He paused in his stride, waited for her to catch up. 'You're not as fit as you once were.'

'You're right.' She was breathless with the effort of the climb, her chest heaving.

'You used to be able to outrun me on this hill any day of the week, Kirsty Galbreath.' He would never call her by her married name.

'I know I did.' Her mouth was open, snatching at air. 'I know. I should take more exercise. I sit or stand and paint. But I don't walk enough these days.'

'You should come up here more often. Work up here if you like.'

'I don't think Nicolas would like that.'

'Fuck Nicolas!' he said, with sudden vitriol. 'Oh. I forgot. You already do.'

She stood still, looking up at him. There was a pain in her chest that wasn't entirely due to over-exertion. 'That was uncalled-for.'

'I'm sorry. But you're so fucking complacent about it all sometimes.'

'Complacent?'

'Yes.' He reached down, grasped her by the forearm and hauled her up to stand beside him. She rubbed at her arm where his fingers had left red streaks, like the Chinese burns they used to give each other when they were young, gratuitously cruel, seeing who would snatch his or her arm away first. The farm was behind and below them. To their left was the high summit, with the round eminence of Hill Top Town. In front of them the land was folded into ridges, scattered with big grey boulders, sloping away to end abruptly in a vertical drop to the sea. To their right, the rest of the island was spread out like a green and brown quilt, embroidered with sulphurous patches of whin.

'Don't think,' he said with sudden vehemence, 'Don't think that I'll put up with it forever. I know you take me for a fucking fool, Kirsty. Doling out your crumbs of kindness now and then and congratulating yourself on how well you're managing things. How well you're managing me!'

For a moment, she couldn't think of a thing to say in response, but then resentment came to her aid.

'You're not telling me you've been celibate all this time! Because I won't believe you.'

'I didn't get married, did I?'

'You went away and left me with never a word.'

'I've tried to explain why I did that.'

'But not even a postcard to tell me you were alive. So what in God's name did you expect, Finn? Did you expect my life to grind to a halt, because you weren't there? Did you really go for my sake, or just to fuck me up so that I'd be as hopeless as yourself? What the hell did you expect?'

His eyes were dark at the best of times, but now they were opaque and cold.

'I expect nothing,' he said. 'Isn't that what I've got from you, Kirsty? Fuck all. Or should that be less than fuck all?'

They were facing each other on the open hillside. He couldn't look at her any more. He turned and strode off in the direction of the summit, leaving her to follow or go back as she chose. She followed him, stumbling into patches of bog where the moss lay livid green on the surface and the mud beneath tugged at her shoes. She almost lost one; the peat relinquished it only with a protesting squelch. She stopped to retie her lace more tightly and when she stood up again she couldn't see him. 'Finn!' she shouted, but there was no reply.

The sun was sliding down the western sky and dazzling her eyes. She climbed again, hauling on the stringy stems of last year's heather to pull herself higher. And then she was over the edge of the hill fort, with the astringent scent of the sea in her nostrils. She was as familiar with this place as with her own room at Dunshee, but Finn was nowhere to be seen.

She came running down what might once have been a narrow causeway, carried by her own momentum, tripping over heather roots, falling. She put her hands out to save herself and jarred her whole body on a flat stone, like a flagstone, half submerged beneath the moss, grazing her hands and bruising her knees.

'Oh Finn!' she said and the sound of her own voice, half sob, half groan at the pain in her hands and knees, stirred some memory in her of another time, years before. She had been ahead of him that time because he was right, she could always outrun him. His legs were longer but she was more agile. She had been running and laughing and turning back to make fun of him and she had fallen flat on her face, perhaps on this same spot. She remembered biting her lip until it bled, because she didn't want him to think her a cry baby, but he had come up behind her and picked her up and rocked her in his arms.

'You're all right. You're all right,' he had said, and set her down and patted her back until her breathing steadied and the pain left her.

Now she began to cry at the memory and at the sadness of time that ruined all things, biting her lip again to try to stop the tears. But they came streaming down her face anyway, and she rubbed them away, making bloody, grimy streaks on her cheeks, because her hands were dirty and grazed. She was choking, sobbing helplessly and her nose was running and she was trying to wipe it with the back of her hand, trying to stem the salt water. She curled up into a ball, sitting on the cold stone, drawing up her knees and folding her arms around herself, rocking backwards and forwards, chanting 'Oh Finn, Oh Finn !' on each sobbing exhalation.

From nowhere, he was kneeling in front of her. 'Ah Kirsty!' he said. 'What are you doing to yourself?' He put his arms around her and pulled her forwards so that she rolled onto her knees again and said 'Ouch, ouch!' and he said 'Sorry, sorry!'

He held her away from him for a moment and looked into her eyes, shaking his head sadly. 'What are you doing to yourself?' he repeated.

'I can't beat you,' she said. 'I can't beat you any more.'

'At what for God's sake? Beat me at what?'

'At anything. I'd follow you to the ends of the earth and beyond. I'd go to hell in a handcart for you, you know I would.'

He licked his forefinger and wiped at the grimy, bloody tears and the touch of his damp finger on her cheek gave her a small shock of desire. 'And I you. Oh Kirsty I do love you so much!' he said. He took her head in both his hands and pulled her towards him, threading his fingers in her hair, kissing her, only just in control of himself.

'Is this what you want?' he asked her. 'Is this what you need?'

She nodded. 'Yes it is.'

He kissed her again, biting at her lips. They were mouth to mouth, each breathing the other's air.

'More,' she told him, knowing that it was not enough, that it would never be enough. 'Please!'

They toppled sideways onto the stone, their lips still searching for each other. She was fumbling with his jeans, tugging clumsily at them, and he was helping her. She cried out to him to hurry, hurry. I can't bear it, she thought. I can't wait. I can't wait any longer. Only when he was inside her could she let go once and for all, cry out, tell him she loved him, had always loved him, would always love him, pushing herself towards him, closer and closer, trembling and crying out with the exquisite pleasure and pain of not knowing nor caring where Finn ended and Kirsty began, forever.

In the late afternoon, chilled, bruised and battered by too much lovemaking on cold stone, they stumbled down the hill together and into the house, hoping that her grandfather was not up and about to see them. He was no fool and nothing could disguise what they had been doing. Their bodies inclined irresistibly towards one another, two halves of one whole.

Fortunately, Alasdair was still in bed. Dave had gone home, but he had topped up the range fire before he left and the kitchen was warm, with a full kettle just beginning to sing on the hob. She crept upstairs to find her grandfather sleeping peacefully, with the cat curled up in the curve of his body, and the mug of tea that Dave had brought him half drunk and cold beside the bed. She went back downstairs. They spoke in low voices to avoid rousing him.

'You're not going yet, are you?' Finn asked her.

'No. No, I'll stay. I'll stay the night if you'll let me.'

'If I'll let you?' he echoed, and his smile was almost a grimace.

'I'll phone Heather and tell her that my grandad needs me here.'

'Nicolas will find out.' He said this with a certain grim satisfaction.

'It doesn't matter if he does. As far as he's concerned, I'm staying the night to look after my grandfather.'

'Well I certainly hope he believes you,' said Finn.

He made a pot of tea and they sat on the rag rug in front of the range. He set his back against a heavy oak chair, and she leant against him, his long legs angled on either side of hers, her body enclosed by his. She could feel the rise and fall of his chest, could feel him breathing. In between drinking his tea, he folded his arms around her, or leant down to kiss her ear, or rub his lips gently against her hair.

'Grow your hair again.'

'I'm too old for long hair.'

'I loved your hair, Kirsty. Every last thread of it.'

She sighed, leant her head back, pushing it into his chest. 'I wish we could stay like this forever.'

'I wish we could.'

She closed her eyes and listened to the familiar sounds of Dunshee, the quiet rustle of coal and wood settling in the grate, the slow tick tock of the kitchen clock, the moan of wind investigating the gables, the distant cries of lambs and seagulls, curiously alike when heard from within these stone walls. Nicolas and Ealachan receded into the very back of her mind. It was as if they had never existed at all. Even her children, her beloved India and Flora, were not the imperative she always found them. She could hardly visualise them just now. A faint twinge of maternal guilt stirred, then that too faded. They were safe and sound, so why worry? Her thoughts drifted into sleep. She woke to find his left hand on her breast, exploring the heavy shape of it, tugging gently at the nipple while he nuzzled his lips into her neck.

'Kirsty?' he said, and tried to turn her to face him.

'What about my grandfather?'

'He won't hear anything.'

So she turned in his arms and they made love again, on the warm rag rug in front of the fire, more slowly this time and with less desperation. But she was afraid that their cries would wake and alarm the old man who lay sleeping upstairs.

Later, she took a tray up to her grandfather. He seemed to be feeling much better after his long sleep. She sat with him while he ate his omelette, helped him up to the bathroom, fetched him the radio from the kitchen, and settled him in bed again.

'I'll be right as rain tomorrow, after all this pampering. Are you going to have something to eat before you go, Kirsty lass?'

She said that she was planning to stay the night. She would make supper for herself and Finn, and then she might as well stay. The night had turned wet and windy, and there seemed no point in going home to an empty house.

'Where will you sleep?' he asked, anxiously. 'You know Finn has your room now?'

'That's all right' she told him, lying effortlessly. 'I'll take mum's old room.'

'But the bed will be damp.' He seemed querulous and upset. 'It hasn't been slept in for years, Kirsty. You know that's what your mother would say.'

'It'll be just fine. Don't you worry. I'll put fresh sheets on it. And Finn will find me a hot water bottle.'

'Well if you're sure … It'll be good to know that you're under this roof again.'

'I feel like that as well.'

She kissed him and went downstairs.

In the kitchen she made more omelettes for herself and Finn. They tried to eat, but it seemed like a waste of precious time, and eventually they gave in to the inevitable and crept quietly up the stairs to Kirsty's old room. Finn lighted a wood fire in there, screwing up newspaper into twists, like in the old days, while she undressed. She could hear her grandfather's faint snores as she crept into the soft space in the wall, the feather bed beneath her, the eiderdown on top. Finn slipped off his clothes and stood in the firelight, looking at her as though, even now, he could hardly believe that she was in his bed.

She loved the very sight of him, the touch and taste of his skin against hers, the familiar scent of his body, his hair, his hands on her face. He was hard and enduring as oak, cool and long and lovely as clean water, sweet as honey. They found themselves murmuring endearments, words and phrases with meanings only for each other, the poetry of longing and loss and enduring love.

And afterwards, when they lay, exhausted and sated, belly to back, like two spoons, she whispered in his ear, 'You were right.'

'About what?'

'About India. She's your daughter. I was pregnant when you left. It was weeks before I realised though.'

'I knew as soon as I saw her. That photograph just confirmed it. How could I not know? How could Nick not see it?'

'Maybe he does know. Or maybe he doesn't look at her in that way. He loves her, that's for sure. Are you angry?'

He turned to face her, pulling her close.

'I can't get angry with you any more, Kirsty. It's unproductive. Like getting angry with myself.'

'I'm so sorry. I didn't know what to do. It was a while till I realised I was pregnant. At first, I thought it was the stress of losing my mum – and you. Then, Nick was there and he was so kind to me.'

'It doesn't matter.'

'It does.'

'It's over and done with.'

'Do you think we should tell her?'

'What good would it do?'

'Doesn't she have a right to know?'

'Not if it does more harm than good.'

'You're a lovely man, Finn.'

He stirred uneasily. He had to be honest with Kirsty of all people.

'I'm not lovely at all. Oh God, don't credit me with more integrity than I actually have, Kirsty. I like India, and I admire her. But I only love you. Only feel for you. I can't be more than I am. I can see that it would be disastrous to tell her. I know what I should feel, but I don't feel it. I never will now.'

'Hush,' she said. 'I know, I know.'

In the night, she awoke, roused from sleep by some sound outside the farm, and, just for a moment, wondered where she was, alarmed by the strangeness of it, but instantly comforted by the familiarity of her surroundings. She was curled around his body and he was warm and relaxed in sleep. She lay quietly and listened. The call of the corncrake, nesting somewhere in the reeds by the shore, floated in at the window.

In the morning she went back down to Ealachan, told Heather that she had to look after her grandfather for a few days more, packed a bag, not forgetting drawing paper and charcoal, and returned to Dunshee, where she stayed until the day before Nicolas was due to come home. Every day she drew pictures of Finn and herself, a series of strange sketches of the two of them as children. Every night, she pretended that she was sleeping in her mother's room, while in reality she joined Finn in her old bed in the wall. They did not sleep very much. They tossed and turned like seals in the water and cried out with pleasure. In their element.

Later in the week, though, thoughts of India and Flora stirred her conscience.

'I'm fine now,' said Alasdair, who had been up and about for a day or so and was, frankly, puzzled by her continued presence. 'Time you got back down the hill, Kirsty. I know you're enjoying being at home again, but India will be coming home too, looking for her mother.'

Finn had overheard this conversation. He had been standing in the doorway listening, and he shrugged, almost imperceptibly.

'Don't worry,' she said. 'I'll be there when India comes back.'

Nicolas telephoned. He too sounded faintly puzzled by her prolonged stay at Dunshee. 'Is your grandad very ill?' he asked.

'He was quite poorly. But he's much better now. In fact I was planning to go back to Ealachan today. Get ready for the girls.'

'That's what I'm phoning about. India's been invited to stay with a friend outside Oxford for a week or so. And Annabel's flying into Heathrow with Flora, so she thought they might as well go to Maida Vale for a while. India's going to join them there.'

'I see.'

'You don't mind, do you?'

'No. No that's all right.'

'So I'll just be coming back on my own.'

There would never be a better time, she thought, but how could she bring herself to tell him?

When she went to her mother's old room, half heartedly packing up the bag she had kept there, for appearance's sake, Finn followed her and pressed her against the wall, kissing her hungrily.

'What will you do?' he asked. 'What are you going to do? Hadn't you better just leave your things here?'

'I can't bear to hurt the girls.'

'It isn't a choice between me and the girls. It's a choice between me and Nicolas. I would never, ever ask you to abandon your kids. Me of all people. You should know that.'

'I do know that.'

'Please don't choose him all over again. I can't bear it if you do.'

'I think I've already chosen, don't you?'

The inevitability of it swept over her. Finn had the prior claim. Fear for her daughters, guilt over what she was about to put them through, flooded her mind but didn't change anything.

'We can do this Kirsty. We can make it right, you know. For the girls as well as you and me.'

'But nothing can make it right for Nicolas. And I have to tell him about us,' she said suddenly. 'I have to tell him properly. To his face. I owe him that at least.'

'But you will tell him?'

'I have to. I can't carry on like this. I can't tear myself in two like this. Not any longer. Not even for another day.' She looked around. 'I'll leave my things here. And fetch the rest up later.'

'I'll put them in my room.'

'What about my grandad?'

'He's not daft, Kirsty. He must have an inkling. I mean look at us. We can't keep our eyes or our hands off each other. Do you not think he might have noticed?'

'I don't know. I can't think straight.'

'Do you want me to come with you? We could face Nicolas together.'

'No.'

'Are you sure? He'll be angry.'

'He will. And he has every right to be angry. But this is something I have to do all by myself.'

Chapter Thirty Four

SHE DIDN'T KNOW how to start. It would have been much easier to have blurted it out in the middle of a row, but Nicolas wouldn't argue with her. Whenever she lost her temper, he simply removed himself from the situation until she had calmed down, although he could be sulky when he chose. Kirsty would flare up and have done with it. Nick could keep a disagreement going for days, waging minor wars of attrition that wore her down. So she waited until the evening, when they were alone together, and then she just came right out with it.

'I have something to tell you.'

He looked up from his paperwork.

'Can't it wait? I really have to finish this before tomorrow.'

'No. It can't wait.'

He sighed. 'Is this something to do with your work? I've told you. You'll be much better off in London. I have gallery contacts there and so does Annabel. There's nothing for you in Scotland.'

'Oh for goodness sake, Nick.' Exasperation lent her courage. 'London isn't the centre of the universe, you know. Something's happened and I need to tell you about it. We have to talk.'

'Talk about what?'

'I've decided to move back to Dunshee. To live with Finn.'

He shuffled the papers together, as if he hadn't heard her properly.

'What?' he said again, so she was forced to repeat herself.

'I'm leaving you,' she told him and the words sounded over-dramatic, a childish threat rather than a promise. But then, perhaps the language of separation was always like this, banal, a parody of itself.

'Is this some kind of joke, Kirsty? Because it's not very funny.'

'I'm sorry, Nick, but I'm going back to Finn. '

'*Back* to Finn ?'

He pressed his pen so hard into the pad that the nib broke.

'I mean I'm going home.'

Worse and worse, she thought.

'I thought this was your home.'

'It was. It is.'

She couldn't think of anything else to say. Her heart was pounding with anxiety, her mouth dry. He turned around and looked at her, really looked at her, gazing into her eyes for a moment, his thin face flushed and angry. He had never looked more handsome.

'This has been going on ever since he came back, hasn't it?' he said, slowly.

'No. No it hasn't.'

'How long then?'

'Just this last week.'

'Do you take me for a fool? Do you really expect me to believe that?'

'You can believe it or not. I don't care. But it's true.'

'No,' he said. 'It's been going on for years. In your head at least. It's been going on for years and years.'

'It hasn't.'

'Oh but it has. I've been such a fool. Such a bloody fool.'

He got up and blundered out of the room, moving blindly. She heard him go out of the house, slamming the heavy door behind him, the sound of it echoing through the empty corridors.

A little while later, the phone shrilled, making her jump. It was Finn.

'Have you told him yet?'

'Yes.'

'How did he take it?'

'I'm not sure. He just got up and went out of the house. It's what he always does. I don't think he can bear confrontation of any kind.'

'Do you want me to come for you?'

'No, Finn. I have to wait for him. I have to speak to him. We have to talk it through'

'You are coming back to me, aren't you?' he said anxiously. 'You haven't changed your mind. He hasn't made you change your mind, has he?'

'No, he hasn't. But we have to talk. I have to wait for him to calm down a bit, so that we can at least begin to talk about it. I can't just walk out!'

'How long will that take?'

'How should I know? Just have patience and let me do this my own way!'

Nicolas came back into the house an hour or so later, his hair damp, his nose red with the cold, his shoes muddy. It was a rainy night. She was in the kitchen, making a pot of coffee. Automatically, she got down two mugs, used full-cream milk, the way he liked it, added his spoonful of sugar, not too little, not too much.

'Where did you go?' she asked him.

'For a walk. Oh don't worry. I didn't go anywhere near your precious Finn.'

'I was just worried about you.'

'Bit late for that. Unless ...'

'I haven't changed my mind.'

'Well good for you. Why don't you go and pack your bloody bags then!'

She took her coffee, went upstairs and began to pack a few essentials, methodically folding clothes into an old leather suitcase. After a while, he followed her, a glass of whisky in one hand and the bottle in the other.

'You're not really going through with this are you, Christine?' he asked, sitting down on the bed. The sight of the suitcase had sobered him.

'I'm sorry, Nick, but I am.'

'I knew it,' he said. 'As soon as he came back, I knew what would happen.'

'You didn't know any such thing. Because I certainly didn't.' Was that the truth though? She had always known what would happen if ever Finn reappeared. She just hadn't expected him to come back.

'He's been away for – what was it? Ten years? Twelve? He comes back and the two of you are as thick as thieves again. It was as if nothing had happened.'

'Eleven,' she said. 'It was eleven years.'

'Yeah' he said, wryly. 'Eleven years and how many months, weeks, days? Were you counting? You're lying to me. This must have been going on ever since he bought Dunshee! You knew it was him and you didn't tell me. You betrayed me, Kirsty. This has been going on for years.'

'You can believe what you like, but I only knew he'd bought it when he turned up at the door. And I thought I could just have him as a friend. I thought we could be the way we used to be, when we were kids. The way we always were. Like brother and sister. You don't know what a struggle it's been, Nicolas. I did my level best.'

'Then your level best obviously wasn't good enough. Christ, it's practically perverted. Why did you marry me when you loved him?'

'I loved you too. I still do love you.'

'But not in that way. Never in that way.' He sounded more sad than angry. 'The thing was, I didn't know it. I couldn't see it. I really thought you loved me.' He paused. 'Everyone loved me,' he added, reflectively.

'I know. You always got what you wanted, didn't you, Nicolas? Even me.'

'I thought you were just playing hard to get. And then when your mother got so ill and you seemed so vulnerable …'

'I was confused. And I was so worried about him. He had nothing at that time.'

'He had you.'

She didn't contradict him.

'I think he should have had the guts to come down and face me himself.'

'He wanted to. I wouldn't let him. This has nothing to do with him.'

'How can you say that?'

'I mean this is my decision. My fault. Mine. Nobody else's. He didn't persuade me or seduce me. You must believe that. And he would have come. But I said I had to speak to you alone. I owed you that at least.'

'Yes. You owed me that at least.'

She closed one case and opened another.

'What about the girls?' he said as though the thought had just occurred to him. 'So what's going to happen about my girls? Will I tell them that their mother has bolted? Gone off with her fancy man?'

'I'll tell them. Or we could tell them together. I'm only going up the road.'

'Well I can tell you right now, they won't be visiting you. Not at Dunshee.'

'Of course they will.'

'I won't let that man near them!'

'You may have to.'

'Try me!'

She could see that they were spiralling inexorably towards custody issues and that this was neither the time nor the place.

'I think we should talk about all this later, Nicolas. When they come home. Maybe by then we can be civilized, convince them that we don't hate each other.'

'Don't we?'

'I don't hate you.'

'You just don't love me the way you love him.'

'No.'

'Well don't expect me to be quite so civilized as all that, Christine. I feel fairly murderous right now.'

'I know.'

'I don't think you do.'

'Let's talk about it later.'

She moved about the room, opening drawers, taking out folded clothes, the simple, commonplace actions soothing her. He watched her and poured himself another large whisky.

'You won't come to London?' he asked, as though still unable to bring himself to believe it.

'I never did want to go to London, you know. It would have driven me mad. I can't leave the island. Everything I love is here. All my inspiration is here.'

'Your inspiration!' he said scornfully.

'Yes. Inspiration. Everything that makes me the person I am. The person you're supposed to love!'

'How can you be so cold? So cruel?'

'I'm sorry. But it matters to me, and you can't see that. I don't think you ever saw that, not really. You just paid lip service to it. I'm not one of those artists who can switch focus. I realise that now. This is my canvas. This place. This is where I belong.'

'How do you know if you've never even tried? London might be just what you need.'

'But it isn't. I know it isn't. In here and here.' She tapped her hand on forehead and breast, a strangely religious gesture. 'I think I'm destined to go on exploring this small piece of the world in greater and greater depths. Two or three lifetimes wouldn't be enough. But you've never really understood that, have you, Nick?'

'No. I think it's all arty farty nonsense. You're using it to justify your infidelity. I think you could have given London a try. For me and the girls.'

She stifled the angry observation that the girls would be at school in Scotland for much of the time, and now he would have to find somebody else to help nurse his father. What was the point? It would only make things worse.

'So I'll go to Dunshee,' she repeated. He had gone very white and the whisky didn't seem to be helping at all. 'And I'll take the car, if that's all right. I'll bring it back tomorrow.'

'Whatever. But, dear God, there's so much to sort out. Money for instance.'

If he sold Ealachan and the other island properties she would have a considerable claim on the family finances. She hadn't even thought about it until this moment.

She said, 'Oh, you needn't worry. I don't want any of your money!'

Nevertheless, it crossed her mind that it would give Finn a certain malevolent satisfaction to fleece him of a large slice of his capital. Well, Finn could have her, but none of Nick's money. And she needn't have worried because later on, Finn, pride outweighing malice, would say, 'Tell him to give his cash to the girls. You need none of it. I have enough for both of us. I don't want you to be beholden to him in any way.'

'We'll just have to sort things out properly, Christine.'

'We will.'

Your grandfather won't approve,' added Nicolas, with a sort of dreary triumph.

'No he won't. But he'll get used to the idea.'

'Full circle eh?' he said stiffly. 'But I still say you're not taking my girls up there.'

'Not to live maybe. But India spends half her holidays there. You wouldn't deny her that pleasure.'

'Pleasure? Pleasure?'

'They're at school so much of the time anyway. If you sell Ealachan, I thought maybe they could divide their time between us. Come to Dunshee, go to London. We could work something out, couldn't we?'

'Would he allow that?' Nicolas couldn't bring himself to say Finn's name.

'Of course. He isn't a monster, however much you hate him!'

'So how would he be with another man's children? My children. How the hell could I ever trust him?'

'He isn't a monster,' she repeated. 'And they're my children too.'

'Meaning?'

'Meaning whatever I ask him ...'

'He fucking well does.' The expletive tumbled out of him. He had never sworn at her before. 'I know. I know. So what do you want me to do, Christine, since you seem to have this all planned out? Do you want a divorce?'

She said again, 'Can't we be civilised about all this?'

'I think we're going to have to be, don't you? Otherwise I'll just go up there and kill the bastard.'

You and whose army, she thought. But she didn't say it aloud. Not this time.

As he got up to go out of the room, she said, 'Kirsty.'

'What?' he asked. 'Kirsty what?'

'My name is Kirsty, you know, not Christine. It's Kirsty or Cairistiona. That's who I am.'

'What are you talking about?'

'I was never Christine. I don't even like the name. It's not me and it never was. Nobody has ever called me that, except you and your sister. I'm Kirsty.'

'Hell mend you then!' he said, flinging himself out of the room. 'Be whatever you like! And don't worry. I wouldn't care if I never mentioned your sodding name again!'

She put a couple of suitcases in the car, hauling them down the long flights of stairs all by herself. She would have to come back for the rest later. He was nowhere to be seen. She suspected that he had taken refuge in some remote part of the house with the bottle of whisky. She felt so weary that even the effort of driving up to Dunshee in the rainy dark was quite beyond her. She had to sit there for a few moments, trying to pull herself together, resting her forehead on the steering wheel.

Finn was waiting for her, his face strained and anxious. She got out of the car but although he stretched out his arms to her, she didn't want to be touched.

'Not yet,' she said. 'Let me get inside. Just let me get inside.'

'I was afraid he might not let you go.'

'Of course he let me go. How could he stop me? Don't dramatise things, Finn. They're bad enough without that.'

'You don't know what was going through my head. I still thought you might not come.'

'I said I would, didn't I?'

'I had to tell your grandfather what was going on.'

'Oh God, you didn't.'

'Well, he was asking questions. I couldn't lie to him. He had to know.'

'What did he say?'

'His main concern was for the girls.'

'What did you tell him?'

'I said we'd sort something out. They could come up here in the holidays.'

She started to cry, tears of strain and relief. 'We will, won't we, Finn? We will sort something out?'

'I promise you. I'll do anything. I'll even go away while the girls are here if you want me to. If Nicolas wants me to.'

'But I want you to get to know India … to get to know them both better.'

'They might not want to know me.'

'So where is he? My grandad? How did he take it?'

'He's not happy. He's gone up to bed. He said he's getting too old for all this upheaval.'

'It's not fair on him. It isn't fair to do this to him. First Nick. Now Grandad. And the girls. We're making all of them miserable, just for our own satisfaction.'

'You know it's more than that. Give it time. It will be all right you know.'

But she realised that he would say this because he believed it. He had to believe it. Nothing else mattered to Finn. Nothing else would ever matter now, except that they should be together. As for her, she wanted to see her girls, had a great craving to speak to them. Flora was still abroad, so she phoned India in Oxford.

'Hi mum!' said her daughter, brightly. 'We've just come in from the theatre.'

'Are you having a good time?'

'Yes thanks.'

'Good. I just wondered. You know? Just wanted to hear your voice really. Just wanted to say hello.'

'What are you doing, mum?'

'I'm at Dunshee.'

'Lucky you. Is grandad OK?'

'Yes, he's fine. He's been ill, but he's much better now. Everything's fine.'

'Listen, must go. We've ordered pizzas. See you soon then.'

India made kissing noises and hung up.

'Can I get you something to eat?' Finn asked anxiously.

'No. I'm not hungry.'

'Well, something to drink then.'

She looked round the kitchen. 'I wish my mum was here.'

'I don't think she'd be very happy either, do you, Kirsty?' said Finn, drily.

'She'd have my head on a plate. Yours too. But she'd still make me a cup of tea.'

'I can make you some tea.'

'Yes. Tea would be nice.'

She sat in the warm kitchen, watching him moving about the place with a slight air of clumsiness. His gaze kept swivelling in her direction. He couldn't help himself. At last he brought a mug over and set it down beside her.

'Mind. It's hot.'

'Thank-you, Finn. '

'I'll bring you tea every morning. I always bring tea to your grandfather.'

'I'd like that fine.'

He sat on the floor beside her chair. She reached out and touched the top of his head, feeling the sooty softness of his hair beneath her fingers, closing her hand around the darkness.

She drank her tea, and then they went up to bed together, too exhausted to do more than lie in each other's arms, listening to the rain on the window, and the sounds of the old house settling around them, waiting for sleep to come.

Chapter Thirty Five

ON THE LONGEST day of the year, Kirsty and Finn climbed to Hill Top Town together and sat on the westernmost edge of the island, watching the sun dip towards the sea, where it would just sink below the horizon, only to rise again. There would be no darkness tonight.

'Here we sit, on the edge of the world,' he said.

Many things had changed over the past few months, such sweeping changes that Kirsty would not have believed them possible if somebody had told her about them beforehand. Ealachan, contents and all, had been sold to an American film maker called Charlie McNeill, although he had not yet moved in. He was a plump, untidy man, very proud of his Scottish ancestry. He had brought his Porsche over from the mainland on the ferry and he would sit in the pub, talking to the locals about island history. They were suspicious of him at first, then beguiled by his enthusiasm, touched by his friendliness. Kirsty liked him. He had already visited them at Dunshee. While Finn sat listening to their conversation, she and her grandfather had chatted to him and he had told them about his plans for the house. He loved Kirsty's paintings. When he asked her if she would be prepared to keep the gallery going, she agreed.

A couple of weeks previously, Nicolas had finally decamped to London. Later in the summer, he would be going to America and India and Flora would be coming north to stay at Dunshee for a little while. India had been remarkably philosophical about the whole thing and, after her initial shock, seemed to be starting to take the separation in her stride. So many of her friends' parents were divorced that it was more the norm than the exception and she had plenty of people to confide in. Flora, younger and altogether more vulnerable, had been much more distressed, blaming Finn, her mother, and even herself for the whole upheaval. It didn't help that she felt as though she had lost Ealachan at the same time.

'Don't be so silly,' said India when she caught her sister in tears yet again. 'It isn't uncommon, Lolo. In fact it happens all the time. Just because they're splitting up, it doesn't mean they don't love us.'

'She must love Finn more. Else why would she go away with him?'

'But she hasn't really gone away. Only to Dunshee. She's sort of gone back there, hasn't she? And that's home as well. Or as good as.'

'Not to me. Besides, he's there. And I don't like him.'

'If you mean Finn, it'll be all right. You'll see.'

'How do you know?'

'I just do. Besides, it has its advantages, you know.'

'What?' asked Flora, blowing her nose. 'I can't see any.'

'Well, we get two of everything for a start.'

'Oh Indie!' said Flora, and started to cry all over again.

So long as she was allowed to come and stay at Dunshee with her beloved great grandfather, and play the fiddle with him, so long as she was allowed to see plenty of her mother, India found that she didn't much care what else happened. She was already planning trips to the States with her father, but Dunshee had always been her favourite place, her lodestone, a still point in her busy world. She didn't even mind Finn being there. She didn't like him very much, it was true, although he was always kind to her, in a detached way. He seemed aloof and unemotional. But she could put up with him.

Flora, on the other hand, missed Ealachan, missed its flower garden, its woodland paths where she had once walked the dogs, its summer house where she had organised picnics for her soft toys. Charlie McNeill was accommodating, and when she was on the island, she would always accompany her mother to the gallery, but Charlie had made changes, and her sense of ownership had gone. When her father was away on business, as he so often was these days, she chose to spend most of her free time in London with Annabel. Annabel took Flora shopping for new clothes, let her dress up in her high heeled shoes, showed her how to use make-up, allowed her to watch unsuitable programmes on the television.

Alasdair had taken a long time to come round to the new state of affairs. They suspected that he had still not quite come to terms with it. Kirsty sensed that he was disappointed in her and that was worse than if he had been really angry.

'You shouldn't be doing this' he said, severely. 'I understand how you feel, but there are some things that are just wrong.' He shook his head. 'Just plain wrong. Those wee girls ...'

There was nothing either Kirsty or Finn could say or do to make things better. Oddly enough, it was India herself who started to talk him round.

'These things happen,' she said, airily. 'We just have to make the best of them.'

'Is your sister making the best of things?'

'No, not at the moment. But she will. Once she's settled down at school.'

'And that's a good thing, is it?'

'It will be. It'll be fine. You'll see. And at least mum hasn't bolted completely.' India, always a precocious child, had been reading Nancy Mitford.

'Bolted?' asked Alasdair, bemused. 'What are you talking about?'

'You wouldn't believe how many mothers do that. My friend Tanya, at school, her mother ran off with the postman. Bolted, you know? Her mother literally ran off with the postman and set up house with him. Well it was a squat actually. Somewhere in Glasgow. At least mum's only run up here to Dunshee. And we love it here, don't we?' She flung her arms around him and kissed him lavishly.

'Aye, right' he said, sceptically. But she made him laugh. 'The postman eh?' he said. 'What a thing to do! And what's a squat when it's at home?'

Kirsty's hair had grown a little longer. Now it fluffed in untidy red wisps around her face. They had brought a bottle of wine to the western edge of the island, in celebration of the solstice. She was wearing a long cotton skirt, green wellington boots, and one of Finn's old sweaters. It was stiff with oil paint. Her nails were bizarrely pitted with the stuff. She could never get them clean. It had been a constant source of irritation to Nicolas, but Finn didn't even notice. She was sitting on a blanket and sketching him. He sat up on a rock, gazing down at her.

'Are you cold?' she asked him. 'Do you want your pullover?'

'No. I'm fine.' He grinned at her.

'What?' she asked him. 'Why are you laughing?'

'I was thinking what a fashion plate you make.'

'That's a very old fashioned expression.'

'I know. My mother used to say it. I have this memory of walking through Dublin with her. "Would you look at that fashion plate, Finn?" I think she kind of wanted to be a fashion plate herself.'

'You've never told me, you know.'

'Told you what?'

'What happened. To your mother, and you. You've told me bits of it. But not the whole story.'

'Even I don't know the whole story. I was too young.' He gazed at her. 'But it's true that I found out more. During those years when I was away. I made it my business. It was one of the things that kept me sane, when I was – without you. I studied, I worked. And I tried to find some explanations.'

'And did you? Find them I mean?'

'Sort of. The school I was sent to, well, you know a bit about that. It was an Industrial School. They used to have them over here once upon a time. They were a Victorian idea. For the poor. To teach useful skills to the sons and daughters of toil.'

'Like in Dickens? Dotheboys Hall?'

'I don't know. Maybe. Anyway, they were very hot on Industrial Schools in Ireland. England abolished them early on. In Ireland, the church and the state were hand in glove, and they managed to keep them for a lot longer. There may still be some around for all I know. But the one I was in, it's a ruin now, derelict.'

'So you did go back?'

'Just the once. I went to Dublin, and drove out into the country-side, to the school.'

'What was it like?'

'A wreck. A ruin.'

'Did it help?'

'A bit. I used to think I'd like to go to Ballyhaunis, to see if my mother's family are still around. I used to think about that a lot.'

'I'll come with you if you want to go.'

'I don't need to go now. I don't need anything or anybody else. Not now I've got you, Kirsty.'

'So these schools …?' she prompted.

'They were run by the Christian Brothers. Those were for the boys. Or the Sisters of Charity, for the girls.' His mouth twisted into a little smile. 'Ironic, eh? Neither very Christian, nor very charitable. But we had it drummed into us that we were charity cases and should thank God for what we were given, and believe me, that was little enough. It was … well, I'll tell you what it was, it was a form of slavery. We were like slaves. We were taught a little, but we had no rights. And for the rest of the time, we worked.'

'Not charity cases then?'

'Not at all. No. Apparently, we were government funded and quite handsomely. I told you, I made it my business to find out. But the schools were paid per child, so it was in their interests to squeeze in as many kids as possible. Capitation. Bloody disastrous. The cruelty men were on the look out for any children that could be swept in and they seemed to wield a very large broom. If you were poor, destitute, they called it, if you were morally at risk, whatever that meant, if you skipped school or stole a handful of apples – all that was enough reason. You would be taken to court and committed until you were sixteen. The day before your sixteenth birthday, to be precise. I was seven when it happened to me.'

'Dear God! But you weren't destitute, were you?'

'Not really. We were poor. But my mother was properly married, in the church too, even though my father had left her. She took me to mass on Sundays. She worked in a factory. She was a machinist. There was no money to spare, but we managed.'

'Have you spoken to your mother about this?'

'No. She'll talk to me and about me, but not about the past. Just once, that first time we met, I think she maybe wanted to talk about it then, but I wasn't ready. And now, if ever she writes, it's about the here and now. She prays for me a lot.'

'Well, I don't suppose you should turn down prayers. They may come in handy. One day.'

When he thought back to that time, before the school, before he lost her, it seemed very happy, maybe happier than it really was.

'I don't remember my mammy even so much as raising her hand to me.'

'So what went wrong?'

'Mrs Maguire went wrong.'

'I remember you telling me about her. Mrs Maguire with her flowery hat and her shiny handbag.'

'That's right.'

Mrs Maguire had been a bit of an anomaly, or so he had discovered later. The Legion of Mary weren't exactly friends of the Industrial School system. They were all about keeping families together. But Mrs Maguire had been different.

'She was a nosy old cow, really. My father had been away for years. There was man who worked at the factory. I think his name was Johnny, but I don't remember his second name. Maybe I never knew it. He was nothing important. In fact I think he hauled the stock around or something. He always looked knackered. So God knows how they even met, but he and my mother did meet and he liked her. And she seemed to like him. They started seeing each other, now and then.'

'Do you remember him?'

'I do. A little. He was older than she was. He had grey hair. A sad old raincoat.'

When he thought about it now, Finn realised that it had probably been his demob coat, from after the war, and he had still been wearing it. But he had been very kind.

'They were as gentle as each other. No fight in them. He would come to the house but he never stayed over, as far as I remember. I think Mrs Maguire found out about them and reported her as an unfit mother. I don't know. Maybe he was married. But that was when it all kicked off.'

He gazed at the sea. What had kicked off? He had let her in. It was all his fault. But why had that been such a disaster? A pebble, causing an avalanche? He still couldn't remember. They knew Mrs Maguire, saw her at the church each week. Why should it have been such a crime to let her into the house?

'They sent me to the school and my poor immoral mother finished up in one of those laundries, a Magdalene, washing away her sins. Except that eventually, she changed her mind and joined the enemy. Stockholm Syndrome, isn't that what they call it? You identify with your captors. But maybe that isn't the whole story. I think she's genuinely contented now.'

'And was the school terrible?'

'You can't begin to imagine. And I'm glad you can't imagine. It was terrible in ways you couldn't conceive of.'

'But did nobody stop them? Was there nobody to see it happening?'

He gazed at her helplessly. 'I don't have the words, even now. But I think the beatings were the worst thing. Not just the savagery but the sheer unpredictability of them. We were beaten constantly for nothing that I could see. In all the years I was there, and with all the beatings I had, every week, sometimes every day, none of them ever seemed to make sense. It wouldn't have been so bad if they had been punishments for something. But they never were. I've thought since, it was the sheer lack of cause and effect that was so terrifying.'

They had slept in big dormitories, dozens of beds in rows, and they would be dragged out in the middle of the night, spread-eagled on the landing, shirts up round their armpits, and beaten on their naked buttocks. He remembered the faces of the men wielding the canes, alight with a sort of avid pleasure. He couldn't tell her properly, not even Kirsty. He was still ashamed to talk about it. As though it were all his own fault.

'I think some of those men were crazy. Crazy. I think they should have been sectioned. I've wondered about it since: the violence, the ignorance. What made them do that to defenceless children? How could they? And why did everyone else turn a blind eye to it? Did they think we were less than human? I know they were different times and kids were beaten, but they weren't beaten like that.'

'Not all kids were beaten. Nobody ever laid a finger on me.'

'It was like prison without the rules.'

'You'd have been much better off in prison.'

'We would. When I got older, I used to think that. Some of the older boys fought back, sure enough, but the younger ones – what could we do? We were half starved and filthy, we were cold, we were abused, and nobody came to our aid. The food was like pig swill, in fact the pigs had it better than we did; we had maggoty potatoes, bread and marge. You would eat the turnips out of the fields you were that hungry. You never had your own clothes. Didn't you wonder why my clothes were always too small for me when I came to the tatties?'

'I remember my grandad giving you some of my dad's clothes.'

'He did, and I went back with them, but I never saw them again. Too good for me. They were whisked away and that was that.'

'But did they not have inspections? Did people not come in from the outside?'

'Oh, they were fly. All of them. When the inspector was coming, they always knew, somebody must have tipped them the wink. They always had enough time to clean the place up. Put on a good front. Like a stage set. There would be proper delft on the tables. You'd get clean clothes. But as soon as the visitors went away, that was it. Back to what passed for normal.'

'Didn't people ever run away?'

'They tried. But if you ran away, the guards, the police always brought you back, no questions asked, and the Brothers half killed you. I wet the bed every night for the first couple of years in that place. Why wouldn't I? I never wet the bed at home, but I wet the bed there. They used to make you walk about with the pissy sheet on your head, to show the world what a devil you were. And I was doubly demonic because I wrote with my left hand. There was no hope for me at all. God, Kirsty, I haven't the words. Even trying to put it into words for you makes it seem less than it was. Do you remember Francis?'

'I've never forgotten him. He died, didn't he?'

'He always got it worse than me. I had a thick skin and a knack for keeping my head down. You become kind of invisible after a while. You learn how to do it. But Francie never did. There was a farm at the school and we worked on that. Never saw any money for it, but as we got a bit bigger we were useful to them, I suppose. And one of the lay brothers, he was nicer than the rest. I don't know if he did it to give us a break, but he managed to persuade them to send us away to the tatties, and that's how we came here. It was Francie that needed the break. I was just sent along to look after him, I think. Francie would have got away. He'd have been home free if he had managed to hang on for a bit. When you got to sixteen, they used to find a job for you, and mostly you stuck it for a few years, because you thought that you had to. You didn't know you could escape. But sooner or later, you would realise that you didn't have to stay and there was nothing much they could do if you high tailed it over the water to England or Scotland. I didn't know it myself till your grandfather sent that priest packing.'

'So what happened to him? To Francis? You told me he fell down some stairs.'

He shook his head, his face grim, lost in the past.

'I think there was more going on. He was this sweet lad, Francie. I think there were other things going on. Even worse things. Other kinds of abuse. He would try to tell me sometimes, but I didn't want to know. Things were bad enough without that. I don't think he fell. I still don't know whether he jumped. Or was it even worse than that? He could have been pushed, for all I know. They said it was a terrible accident, but I'm still not sure, even to this day. That was when I knew that I had to get away. But I couldn't see how I could do it. Until your grandfather helped me.'

'Thank God he did.'

'When I came here, that was the first real act of kindness I had known since I left my mother. Can you believe that? Your grandad saying "take a break, lad." I remember it to this day. And you, of course. I couldn't understand why you were both being nice to me.'

'If I could have put everything right for you, I would.'

'I know you would. But it doesn't matter. Not now I have you. Not now we're together.'

The terrible thought came to Kirsty that perhaps she had sacrificed her own children for Finn. To try to put something right that never would or could be right. Not completely. Finn was damaged and there was nothing she could do except give him unconditional love. But that wasn't really the truth of it either. The children seemed happy enough now, and no life was without upheavals. They had been very civilised about it all, she and Nicolas. That was always Nick's way. The perfect gentleman. But how could you ever tell what damage might have been done? How could you ever tell what might lie ahead?

Chapter Thirty Six

Kirsty and Finn were married very quietly in a mainland registry office, as soon as the divorce came through: just the two of them with Alasdair and a couple of witnesses from the island, but no other guests, no party, not even the girls. Alasdair lived with them for three more years. He had accepted the situation and admitted that he was delighted to have both Kirsty and Finn back at Dunshee. It was, he told her, what he would most have wished for and he was happy that they were all together again.

'But I wouldn't have wanted you to go about it in this way, Kirsty,' he said. 'Not quite in this way.'

'I know. But the girls seem to be happy enough now.'

He died peacefully at his beloved home in early summer. His funeral was more of a celebration than a wake. Nicolas didn't come, but Annabel picked up India and Flora from school and brought them to the island. Flora was sad but India was distraught.

'I'm so used to him being here,' she said to her mother. 'If I had any troubles, I could take them to him. What am I going to do without him?'

Just before the funeral, Finn took her into the kitchen at Dunshee and presented her with her great grandfather's old fiddle.

'He asked me to give it to you. My playing isn't a patch on yours. It's a lovely instrument, and I think you must have it. Why don't you play something for him at the service?'

She played a series of light-hearted jigs and reels that her great grandad had played at weddings, and that made everybody smile, but she finished with the sad song of the fairy folk that Finn had learned all those years ago, and made her mother cry.

For ten years, like the characters in Kirsty's favourite childhood book, they lived together in great joy and contentment. Afterwards, looking back on those years, Finn thought that he had hardly noticed so much time passing, so absorbed had he been in the small but keen pleasures of everyday life with Kirsty. She was the sun in his sky, each day a small miracle of recognition and recollection that he was with her. Passion became familiarity, but never ceased to delight them. She had carried on painting, working almost every day, but with each year that passed, the commercial imperative seemed to grow less important to her. It was the work itself that absorbed her. After her grandfather's death, and with Charlie's blessing, she had resigned from the day to day running of the gallery at Ealachan. Instead, Charlie employed a young man to work there, much as Kirsty herself had once worked in the Edinburgh gallery, while Kirsty advised about exhibitions and sometimes liaised with artists. She was still drawing and painting aspects of the island in all its seasons. Her island paintings sold reasonably well, especially to Charlie's guests at Ealachan. But her work often involved Finn, and those images were never for sale.

'Not again, Kirsty,' he would say, but the truth was that he would do whatever she asked of him, and if that meant sitting on a rock for hours at a time while she produced interminable sketches, who was he to argue?

For the first few years of their marriage, they grew potatoes in the sandy fields beside the shore. Finn bought an old harvester from a neighbouring farm and sold the crop to the island shops. Instead of the tattie howkers of old, a few islanders came up to help. They sold the few remaining sheep after Alasdair died but they kept half a dozen hens, and Finn dug a vegetable garden. At first, a little consultancy work came his way, and it paid well, but the truth was that he hated to be away from the island and from Kirsty for more than a couple of days at a time. Their needs and wants were very few. They lived happily, mostly on Finn's savings, on the occasional sale of Kirsty's work, and on a small monthly payment from Nicolas, that he had insisted on including in the divorce settlement, in spite of all they could do to deter him. He pointed out that since the girls would be spending time at Dunshee, it was only fair that he made a contribution, and they didn't have the heart to reject his generosity.

Around the time of the millennium, Kirsty fell ill. Her symptoms were vague and worrying: shortness of breath, fatigue, night time sweats, inexplicable bruising. Eventually, Finn took her to a mainland hospital, the same one her mother had spent so much time in and, quite quickly, she was diagnosed with leukaemia. She kept her illness a secret. India and Flora still went to visit their mother at Dunshee, but she always managed to hide it from them. She only told them that she was run down, a bit anaemic, had been advised to take it easy. She had treatment, lost her hair, grew it again, just in time for the girls' next visit.

'Why have you had your hair cut so short again, mum?' asked India.

'The hairdresser got carried away.'

'It isn't very nice,' said Flora, thoughtfully. 'You ought to grow it.'

'I'm doing my best.'

'You should tell them,' said Finn, when they had left the island.

'No. I don't want any fuss. I don't want anyone feeling sorry for me.'

She fought the disease long and hard, with every possible treatment. Finn would have moved heaven and earth for her. He would gladly have taken the illness upon himself, if that were possible. But after the last remission proved to be only a temporary respite, Kirsty put her foot down. She didn't want to be away from the island and she didn't want to be away from Finn any longer. Nothing he could do or say would change her mind. She took such palliative treatment as they could offer her, while she stayed at home, but refused to go back into hospital and her health steadily deteriorated throughout that winter and early spring.

At Easter, her daughters came to Dunshee for a few days, and Kirsty rallied all her strength to behave normally with them; so much so that India and Flora noticed little amiss with their mother, beyond the fact that she seemed very tired and needed constant catnaps.

They spent more time with Finn than ever before. He was shy, but kind to them. Afterwards, India suspected that Kirsty had asked him to be nice to them and, as always, he had obeyed. He carried their picnic things down to the beach, arranged fishing trips for them with good looking young islandmen and escorted them to and from ceilidhs in the village hall or quiz nights in the hotel, where they could chat to visiting yachtsmen. With the self centredness of youth, they seemed not to notice how few of these activities involved their mother.

India had finished college by then, had managed to find herself an agent and was intent on making her mark in the world of music. Flora was doing a Business Studies course in Edinburgh. Physically, Flora was the image of her mother, but much more reserved and precise. She had a lustre about her, as though she had just stepped out of a photograph. There was never a hair out of place, and she was never seen in public without carefully applied make-up, in sharp contrast to her sister. India only wore make-up on stage, and even then, usually had to be reminded about it. Once, when they had gone on holiday to Italy with Annabel, their luggage had gone missing, along with Flora's make-up case. India watched in astonishment as her younger sister dissolved into angry tears.

'But it's Sunday,' she kept saying. 'I can't buy anything!'

She was only placated the following day when the shops opened and she was able to replace her lipstick and mascara, even though the missing luggage turned up within a few hours.

'I love her, but she drives me nuts!' said India to Finn, in an un-guarded moment. 'She's so high maintenance now. She was never like that when we were younger. I was the neat one. Now she takes an hour to do her hair and makeup. A whole hour every day and then she has to take it all off again at night. What a waste of time!'

'That's just the way she is,' said Finn, mildly. 'And perhaps it's just her way of ordering her world, making herself feel safe and unassail-able, you know?'

Much later, India remembered those words, wished she had been able to talk to him, ask him what he meant by them. But she had a feeling he would have clammed up as he always did, after that one rare insight.

By May, Kirsty was desperately ill. Again, Finn suggested that he must tell the rest of her family what was going on, but she refused. She became so agitated when he argued with her that he couldn't bring himself to do anything but capitulate. She knew that she was being impossibly selfish, but she didn't care.

The morphine made her sick and vague and she would take the tablets only when she couldn't bear the aching in her joints any more. Her temperature fluctuated alarmingly and she had terrible nosebleeds. Just lifting her would cause her skin to bruise. Where Finn had held her, and there was no doubt that she needed his support, there would be two sets of five blue fingerprints on the white flesh. He feared all the time that his touch would damage her, but she told him that she didn't care. She needed to feel his hands on her. Finn couldn't bear to think of her illness. He sometimes found himself pretending that it was some minor condition from which she would recover in time. He couldn't bear his sense of panic, a terror that could only be controlled when he focussed on caring for her, on her day-to-day needs.

She was so frail that he wondered how she could stand upright, but she would insist on getting up and going into the garden, so that she could watch the sea from a basket chair, or smell the sweet coconut scent of the whins on the winds that blew down from Hill Top Town.

'I wish I was sitting up there with you,' she said to Finn, one May evening, when she had been more restless and unwell than usual. 'I wish we were there, the two of us together, watching the western sea. It would make me better just to be there, I'm sure it would! Can't you carry me up there? Can't you? Please Finn!'

'Kirsty how can I? There's no strength left in you! It would kill you to go up there. I'm as strong as a horse, but I couldn't carry you up there safely, sweetheart. I'd be afraid that you'd break in my arms. We'll go when you're better. I promise.'

She was silent for a moment, gazing up at him.

At last, she sighed. 'Well, Hill Top Town will just have to wait then. We'll get there eventually, I know. But what about the boat? We could go out in the boat, couldn't we? I wouldn't have to do a thing. You could bring it in to the beach and carry me down there. I don't weigh very much.'

'You're thistledown. And just as fragile. But I'm so afraid of breaking you.'

'I don't care. What's a few broken bones? I want to be out there on the water with you, one last time.'

He winced, but said nothing, shaking his head.

'Listen, you have to do what I want.' She smiled at him, with a look of sheer devilment, a flash of the old Kirsty. 'You never know, it might be my last request.'

'Don't!' he said. 'Don't do this to me. I can't bear it, Kirsty!'

'Well I won't,' she relented. 'But it's a very calm night. It'll be all right, really it will.'

'I'll fetch the boat in,' he said.

It was the nut brown, clinker-built rowing boat that had belonged to her grandfather. It was afloat already, tied to the iron stanchion on the beach below Dunshee. Finn wrapped Kirsty in the black and white shepherd's plaid that he had found in one of the upstairs cupboards.

She snuggled into it. 'I'd forgotten all about this. Do you remember how we used to wrap it round us in the barn, when we were young? My grandad used to wear it on the hills sometimes. He once told me that it was more than a hundred years old. I wish I'd worn half so well.'

Finn gathered her gingerly in his arms. She winced, but set her lips in a firm line, and would not cry out. He carried her carefully down the meandering track to the beach, trying hard not to jar her bones, trying hard to take small, safe steps. Afterwards, he would remember the powerful scent of bluebells. He left her sitting on a low rock, still wrapped in the shawl, while he went down, drew the boat onto the beach, made a nest of cushions there and came back for her.

'How are you?' It seemed a foolish question, she was so obviously unwell, but what else was he to ask?

'I'll do. Come on. Let's go.'

Lifting her as though she were made of blown glass, he walked across the beach and lowered her gently among the cushions. Then he pushed the nut brown boat over the white sand into the water and stepped in at the last moment, holding his breath, trying to steady the boat, trying to give Kirsty as little discomfort as possible.

It was a warm evening and very light. The sea was glassy, the bland, impassive face of the moon just showing in a blue sky. Finn faced Kirsty, took up the oars and sculled quietly out into the bay. Kirsty trailed her fingers in the water and relaxed into her cushions, saying nothing. Finn seemed beyond sorrow, gazing at her as though he could never have enough of the sight of her.

He shipped the oars and sat very still in the centre of the boat. They drifted below Dunshee, listening to the sharp calls of wading birds along the shoreline, moving with the tide. A big seal came to look at them, popping its head out of the water a couple of times and snorting at them, to Kirsty's absolute delight.

'Do you remember?' she said to Finn, 'Do you remember how the seals would always come when we were fishing? And you could have seen them far enough because you said they always scared the fish away? But I liked them so much that I didn't care.'

When an evening breeze sprang up and ruffled the surface of the sea, he leant forward to arrange the shawl more closely around her. She caught at his fingers and kissed them.

'My darling!' she said with infinite tenderness.

'All of me. To the last drop of my blood.' He rubbed at his eyes and cheeks. 'The wind's in my eyes, that's all.'

'I know, my love,' she said. 'I know.'

The light drained slowly out of the sky. He wanted to bring the boat in, but she protested. 'Wait,' she said. 'Just a while longer. Just a little while. It's all right. I'm warm enough.'

She dipped her hand in the sea again and, as she raised it, her fingers left an iridescent trail, a stream of opals, tumbling and shimmering into the water, tiny life forms, each generating its own spark of light.

'I'm sorry,' she said, at last, her voice slightly slurred.

'Oh my darling, you don't have anything to be sorry about. It's me who should be sorry. I should never have left you. Never. It was the worst thing I ever did. Unforgiveable.'

'I forgave you long ago. But will you forgive me?' He saw that she was gazing at the shoreline, her brow creased in a frown. 'Whatever possessed me to do that to you, my love? Where is a knife that will cut it? Search the sheathe where you left it. Do you hear it? Do you hear it, Finn?'

'Hear what?'

'The heron screaming and the sad song of the corncrake in the meadow.'

At last, she allowed Finn to row her back to shore. He hauled the boat onto the sand, lifted her out and carried her tenderly back to Dunshee. As they approached the house, she reached up and clasped his neck so that her head was nestling against him. In the warm kitchen, he tried to put her down on the sofa while he went to get her a drink, but she wouldn't let him.

'Don't!' she said. 'Don't let me go, Finn, please. Not just yet. Let's sit for a while. Till I feel better.'

He sat down on the nearest chair, her grandfather's old rocking chair, with Kirsty all bundled up on his lap, his arms fast around her.

He bent to kiss her. 'Ah Kirsty, my darling Kirsty! We wasted so many years. We should have had our whole lives together!'

'We have,' she said. 'We have been together our whole lives, haven't we? Just not always in the same place. Don't be angry with me now. I can't bear it if you're angry!'

'I'm not angry with you. I was never angry with you. I would have gone to the ends of the earth for you, Kirsty, my dearest, darling Cairistiona!' He rocked her gently.

She tried to say, 'To hell in a handcart!' but her lips were dry and she could only whisper the words.

'Listen to me now. Close your eyes. I'll rock you till you fall asleep. You'll feel better then. Go to sleep, my darling, my sweetheart. Go to sleep.'

The room fell very quiet. At last, the only sounds were the muted rustle of the fire in the grate as a log slowly dwindled to white ash, and the squeak of the chair, moving back and forth, back and forth.

Time passed. When, holding her close as ever, he looked down, he could see that she lay cold and still in his arms.

Finn carried Kirsty upstairs and placed her gently on the bed, in her old room. She looked peaceful, lying there with the plaid still wrapped around her, but she looked strange and empty as well. Everything that had animated her, everything that had made her so uniquely his Kirsty, had gone and he did not know where to find her. He didn't stay in the room long. Instead he went downstairs and phoned the island nurse who said that she would inform the doctor on the mainland. Then he called the minister, who seemed very shocked. He hadn't realised quite how ill she was, but she had hidden her illness well, even from her family.

The minister came driving up the track in his elderly Golf, said a prayer over Kirsty, and sat with Finn for a while, but seemed embarrassed by his silence and scared by his stony face. He left just as the district nurse arrived. She was professionally brisk and left Finn a couple of sleeping tablets, promising to send the undertaker up as soon as possible.

'It will be tomorrow morning, now.'

'No hurry,' he said.

'Will you be all right?' she asked. 'Sometimes people get very frightened. You know?'

She glanced upwards, indicating the room where Kirsty lay.

'I was never scared of her when she was alive, so why the hell should I start now?'

Nevertheless, he could feel the intense silence in the house, pressing in on his ears. He had never known it so quiet before. He switched on the television, but the foolish babble was unbearable, so he drank a glass of whisky and then went out, climbing up to Hill Top Town. Already, there was a gleam of light in the eastern sky. The short night-time was ending. He stumbled among primroses, violets and bluebells, their colours muted and strange in this light. Gradually they gave way to willow scrub and last year's dried heather with the wind whistling through the stems. And then he was on the open hillside, with seabirds whirling around him, angrily, and he shouted with them, screamed wordlessly into the breeze that came from Ireland. He lost all track of time, but eventually hunger and thirst and the weakness in his own legs forced him back down to the house. He couldn't remember when he had last eaten, and all he had drunk had been the whisky. He made a pot of tea, put sugar in it, sliced and buttered bread, set it aside and forgot about it. Overcome by dizziness, he sat down next to the kitchen fire.

The old cat came and tried to sit on his lap, but he pushed the creature away, sweeping it off with his hand. It mewed a protest, then crouched uneasily in front of the cold range, looking up at him with accusing eyes.

Eventually, he went up to the room where Kirsty lay. He thought that he could lie beside her a while, but she seemed so cold, and he couldn't warm her. He pulled up the blanket from the bottom of the bed and tucked it round her, as well as the plaid, with some confused idea of warming her. The cat had followed him and, before he could stop it, it jumped onto the bed. It crouched beside her for a moment, looking into her face, and then it gave a single, wailing cry and was gone, leaping down the stairs. He followed after and found it crouched in the hearth, its fur standing on end, its eyes wide and fixed. He sat down again and, presently, it jumped onto his knee and when it padded a bed there, he did not move it.

He dozed for an hour or so, warmed by the weight of the animal on his lap, soothed by its gentle breathing, until full daylight crept in the window. Then he got up and phoned Nicolas, who sounded shocked and tearful, but surprisingly calm. Finn wondered if maybe he had seen it coming and then the thought struck him that Kirsty may even have written to her ex-husband without his knowledge.

'Did you know she was so ill?' he asked.

'She told me she was ill. But she also asked me not to visit. Not until she was feeling better. I thought she was getting treatment. I thought things would improve again.'

'I hoped for the same thing. How do you think the girls will take it?'

'They'll be devastated.'

'I'm sorry.'

'Just tell me, Finn. Tell me that somebody was with her. You didn't let her … you didn't …' Nicolas's composure deserted him and he choked on the words.

'I was with her. All the time. Right to the end. What do you take me for?'

'You should have told me.'

'I wanted to. But she didn't want the girls to know. She was adamant.'

'I know.'

'She wanted them to remember her the way she was.'

'And do you think that'll be a comfort to them? Or do you think they might just be furious. Hurt and furious.'

'I don't know and to be honest with you, I don't have the energy to argue with you right now.'

'All right, Finn,' said Nicolas, and Finn could hear the capitulation in his voice. 'I understand. I do understand.'

They spoke briefly about funeral arrangements and all the people who would want to come. Kirsty would be buried not far from her mother and her grandmother in the island cemetery.

He made a few more phone calls and then he sat in the kitchen, listening to the sighs and creaks as the growing warmth of the sun woke the old building. He was aware that he was exhausted, but sleep still seemed very far off. He dozed and woke, made tea, took a shower and then went out, striding down to the beach, and only returning when he saw the undertaker's car, pulling up at the house.

'I'm sorry for your trouble,' said Hamish, who had lived on the island for years. He looked narrowly at Finn. 'You look very poorly, Finn, if you don't mind me saying so.'

'I was looking for her,' Finn said, thickly, shaking the proffered hand. 'But I couldn't find her.'

Hamish knew something of their history. 'It's always a shock,' he said. 'Even when it's expected, it's always a shock.'

'But she wouldn't go without me, would she? She wouldn't go off and leave me all alone. I never thought she would do that. You would think that she would still want to be with me, wouldn't you?' Finn covered his face with his hands. 'But I can't find her anywhere. She left me and I don't know where she's gone. Jesus Christ, what will I do if I can't ever find her again!'

Other people began arriving: the minister, the doctor, various islanders, and then friends and relatives from the mainland. Finn sat in the corner of the room and watched while other people came and took charge. Soon, the hotel too was full of mourners but he kept well out of their way. In the days before the funeral he took the boat out and just drifted about with the currents. Kirsty's daughters came to the island the day before the funeral and stayed at the hotel with their father. Flora sat close to Annabel in the lounge, a damp tissue balled up in her hand, while India seemed more angry and hurt than sad. Eventually, however, and much against Nicolas's advice, she went up to Dunshee and sought out Finn.

'Why didn't you tell us? Why the hell didn't you let us know that she was so ill? What right had you to keep it from us?'

'I couldn't say anything. She didn't want me to.'

'Oh yes. And your first loyalty was always to my mother, wasn't it? You didn't think about our feelings, did you? You never really wanted us here.'

'It was nothing to do with you, India. I always wanted you here. Always. But you're right. My first loyalty was to Kirsty. It had to be. It still is. She was all I had, and I couldn't go against her wishes. If you can't be selfish when you're dying, when can you be?'

Chapter Thirty Seven

AT THE FUNERAL service, India played the fiddle, her great grandad's old fiddle, to which she had fallen heir, filling the kirk with the most glorious, heartrending sound. She played a lament, her grief stricken and gravely beautiful face bent over the instrument. The music would have wrung tears from a stone. That was what everyone said afterwards, curiously comforted by the perception that they were in the presence of an uncommon talent. Flora, her hair a cap of neat red curls, recited a sad poem that she had made up especially for Kirsty. Nicolas assumed the role of chief mourner which caused a few raised eyebrows on the island, but it wasn't really his fault. Finn seemed to have abdicated all responsibility and somebody had to take charge. Who else, if not Nicolas?

In fact, Finn almost missed the funeral, but at the last moment, he crept into the back of the church, swathed in an old sheepskin jacket, shivering, although the day was warm. His mind was elsewhere. None of this was real to him. In the cemetery, he came forward to take one of the cords and then threw a posy of spring blossoms: primroses, violets, celandines, in on top of the coffin, but went off again soon afterwards without speaking to anyone. He didn't even go to the funeral tea that Annabel had organised in the hotel.

The evening after the funeral, India walked up to Dunshee again. Finding the house empty, all her cousins having left on the last ferry of the day, she walked down to the beach. Finn was sitting in the boat that was floating in a few feet of calm water, gazing up at the hill behind the farmhouse.

She hovered on the sand, watching him, willing him to speak first, but he said nothing.

'You should have come down to the hotel, Finn,' she said at last.

'Why?'

'It might have done you good to speak to other people.'

'Who?' he sneered. 'What people? You mean Nicolas? I'm sure that would have done me a lot of good.'

'No. I mean me. And Flora.'

'Flora hates me.'

'No she doesn't.'

'Dislikes me then. She does dislike me. You can't pretend she doesn't.'

'I think she's afraid of you. Quite a lot of people are, you know.'

'What about you, India?'

'I don't hate you. How could I, when mum loved you so much?'

'Are you afraid of me?'

'No. Of course not. I've told you. I'm my mother's daughter.'

He looked at her, briefly, then transferred his gaze back to Hill Top Town.

'But you should have made the effort to talk to people, you know. People from round here. People who knew and loved my mum.' India could feel the tears starting as she said the words. She swallowed hard.

'I loved her better than anyone,' he said.

'Oh Finn!' She gazed at him, helplessly. 'I know you did. I know.'

'What's she playing at? Why is she hiding from me? Is this to pay me back? Is this what she felt like when I went away? Being left behind is worse than going. Being torn away from somebody. Being torn apart. I know what I'm talking about, India. I swore I would never let it happen to me again. But now it has.'

'Do you mean when you were little? When you got taken to that school? When your mother had to leave you?'

He turned on her, fiercely, rocking the boat. 'How do you know about that? Did she tell you?'

'Mum? She told me a bit.'

'Well she shouldn't have. It was private.'

'She said that your mother had been sent to one place and you'd been sent to another. And we had to understand how difficult that would be.'

'And make allowances for me?'

'No. She just loved you with all her heart and soul, Finn. She wanted me to understand a bit about you. She didn't tell Flora. Only me. And she said she didn't know very much and it was really none of her business, but she would tell me what she knew, anyway, because I ought to know.'

'My father left us when I was a baby. He went to England, for work, and never sent a brass farthing back to us. Did she tell you that?'

'She said you and your mother were on your own and it must have been difficult for you back then.'

'It was. But she had a job, when I started school.' He frowned, rubbing his forehead. 'That was my first school. And then my mother lost that job and she didn't get another one for a while, and things were difficult. It was hard. We were cold. I remember going to bed to get warm, the two of us cosied up together. She had a friend called Phyllis. I couldn't say her name. I called her Phissie. She used to lend us things. She gave us food, I think. Groceries. And then, my mother managed to get another job. That must have been what happened. But it all went wrong. It was my fault.'

'Finish the puzzle, Finn. You have to finish the puzzle.' That's what she had said to him. In the dream. He still had that same dream, even now.

'How could it be your fault? You were just a little lad. What on earth could you have done wrong?'

India wanted to reach out and touch him, but he was in the boat, there was a small stretch of water between them, and it wouldn't have helped anyway. The only touch Finn wanted was the one he couldn't have.

'Open the door. Open the door, Finn!' That's what Mrs Maguire had said. She knew his name. And he had recognised her voice. He was there, seeing himself, watching it happen all over again.

Pulling the chair over to the door. Finding the big iron key. The spare key. Climbing up onto the chair and turning it in the lock. He needed his two hands. It was hard but he managed it. Proud of himself, like a big boy. She came through the door so quickly that she almost knocked him off the chair.

'I let her in,' he said, gazing at India.

'Let who in?'

'Mrs Maguire.'

'Who was she?'

'The Legion of Mary woman. I told your mother about her. She was a nosy old bitch. She had her suspicions about us. And she came snooping around. I wasn't supposed to let her in. My mammy was at work. Mrs Maguire came to the door, and I thought it would be all right because she had said not to let any strangers through the door. Don't open the door to strangers, she said.'

'You were all alone? A little boy?'

'I told you. But I didn't think Mrs Maguire was a stranger. We saw her in the church on Sundays. She was friendly with the priest. I thought I'd better do as I was told. So I got a chair and I stood on it, and I unlocked the door.' He paused, the memories flooding through him, wave after wave. 'Oh Jesus, I unlocked the door. And she was so angry! Mrs Maguire was so angry with me!'

'But why would she be angry with you? I don't understand! You were a little boy, and you were alone in the house. Was that it? Your mother had left you alone while she went to work?'

'The woman downstairs was supposed to be looking after us. But she was ill. And my mammy had been ill too. We had both had the flu. She couldn't take any more time off work or she would lose the job. She would lose this new job and she said she couldn't afford to do it. It had taken her months to find it. So she said, you'll have to stay here, Finny. You'll have to stay here with her. Mind her.'

'Mind who? The woman downstairs? I don't understand, Finn.'

'You don't understand. She'd told me what to do. I knew what to do. I was sensible. It would have been all right. I was her little soldier. I knew everything I had to do, and she would come home and see us in the middle of the day, and … Jesus, I did the wrong thing. I did a bad thing. It was my fault. I let Mrs Maguire in. She could see that there was nobody to look after us. And it was criminal, she said, criminal!'

'Your mother left you on your own so that she could go to work, and this Mrs Maguire reported her?'

'No. No! You don't understand!' He was shouting at her, seeing it all in his mind at last, the words tumbling over themselves. 'I wasn't on my own. There was Grania. Grania was there too!'

A pair of oystercatchers flew overhead, calling plaintively to each other, their golden beaks catching the last of the light.

India drew a deep breath. 'Finn, who was Grania?'

There was a long silence. It was as though some door to memory had been suddenly, forcibly thrown open. He had turned the key, and Mrs Maguire in her blue hat had come bursting through. Finn rocked back and forth in the boat.

'Oh Jesus! Oh Jesus! Grania! She was the baby. She was the baby. She was my little sister. My Grania. I loved her. I loved her so much! My Grania!'

Finn and his mother had caught the flu and it had gone through the whole warren of a house. Only the baby, Grania, stayed healthy. Mary was on a warning, no more time off work, but then the old woman who usually looked after the baby took to her bed with the flu as well. So Mary, in desperation, left Finn and Grania in the room on their own. Finn was a bright little boy, who knew what to do and loved his baby sister. He knew how to heat up the bottles and test them on his wrist to make sure that the milk wasn't too warm. How to hold the baby and feed her. How to make sure she didn't choke. How to burp her and change a nappy. He knew all of that. And his mother was coming home at dinner time to make sure everything was all right. But Mrs Maguire came to the door first. Maybe she already suspected something. A lost job. A new baby. No husband in evidence. The baby woke up at the furious knocking and started to cry, that hungry, fretful wailing, like a wild bird, and Finn didn't know what to do between the fierce demands of the crying baby and the noises at the door, so he let the woman in. He wasn't supposed to let anyone in, but he knew her from the church, so he let her in. It was all his fault.

It seemed fine at first. Mrs Maguire was plainly angry, but then she calmed down and smiled, a wide smile, showing all her teeth, and she gave him a sweet out of that big shiny handbag. It was a rotten sweet, stale and soft and it hurt his mouth. She started asking all kinds of questions and the next thing Finn knew, the Gardai were there. He blamed himself. They were put into a big black car and taken to court, the baby all bundled up in a blanket on Mrs Maguire's knee. At the courthouse, they were left outside while the authorities did the business inside. And then, Finn was taken off to school. He never saw his mother again, not till that meeting in the convent. He never saw the baby again. Worse, he didn't remember her. He had erased her from his memory as surely as though she had never existed.

The tide had brought the boat gently onto the sand. India reached out to him, but still he sat there, unwilling to move.

'Don't tell me they sent a wee baby to one of those schools as well?' she asked him.

'I don't know what became of her.'

'But you remember her?'

'Just this scrap with dark hair. And not very much of it. Little fingers, little toes. I used to watch my mammy giving her a bath. She would wave her arms around and I would tickle her. I liked the back of her neck. I remember that. But I don't remember anything else. I don't think I want to remember anything else. I'm sorry, India. But there's nothing in here.' He touched his chest, his heart. 'There's nothing left in me. I'm empty. I wish I hadn't remembered. Do you think that's what she's doing? Paying me back?'

'Do you mean my mother? But she didn't know about Grania, did she? She didn't know you had a sister. Besides, my mum never did you a bad turn in her life.'

'She married Nicolas, didn't she?'

'Only when you left her. She would never have done it, if you hadn't gone. Never. And besides, I'm glad she married my dad. She was happy with him.'

'Your father ...'

'What about him?'

He stared at her, seemed on the point of speaking. Then, she saw his gaze slide away from hers, as though momentarily distracted by something beyond her. She turned to follow his line of vision, and realised that he was again looking up, way beyond Dunshee, towards Hill Top Town, where birds soared and tumbled up there. He didn't know what they were, but they looked like flakes of ash from some great bonfire.

'Never mind, India. It doesn't matter.'

'Come back up to the house with me.'

'Where is she now? Tell me that!'

'I don't know. I wish I did. But I know how it feels. Because I feel the same. There's no point in us arguing. We just have to try to help each other.'

'Nobody can help me now. Nobody. Not even you, India.'

All the same, he got out of the boat. She helped him to haul it onto the sand, above the tideline, and walked back up to Dunshee with him. She made him some beans on toast, which was all she could find in the house. She sat with him while he ate it, and then washed up the dishes. Nicolas phoned her on her mobile, from the hotel.

'I was getting worried about you. We all were. You've been there for hours.'

'It's all right dad. I'll be down soon.'

'Well just see that you are.'

Chapter Thirty Eight

KIRSTY HAD DIED just when her daughter was about to become wildly successful, playing what the critics called a celtic classical fusion fiddle. Whenever she read these kind of reviews, India could hear her mother roaring with laughter at the very expression. 'Fusion fiddlesticks,' she would have said. It was what India did say, in exactly her mother's old fashioned tone of voice, when she went to spend a couple of nights in London with Flora and Annabel.

It was almost two years after Kirsty's death and India, who now had her own flat in Edinburgh, was performing at a small venue in Covent Garden.

'Have you been back to the island?' Flora asked.

'I went in February. Just a flying visit. I had a gig in Oban. So I thought I would go. Have you been yet, Flora?'

Flora shuddered. 'No, and I don't want to.'

'I'm sure Charlie would put you up at Ealachan if you wanted. You wouldn't have to stay at the hotel. He's very fond of Aunty Annabel these days.'

'He is. And I'm sure he would, but I can't bear the thought of the island. Too many painful memories. I'm surprised you can stand to go.'

'It wasn't all bad. In fact, most of it was pretty good, you know. We should count ourselves lucky. We were blessed with a happy childhood. And loving parents.'

'Until *he* came back into our lives.'

'I think that was inevitable. Don't you?'

'I wish he had died on that rig. I wish he had never got off. I wish he had drowned.'

'Don't say that, Lolo.'

'Why? I mean it! If he had never come back, our mum would have stayed with our dad, and maybe she'd be alive now. He would have got her better treatment, and got it sooner, you can be sure of that.'

'We can't be sure of anything.' India gazed at her younger sister, distressed by her bitterness.

'We haven't turned out too badly, have we?' she asked, in an effort to lighten the mood.

Flora was working with Annabel in the design business and they were doing quite well. Once they had abandoned Annabel's fiddly jewellery and concentrated on interiors, things had started to go better. Flora had flair, a sense of style, and she was very efficient. Annabel had contacts and charm. Together, they made a formidable team.

'So, what did you do, when you went to the island?' asked Flora, unwilling to change the subject.

'I went to the cemetery. Took some flowers. The weather was appalling. Somebody had left a bunch of evergreens there. Maybe it was Finn.'

'At least he looks after the grave then.'

'Mum and great grandad and granny. They're all there. Quite a party. I know it sounds daft, but I always think what a nice part of the cemetery it is.

Flora shuddered. 'Did you go up to Dunshee?'

India nodded. 'It was difficult but I thought I should.'

'So how was he?' Flora still couldn't bring herself to say the name aloud.

'Not good. I think he's drinking too much. I wanted to tell him that I've been trying to find out about his sister but we didn't talk about it. Not really.'

'What sister?'

'He had a sister. Not even mum knew about her. A baby called Grania. I think she was put up for adoption, but I can't find out where she went. Nobody will give me any information. I was going to tell him that I'd been searching, but there didn't seem any point. He's in his own wee world up there. He doesn't seem to care about anything. He didn't want to let me in, but I kind of made him. He wasn't really rude. Just indifferent.' She hesitated, aware that she wasn't quite telling her sister the truth. She had thought him indifferent, but then there had been the parting gift of the folio.

'He gave me some of mum's drawings, you know.'

'He didn't ever care very much about anything ...'

'Except our mum.'

'Except our mum,' Flora conceded.

'Her paintings are fetching quite good prices now. Somebody told me they'd seen one in a London saleroom only the other day.'

'You're right. Dead artists always fetch more. Sad isn't it? So are you going to sell those drawings, India? You can, you know. I don't want them. I have her few bits of jewellery, plenty of photographs, some of her clothes. I don't need her drawings.'

'There's this fabulous, life-size picture of Finn.' India hesitated. 'It was down in the gallery, on the island, stored away with its face to the wall. Charlie phoned me about it from Ealachan. He was having a bit of a clear-out himself, after mum died, and he said it almost gave him heart failure, it was so lifelike.'

'Yeah. Well it would give you heart failure if it was Finn,' said Flora, morosely.

Her sister ignored her. 'I don't know why it was there and not at Dunshee, but she still painted down there sometimes, and maybe they just never got round to taking it up the hill. I don't think they ever intended to sell it. Charlie asked me what he ought to do with it. He thought one of us should have it.'

'Why would we want it? Why didn't he just send it back up to Dunshee? To its owner.'

'Because he thought it was a very fine work of art. And he thought Finn might destroy it. Or neglect it at least. Dunshee's a damp old place, these days. Mice, mildew. It wouldn't have survived.'

'I suppose not.'

'And it would be the very last thing our dad would want. Charlie thought he might put his foot through it.'

'I wouldn't blame him if he did.'

'So he phoned me. And then he sent it to me in Edinburgh. Do you mind if I keep it? It's such a beautiful picture.'

'Beautiful? Of that monster?'

'It is beautiful though.' Her voice was a whisper.

'What have you done with it?'

'It's just in my flat. In my bedroom.'

'Yeuch.'

'It's a bit spooky. He's down the shore. Sitting on a rock. I think it must be the shore at Dunshee, though it's hard to tell. At first, you think the eyes are following you. But they're not really watching you at all. They're watching the artist. And the expression on his face. I can't describe it. You'd have to see it. There's a heron in the picture. And just the suggestion of Hill Top Town in the background, but you wouldn't know that, if you didn't know the place. It's the most wonderful piece of work. It's Finn, looking young and absolutely gorgeous and he's gazing straight out of the canvas at my mum. A real woman's perspective on her lover. You don't often get that. It's usually the other way round with art. But they're so complicit. That's the word. As though they share some amazing secret. And yet, here's the really spooky thing, there's something wrong. You don't see it at first. I didn't. But he has his hand, down by his side and there's a knife, a dagger of some sort, in his thigh. Somebody has stabbed him. He's holding it and yet he's looking at her. With love.'

'God's sake, India, it sounds dead creepy. Just like him. You're welcome to it. I certainly don't want it.'

'I love it. It's so sensuous and so beautiful. I look at it all the time. Mind you, I put it in a cupboard whenever dad comes to visit.'

'Just as well. So what were the drawings he gave you?'

'They were mostly of Finn as well. Charcoal sketches. Very strange and disturbing. Hard to describe. I can show you some of them, if you like.'

'No thanks, Indie.

'I keep feeling I should show them somewhere though. Arrange an exhibition. They're so good. But I can't do it. They seem so very personal, somehow.'

'Keep them. Do what you like with them.' Flora hesitated. 'I hope to God I never fall in love like that.'

'Most people go through life looking for that kind of passion. Reading about it. Hankering after it.'

'Then they're crazy. And isn't it lucky that most of us never find it? It destroys you.'

'Not necessarily.'

'You wouldn't want anything like that, would you, India?'

'I don't know. Sometimes, when I look at those pictures, I envy them.'

'But look at what it did to them. And to other people. The harm it caused.'

'Mum was her own worst enemy. She didn't ever want anybody to get hurt.'

'Besides, you've found that kind of passion already.'

'You mean my music?'

'Yes. Your music.'

'It's true. When I'm playing there's nothing else and nobody else in the whole world that's more important. I suppose our mum was like that with her art. I understand her very well. But it was all tied up with Finn, somehow, wasn't it? For mum I mean. There was something uncanny about it. He was such a part of it for her, even when he wasn't there. Like a muse. I know all these dead male artists used to go on about their muses, but I think in some strange way, Finn was essential for mum. She couldn't do without him. She was essential for him too. He was part of the island, the landscape, part of her inspiration. In a way, he was in everything she did. And she was, well, I'm not quite sure what she was for him, but she was certainly vital.'

'I can't see me ever feeling like that about any man. Although it might be good to find some nice guy, make a couple of babies, and then carry on working, of course.'

India hugged her. 'Which is exactly what I hope you do!'

In May of that year, not long after India's visit to Flora, Charlie McNeill phoned her with the news that Finn O'Malley was dead. He had wandered up to Hill Top Town and passed out up there, probably from too much drink, or not enough food, or a combination of both.

It wasn't a particularly cold night, but all the same he had died of exposure.

'That does happen from time to time, seemingly,' Charlie added. 'People dying of exposure, on nights when they should be fine. They become disorientated and confused and then just lie down and fall asleep.'

Finn hadn't been in the habit of visiting the village much, and even the postman seldom came to Dunshee, but eventually he had driven up with a council tax demand and found the house deserted, the doors wide open, the hungry cats roaming around. Search parties had been sent out and when they found Finn, he had been dead for some time. Charlie told her that he had been clutching a piece of agate in his hand and it was buried with him. If India had been of a more sentimental turn of mind, she would have imagined that he had died of a broken heart.

India cancelled a recording session, went over to the island and paid for the funeral herself. She had Finn buried with her mother in what she had called that 'nice part of the cemetery', though she couldn't imagine Finn wanting to have much posthumous conversation with Isabel.

No other members of the family attended the funeral but, however reclusive he had become, the islanders still counted Finn as one of their own and turned out in force to bury him. Kevin Gleason came over from the mainland and assisted the minister with the service. He was older, more portly, a little more cynical about almost everything but still a kindly man, in his own remote and rather bookish way. He told India that he had brought the news to Finn's mother himself, but Sister Dominica was very vague these days. The nuns explained that she was suffering from Alzheimer's and her short term memory was all but gone.

'My son?' she said. 'My Finny, dead? Ah, God rest his soul!' She dabbed at her eyes, but only a few minutes later, she smiled brightly at Kevin, and asked, 'Are you conducting a retreat here, Father?'

After the funeral, it was discovered that Finn had lodged a will with his Glasgow solicitors, leaving everything, Dunshee included, to India. This caused a minor sensation on the island, but the rumour and speculation soon died down. Finn had always been strange in the head, and this was just one more piece of odd behaviour.

India, however, was profoundly disturbed by her inheritance, because it served to confirm a suspicion that, only a few months earlier, had become a certainty for her. She could date it with some precision. It was the day her mother's huge portrait of Finn had arrived. Charlie had sent it by carrier, and she had been alone in the Edinburgh flat when the delivery men carried it upstairs. It had been securely wrapped in many metres of bubble wrap, inside rigid cardboard and a layer of brown paper, and the men staggered beneath the weight of it. She had signed for the parcel, and then sat, gazing at it for a while, reluctant to open it, remembering the folio of drawings and how much they had disturbed her. At last, she went and fetched scissors and wrestled with wrapping and cardboard.

When, finally, the portrait emerged safely from a sea of paper and plastic, she breathed a sigh of relief and propped it against one of her plain white walls. It was beautiful. He was beautiful. There was still, within the picture, something of the boy within the man, uncertain, long-legged, arresting, with dark, troubled eyes fixed on the artist. Who could not love him? But there was something else about the picture and just at first, she couldn't identify it. It seemed disturbingly familiar and yet she knew that she had never seen this picture before. So it must be something about the man, the depiction of the man himself.

Her eyes strayed to the small bookshelf where she kept her favourite novels. On the top shelf sat one of her mother's many sketches of India herself, as a young girl. It was a lovely, swift, charcoal drawing. Kirsty had caught her daughter as she perched on a rock, down on the beach at Dunshee, long legs apart, hands on knees, feet firmly planted on the sand, as though she were about to spring into action and run away. India found herself looking from the sketch to the portrait and back again. The resemblance between the two was uncanny. But then, why wouldn't it be? She gazed at Finn, tears running down her cheeks. She tried to dash them away, but still they came, blurring her eyes as she stared and stared into the face of her dead father.

India made many attempts to find Grania. Her sole confidant about her own parentage was Kevin Gleason and she trusted him to keep the revelation secret. With his help, she managed to identify the Dublin convent where the baby might have been taken. He offered to intercede on her behalf. She made a special trip to the convent, met with the Mother Superior, begged, pleaded, cajoled. When none of this had any effect, she tried a solicitor's letter. But she met with absolute silence. The information was a secret and must remain so. Finn's mother had been persuaded to sign his sister, Grania, away for adoption, and there was not a thing anyone could do about it now. All other details were confidential.

She had another meeting with Kevin in Glasgow. He pointed out that the child could have been sent anywhere: America, Australia, Canada. Nobody would divulge these secrets, not the Irish State, and certainly not the Church. But he thought that if somebody would go to the trouble of adopting a wee baby, then they wouldn't be looking for unpaid labour. They may well have been looking for a child to love.

'Some of the nuns had a good thing going with wealthy families, overseas. Good Catholic families, with a bit of cash,' he said. 'Grania was probably much more fortunate than Finn. Let's hope so, anyway.'

India was surprised by his openness, but he had been very fond of Finn and very sorry for him. All the same, whenever her work took her to the States, which it did quite often now, she would find herself gazing at the faces of middle aged women and wondering, is that my Aunt Grania? Or that? Or that?

Afterwards, when she began to stitch the revelations of the past couple of years into the fabric of her life, India thought long and hard about Finn and her mother. No matter how often she rehearsed what she knew about the relationship, there was always something that eluded her. It was like a glimpse of something out of the corner of her eye, a footstep of somebody who had just left the room, a distant, magical air that she couldn't quite catch. The more she tried to pin the melody down, the more it slid away from her. Sometimes, on stage, she still played the old fairy tune that her great grandfather had taught her all those years ago. She dimly remembered that she had heard Finn playing it too, although he had no great talent with the instrument. Whenever she ventured to play it, it always brought Kirsty and Finn into her mind with renewed intensity.

Love? Could it be their love that eluded her? And if so, just what kind of love? That was what she asked herself, constantly interrogating what she knew about her mother and Finn, not obsessively, but with a kind of insatiable curiosity about them. She thought that Flora was right. People might fantasise about the kind of passion that lay between Kirsty and Finn, but it burned into you, that kind of love. It consumed the lovers. Nothing was ever enough. It sprang from some terrible need, some wound that could never quite be healed. Finn had been so grievously damaged that nothing could really heal him, not fully. She thought uneasily about her mother's illness, about her last sight of Finn, literally dying of grief.

Sometimes she would lie awake, thinking about her mother. If Kirsty had really loved Finn, how could she have thought of marrying Nicolas? If he had loved her, how could he ever have left her? She always came to the same conclusion. Of course she had loved him. That was her tragedy. And Finn had certainly loved Kirsty. That was his.

And yet, there was something primitive, something deep inside her, that was forced to acknowledge its attraction, the romance of it, the way in which so many people could be so enthralled, so spell-bound by the prospect of such a passionate obsession. Everyday life could be so prosaic that even the most practical and pragmatic of us might dream about selling our very souls for love. A world well lost indeed. But then, she thought uneasily, was that only because she truly was her father's daughter?

She had Finn's name added to Kirsty's on her mother's headstone, a smooth slab of black granite with a simple engraving, like a child's picture of a hill, just like the land behind Dunshee. Somebody – India had no idea who – carried on leaving posies of wild flowers at the foot of the headstone, even after Finn's death. In summer it was wild roses and honeysuckle; in autumn it was late harebells and heather.

During the following wet and windy summer, India spent some money on Dunshee, tidying it up, making it windproof and water-tight again. She got Cats Protection to come over and move most of the cats, though two of them escaped, only to come back and lurk about the barns, a moth eaten black tomcat and his companion, a ragged marmalade female, but they seemed to be beyond breeding, and eventually she left them in peace.

'If they don't bother me, I won't bother them,' she said to her sister.

She had decided almost immediately that she would keep Dunshee. One of these days, she thought, she would want to settle down and when she did, Dunshee would be waiting. Until that day she went there only occasionally. But then, she would light a fire in the range, sit in the old rocking chair and each night, she would sleep in her mother's bed in the wall, where it was warm.

Flora would sometimes come for a day or two, but she always said it was too spooky. Too sad. Too nostalgic.

'I don't know how on earth you can bear to be up here all alone. I couldn't do it.'

'I don't mind. There's nothing to be afraid of here, Flora. Not now.'

'Well I wouldn't like it. It's a noisy old house. Too many creaks and bumps for my liking.'

'There are mice in the attic.'

'They must be wearing hobnail boots then.'

'I play the fiddle for them and I'm sure they listen.'

'Who listens, India? What are you talking about?'

'Oh …' She stretched out her long legs and smiled enigmatically. 'You know? Such ghosts as choose to inhabit this place. Our great grandad for one. Don't you sometimes imagine that all the layers of times past are still here, with people just carrying on, living here, all of us at once?'

'No I don't,' said Flora with a shudder.

'Well I do. Sometimes I could swear that I can smell great grandad's tobacco. You know that lovely vanilla stuff he used to smoke?'

'You're kidding me!'

'I'm not. But maybe it's just in the walls.'

'And our mum?'

India didn't answer immediately, but at last she said, 'The old loft above the kitchen.'

'What about it?'

'It makes me a bit uneasy. I wouldn't like to sleep up there, that's for sure.'

'You're scaring me, India.'

'I don't mean to. And it isn't exactly scary. Not really. Not in any sinister sense. This is our mum I'm talking about, after all! Just strange. A strange feeling. As though the whole room has the weight of the past in it. It's a sad room right enough but not in a bad way. Self contained. Private. Keep out. That's what it says.'

'I don't think I want to know any more.'

India regarded her sister thoughtfully for a moment.

'You know the old hill fort?'

'Of course. Hill Top Town. I haven't been up there for ages though. And if you're going to tell me something horrible about that as well, don't bother.'

'No, it isn't horrible at all. It's rather nice. It was a special place for her. For her and Finn both. I think they were very happy there. Really happy and whole.'

Flora shrugged. 'So?'

'Well, I went up there, the last time I was here. It was such a beautiful day. I was tired and needed to recharge my batteries, so I came here to Dunshee. I woke up in the morning and the sun was streaming in the window, so I took a picnic, just like we used to do when mum brought us up to see great grandad. I packed a few sandwiches and some fruit juice. Then I climbed the rocks behind the house and went up towards Hill Top Town.'

'And?' Flora was interested in spite of herself. It was a calm night and the windows were open. She could hear the faint rasping of the corncrake in the meadow by the shore. India paused to listen for a moment.

'Summer visitor,' she said. 'He's in lots of mum's pictures. Have you noticed? Even if he's only lurking in a corner.'

'I never saw that.'

'I did. It's like a game. Hunt the corncrake.'

'Typical mum.'

'Anyway, I remembered Hill Top Town so clearly from when I was a wee girl. Before they sent me away to school. I loved it up there. I know it was never your favourite place, Flora.'

'No. It was always Ealachan I loved. The gardens. The trees. The avenue of camellias.'

'Anyway, there's a sort of saucer of land at the very top of the hill. You think it's flat topped when you look at it from below, but actually it's not. There's a kind of depression, with a jumble of rocks at the bottom of it. There are blueberry plants and myrtle and a few harebells. The heather was just coming into bloom. I hauled myself over the lip of land at the top and I could have sworn I heard voices.'

'It would have been visitors, hill walkers.'

'No. Listen. There were two people talking nearby. Quite close to me. That's what it sounded like. A man and a woman. You know that kind of low murmuring you sometimes hear when two people are very intimate and are chatting to each other, with comfortable pauses? You can't quite make out what they are saying, but it doesn't matter, because it isn't for your ears anyway. Two people, their words only for each other. I looked around, expecting to see … oh I don't know … somebody. Anybody. Tourists who had walked up from the hotel maybe. But there was nobody to be seen. Nobody at all.'

'Weren't you scared?'

'No. It was good to hear. It made a kind of music. I sat there for a while in the sunshine, listening to them. Soothed by them. I think I fell asleep for a moment and when I woke up, all I could hear was the wind rustling across the heather.'

Flora cast about for an explanation. 'Maybe sound travels. And maybe Hill Top Town holds it, traps it there.'

'Maybe it does,' said India. 'That's exactly my point. Maybe it does.'

— THE END —

Author's Note

Many thanks are due to all the friends, family members and readers who have encouraged me to keep going with this novel. There is a sense in which it is a beloved child, but like so many favourites, it has been a difficult child too. So perhaps some background information might be of interest.

Wuthering Heights was my late mother's favourite novel. I was a Yorkshire lass, although one with a rich Polish and (like Emily) a rich Irish heritage as well. We lived in Leeds until I was twelve years old. You can read more about my family background in a book called A Proper Person to be Detained (Saraband 2019), part personal memoir, part family history. I was named for the heroine of Wuthering Heights, a doubtful compliment some might say, and I was trundled over the moors in my push-chair to Top Withens, the setting for the Heights in the novel, if not for the house itself. As soon as I was old enough to read and begin to understand the novel, I fell in love with it, although I soon realised that it was a powerful and absorbing evocation of cruelty, loss and obsessive love, with very little of romance about it. Since then, I have reread it almost every year, and have found more to marvel at on every reading.

Throughout my previous long career as a radio dramatist, I would periodically ask the powers-that-be if they would allow me to dramatise Wuthering Heights. They would let me dramatise all kinds of classics, from Kidnapped to Ben Hur, so why would they never let me work on the novel I loved? Instead, every dramatisation by somebody else infuriated me, obliterating the genius of the novel under odd, quirky interpretations. Or was that simply my natural envy asserting itself?

Cue forward some years, and after a spell of writing for the stage, I began to focus almost wholly on fiction, with occasional ventures into non-fiction. Most of my work since then has been beautifully published by Saraband. But before I ever began to work with them, I had written several drafts of Bird of Passage. Most writers have 'bottom drawer' novels: the books that you write before you are ever published. I have several, and most of them should never see the light of day. But Bird of Passage always felt different. By the time I came to draft it out, I was experienced enough to know that I was writing a kind of homage to Wuthering Heights and that it was a labour of love. This is not a retelling. How would I dare? But as one reviewer so perceptively describes it, it is a dialogue with that novel, an exploration of the nature of obsessive love and of the relationship between character and landscape.

For some reason, the connection between Bird of Passage and Wuthering Heights has always scared off both agents and publishers and – strangely – I could never persuade any of them to read it. Perhaps the subsequent over-romanticising of Wuthering Heights meant that they misunderstood my intentions. Emily wrote a savage novel, a story with a deep vein of cruelty running through it, an extraordinary book about the destructive nature of passion, and about a damaged individual. It is that same obsessive and destructive love that I have tried to explore in Bird of Passage. This is, of course, a very different story, with a different setting, but every now and then, there is a glance back at the much loved source of my inspiration. Those people who have read the novel as an eBook tell me that they have been moved by it more than by any of my traditionally published novels. With this new edition, I hope that you too can enjoy the story of Finn and Kirsty just for itself.

– *Catherine Czerkawska*

About The Author

Catherine Czerkawska is a Scottish based novelist and playwright. She graduated from Edinburgh University with a degree in Mediaeval Studies followed by a Masters in Folk Life Studies from the University of Leeds. She has written many plays for the stage and for BBC radio and television, and has published nine novels, historical and contemporary, including the Physic Garden, the Jewel, the Curiosity Cabinet and the Posy Ring (all published by Saraband). Her short stories have been published in many literary magazines and anthologies. She has also written non-fiction in the form of articles and books as well as A Proper Person to be Detained, a highly praised memoir that is a blend of true crime, family and social history. Wormwood, her play about the Chernobyl disaster, was produced at Edinburgh's Traverse Theatre to critical acclaim in 1997. Catherine has taught creative writing for the Arvon Foundation and spent four years as Royal Literary Fund Writing Fellow at the University of the West of Scotland. When not writing, she collects and deals in the antique textiles that often find their way into her fiction.